THE PROTÉGÉ

WATERFYRE RISING 6

NADIA HAN

PROSE CONCEPTS

For those with the "fyre" to reach beyond the stars.

.

.

.

"Love is the bridge between you and everything."

– Rumi

COPYRIGHT

Special edition paperback ISBN: 978-1-952820-59-5

Hardcover ISBN: 978-1-952820-60-1

PROLOGUE
ORION

MY PALMS WERE SWEATING as I stared at the group of people in the busy park. Nerves knotted my stomach as I scanned the crowds, making sure my father, the nanny, and the security guards assigned to monitor me weren't around. I was supposed to be inside my fancy hotel room, eating caviar and studying like the disciplined and astute boy my father wanted me to be. Though it was summer, I had a full schedule of studying so I could take over the family business one day.

They'd be surprised to know what sustained me during these grueling days.

A fifteen-year-old boy didn't need a nanny. That was embarrassing. Though I didn't mind Molly watching over me, I preferred my solitude. My mom was meeting up with some of her astrology friends, and Dad was at a business meeting. Mom had asked me to join her, but I had told her I was busy studying, which wasn't a lie. I was studying how to be the best thief.

"Ready for this, boy?" my mentor said into the earpiece. "It's not too late to back out now."

The Condor wasn't with me in Providence, Rhode Island, but somewhere in Europe. But because today was my debut, I kept him informed to prove that I'd learned something from him.

I'd met The Condor in Paris during a vacation trip with my parents. He'd started a conversation after seeing my mom's astrology book on my lap. We started a strange friendship discussing the constellations and weird shit. When he started telling me stories about a prominent thief, I was hooked. He was sharing his personal stories with me. Fascinated by his life, I had *begged* him to teach me, and my persistence paid off.

I didn't want to fail The Condor. He had one other disciple called The Raven, but I'd never met him. I felt privileged that The Condor had chosen me to be his next disciple, and I wanted to make him proud.

"I'm ready." I walked toward the playground, looking for the perfect victim. "Chat later."

Fear crawled up my spine as I glanced at the people around the picnic tables, the couples cuddling on blankets sprawled on the grass, and groups of kids hanging out.

Wearing khaki shorts and a T-shirt, I shifted my backpack as I observed the surrounding people. No large groups. Too many eyes. Too much room for mistakes. It had to be someone isolated. I had accompanied The Condor a few times when he'd stolen precious items, and I'd watched plenty of videos he'd recorded of his adventures.

Three teens stood by a tree, but a dog wagged its tail by the tall kid's feet. Not a good option. I swung my attention farther down the path. My eyes settled on two teens busy looking at a magazine. Excitement rushed through me as I took out a book and walked toward them, pretending to read.

I bumped into the girl, snatched the brooch from her shoulder bag, and said, "Shit. Sorry!"

She fell against her friend, probably her boyfriend.

"Yo, watch it," said the boyfriend, looking annoyed.

"Sorry," I apologized again and walked off, smiling like a fool.

The brooch warmed my hand as I made my way out of the park. My heart raced with excitement and fear. No one called after me. No one shouted for the police.

I'd succeeded.

When I'd gotten far enough, I glanced back and saw the two teens still engrossed in the magazine. Smiling to myself, I opened my palm and examined the gleaming brooch. I didn't know if it was worth anything, but it had glistened from afar, calling me.

I snapped a picture and sent it to The Condor on a phone that my family didn't know I had.

Orion: *My first souvenir.*

My first treasure.

The Condor: *Not bad.*

Orion: *Thanks!*

A thrill rushed through me.

The Condor: *We'll chat when you're back in Sweden.*

What would happen if my parents found out about my new hobby? Disown me? That would be my father's reaction if I weren't his only son. He needed me to carry on his lineage. Thinking of the responsibility bestowed upon me stressed me out, so I shoved it away.

Mom would ask me the reason for my choice. She'd always looked at things differently. I loved her for that. The world needed more people like my mom. Dad's family thought she was weird, but Mom didn't care. She had worked for NASA before she married into the Reimann family. Though she was a scientist, she also liked mystical things. My dad's family was probably jealous of her intelligence. Especially my aunt, Madelyn, who had a lot of plastic surgery and wore too much makeup. I'd heard her talk about my mom behind her back.

I didn't like being around Uncle Ray's family. His sons Jonah and Jasper attended the same private school as me. Jonah was two years older, while Jasper was my age. I didn't mind Jonah, but Jasper was a different story. My cousins wouldn't dare steal like I just did.

The idea of breaking the mold fascinated me. Liberated me. I chose to do something that intrigued me rather than follow the rules set by family—society's fucking boring rules that suffocated me.

Satisfied with my work, I headed back toward the hotel. My phone rang, and the ringtone signified it was my family phone.

Shit. Had my dad discovered I'd been gone? I reached for the phone in my backpack.

Relief settled when I saw Molly's number. I had told her I was going out for some fresh air.

"Hi, Molly."

"Orion," she breathed, followed by a pause.

Was I in trouble? Was she mad at me for sneaking out?

"I'm heading back now. Sorry I took a while."

"Just wait for me in the lobby. I'll take you to the hospital."

"Why?"

"A car... hit your mom." She finally burst into tears.

My chest felt as though it had caved in at her words, and I knew without her having to say it that my mom was dead.

CHAPTER ONE

ORION

WITH VENGEANCE STIRRING in my blood, I followed the attractive hostess wearing a fitted black skirt and a cream blouse through the luxurious Wellness Center. She walked up to a set of wooden doors with a metal sign that read Exclusive Members Only and pressed her thumb and index finger to the screen. The screen illuminated, signifying a match, and the doors opened.

"Your first time here?" The brunette raked her gaze down my body and flicked me a seductive look. "I'm Daniella."

"Yes," I replied, not in the mood to feed whatever she had on her mind. If it had been a month ago, I'd have taken her up on the offer. She had an attractive face and body. Those were perfect distractions to keep me relaxed.

But not today. Not when I was in search of my mentor's killer. My mentor, Pablo Toledo, also known as The Condor, had been found dead in a street of Providence. The person who killed him made it seem like a bad robbery gone wrong, but I saw through the lies.

The Condor wasn't your average man. He was the best thief I'd ever met, my hero. He taught me how to be a man. The Condor redefined thievery to me. He stole from those who had taken from him. I admired his ability to set the moral scale into balance.

Making the killer pay for the crime was my method of righting a wrong.

"Enjoy, Mr. Reimann." Her voice interrupted my thoughts.

She gestured to the arched hallway that opened to a luxurious club entertaining the wealthy and powerful. "If you need anything, please let me know." She took out her business card, flipped it over to the back, scribbled her phone number on it, and gave it to me.

"Thank you." I tucked it into my pants pocket, intending to toss it out later.

I scanned the room surrounded by burgundy walls, gold sconces, crystal chandeliers, velvet lounge chairs, and elegant tables. The gentle music should have soothed me, but nothing could do that. I had to find the killer.

After a month of research, my team informed me a person of interest was in this city. His fingerprint had been found on a piece of paper inside my teacher's pants pocket. I'd directed my team to run an international scan. They found a match when the club scanned in a new fingerprint as part of their membership signup requirement.

After today, my name and fingerprint would be deleted from their system without a trace.

I looked around the room, searching for a man who went by the name TR. The image I'd received showed a dark-haired man with hollow cheeks.

Men and women in designer clothing eyed me, gauging

the size of my bank account, my status in the public arena, and how I could benefit them. This was how most elite clubs operated. Everyone in the club wanted something from somebody. Though the clubs were always full of people and conversation, I often felt alone. Like I didn't belong anywhere.

In this glamorous arena, it was difficult to know who was friend or foe. To be safe, I viewed everyone as a foe.

As I scoured the area, cold eyes continued to stare at me. I stared back, colder, harder. If I wanted to, I could purchase this damn club—this entire block—and completely demolish it. Then where would these judgmental people go to meet their multiple mistresses? How would they hire an assassin to destroy their enemies or buy drugs to numb their pain? So many illicit transactions occurred in these clubs, but I didn't have time for that kind of shit.

Especially today.

I had too many things on my plate. I needed to locate TR, then rush to an important meeting that couldn't be rescheduled.

A sudden surge of panic rose in me, sending heat all over my body. The fear of losing control gripped around my throat, making it hard to breathe.

Fuck.

I slowed my steps, spotted an empty chair, and sat down. I took out my phone, pretending to look at it while I concentrated on my breathing. Then I looked around the room for two red things, two orange things, and then went through the colors of the rainbow. This was a method my mother had taught me.

I thought I had these panic attacks under control, but

Pablo's death had overwhelmed me with grief. The same grief I'd experienced when my mother died.

It had been a month since my teacher's death, and grief was still a fucking monster devouring me from the inside out.

When the heat subsided, I took another breath, rose from the chair, and continued wandering around. The eyes kept following me, probably speculating about what I was up to.

Let their imagination go wild.

I wasn't going to leave this room until I got answers. The Condor was more of a father to me than my biological father. He'd given me a thief name, The Roc, a mythological bird more powerful than a condor. I grew into a man because of him. The Condor was only a month from retiring when someone took that from him.

When I got the call about his death, I'd been in Paris preparing to join Arrow Holt in Monaco to take down members of The Trogyn, a dangerous crime organization that spanned multiple continents with elite members ranging from politicians to royalty. Uncle Ray and Aunt Madelyn both died in a car accident in Milan two months before The Condor. My uncle and aunt had their children, my father, me, and countless friends at their funeral. The Condor only had me.

Death had surrounded me the past few months, draining my energy. It needed to get away from me.

A man sat in the far corner of the room wearing a gray suit with his black hair tied back in a leather band. Could he be TR? His back was facing me, so I couldn't see him.

This man either knew my mentor, was the last person to see him, or knew the killer. Excitement thrummed in me as I walked toward him.

A man with a white beard nodded to a blonde woman standing beside a tall table.

She sashayed over to me. "Can I help you with anything, sir?"

"No. Just browsing."

Blondie gestured to the bar on the other side of the room. "You must be new here. Do you need me to show you around?"

"I have a friend waiting for me." I jerked a chin toward the black-haired man.

Nodding, she smiled. "Wonderful. If you need anything, please let me know. My name is Yvonne, and I'm the manager here."

"Thank you, Yvonne."

I strode over, pulled out the empty chair, and folded myself into it. The man didn't have a hollow face like the image I'd seen. He placed his cocktail down and considered me with brown eyes. I had expected him to look surprised and demand to know who I was. Instead, his expression told me otherwise. Who was he? Had I met him before and somehow forgotten?

"It's about time you showed up," said the man. "Want anything to drink?"

What the hell?

"No." I studied him, trying hard to remember if I'd met him somewhere. He had a long scar on the side of his neck and a strong face that could maneuver the dark world. Sharp brown eyes studied me as I studied him. He appeared older than me, but younger than my mentor.

He sat back, looking relaxed. "Ask your questions."

This turn of events threw me off, but I kept my composure. Remaining calm and cool ensured I had the upper hand. I came here expecting to interrogate a criminal, only to have him take charge of the conversation.

Leaning back in the chair, I asked, "Who are you? How did you know I'd be here?"

"Grief has clouded your judgment. I expected more from The Roc."

The fuck? No one knew my thief name except my mentor . . .

"What's your relationship to The Condor?" I asked.

He leaned into the table. "He was my mentor too."

My mouth dropped. "You're The Raven?"

The initials TR clicked in my head. The Condor had mentioned his student had retired to settle down with his woman.

He was right. My mind had been muddled and missed this important detail. What else had I missed?

"Nice to meet you, Orion Reimann. Though I've retired from that art, I still kept in contact with our teacher. He spoke highly of you. Said you were better at the art form than he was."

Thievery was a work of art, indeed. It took skill, calculation, and craftiness to ensure a smooth undertaking without being caught.

I released a disbelieving laugh. "Impossible. *He* taught me everything I know."

"According to him, the student surpassed the teacher years ago." The amusement flickering in his eyes turned to seriousness. "He knew someone was after him, so he reached out to me a week before his death."

Why didn't he tell *me*? I could've helped.

Maybe he thought I was still grieving for my uncle and aunt. He should've known I wasn't close to them.

The Raven probably sensed my irritation and said, "You were swamped assisting your friends. He didn't want to burden you. The Condor was going to share everything with you." He paused and swallowed. "I wish he hadn't delayed it."

Me too.

"How did he know someone was after him?" I asked.

"He discovered something about The Trogyn. He said it's a highly intricate scam that spans several continents. It would need careful unraveling. We were supposed to meet so he could share what he found out." The Raven finished his cocktail and met my gaze. "When he didn't show up at our scheduled meeting, I knew something was wrong. The Condor was someone you could depend on. He had saved my life years ago."

"He had saved mine too," I said.

"And we failed to save him." The Raven's jaw tightened. "He may have been a thief, but he was a better man than those who preach love and respect on the public stage." He pressed his lips into a thin line. "The killer made certain The Condor's discovery died with him."

I scrubbed a hand over my face, trying to absorb this information. Did The Trogyn kill my mentor?

What did he discover? This crime ring was a virus under my skin, and I vowed to destroy it.

"He left something for you—his treasure box." The Raven smiled.

"He did?"

Like my treasure box, his probably contained important items like the first artifact he'd stolen and other important items. Though I was honored, I wasn't ready to look through it yet. His death was still too raw for me.

"You deserve it. I guess he never told you that?"

"No." Regret clawed at me. Apparently, I'd been too busy to make time for him. "Is the box in Sweden?"

"It's in his Providence apartment," said The Raven. "He wants you to take care of it."

"How did you know I'd be here?"

He lifted a shoulder. "Educated guess. I left traces of myself because I knew you'd be ferocious at tracking down every person who had been in contact with him. So here we are."

My phone buzzed, and I retrieved my phone to see a reminder for a meeting I couldn't reschedule. "I have to go."

"Me too. My wife and kids are waiting for me. If you need anything, call me." He gave me a piece of paper with his number on it. "Don't hesitate. I want the killer to pay."

"Thank you." I took the paper, shoved it into my pocket with no intention of involving a family man who had left the underworld to be with his family.

I had plenty to work with.

CHAPTER TWO

ELENA

FRUSTRATION WAS a deadly mosquito hovering around me as I sat in my boss's office, glaring at him. Alvin Coolidge managed Channel 7 News, and I needed his assistance with a personnel matter.

"Chantel is lying," I said, trying my best to hold my composure.

My competitive coworker—who had a face like Catherine Zeta-Jones and the body of supermodel Gisele Bündchen—was like the dirty water that bred mosquitoes. She created a dangerous working environment for me and others. But nobody seemed to care.

Alvin leaned back in his leather chair and looked at me with deep-set blue eyes. "Why would she lie? She has no reason to."

She has every reason to. I'm a threat to her.

"Ever since the ratings for Uncover the Truth skyrocketed, she's been making up shit about me. I've let things slide. But accusing me of working with a drug dealer to get the scoop for my episode is crossing the line." Anger bubbled in me. "Do you know how many phone calls and emails—not to mention the social media frenzy—I had to deal with because of her accusation?"

"She said she was just being sarcastic."

"That's a fucking lie. And you know it." I'd never cursed at work, but Chantel had stepped on my last nerve. Shifting in my seat, I fumed. "Her 'sarcasm' was on a popular podcast. She's ruining my reputation!"

"You're overreacting," Alvin said calmly.

"Are you serious?" His indifference fueled the fire in me. "It's not overreacting, Alvin. It's called *defending* yourself. You would understand this if you weren't fucking her."

His eyes widened at my bluntness.

I knew I shouldn't have said that, but I couldn't help it. If I didn't need this job, I would've resigned a while ago. But dammit, life had a chokehold on me. I wouldn't pretend he was being an objective manager.

I waited for him to deny it or make up some stupid excuse. I'd seen her get into his car after work and caught them kissing at a restaurant.

"That's my personal business."

"Which is *affecting* your ability to do your job: be objective in this matter."

Chantel's father was a senator in New York, and her uncle was an influential agent representing several celebrities. Alvin Coolidge was a man who wanted to be in her circle.

Dropping the subject, he said, "Upper management has been on my ass about your latest investigation. They don't think it's viable."

My mouth dropped. "It *is* viable when people are dying for no good reason."

"People die every day, Elena. They get sick and they die. They get into car accidents and they die."

I couldn't believe what I was hearing. "Do you realize how cruel that sounds? Concerned people are asking for my help about their family members' suspicious deaths. People want the truth even if it's ugly. What I'm hearing is that *you* and *upper management* believe the truth isn't worth it." I narrowed my eyes at him. "Why?"

He shrugged. "Channel Seven has a new direction now. I'm sorry to say there won't be any more Uncover the Truth."

A heavy boulder dropped into my stomach.

"What?" My heart stopped as tears filled my eyes.

This was *my* show. I'd made it popular from the day it first aired. I'd put my heart and soul into every story, and those stories had made me a better person.

"Upper management is reorganizing everything. You're being reassigned to other projects."

Uncover the Truth was the most successful segment of Channel 7 News. There had to be another reason for the sudden shift. Was Chantel paying them to squash my show? Were they creating a show just for *her*?

I needed to get out of here because if I had seen Chantel in the hallway, I might have strangled her. But that would put me in jail and keep me from taking care of my mother. Who would pay off the monstrous debt . . .

Shit!

Anxiety tightened my stomach. I'd forgotten to make the payment that was due yesterday. This fiasco at work was messing with my head.

"I'm taking my four-week vacation starting right now." I rose from my seat. "Sorry for the late notice, but this stressful work situation is detrimental to my mental health. I need the extra time to adjust to the sudden changes. You and upper management will have to understand." I inhaled and exhaled to loosen the knots in my stomach. "If you don't, there's a mental health clause in the company policy handbook that would remind you. Check chapter five."

I didn't give him time to respond, stalking out of the room and heading to my office. Then I grabbed my purse and the box of folders containing all my research and rushed out to my car. I dumped everything into the passenger seat, rounded the hood to the driver's side and got in. Once inside, I exhaled a long breath. After a few more breaths, my body calmed.

Switch gears, Elena.

Shrugging off the anxiety as best I could, I switched my focus to bills. Compartmentalizing things had helped me manage my life during stressful moments. I could dump all my concerns into a box, cover it up with a lid, and shove it aside until later.

I didn't know how I came to that method. It was a personal mechanism birthed from extreme stress.

Opening the list of bills on my phone, I saw two bills that were unchecked, which meant unpaid.

You're losing it, Elena.

I should have felt bad leaving work early, but right now I didn't care. Why should I care about ethics when my employer didn't give a damn about me? I'd worked so hard there, and for what? A false accusation and my show pulled from the air. Money had power. It talked louder than someone like me who was struggling with finances. Who didn't have powerful family or friends.

I'd use the time off from work to think about what I wanted to do. Should I return to work and do mundane news? Though my heart wasn't in it, I needed the money. Maybe I'd spend the time looking for another job.

I drove out of the parking garage and headed to pay my bill, which had incurred the massive late fee of five hundred dollars.

"Remain calm. You can do this," I told myself. "*Mamá* doesn't need to see you stressed out. She won't retire if she knows about your financial predicament."

The late fee to my phone bill—which included my mom's mobile phone—was something I could deal with even though the extra money could've gone toward the insurmountable debt looming over me like a dark cloud that had just gotten darker.

Only three hundred thousand dollars left. I'd be free after that.

The loan shark was cold and ruthless. I couldn't negotiate with him without fearing he'd hurt me or my mom. I knew he'd create trouble for my family if I didn't pay up. The worst of it all? The loan shark was my uncle Carlos, my deceased father's older brother. Money was blood to him. Everything else was just . . . everything else.

My father had incurred an obscene amount of debt to my uncle, a greedy man who valued money more than his family. Maybe that was why he didn't have a wife or kids. Who would want to be with a heartless man? The day after my father died from a stroke, Uncle Carlos came to me and my mom asking for the money. The asshole didn't even have the courtesy to let us grieve. Did he even grieve for his brother?

I'd lied to my mom, telling her everything was taken care of. I didn't want her to stress about it. She was recovering from a thyroid condition that had made her thin, pale, and losing a lot of hair. Her hair was just growing back. The financial burden would destroy her. She was all I had left.

As a journalist, I'd seen all kinds of people doing all kinds of callous things to each other. But it still shocked me that a family member considered me and my mom as enemies. Money could do that to people—turn their hearts black, their eyes blind, and their emotions cold.

I'd met strangers who were kinder to me.

Even though my mom was officially retired next week, she would continue to volunteer at Wild Roots a few days a week. I didn't object because it would keep her mind active. She deserved a retirement gift, but there was no extra money for that. I'd used up my savings and my 401k money to pay an enormous sum to Uncle Carlos. These days, I was living paycheck to paycheck.

Should I ask Uncle Carlos to waive the late fee?

Nerves returned as I imagined his harsh reply. *"I have a family to feed too, Elena."*

He considered his violent men family. Did my father know his brother was a coldhearted loan shark?

There's no such thing as a compassionate loan shark, Elena.

Did my father assume Uncle Carlos would be kind to his family and dismiss his debt?

Some days it infuriated me that my dad had left this mess to me and Mom. What could I do but pay it? I couldn't call the police on Uncle Carlos. My dad had borrowed money from him, signed the agreement. This was a family dispute, and dragging him to court would bring shame to our family. I knew without a doubt Uncle Carlos would send his men to hurt us. Besides, I didn't want the world to know about my family's issues.

Bam!

A crunching noise cut through the air.

Holy fuck.

The loud noise yanked me back to the present moment. With trembling hands, I pulled over to the curb. I'd hit a parked car. *Shit.* Now I'd probably owe a lot more from the damages to this luxury car.

Shame on you, Elena.

Trembling inside my car, I glanced around and waited for someone to come screaming at me, but no one did. I could just drive off. No one would know . . .

But *I* knew. That act would forever live in the back of my mind, eating me up.

Karma catches up to you. You can't escape it. Always do the right thing.

Mamá's words rang in my ears. What if someone hit my car like that?

I inhaled a breath, got out, shut the door, and walked over to the beautiful black car I'd dented.

Shit.

Shit.

Shit.

If I thought my uncle's debt was too much, I was wrong. The amount of money required to repair the damages to this beautiful car could make me homeless. This car lived in another world—a world I could never enter. A world I didn't understand.

What had I gotten myself into?

My body quivered as anxiety slithered around me. I stared at the Bugatti La Voiture Noire, admiring the sleek design that demanded attention. It was magnetic, compelling, and legendary. How did I know about this car?

I'd accompanied my best friend, Elliot, to the Geneva Car Show last year. He loved fashion, beauty products, and expensive cars. This one-of-a kind car had sold for about nineteen million dollars to some anonymous car freak.

If Batman had a big brother in a car form, this haute couture car would be it. A special edition like this shouldn't be parked in the busy streets of Providence. It should be in a garage somewhere. It should have bodyguards all around it.

"Doesn't look good." An old man with short silver hair approached me. He took off his shades, studied the car, made a face, and shook his head. He wore shorts with frayed edges, a brown safari jacket over a green T-shirt, and sneakers, making him appear like he'd just stepped out of an Indiana Jones movie. "Did you do that, dear?"

"Unfortunately, yes."

He glanced around, then shifted close to me. "There's no one here. It's gonna cost you. You should go. I won't say a word. I swear." He zipped his lips with his fingers and tucked the invisible key into one pocket on his vest.

His harmless gesture made me smile. "I can't do that."

"Why not?" He scrunched up his face, placing the sunglasses back on. "It's gonna cost an arm and leg."

"If this were my car, I'd want to know who dented it. Leaving would solve one issue for me, but I'd be thinking about it all night, wondering when the owner would find out and come after me. I wouldn't be able to sleep."

The man pursed his lips, nodding slowly as he looked at the damages with me.

Nausea rose, making me feel sick. "I'll be in debt forever."

"But it was an accident, right?" he asked.

I nodded. "I should've paid more attention to the road."

"Rough day?" He studied me.

Who was this stranger who brought a little comfort to my horrible day? "The worst."

He waved a hand. "It happens, dear."

My body stiffened as I sensed a presence around me.

"Uh-oh," said the old man. "I'm gonna take off. Good luck." He walked across the street and disappeared behind parked cars.

I turned and faced a man who sent my nerves skyrocketing to another level. Every time I saw Orion Reimann, my legs wobbled. There was something extremely powerful about him. If there was a man who suited the car, it would be him.

Orion Reimann was a man that emanated power and magnetism. He looked like a contained storm that could unleash its relentless force at any moment. A strong-boned face, high cheekbones, intense gray eyes, and a square jawline stirred something in me. Standing well over six feet tall, he wore a tailored black suit, a cream shirt, and a gray tie that cut him a wealthy man dwelling in a world way out of my reach. A world I didn't understand and didn't trust.

He resembled a sleek jaguar, wearing a perfect coat, dominating his terrain with his mere presence. I was prey frozen in place, even though he hadn't said a word to me. He radiated an air of power that could part the Red Sea.

Earth to Elena!

What the hell was wrong with me? My mind should be on practical matters, not some fantasies that weren't any help to me right now. I could owe him thousands of dollars I didn't have.

He ran his fingers over the dents and scratches. My eyes followed the long fingers and the expensive watch that looked more intricate than a Rolex. Orion seemed like a man who liked one-of-a-kind things.

I couldn't tell if he was angry.

"Sorry about the damages," I said, wanting to get the ordeal over with. "How much do I owe you?"

He walked up to me, and I was overwhelmed by the raw masculinity he exuded. My nerve endings sizzled from the close proximity. I panicked from the powerful reaction and fell a step back. Normally I held a barrier protecting me from exterior influences because it kept me safe in a bubble so I could do my job. Being a reporter put me close to the powerful and wealthy. Not all of those experiences had been good.

Stress had weakened my barrier today, and I felt Orion's energy thrum around me. He was a gorgeous man, a danger to women everywhere. What did a man with that kind of power do on a normal day? Did he wake up with a strict agenda, a disciplined diet, three assistants to help with whatever he needed, and several financial advisors to guide him to earn more than what he already had?

Boring.

I couldn't live a life based on charts, profit margins, and strict rules that would suffocate me. It would be like me trying to shove my foot into a fancy shoe that didn't fit.

Though he was out of my league, I could appreciate an attractive man when I saw one. It was healthy to acknowledge what you liked so that things you didn't like could stay away. What woman wouldn't be attracted to him? He was on the news a few weeks ago with a pretty woman in his arms. Every time I saw him, he had a new woman beside him.

Men like that were noncommittal. Just like my ex, they liked variety.

"You're a journalist, correct?" he asked in a baritone voice that made my inner thighs quiver.

"Yes. Why?"

His gaze raked down my body, and embarrassment washed over me. I wore gray capris with dirt stains I hadn't been able to remove and a T-shirt that read: *I can be held, but not touched. What am I?*

He stared at my chest, sending all kinds of sensations through my body. "What's the answer?"

"Huh?"

"The riddle on your shirt."

"Oh. It's a grudge."

"Do you hold grudges?" he asked.

I tried not to, but Chantel had been testing me. "It depends."

"On what?"

Why was he asking me these weird questions?

"Circumstances."

"I don't hold grudges—I just get even." His gaze intensified. "I have a proposal for you."

"What?" I thought I heard him wrong. "For what?"

The corner of his lips tilted. "What else? The damage to my car."

Why couldn't I think clearly? I needed to get this situation resolved so I could get to Uncle Carlos. The last thing I wanted was for him to slap on another late fee. He'd do that without remorse.

"What's the catch? I'm not interested in fine prints, Mr. Reimann."

"There's no fine print." Something sparked in his eyes. "You might change your mind after you hear what I have to say, Ms. Sanchez."

He knows me?

Well, that wasn't hard. I worked for Channel 7 News in Providence. He probably saw me on the news.

Orion leaned against the hood of his car, folded his powerful arms in front of his chest, and studied me. I believed God was playing favorites when Orion was born. I'd never met any man with his captivating features. I couldn't even describe him in words. He was beyond stunning. A new word had to be invented for him.

Don't wobble. Don't stumble.

The bones in my legs felt like they were dissolving, leaving me with nothing solid to stand on. Fearing I'd collapse in front of him, I stepped onto the curb and leaned against the pole with a one-hour parking sign. I inhaled and exhaled, trying my best to stay balanced. He probably thought I was acting strange, but I didn't care.

I'd never reacted to a man like this. I blamed my condition on this terrifying situation, the blazing sun, and financial doom.

"Why aren't you mad about the damages?"

"What makes you think I'm not?" he countered.

I didn't have time for games. "How much do I owe you?"

CHAPTER THREE

ORION

"YOU CAN'T AFFORD IT," I said, feeling a little better than I had earlier. Her beautiful face was the perfect distraction from my shitty day.

Elena didn't even bother looking away when she rolled her eyes at me. Sexy. Challenging. Like a secret dare only I understood. I admired the brave gesture. Most people would surrender and agree to everything I demanded, especially given the situation. She damaged my car, so I had the upper hand here.

The more I studied Elena, the more she fascinated me. Caution and suspicion gleamed in her brown eyes. If I were her, I'd do the same thing. She had smashed into my precious car, and her salary couldn't cover it. She knew this, and yet she hadn't run away. That intrigued me the most.

Her luscious lips formed a defiant pout. She was a beautiful woman trying to contain the fire within her. From my experience, a passionate person got things done properly.

I'd seen when her car slammed into mine. The camera from my car, the cameras from the street, and the ones on the building had all showed up on my feed. Normally I used my parking spot in the garage, but it would have cost me a few more minutes, and time had been scarce today. So when I saw this open spot, I pulled in. The conference room was just through the set of doors. Promptness was my forte, as it should be with people who ran multiple empires.

"Why don't you stop playing games and just tell me?" Irritation coated her voice.

I enjoyed the gorgeous view more than I expected.

"I don't have time for games."

The first time I'd seen her was at the Mount Centauri Museum, when I revealed my identity to Arrow, Remington, Grayson, Royce, and Forrest—the WaterFyre Rising boys. The second time was at Aimee and Kaylee's stuffed animal debut.

"Stop being an arrogant ass," she said without blinking.

I wondered if she'd hold a grudge against me.

"Just because I want to take my time doesn't make me arrogant, Elena." I liked the way her name sounded on my lips. "Why don't you want to hear my proposal?"

She pushed herself off the metal pole and flicked me an annoyed look. "It's probably wrapped in thorns. Not interested. What's the damage?"

"Do you know how much my car cost?"

"Why do you people spend so much money on a car?"

"Why not? I work hard for my money. I like beautiful things."

She pulled out her phone, glanced at it, and muttered. "Shit."

Anxiety strained her face as she tossed the phone back into her purse.

"A businessman like you should know that time is precious and costly. What's your proposal?"

I pushed myself off the hood and gestured to the scratches and dents. My finger traced the silver paint left from her car. "To pay for this dent here would require your annual salary. Mind you, there are more scratches over here."

The offer swimming in my head also surprised me. After hearing the story surrounding The Condor, I needed someone in this city to help me find answers. This was Elena's turf. She could assist me, help me see things I might've missed.

When she didn't take off after hitting my car, she became the perfect candidate. She possessed a character trait required to work with me. Elena Sanchez demonstrated she had an integrity that many people in the media lacked these days.

I'd encountered numerous respected journalists and trusted none of them. I could still be wrong about Elena, but I'd give her the benefit of the doubt. Besides, this was my opportunity to resolve an attraction I'd felt when I saw her at the museum.

I didn't have time for relationships. My concentration was on finding who had murdered my mentor.

Elena Sanchez intrigued me not only from what I'd witnessed on the recording, but from the way she made my heart race. There had only been one woman who'd done that, but she was no longer on this Earth.

You need to get laid.

That was probably true, but time had been scarce for that too.

Would she agree to help if she knew the reason for the proposal? Probably not.

She seemed agitated, so I'd give her the short version. Once she agreed, I could make adjustments.

"I need help that requires extensive research around Providence. You live and work here. I'd appreciate your perspective."

She arched an elegant eyebrow. "What kind of research?"

"The kind that takes down bad people regardless of who they are."

Her face brightened, lighting up something within me.

"Why me?" she asked.

I shrugged. "Because you report the truth, even if it costs your career."

She flicked me a curious gaze, studying me for far too long. "How did you know about that?"

"Work with me and I'll tell you."

"Why does it sound too good to be true?" she countered.

"You're overthinking it." I studied her reaction.

She gave me a half-laugh. "I'm certainly not." She jerked her chin toward my car. "That stunning beast of a car cost more than most mansions. I fear your proposal might lead me to my demise."

I laughed. "You have an interesting imagination."

"No, I'm being practical. You're a rich guy who can pull all kinds of strings. I work in the media and I've seen, heard, and witnessed countless things requested—no, *demanded*—by privileged people like you. Frankly, I don't trust them."

Such admirable honesty.

"You believe I'm untrustworthy because of my wealth? That's prejudice, isn't it?"

There goes the sexy eye roll. Fucking hell.

"I didn't say that." She scoffed. "But what you just did

was twist my words into some retort that makes you seem glamorous while I look like a jerk."

Was I trying to do that? *No.*

Would she believe me? Probably not.

"I guess a journalist suspects people the same way the people suspect a journalist."

"What do you mean?"

"No one trusts the media. They can twist things to suit their agenda." I stepped closer. "You know I'm right."

A privileged family had tried to pay her off for not reporting about their son's rape of two college girls. Elena was the witness who had stumbled on him with the two intoxicated girls. When she refused, the family threatened to destroy her career. Not only did she report it, she also discovered evidence to help the police. However, her career suffered. That family owned a share of the news station, and she'd been demoted ever since, only reporting on a smaller scale and focusing on Uncover the Truth.

Her elegant eyebrow arched. "Why me?"

"You're a seasoned journalist who can do what I need done efficiently."

"But there are others out there who are better."

"I'd say 'better' is a subjective adjective, wouldn't you agree? For example, Robert Banks from Channel Five News is respected and revered. And yet he just admitted to fraud, among other things. Kelly Connelly is a beautiful and experienced anchor. The City of Providence loves her, and yet she took someone's hard work as her own."

Elena's mouth dropped open. "How do you know that? That's confidential."

I lifted a shoulder. "I'm good at research too."

Intrigue glimmered in her eyes.

"I'll give you fifty-thousand dollars for a two-week trial."

"What?" Her eyes widened.

"That wouldn't even cover the paint job for my car."

She ran a hand through her hair, stress reappearing on her face.

"And after the two weeks, if you decide to stay to finish the project, you'll get three hundred thousand dollars."

Her jaw dropped. "You're kidding!"

"I don't kid around with important things like this."

Her eyes sparkled. "What's the timeline for the project's completion?"

"Probably three to four months, with some wiggle room to adjust for unexpected events."

"I have a full-time job."

"Make your own time. Work whenever you can. I'll have a secured drive where you can upload and share information with me. I'll provide everything you need. You won't need to spend any money."

She looked at me for a moment, took out her phone, glanced at it, sighed, and dropped it back into her purse. What was she worried about?

Looking nervous, she asked, "If I agree to help you now, is it possible to get an advance?"

"That could be arranged. But why?"

I didn't know why I asked. She didn't need to tell me, but I got a sense that something was bothering her.

"To buy my mother something for her retirement gift."

"I can wire it right now. We start next Monday."

"Okay. Do you need me to fill out some forms?"

"We can do that later."

She took out her phone, showed me her bank account number, and smiled. "Here you go."

CHAPTER FOUR

ELENA

I DIDN'T HAVE time to contemplate the strange encounter with Orion or how his presence overwhelmed me with need. I'd save that for later tonight. My bank account had grown an extra twenty-five thousand dollars, which I desperately needed to feed my deflating balance.

I drove toward Uncle Carlos's business as a series of nerves tumbled inside me. They were different nerves. How did I know that? I wasn't sure. My mind could tell the difference as though a clementine sat next to a tangerine. From a distance they looked the same, but close up they were two different things.

I knew I was going insane when I started comparing my nerves to fruits. But the analogy kept my brain functioning properly. For now.

I should have collapsed in a heap on the floor with the multiple jobs I had to juggle and the increasing stress taking a toll on my mental and physical health, but somehow, I was still standing. Maybe my dad and grandmother were watching over me from up there. I'd never met my father's parents. They'd passed before I was born.

My mind swung back to when Orion looked at me, making my knees wobble. He had created a new anxiety that had nothing to do with my debt. I'd felt this when I encountered him at Kaylee and Aimee's stuffed animal debut. My Musepaper subscriber list had tripled after that segment, featuring young entrepreneurs. He'd been there to support them. I'd dismissed the sensation because I wasn't the only woman ogling at him.

Vivian, Audri, Michelle, Kiera, and Natalie all made comments about him and the women. He probably had several girlfriends.

Why was I thinking about this right now?

Stay focused or you're gonna hit another car.

Ugh. Pushing everything aside, I pulled into a parking lot, got out, and looked at my sad car with the damages that wouldn't get repaired. His car could be fixed, but my Honda Civic had to wear those scars. It wasn't worth the money to fix it, and I didn't want to report it to my insurance company because they'd hike up my premium.

"Sorry about today," I said to my car and ran my fingers over the damage. "Stay strong for me, okay? I need you."

I couldn't afford a new car, but I had to get new winter tires this year for the snow. My all-season tires were all worn down.

Huffing out a breath, I headed into the brick building my uncle owned. The ten-story building had other businesses, but Sanchez Financial took up the entire first floor. Though the building didn't look gloomy, a shiver ran down my spine as I yanked the door open, heading to his office.

My grandmother used to tell me that some places

were homes to dark energy. She was a mystic and believed in that stuff, especially when she was living in Peru. I believed it to a certain extent.

I was certain my father wasn't the only person in debt to Sanchez Financial. From the outside, their business seemed like a normal financial firm loaning money to homebuyers and such. Maybe he had a different department that dealt with gamblers. I'd done some research on him and the legality of loan sharks, but nothing could help erase the debt my father owed him.

My father had owed him eight hundred thousand dollars in loans over the course of three years, which neither my mother nor I heard about until after his death. I didn't know my father had a gambling issue. My mother had been sick for a couple of years and hadn't been able to work as much. I could see why he went this route. But he should've talked to me. We could've found another way to pay medical bills and the mortgage without a dangerous loan shark breathing down our necks.

I walked up to the receptionist, a pretty girl wearing a black dress with a nametag that read Sofia. Monique had greeted me the last time I was here. Before Monique was Tamara. He probably had a lot of part-time secretaries.

"I'm here to see Carlos."

Sofia smiled, picked up the phone, and informed him of my arrival.

"You can go right in. He's waiting for you."

I walked down the hallway to the double doors. A man dressed in a suit opened the door and gestured for me to go in.

A man in a brown suit with a bushy beard sat on the

couch beside Uncle Carlos's desk. They were drinking wine while discussing how much they earned from people like me. Both men glanced over at me. Burly Man raked a gaze over me, and my body felt dirty. I wanted to get out of the office immediately.

I'd give my uncle ten thousand dollars today. That would reduce the loan to three hundred thousand dollars. The burden had weighed heavily on me for the past two years. His interest rates were insane. These loan sharks made up their own rules and robbed people of their hard-earned money.

I was trying my best to not let my mother know anything about this debt. If she did, she'd want to return to work to help me pay it off.

Only three hundred thousand dollars left. I could do this.

If I didn't, he'd take over my mother's house and my house, which I'd inherited from my grandmother. He couldn't take it legally because we owned it. But he could create enough trouble for me and my mom, forcing us to let the homes go.

Why was I related to such an evil man?

I was ashamed to be his niece. I wanted to pay off the debt and be done with him forever.

Uncle Carlos smiled, got up from his chair, and walked over to me. "Elena." He took my hand in his as though he adored me.

My hand felt icky from his touch, and I needed a hand sanitizer once I got back into my car.

I reached into my purse, pulled out the check, and gave it to him. "This will cover the next three months. I won't be late."

Nodding, he looked at the check and arched an eyebrow. "You won the lottery?"

"Thanks to you, I've been working a lot." I pasted a fake smile on my face.

Uncle Carlos smirked. "That mouth of yours could get you in trouble."

I'm already in financial trouble.

I wanted to say so much more, but I heard the threat in his sentence.

"Who's this, Carlos?" Burly Man asked.

"Sam, this is Elena, my niece."

Sam's stare made me feel like a snake had slithered down my back.

"Thank you for the payment. I'll send the invoice with the updated balance to your email. You're doing a great job."

"I know my balance. See you later."

When the door closed behind me, I blew out a breath. But I didn't breathe normally until I got into my car. I wished I could've just paid for everything online so I didn't have to come here. But he had insisted on a check payment handed to him.

Then I headed to my part-time job waitressing at Let's Ketchup restaurant, a fusion restaurant that made the best fries I'd ever eaten. The owner, Mario, knew my mom, but I asked him not to tell her I was working there. It was just two days a week, but the tip money had helped me in the past few months.

I was a battery going into overdrive. Hopefully I'd bring home great tips tonight.

CHAPTER FIVE

ORION

"YOU GOT IT," said Sebastian, my mechanic and longtime friend. I didn't trust anyone but him and his team to work on my cars. He only worked for me and traveled to wherever I needed him. He got paid well for keeping my collectibles top-notch.

"I'll be taking the black SUV for now."

"How did you get these dents?" He studied the damage to my Bugatti.

"I parked on the street instead of in the garage because I was running late for a conference."

"Did you find out who did it?"

I didn't know why, but a strange protectiveness rose in me. I didn't want him slandering Elena.

I nodded. "It's resolved."

"Who the fuck would dent this masterpiece?" He patted the car, talking to it like it was his pet. "You didn't know what hit you, huh?"

Though the question wasn't directed at me, I answered it in my head. *No.* I didn't know how strong the force was until

I couldn't remove her from my mind. Elena figuratively slammed into me today, unsettling me.

Though I considered Sebastian a good friend, I didn't want to rope him into my business.

But you just yanked Elena Sanchez into your business, my inner voice sounded, and I shoved it away. She knew the area, and that was an advantage I needed.

Liar.

Working with a smart and attractive woman was an added benefit any business executive would agree with, and I was a man who valued profit.

"Have Ralph drop off the Bugatti at the garage." I hopped into the black SUV and headed to my apartment, which was an entire floor in my office building.

I pulled into my garage, and my phone rang. Getting out, I groaned at my cousin's name.

"What is it, Jasper?" I asked, not in the mood to deal with him.

His parents had left him a lot of money, but nothing he'd done in the past two years had garnered success.

"Can't I call to see how my cousin's doing?"

"That would make you too considerate, and that's not you."

"Asshole," he said.

I grinned, thinking about his missing Rolex and the Bugatti watch that were inside a safe of things I'd soon sell on the black market. I didn't want his watches; I just liked knowing he'd suffer because someone took his belongings.

"You sound cheerful. Did you just buy a new watch or something?"

"You know me so well. Got a watch *and* a car."

"You don't have a good track record holding on to things."

"Not my fault! I've been searching for them in the market. I'm going to destroy the fucker who took them."

"Probably one of your friends."

"Nah, they can afford their own Rolex and car. It has to be some lowlife. Anyway, have you reconsidered my proposal?"

This was the reason he called.

"I already told you no. My answer is final, Jasper. I'm not selling Quintile Island."

"Your father said you might change your mind if I gave you enough time to think about it."

That was a lie.

"First, there's no price that would make me sell my island. Second, if you don't already know, my father and I don't have a relationship other than a DNA match. He doesn't know what I want. You've been misinformed."

Speaking to Jasper drained my energy. He was an irritating person who never listened to anything that didn't align with his needs. He should take lessons from his older brother, Jonah, who had more business experience and common sense. Jonah had taken over his father's position, helping run the Reimann Sienna Bank along with my father. But Jonah also had his real estate company to manage. It was recently voted one of the top ten firms in the world. I often wondered if he ever had the same pressure placed upon him the way it was bestowed upon me.

Did he have panic attacks? Did he suffer in silence?

Jasper had asked me to collaborate with him on several business ventures. I'd declined all of them. Even his brother had declined him.

I didn't enjoy collaborating with family. Too much potential to get messy. Besides, I'd never forget how Jasper and my aunt had talked about my mother behind her back. Or how they had shamed Kate for being open about her battle with depression. My chest tightened as my hand went to the gold ring dangling from my necklace. Kate and I were supposed to get married before mental illness took her from me.

That familiar sadness crept in, and I hated Jasper even more for souring my mood. "I'm done talking."

"I'll give you another week to think about it. If your answer is still the same, I'll stop bugging you. I really want Quintile Island."

Frustration flared, and a headache bloomed in my temple.

"Why?" I seethed.

"Because it's a great location. I want to develop a tourist resort that could bring in a lot of money."

I rolled my eyes, and the gesture reminded me of Elena. Then a surge of desire swarmed through me.

"Let me save you time. The answer will always be no. Don't ask me again." I hung up and leaned back in the seat.

A part of me felt guilty for wanting Elena. Though Kate was no longer with me, I still respected her. She was like me in so many ways. She could finish my sentences and knew me better than my family. There hadn't been a serious relationship after her. Just temporary flings that had no strings attached.

Elena's beautiful face flashed into my vision, like a rebel with her own agenda. She was the first woman who had intrigued me this much. The first woman to squeeze herself into my thoughts, anchoring herself there.

I couldn't shove her away.

Maybe it wasn't a good idea to have her working for me. The contract would be only four months at the most. Then she would be on her way and I'd return to Sweden.

Huffing out a breath, I exited the car and entered my home. The quiet welcomed me, but the sadness still clung like gloomy clouds. I walked over to the kitchen counter, poured myself two fingers of whiskey, and brought it into my office.

Working had always kept my mind focused. Right now, I needed to concentrate on the reason I was in Providence.

Who had killed my mentor? I owed everything to him. He'd made me into a man who followed his dreams despite what his environment demanded. A man who had stolen in order to right some wrong. Sometimes crimes were necessary to catch the criminals.

The Condor had given me a sense of purpose. Without purpose, a man had no direction.

I was born into a wealthy family with everything provided for me. I didn't have to work hard or finish college to receive a privileged lifestyle. I was predestined for it. Despite having all of that, I felt so alone and vulnerable, especially after my mother died. She had been the person who knew how to ease my panic attacks.

Money couldn't solve it. The best therapist in the world couldn't help me. No one could.

The pills helped a little when life became too much, too dark. Over time they stopped working too. But I'd learned to recognize the life patterns that could trigger my anxiety. Most things were just phases that would soon pass.

That was how I'd been living my life.

People didn't know what lay behind the glossy façade.

I finished my whiskey, letting the taste linger on my tongue before swallowing.

Then I turned my attention back to the investigation and opened The Condor's file. It held everything I'd gathered about him and those he'd been in contact with. His routine, what shops he visited, where he went for coffee. People he saw regularly when he was in Providence.

The Condor was like a father to me when my father was too busy to even look at me. My mentor was a meticulous man who had his own wealth, but he lived a simple life. He didn't drive expensive cars or dine lavishly. He blended in with everyday people.

Who wanted him dead? Why?

I browsed the list of names and businesses he'd visited over the years. Digging into my mentor's personal life was something I didn't want to do. I didn't want to violate his privacy, but this had to be done.

Did he know an elite member of The Trogyn? He'd never mentioned them to me. But then again, maybe that was what he'd been waiting to tell me. I flipped back to the few times we'd met up. The Condor had seemed normal. He gave no indication that something was wrong.

The past few months had been chaotic, throwing my thoughts in many directions. I needed to see this investigation clearly, otherwise I'd miss an important detail that could lead to the killer.

Exhaustion pulled at me. Leaning back against the chair, I closed my eyes, and a memory flashed.

I sit on the couch in my father's library, my cousins Jonah and Jasper sitting across from me. Jonah is reading a comic book, and Jasper is watching something on his phone, laughing like an idiot. Jonah has dark hair, while Jasper got his mom's genes of dirty blonde hair.

"Look at her." He elbows Jonah. "Remember her?"

"You still have that?" Jonah shakes his head.

"Yeah! She's got a pretty face. I wish we had more time with her."

Jasper is such a prick. He's probably bullying someone and recording it.

I don't want to be in the same room as him. I get up and walk toward the door.

"Where are you going?" Jasper rises from the couch and follows me, tugging at my backpack.

Uncle Ray is discussing something with my father in his office.

"Out," I said.

"Where? I heard your dad tell you to stay in the library to study."

I flick him an annoyed gaze. "I don't need to study. But you do."

I'm an excellent student with an excellent memory.

Why are my cousins so annoying? They should both go home.

Jasper flicks me an annoyed look. "I heard you cheated on your math exam."

I'm surprised more kids didn't beat the shit out of him. They're probably afraid my aunt and uncle would sue them.

"Unlike you, I don't need to cheat or pay another kid to write my essays," I mock.

Dumb fuck.

"Your mom's into weird shit." He laughs. "Bet her death was written in the stars."

Rage surges through me. I drop my backpack on the floor,

walk over, and punch him in the face. "You talk shit about my mother again and I'll break all your teeth. Then I'm going to tell the dean all the essays you've submitted this year were by other kids you paid off." I seethe as anger pumps through me. "I'll even name them."

"You wouldn't dare!" He holds a hand to his face while pointing at me.

"Try me!"

Jonah jumps up from his seat to stand in between us. "Stop it!"

"Your mom was nothing before she married Uncle Rex!" Jasper shouts.

"At least my mom isn't fucking her accountant or her security guard like your mother." I try to reach for the asshole, but Jonah stops me.

"Just go," Jonah told me. "I'll take care of him." He whirls around to his brother. "Shut up! Dad's gonna hear you."

I leave the room, seething. Jasper is such an asshole. He probably gets it from his mother. I don't understand why Uncle Ray doesn't divorce her. Maybe he has a mistress on the side too.

I hurry into the backyard, escape through the garden to the park, and call The Condor to let him know I've arrived. While waiting for him, I kick a rock, imagining it is Jasper's head.

I reach into my backpack, open a bottle of lavender oil my mom got me before she passed. Whenever I sense a panic attack, I'll sniff it and look around me to find three things, starting with the color red. I continue the process until I've used up all the colors in the rainbow.

It's her method to train my brain to calm itself. I miss her so much.

"Hey, buddy," he says with an accent. He drops beside me

on the bench and slings an arm around me. "Sorry about your mother. She's watching over you."

Not sure if I want her to, especially with the things I've been doing.

Sorry, Mom.

"Everything okay?" His brown eyes search mine. He's grown his brown hair long past his chin. I almost don't recognize him.

"What's with the beard?"

He laughs. "New trend."

"Yeah, right." I don't believe him. "You're in disguise. What are you planning? Can I come?"

He studies me. "Would that make you feel better?"

I nod fiercely. "Yes."

"Okay, we'll talk later. I want to see that prize."

I reach into my backpack for the brooch I've stolen, placing it into his hand.

Smiling, The Condor holds the brooch, studying it like a precious gem. "You did a fabulous job. Looks better than the photo you sent me." Tears and pride gleam in his eyes. "This is a fine treasure. Keep it safe, okay? Every thief has his own treasure chest to store his favorite prizes. Here's yours."

A reminder buzzed on my phone, bringing me back to the present moment. I had a conference call tomorrow and a meeting with Remi and Attikus the following day to discuss The Trogyn. All the boys were monitoring various angles of the crime organization. Though we had eliminated many elite members, there were still plenty around.

CHAPTER SIX

ELENA

BY THE TIME I got home from Let's Ketchup, I was exhausted but too wired to sleep. I could have called in, taken a day to rest because of the extra income that I'd stumbled into, but I couldn't do that to Mario. He'd been good to me.

After a quick shower, I crawled into bed and Orion's gorgeous face popped into my vision. Heat swirled in my lady parts, forcing me to stay wide awake.

I had an entire week before the new gig started. What would it be like to work with an intense man like him? Was he a micromanager? Or did he trust his team to do their job?

What exactly did he need me to research, anyway?

I couldn't deny my attraction to Orion. He probably didn't know I existed until I smashed into his car. His type of woman hung out with celebrities and rich folks. That world was beyond me. I'd searched his name after seeing him at the museum. There wasn't a lot of info on him. I'd browsed the few pics of him at social events with pretty women. A brunette and a blonde. An uncomfortable feeling stirred in my stomach, and I did something against my better judgment—I compared myself to them.

Since I couldn't sleep, I checked my Musepaper website. I'd gotten more subscribers, which meant I needed to create more content. I had plans for this newspaper, but not enough time to do everything. My energy was dwindling, but I didn't know what to do.

Sometimes you just had to trust the universe. That it would guide you to where you need to be.

I had two articles to finish for Musepaper and continue the research I'd started for Uncover the Truth, even though I didn't have that platform to share my results anymore. I could release my findings on Musepaper, so those families who had trusted me would get some answers.

Had Orion seen my show? Heat warmed my body as I recalled the intensity of his eyes on me. He had the potent stare that held command and secrets. Who was the real Orion Reimann beneath the fine clothing, gorgeous face, and perfect body?

The man seemed like a pressure cooker today. But I guess I was one too. We were both holding something within us. What was he trying to contain? Or was he intentionally giving off an intense energy that made those around him jitter?

Stop thinking about him.

I scrolled through the emails in the general inbox for Musepaper, browsing all the inspiring stories people had sent me. Once in a while, I'd request my readers to send me stories about their town. But that kind of request opened doors to a slew of things.

I'd gotten emails from men asking me out on dates. Some asked for relationship advice. So many people were just lonely and needed an outlet. Online dating could be a dangerous place. I'd reported on several people getting scammed, raped, or killed from meeting someone on a dating app. Though I also heard about happily ever afters, the terrifying ones had stayed with me.

No online dating for me.

I hadn't dated anyone since Liam Fleming, my ex-boyfriend, who didn't have trouble moving on to New York City to be with the heiress of a luxury handbag company. He now worked as the news anchor for the popular show World News Recap. I didn't have her influence, and I couldn't help his career.

Was that important to all men? Would Orion choose a woman with influence to help his career over someone he loved? Liam didn't love me. He didn't understand the meaning of unconditional love.

My chest ached, and I placed a hand over my heart. Though I was attracted to Orion, I couldn't let my heart be broken again. I'd put in a lot of effort to make things work with Liam, but in the end, he chose someone else. He'd left me during a time when I was grieving for my father.

That said a lot about a man, right?

Stop thinking about him.

I hated when I couldn't sleep late at night. All the muck from my life floated to the surface, taunting me.

To lift my mood, I browsed previous articles on Musepaper. I smiled as I reviewed the recent write-up on Stuffed Cuteness, an adorable collection of stuffed animals from Vivian's younger sister Kaylee and their friend, Aimee. That story had gone viral and gotten me a lot of subscribers. Young girls had written to me asking for more information on Kaylee and Aimee.

My phone rang, startling me. I grinned at my best friend. "Hey, Elliot."

"What kind of greeting is that?" he asked.

"What do you mean?"

"Where's the enthusiasm for your best friend you haven't seen in a month?"

"It's eleven at night. I'm about to go to bed."

"Shit! Sorry, darling. I'm still in California. Be back in on Wednesday. What have you been up to?"

"Working. You know my situation," I said, appreciating him more than he knew.

We'd been best friends since the sixth grade. Elliot was a handsome gay man, and I'd used him to keep creepy men away from me when we hung out. He owned Salon Oasis and knew how to dress to impress.

"You need a break. You're not a machine."

I knew that, but there was so much to do and not enough time. Bills needed to be paid.

"I will. Don't worry. I'll take a few days for a staycation. Not in the mood to travel." I didn't want to spend unnecessary money for a hotel and other travel expenses.

"Did you fix the leak in the roof yet?"

"On my to-do list. Guess what? I slammed into a Bugatti Voiture today."

"What? Holy shit. What happened?" he gasped, knowing how much that car cost.

I gave him a brief version of the events.

"He offered you a job just like that? What's the catch?"

"He needs my help with an investigation."

"What kind? Nothing shady, I hope."

I smiled at his protectiveness. Elliot was like the brother

I never had. "I'm not sure. I start on Monday at a building downtown. He's a rich guy."

"An extremely rich guy. Only Richie Rich could afford that car. Can't believe he let you off that easily."

"Maybe he really needs my help. He's not from here, and he said he needs someone who knows the area."

"The wealthy can commit crimes and pay others to erase the proof. Just be careful, okay? Promise?"

I'd encountered a few of those stories before. "I promise."

"The reason I'm calling—without even thinking about the time—is because one of my clients is hosting a charity event to support a fashion designer. It's a silent auction, and the proceeds will go to a couple of local charities. One model had a family emergency and can't make it to Monday night's event. You interested?"

My new job started on Monday. It might be too stressful?

"I'm not a model, Elliot."

"But you've modeled for me before. Besides, you'll make three grand for wearing clothes and walking around for three hours of work. It starts at seven PM."

Anxiety tightened my shoulders. I should be resting . . . but the extra income would definitely help me out.

"Showing off your hairstyling skills isn't modeling, Elliot. I don't know how to walk or pose like those models."

"This isn't a Paris fashion show. It's a charity event where regular people wear clothes to mingle. I'm going too. My team will do the hair and makeup. Come on, darling, let me help you."

That money could be added to the fund for a new roof, or new car tires. Or take care of my check-engine light, which just came on tonight.

"So I don't need to do the catwalk? Just be myself?"

"Yup. Karina is modeling too. You know how clumsy she is."

Karina worked for Elliot and had done a phenomenal job with my highlights last year when he was out of town.

"Okay. I'll do it."

"You haven't been in for highlights. Come on Wednesday, and I'll squeeze you in."

I felt bad going to him because he always did everything for me for free.

"It's okay. I can skip this year."

"You are NOT skipping. Don't think I don't know why you're hesitating." He sighed. "You're like a sister to me. We're family, darling. I don't charge you because it makes me happy to make you look beautiful and to see that smile on your gorgeous face. So stop acting weird."

"I'm not acting weird. You're running a business. And I don't want to take advantage—"

"Stop it. How many times have you modeled for me at my shows for free? You helped me build a successful career. Not to mention all those essays I had to do in college. You were there for me." He inhaled and exhaled. "If you don't come in tomorrow, I'm going to be mad. You don't want to see furious Elliot."

I smiled at my dear friend. Why couldn't any of my previous boyfriends love me like him? Unconditionally. No one had put me first except my dad. But that kind of affection was different from lovers.

"Okay. But I don't want to get Jake jealous."

Jake was Elliot's longtime boyfriend. He often traveled with Elliot, attending the latest shows on beauty, hair, and fashion.

Elliot laughed. "Jake loves you, darling. He knows where

he stands with me. Because you're my sister, you're his sister too. That's a given."

Someone shouted something to him in the background. "Gotta go. See you tomorrow!"

After I hung up the phone, I returned to my computer and saw Orion's email.

My heart raced seeing his name. What the hell was wrong with me?

Apparently, he'd stayed up late too.

I reviewed the email from Orion. He sent me the link to the shared drive, a login with a temporary password, a guideline of the files and their contents, and a brief explanation of what he needed me to do.

He wanted me to help investigate the murder of The Condor. I'd never heard of this person. Orion ended the email by saying he'd explain more on my first day.

I admired his organization skill because I couldn't master it. It seemed too strict for me. I preferred leaving space in between just to breathe. One time I tried to organize my schedule months in advance and got bored. Managing an online newspaper required a schedule, and I had and followed that. But it had flexibility for me to shift things around.

Was Orion a man always on a disciplined schedule? I didn't know why, but I wanted to rearrange his schedule just to see how he'd react.

What would it be like to get him flustered?

CHAPTER SEVEN

ORION

I STAYED up late researching Elena and Musepaper, which I hadn't heard of until she wrote an article for Kaylee and Aimee. I'd rescued Aimee from sex traffickers, and she'd charmed me with her intelligence and impressive memory. Kaylee, who was Arrow's half-sister, was also a genius. I knew these two girls would contribute immensely to society one day, and I loved supporting children with big dreams.

I browsed Musepaper's website and stopped at a section called Random Riddles. The latest riddle was posted a month ago. It made me think of Madame Sarcasm, a blogger I used to follow.

Tenting my fingers, I studied Elena's riddle.

I have a bank, but no cash. I like to run, but not walk. I wave, but never say hello. What am I?

What could it be? I didn't want to cheat and look at the answers by clicking on the link at the bottom of the page. After a few minutes, I gave up and found the answer: a river.

I smiled, appreciating the little joys that took me out of

my stress bubble. Doctors couldn't prescribe remedies like these. This was a completely new way for my psyche to shift itself. Madame Sarcasm had done this for me years ago.

I searched for Madame Sarcasm in my email inbox and brought up the last reply, which was her last blog post. Some people called her a unique therapist with no degree.

Inquire at your own risk.

That had been her warning for those who wanted to ask a question, but didn't know what to expect. Over the course of two years, I'd read her replies to people. She'd replied to three of mine. But her last reply was the most interesting of the three.

I'd never heard of her until I overheard a couple talking at an airport. The wife claimed that Madame Sarcasm had helped her untangle her anxiety. Since I had my own psychological issues, my curiosity had been piqued. No therapist had helped me, and I'd paid a lot of money for the best of the best. I'd checked out Madame Sarcasm's website and realized it was her ability to take people out of their confined head space that made her successful. She did it indirectly by making it fun and not forceful. I didn't know if she knew what she was doing, but many people had benefited from her style.

The bio picture that had been on her website showed a lady with silver hair wearing eccentric glasses with catlike eyes. I wondered if my mother knew her. They would've been great friends.

I reread her reply to my inquiry from a year ago.

Dear Asteroid Curious,

You have a very fascinating name. Great way to catch my attention. Your question piques my interest. Life is all about exploring unfamiliar areas, and you've allowed me to step into a place I hadn't been before.

I'll put your question below for everyone's reference so they know I didn't come up with this weird shit.

Question: If you were an asteroid floating in space and a bright star blocked your view of Earth, what would you do?

Answer: First of all, it would make sense for me to give myself a name. Please call me Sassteroid. I love traveling through space with my partner, but then he strays, gazing at other asteroids. He tells me he needs some space, pun intended.

The Universe hears him and answers the request. I'm minding my own business, admiring the mesmerizing nebula, when a dying star bursts and tosses me away from my home—away from him.

I suppose my ex's wish comes true. He has all the space he wants now. Thank the gods.

With renewed independence, I explore the vastness before me because staying stagnant is boring. I approach a cluster of glittering stars. But there's one particular star that's so bright, it blocks my view of the Earth.

I quiet my mind and hear the stars whisper to each other. The cosmic chatter is quite interesting. I understand their conversation through the cosmic vibration. Do they know that I'm close by? Probably. Do they care? Probably not.

Why?

Because I'm a small asteroid, not a big and respectable planet. What exactly can I do to them?

Perhaps a kind approach will suffice in this situation. If he says no, then he doesn't deserve to be a shining star.

I come up to him. "May I please join your cluster?"

To my surprise, he replies, "Oh dear little asteroid. Come into the light. Let's all get along and not fight."

My asteroid brain is stunned. I don't know what to say to this poetic star that just made my universe brighter and more hopeful.

I hope my reply puts a smile on your face. Thank you and all of my readers for three years of wonderful sarcasm and support. When I started this blog, it was just for fun. I didn't think people would send me so many questions.

But it's time for me to move on. Maybe I'll return one day.

For now, ciao ciao.

Madame Sarcasm

The first time I read her reply, I cracked up so hard. All the comments below the post were mostly laughing or heart emojis. I knew her reply would be unique, but I didn't expect this level of personification. Her response took my imagination to new places.

Whenever I looked up at the sky, I wondered if there was an asteroid making friends with some stars. Of course, no one would ever know this about me.

Sometimes people appeared in your life for a specific reason, and Elena had reminded me of a person who had helped me deal with my anxiety.

I should have gone to bed, but since I was feeling extra energetic now, I reviewed the notes regarding my mentor's death. I looked at his apartment documents. He bought that apartment a long time ago, before we even met. I thought he bought it only five years ago.

But then again, I owned several properties all over the world and had never told him either. Maybe he needed a place to store his treasures. I didn't know if The Trogyn knew about me and him. Regardless, I had to be a few steps ahead of them.

CHAPTER EIGHT

ORION

THE NEXT DAY, I walked around my office like a fool, trying to shrug Elena out of my mind. Irritation still clung to me after waking up from an erotic dream about her. I had just finished a conference call with my team, but I could still sense her presence as though she were right beside me. Even her floral perfume scent stirred in my office.

She was like a cunning thief stealing my sanity, time, and energy.

I stopped at my desk and stared at her reply to my email, wondering what she was doing. I should work on the drone prototype, see the status of the software development, check in on the construction of the building on my island, as well as countless other projects on my to-do list. Not to mention I hadn't worked on Level Six for a few weeks because there hadn't been time.

No, I just didn't have energy. Or was it motivation?

You're sex deprived.

Needing to calm my mind, I stepped onto my furnished balcony and took in a big inhale of the late August air. The low humidity offered comfort for my body. I could tell it was on edge where a trigger could start a panic attack.

Over the years I'd learned how to read my body and knew what I needed. The anxiolytics never worked because my mind knew what they were trying to do.

I paced the balcony, trying to empty my thoughts, but the stress had seeped into my bones, my muscles. There was a lot on my plate, but that was my fault for taking on too many things. I dropped to the lounge chair and settled back.

As I breathed, I saw the faces of my loved ones. Over the years I'd come to understand this monster inside me. It had grown with the death of each person I loved. Their presence had been the barrier between me and the monster. When they died, a part of me went with them.

My mother's death took a huge chunk from my heart. Then Kate's death took another portion. I reached for the ring dangling from my necklace. We were supposed to get married, but she lost the battle with the darkness in her. I couldn't help her. Now, with The Condor's death, I felt like there was nothing left in my heart.

Sadness, anger, and the feeling that the world was crumbling around me.

You're the strongest boy I know, Orion. You're the hunter in the sky, and you can achieve anything.

My mother's words echoed in my head.

Pain teaches us compassion.

Kate used to tell me that all the time. She had been my best friend. We were similar in so many ways, and I missed her.

An extraordinary person has to overcome extraordinary obstacles. I admire your strength.

The Condor had told me that once. Even though he

probably said that to encourage me, I had tucked his words away for days like today.

To the outside world, I appeared like a powerful man who had everything under control. Most days, that was true. But some days, the battle with this internal monster seemed insurmountable. Its claws were too big. I didn't have any weapons against it. It consumed me, making me vulnerable, and I hated it. As an adult, I should have the strength to overcome it. And yet I still struggled with it.

I'll destroy you.

The internal war had gone on for too long. I blamed my father for the pressure he'd put on me since I was born. It was as though he had a to-do list for me the second I entered this world.

Be the best at everything. Carry on my legacy. Make me proud.

As a vulnerable child, I didn't have a choice but to follow those rules. He had planted the darkness in me. My childhood wasn't like the other kids who had free time or enjoyed normal vacations. My vacation had tutors for math, science, philosophy, art, fencing, Krav Maga, and other topics that ensured I became the best at everything. I was a bird trapped in a luxurious cage with all the bells and whistles. But those bells and whistles became my nightmare.

I had listened to my father until it broke me one day.

I stumble into my mom's home office, trying to call for her, but nothing comes out of my mouth.

The muscles in my throat tighten as my heart races. My body grows hot, and I'm trembling.

Mom senses me, looks up from her desk, and rushes over. "Oh my God, Orion!"

I collapse onto the floor. The science book in my hand

thuds next to me. My body quivers uncontrollably as I look up at the blurry ceiling.

Mom gathers me up. "Look at me, baby. Breathe in and out."

I'm so mad at myself for not being stronger. For not being able to fight this panic attack.

Tears well in her eyes as she holds me. "You're okay. Just breathe. In and out." She wipes the sweat from my face.

I look at her caring eyes, and a calming sensation washes over me.

Mom has taken me to the doctor several times for my anxiety. She's fought with my dad for not being around much and adding too many things to my day. Though he's reduced my educational workload, the damage has already been done. I'm fifteen now, trying to fight this disorder that's made my life miserable.

"Look around the room. What are three things that are red?"

I look around Mom's eclectic office full of astrology and astronomy decorations and find three things for her.

"Mars, solar flares, and the root chakra on your energy poster."

"Good. Now let's find three orange things."

I've spent time in my mom's office listening to her chat with her astrologer friends at virtual conferences. The cosmos fascinates me, and I can see why mom loves it. There's no absolute meaning to it.

Space is limitless. There are so many galaxies out there, some undiscovered. My mom is a scientist, and she says they don't know everything. Nobody does. Unlike a math equation with a definite answer, astrology is a science and an art that gives a multitude of answers.

By the time I find three things for the last color of the rainbow, I feel ninety percent better.

I sit up on the floor, crisscrossing my legs. "Thanks, Mom."

Mom does the same in front of me. "It's my job to protect you, Orion." She places a hand on my forehead. "Are the meds helping? If not, I can have the doctor prescribe something else."

"They help sometimes. But I don't like taking them."

The constant medication makes me think something is majorly wrong with me. I have a disorder that's invisible. It lives in my mind.

But there is something that has helped me channel my anxiety elsewhere—and my mom will have a heart attack if I tell her I'm a protégé to the best thief out there. So I keep that thought to myself.

Mom continues to study me. "Let's reduce your after-school programs to just two instead of five, okay? You can swap them in a few months. You decide what programs you want to learn. But you do need to maintain your good grades in school." She pats my head and kisses my forehead. "Take Saturdays off. How does that sound?"

My heart leaps. "You mean it? Will Dad be mad? I don't want you guys to fight again."

She cups my face with her hands. "Your dad loves you. He's a private and stern man, but he loves you. Trust me."

I really want to believe her, but my dad spends half the year traveling. When he's home, our conversations are about my studies. I can count on one hand how many times he's given me a hug. But I don't want to make mom sad, so I just nod.

"I'll deal with him, okay? He needs to cut back on his

work too if he wants to live a long and healthy life. Your dad has a lot of pressure on him too. But I'll remind him what's important is his health and his family."

I'm grateful to have my mom with me. She's so smart and works part-time as an astrologer so she can spend more time with me.

"Can you teach me about astrology and astronomy?"

Her eyes sparkle. "I'd be honored. I've been waiting for you to ask me."

"Why?"

"Because that's when I know you really want to learn it. I don't want to force you to study something that might not interest you. I know you're studying a lot of subjects that seem boring to you. But you'll be well prepared for this complex and dangerous world, Orion." She cups my chin. "The cosmos is an elective subject that's fun and unique—like you. I'm passionate about the stars, and I would love to pass that knowledge onto you. I named you Orion, didn't I?"

I smile as I envision the hunter in the sky. It can be seen in the southwestern sky from the Northern Hemisphere and the northwestern sky from the Southern Hemisphere. I've seen it many times from the telescope on the balcony of her office.

"Why do you like that constellation, Mom?"

"Because he's the hero who's going to destroy the big bad beast." She smiles and taps my forehead.

Mom's my savior. I wish my dad were like her.

Tires squealing on the pavement ripped me back to the present. I rose from the lounge chair and glanced down at the streets. Another car accident.

My stomach growled, and I decided to pick up something to eat before diving back to work. On the street, I heard the commotion from the car accident.

"He was crazy, officer! He saw me coming and sped up!" said an older man, looking distressed. A Subaru was smashed against his landscaping truck.

"It's so sad. He must've been on drugs or something," said one woman to another.

Moments like these reminded me that life could end in one second. So I walked across the street to get my dinner so I could enjoy every second of my life. As I stood on the sidewalk with a group of people waiting for the walk sign to appear, a woman exited a familiar car on the other side of the street.

Elena—my new employee—stepped out wearing a FoodHub T-shirt and matching cap and entered an office building carrying a bag of takeout. A FoodHub magnet glowed on top of her Honda Civic, still dented from crashing into my car.

She delivered food? Why? She was a seasoned journalist. I looked at her old car that desperately needed repairs, if not replacing altogether. But I'd learned you couldn't know someone's story from a glance. Some people were experts at hiding their flaws . . . and their monsters.

What was Elena's story? She had asked me for an advance before she even started working. Was she in a financial predicament?

She came out of the office with a smile on her face, entered her car, and drove off. My eyes followed her as she disappeared into traffic. I desperately wanted to order something online so FoodHub could deliver it to my office. Instead, when the walk sign blinked on, I headed to a food court. I could ask her on Monday how many jobs she has.

CHAPTER NINE

ORION

INSIDE REMI'S office at the Krazee Tavern, I sat at the table sipping A Grumpy Old Man while waiting for Attikus to arrive.

"What are you drinking?" I asked Remi, who wore an aqua shirt that made his dark hair stand out.

Smiling, he lifted his thermal mug. "Audri made me chrysanthemum tea. It's good and helps me stay sane on chaotic days. You know how our schedules can be."

I sipped my drink. "You don't look like a chrysanthemum tea kind of guy. Scotch is more like you."

Smiling, he placed the mug down. "It's still my drink on some days. But I'm trying to maintain good health. The tea is superb. Want to try some? I have another mug over on my desk."

"No thanks. Audri made it for you. I'm good with mine."

Remi was a changed man. When I first worked with him, he was a man dwelling in darkness, but now he was beaming with . . . love. I supposed the right woman could inspire a man to change.

Kate popped into my vision. A beat later, Elena's face intruded into my thoughts, startling me. No woman had interrupted my thoughts when I walked down memory lane with Kate.

Feeling guilty, I pushed Elena away to think about something else. Anything but her.

Partygoers cheered in the banquet room, and I focused on that. The restaurant was a hotspot for Providence, Rhode Island, bringing in an eclectic crowd.

Then my mind wandered to my mentor's death. If The Trogyn or someone associated with them had killed The Condor, then they could be anywhere. They could be the guy with spikey hair having a drink with his buddies in the far corner. Or the woman enjoying an appetizer with her friends.

What had The Condor discovered that had gotten him killed?

"You okay?" Remi eyed me from across the table.

I debated on whether I should tell him about my mentor. Remi, Royce, Grayson, Forrest, and Arrow were busy trying to locate elite members of The Trogyn. They were supposed to attend today's meeting but couldn't make it. I didn't want to inundate them with my personal issue until I knew for certain it was connected to The Trogyn.

"It's been a hectic month. I just acquired a new company, and your drones are almost ready. With so much going on, I haven't had time to work on Level Six yet. I know you're waiting for the demo. It still needs some changes."

"Don't stress about it. Let it sit for as long as you need. Don't push it."

"Thanks. I'll share it once I make all the changes."

"The version I saw was fantastic."

"Thanks, man. It needs something I can't see right now."

I didn't know why, but I felt like it needed a change in direction. I hadn't touched the game in a while because of my crazy schedule and the lack of motivation.

These boys were the VATV men I respected—vigilantes against the villains. My circle of trusted men was small. I'd learned a long time ago that the more successful you became, your circle of friends became smaller. Keep your circle of friends tight. In the business arena, it was difficult to trust people. The man standing next you could scheme to overthrow your business or take it over. I'd seen it happen too many times.

Remi glanced at the clock on the wall. "Is Attikus coming tonight?"

"Speak of the devil." Remi jerked a chin toward the entrance.

Attikus walked toward us with his wooden cane etched with an intricate design. He wore a black suit with a white shirt and a silver tie. He had dark hair that appeared darker than his suit and a face that rarely showed any emotion. Older than me by five years, we met when he witnessed me stealing documents from a corrupt police detective. The officer had disrespected a minority family who was distraught and grieving for their deceased family member, who had been shot mistakenly by another police officer.

Attikus had come up to praise me because he'd seen the incident too. I told him I planned on sending the evidence to multiple news stations. He gave me the name of a reporter he trusted. We became friends that summer when I'd returned to Providence at nineteen years old to commemorate my mother's death.

Attikus hooked the cane on the chair and slid into the seat. "Sorry, I'm late."

"Any good reason?" I asked, knowing he was rarely late. Men like us with multiple businesses to oversee followed a tight schedule.

"There was a painting I needed," he said.

"For your museum?" Remi asked.

Attikus shook his head. "My personal collection."

Unlike me, who had a collection of oddities, Attikus was obsessed with fine art. Most of the paintings I'd stolen from other criminals were given to him because he'd appreciate them more than I would. I only did it for the thrill and because I didn't like the men who'd owned them.

"You want anything to drink?" Remi asked Attikus.

"No, thanks." He looked at me and then at Remi. "I heard two elite members are attending a movie premier in Hollywood next month."

"They're funding movies so they can hide behind the glamor of Hollywood," I said.

Attikus nodded. "I'll monitor those members and see where they lead me."

"Grayson and Royce also got the same intel. They'll continue with the elite clubs around the world," Remi said. "Arrow is monitoring an elite member who's meeting someone at the Pentagon. Forrest is focused on a pharmaceutical company that suddenly got large private funding for a new medication that sounds too good to be true. I'm looking into a prominent hotel chain that recently filed for bankruptcy."

"The Trogyn are probably working fast to tie up loose ends," Attikus said.

"Or strategically placing their chess pieces against us.

Anything is possible now. They know about you and your boys." I looked at Remi.

"We'll be ready for them." Remi's jaw tightened.

"I have my team monitoring a club in Sweden that hosts celebrities and wild parties." I leaned into the table. "My team just finished the drone prototypes. You should receive yours in a couple of weeks. Test it and let me know if you'd like any tweaks."

"That's fantastic." Remi beamed. "I can't wait to see what your engineer and designer came up with from my old drone."

Remi and his friends had given their drones to me. They'd created them when they were teens. The devices had recorded the crime that linked them to The Trogyn.

"My team had fun," I said. "How's Slash doing these days?"

I'd never met him, but had heard wonderful things from Remi and the others. Slash had been a member of the crime organization and given these men a second chance. He was their savior.

"He's retired." Remi smiled. "His wife gave him an ultimatum—retirement or divorce. They live in Costa Rica now. In the same area as Royce's parents."

"That's wonderful to hear," I said.

"Slash has helped you enough. It's time for a break." Attikus looked at me. "Do I get a drone?"

I patted his back. "You bet. I need your feedback."

"I heard you bought a company. What is it?" Attikus asked.

"I bought it six months ago, merging with my tech company, specializing in artificial intelligence."

"With how the world's going that's a brilliant invest-ment. Let me know if you need our help with anything."

A loud boom rattled the restaurant. We jumped out of our seats, rushing toward the kitchen.

"It's outside." A girl with curly red hair pointed through the window.

I headed out the door with Remi and Attikus. A crowd of people had already surrounded the area. An eight-wheeled truck had collided with a silver SUV.

The driver from the eight-wheeler gripped his head, looking distraught. A man and a woman were trying to help the SUV driver, who was on the ground. I could tell from the look on the woman's face that he didn't make it.

"He wouldn't stop." The driver of the eight-wheeler told the police officer who had just arrived. "I think something's wrong with his car."

The ambulance arrived, and the EMTs exited, rushing to the man on the ground. Remi and Attikus walked up to the two police officers roping off the area.

A familiar sensation came over me. Looking around, I spotted Elena . . . and a man with bleached blonde hair. He wore a T-shirt with ripped jeans and neon sneakers. He stood too close to her. I didn't like him already.

I especially didn't like this jealousy surging in me. What the hell was wrong with me?

I couldn't take my eyes off Elena and the man. Who was he?

As though she sensed me staring at her, she turned in my direction and recognized me.

Her entire face lit up. Or was that my imagination?

"Hey!" She strode over. "What are you doing here?"

When she smiled, my chest constricted. She was so

beautiful, reminding me of a peaceful night sky filled with stars. She had an easygoing way about her that softened my hard edge. Though she'd been distraught during the accident, I could still sense an easiness within her. I didn't know how I could sense it, but I did. It was as though she were attuned to the flow of nature, where nothing was forced. A wildflower that grew to its own calling, manicured by nature and untainted by society's standards.

The fuck?

Why was I standing amid a major accident waxing poetic? I desperately needed a shower and a good night's sleep.

Christ.

The guy draped an arm around her, and my fingers itched to break his arm.

"Who's this?" he asked her.

He was around my height, but leaner.

Elena met my eyes. "This is my friend Orion. Orion, meet my friend Elliot."

The word friend loosened the knots in my stomach. If he were her boyfriend, she would never introduce him as just a friend. My itchy fingers immediately calmed.

I didn't like this possessiveness in me.

Changing the subject, I asked, "Were you present when the accident happened?"

"Yeah. I was just heading out of the Krazee Tavern." She tapped Elliot's arm, and he extracted it from her shoulder. She stepped close to the caution tape and pointed to the silver SUV. "He was seriously speeding." She snapped some pictures with her phone. "Something feels off."

"What makes you say that?" I asked.

"Gotta go now." Elliot wiggled his eyebrows. "Jake's waiting at my apartment."

"I'll stop by the salon sometime this week. Have fun tonight! Don't stay out too late."

"But that's when the fun starts!" He kissed her cheek and looked at me. "Nice to meet you. Nice T-shirt, by the way."

The discomfort on my shoulders slid off, making me feel ten times lighter. Elliot was a gay man, which meant Elena wasn't interested in him.

No woman had distracted me like this. Not since Kate. Guilt yet again nipped at me, and I touched the ring on my necklace.

It's time to move on, Orion.

Ralph's words echoed in my head. He knew Kate and witnessed how devastated I'd been when she died.

Though I knew it was true, it was easier said than done.

Elena continued taking pictures of the crowd and surrounding area.

I watched her maneuver around, snapping pictures with efficiency. My feet followed her like they were tied to her. *What the hell?*

The more I studied her, the more I wanted her.

And the more it annoyed me.

I was losing control of myself. This desire had to stop.

Irritation rose in me when she got close to the crime scene. "What are you doing?"

Her brows furrowed at the sudden change in my mood. "Investigating."

CHAPTER TEN

ELENA

I COULD FEEL his irritation prickling my skin. What had gotten into him?

Lowering my phone, I asked, "You okay?"

Was Orion having a bad day? He didn't appear frustrated earlier when he first saw me. Butterflies had erupted in my stomach when our eyes connected. The silky butterflies still fluttered in me, but I was trying my best to ignore them. My attraction to this complex man increased every time I saw him.

How would I survive next week when I had to work with him?

"I'm fine," he blurted out, still looking annoyed.

He was obviously upset about something. The man's mood reminded me of the New England weather—unpredictable. I thought I had mood swings, but I always had a reason. But then again, maybe he was experiencing something he wasn't comfortable sharing with me. We didn't know each other that well.

The past few months had been extremely stressful, so I could empathize with him.

The EMT had already taken off with the deceased man. I gestured toward the SUV. "I don't think it was a mechanical error."

He looked at me, and the frustration seemed to have disappeared. "How can you tell?"

"Just a hunch. I've been investigating strange deaths around the city."

"Why?"

Shit.

I hadn't meant to share that much with him.

"Tell me." His gray eyes darkened.

My inner thighs twitched as though they sensed the lust from him. Was it lust? Or was it my wild imagination?

His gaze didn't waver from me as I pondered what I should share. I didn't know if it was the way he was looking at me or how his voice had a huskiness to it that made all my reservations disappear.

"I think it's suicide."

His face tightened. "Suicide isn't something you can toss around like that."

Where did that defense come from? I considered myself a patient person most days, but right now his condescending tone cut into me. Whatever was going on in his mind was *his* problem, not mine. I didn't appreciate him taking his anger out on me. I was done with men blaming me for their shortcomings.

Weren't we having a casual conversation just seconds ago? I'd triggered something, but I was too angry to inquire. He might just piss me off even more.

With the stress I'd been dealing with, I should have been

the one lashing out. Liam used to take out his frustration on me, calling me names and making me feel unworthy, and then apologizing after. I hated his excuses.

Just because Orion had a handsome face and a bazillion dollars didn't mean he could make me feel like shit.

I glared at him. "I don't know what your problem is, but you need to fix it before Monday. Otherwise, it'll be hell for both of us."

Something flickered in his eyes, but I didn't stay to find out. I stalked toward the accident, trying to inspect the scene from a different angle.

Arrogant and moody men could all go to hell.

CHAPTER ELEVEN

ORION

I HOPPED into the shower as soon as I got home, wanting to wash off the irritation from the day. I increase the water pressure from the wall, letting the force beat the muscles on my back. The emotions building inside me needed to be washed away too.

There's nothing wrong with being attracted to another woman.

Maybe the attraction to Elena was a phase that would soon pass.

But so far, the attraction seemed to have increased compared to when I first set eyes on her. Today proved that she had this tug on me. I didn't like it.

At first, I was angry at her for making me lose control. Then I was angry at her for something she wasn't responsible for.

Elena wasn't responsible for Kate's suicide. Elena had made a casual statement about suicide and I'd exploded.

That loss of control terrified me. I'd always been able to

rein in my emotions, but ever since my encounter with Elena, something in me switched off.

Or rather, something in me had switched on. Something fiery, untamed, and unfamiliar.

I felt like a muddy river with so much crap in it I couldn't tell what I was stepping on. Was it a fish, a rock, a log, or just some damn trash?

I needed clarity, and there was only one thing that could help me achieve that. Transform into The Roc, the master thief who could take anything he wanted without a trace.

The act of theft liberated me. It wasn't about stealing something that wasn't mine. The high-octane thrill numbed my anxiety. It was like a rewiring of the synapses in my brain, narrowing my focus to one thing rather than a massive pool of many things.

It was the only cure that helped me survive after my mother's death. I became a better thief because I stole. Life was fucking ironic in that way. The big guy up there sitting on the heavenly throne was probably chilling with his angels and laughing at me.

Look at that fool. He thinks stealing is a sacred gesture that would garner him blessings.

If people knew my weakness, I could only imagine the kinds of blackmail I'd receive. But we all made choices that suited our lives. No one could tell me how to live if they weren't in my shoes. When I stole a precious item, the adrenaline high made me forget myself, dropping me into another world where I became a different person.

You've got issues.

I didn't argue with my other self—it was right. What was I supposed to do when the anxiety medication didn't help? I couldn't afford a panic attack right now. I had too much at stake and couldn't afford any errors.

As I shampooed my hair, I thought of ways to torture my mentor's killer. Or killers. The Trogyn needed to be eradicated, and my empire needed my attention and care as well. I had a dependable management team, but it was still my empire to oversee. My strict upbringing had its pros and cons. I could juggle many projects at once, but at the cost of my mental health.

Closing my eyes, I tilted my face up to the showerhead, feeling the water pressure beat down on my face. Elena's face popped into my vision again, but I didn't push her away. Instead, I focused on her pretty face while the water soothed me.

She was right. I had to straighten myself out before Monday to ensure she got a professional working environment.

After toweling off, my body still thrummed from tension. If I wanted a good night's sleep, I needed to be The Roc tonight. I dressed in dark pants and a black T-shirt. Then I browsed the people on my shit list. I didn't want to stray far tonight. Who was near me?

The list ranged from wealthy individuals to corrupt politicians with skeletons in their closets. We all had them, but some were worse than others. These people valued their money and materialistic belongings more than anything else, and the best way to punish them was to take what mattered most to them.

Over the years I'd stolen from murderers, child molesters, and corrupt business executives who committed heinous crimes. The world was a corrupt place, and it made me feel better to know I had a part in righting a wrong.

I skated on the slim line between vigilante and villain. But that was how I got shit done.

Sometimes I sold the goods to the black market and donated the money to a good cause anonymously. Other times I kept the artifact if it interested me.

I went into my garage and pulled out my duffle of supplies when Jasper called me.

"Why are you calling me again? I already told you I'm not selling the island." Emotions were already high, and I wasn't in the mood to entertain him.

"C'mon, why not? What are you doing on that island anyway? My boat sailed past it. Why do you need security around a construction site?"

"Because of people like you. I don't want my cousin getting injured because he thinks he's invincible."

He snorted. "You building some astronomy shit?"

"Watch your mouth," I said calmly. "Remember what happened the last time you insulted my mother?" The asshole was testing my patience or simply stupid.

"Man, you're too serious. I didn't mean it that way."

Oh, you did, Jasper. I know you.

"I'm glad we're clear about that. Astronomy is too complex for simple minds like yours. It's okay that you don't understand it. Don't insult it. It could be the very thing that stops you from achieving your dreams." I gathered patience. "Just a tip from one businessman to another—don't disrespect another man's interest. Especially a man who has what you want."

I could imagine the annoyance on his face. He wasn't used to people talking down to him. I wasn't one of his fake friends who buttered him up just so they could use him.

Jasper didn't care about protecting the Reimann legacy.

But I did. I didn't want a family squabble to be in the next celebrity gossip magazine. Jasper had paid off many people to keep his shit from getting to the press. But I knew every time he got arrested from bar fights, drove under the influence, got caught doing drugs, or acted inappropriately with women in public. The list was too long and my temple throbbed.

If I continued talking to him, I might not perform what I had to do today.

"Well, if you ever change your mind, let me know."

"Nothing's gonna change," I said firmly.

"Why are you so stubborn?" he asked.

Why are you such an idiot?

"In business, you need to learn when to let things go. It's not beneficial to cling to an unsuccessful venture. There's nothing that's going to make me sell Quintile Island."

The more he couldn't have it, the more he wanted it. This was his MO.

"There's an island for sale near Bora Bora. I'm going to put in a bid."

After a pause, he said, "I already did."

I smiled at the obvious lie. This information wouldn't be public for two more weeks. But he could purchase that island for all I cared. It was well past time for him to focus on something else.

"Okay. Good luck."

My mom had purchased this island and left it to me when she passed. Nothing in this world would make me sell it.

"Haven't you heard that persistence pays off? I'm going to buy my own island and build an amazing tourist attraction."

"Persistence in the right direction pays off. But in the wrong direction, it would lead you off the cliff or into a dead end."

He laughed. "Man, you're morbid. You need to go out and have fun. Want me to introduce you to some ladies? You like them big or small?"

I pinched the bridge of my nose.

"Babe! Party's waiting for you!" a woman shouted from his end.

"See you soon, cuz. Babes are waiting for—"

Hanging up, I turned my attention back to the mission for this evening. Anxiety still dogged my muscles, and I needed a thrill to reset my mind and body.

I opened my duffle bag and chose a disguise.

CHAPTER TWELVE

ORION

ALREADY WEARING a black T-shirt and dark pants, I put on a black wig, a dark mustache, a pair of black-rimmed eyeglasses, and a baseball cap, then looked at myself in the mirror. The Condor taught me that an appropriate disguise helped protect us during unpredictable moments. I didn't want to be caught on camera from a convenience store or someone's mobile phone. It was better to be safe than sorry.

The disguise transformed me into a new character, and the anxiety that had overwhelmed me faded into the background.

In my black SUV, I drove to a residential neighborhood just outside of Providence, toward a house that belonged to a man who had gotten away with abusing three of his ex-girl-friends. This was my small contribution to eradicating evil. Samuel Donatello would lose something he loved today.

With the right equipment, it wasn't hard to hack into the City of Providence's crime files to see recent records and complaints from the city's constituents. Some complaints were never seen by anyone other than the officer who recorded them.

Samuel had been getting away with too many crimes, and the recent one left his ex with two black eyes and broken ribs. He'd paid the officer to cover up his crimes. He'd also paid people to intimidate his other victims, which was why the charges were dropped.

That infuriated me. Kate's ex-boyfriend was responsible for her mental struggle. It was a good thing he died from a drug overdose. Otherwise, he'd have known what broken bones sounded like.

I'd hacked into Samuel's phone and discovered his plans for the rest of the week. He was on a business trip out of state working for Apex Insurance and Financial Investments. His home had a five-year-old security system, making it easy to compromise.

My company, SIGMA—Space Intelligence Generative Machine Applications—produced advanced security among other technologies that had assisted NASA on a few projects. NASA had offered to buy me out, but I had no interest. I didn't need the money, and I didn't want to be owned by the US government, or any government. Orion Reimann was his own man with an empire that stood strong on its own.

My advanced satellites and security capacities interested many countries' defense departments. But I only offered a tiny sliver of information when working with them. Info was dangerous in the wrong hands. Money could buy a lot of things, especially people. I knew that members of The Trogyn had infiltrated several governments around the world.

I had to be careful.

I parked my car a block away from Samuel's home, sat in my seat for a few minutes to gauge the area, and manipulated his security system. Graduate students rented several homes in this neighborhood. Music boomed from a nearby party. With my disguise I blended in with a group of college boys, probably heading to the party. Though it was late summer, there were still a lot of international students around.

After a few minutes, I made my way toward Samuel's home. I scanned the area around the colonial home. I carried a box, pretending to be a delivery guy. If anyone saw me, they'd assume I was delivering a package.

My high-tech jammer was embedded into the cap. It manipulated the internet in the area. No one would know who had interfered. They'd be calling their local service and they wouldn't know either.

If only people knew what their government was capable of, it would blow their minds. People liked comfort and familiarity. When you disrupted that, fear and chaos set in. This was a control mechanism using psychological manipulation. I'd seen it over and over again.

A tabby cat scurried by as I reached the backyard. It darted under the porch, and I lost sight of it. A detached garage sat in the corner with a camera above it. But I had reprogrammed it so that it cycled through the previous days' footage. If anyone were to check, they wouldn't notice the difference.

I walked up the steps, examined the old-fashioned lock, and slid on dark gloves.

"Fucker should have bought a better lock," I said to myself.

He probably assumed that he had a security system and

therefore saved on the lock. But it didn't matter what lock he had—it wouldn't stop me from getting inside.

When I first started learning from my mentor, he taught me how to pick a lock. In the beginning, it took me a while to maneuver the intricate pieces with a pick. In order to understand them, I'd bought various locks, then studied and unlocked them again and again.

I set the box down, pulled out my small supply bag. I took out a paperclip, twisted it, and inserted it into the hole. It didn't take me long to hear the click. I opened the door and walked inside to his living room. He had a few paintings, but they weren't of any value. I was here for an Egyptian sculpture of Thoth in his bedroom. It was worth over five hundred thousand dollars. Samuel had gotten this as a gift from someone. I grabbed the eight-inch copper figurine and placed it into my cardboard box. Next, I scoured the house for his safe. A man like him would have a safe. And just like in the movies, it was behind a painting.

Idiot.

I synced my watch to SIGMA's advanced software and scanned the safe with my camera. I got the maker name, its specs, and a set of numbers with the most fingerprints. After trying a series of potential codes, I got in. It would've been easier if I used my silent drill, but then he would've known someone had gotten into his safe. I didn't want him to know anything until it was too late.

He had a hundred thousand dollars in cash, another hundred thousand dollars in gold bars, and some high-priced watches and precious gems. I put them all into the box. All of this took half an hour. As I headed out, the cat I'd seen earlier looked at me and meowed. It walked to the kitchen and turned to look at me again.

"You hungry?" I asked.

It meowed, and I followed it to an empty electronic kibble feeder. A stack of books had fallen and unplugged the cord.

I plugged it back in, and the cat got its food.

Something about the books intrigued me. I looked at the bookcase that wasn't very tall. The five shelves were occupied with books and magazines. A closer look at the bookcase revealed it was slightly ajar from the wall. The scrapes on the floor showed someone had been pushing it back and forth.

A soft whimper sounded from behind the bookcase. I pushed the bookcase aside, revealing a secret door.

"Someone in there?" I grabbed the doorknob and was surprised it wasn't locked.

The door opened and two frightened faces peered out at me.

"Let's go." I helped them out and glanced at the small space that reeked of urine and feces.

Fuck, how long had they been in there?

They appeared to be in their early twenties, but I couldn't be sure.

Anger erupted in me. I came here tonight wanting to steal a few things from the asshole, but now I wanted him dead. Despite that, there was more to this story. Why was he hiding these women? Were there more of them elsewhere? Was he part of The Trogyn? That was a possibility I couldn't dismiss. I had to remain anonymous.

I grabbed two bottles of water from the refrigerator and made up a story about being the maintenance man who needed to use the bathroom without the owner's permission.

"Please don't mention me to the police. I'll lose my job.

Just say you tampered with the lock and set yourself free. Okay?"

The woman with the brown eyes nodded as tears streamed down her face. "We understand. Thank you for being here. I didn't know if I had the strength to push through the heavy bookcase."

"How did you unlock the door?" I asked.

She reached into the pocket of her jeans and showed me a paperclip. "I found it inside a box he had in the basement."

"I'm Timothy. What's your name?"

"I'm Emma Winters," said the lock picker. "This is my younger sister, Taylor."

They briefed me on how they'd been kidnapped and imprisoned in this asshole's house for a year.

While they called the police from his home phone, an idea percolated in my head. I grabbed the cardboard box, went out to my car, and called the press with an anonymous tip. I thought about calling Elena for this story. She could get the first scoop, but I didn't want her anywhere near this shit. This was too dark for her. I returned to the house, reminded the women not to mention me, and looked for the cat. I didn't see any obvious signs of animal abuse. It wore a gem-studded collar on its neck.

"You wanna help me out, kitty?"

It meowed, so I took that as a yes and added something special to his collar.

Then I checked on the sisters. They sat on the couch holding each other while waiting for the authorities to arrive.

"You'll be okay," I told them. After one last check around the house to ensure I didn't drop or leave anything behind, I exited through the back door.

CHAPTER THIRTEEN

ELENA

"ARE YOU SURE?" I asked Elliot, who was on speaker. My fingers flew across the keyboard, searching. "Okay, I've got the address."

"Don't do anything irrational or reckless."

"You know me." I smiled over the phone. "Very rational and guarded."

"For certain things. Sometimes you get too excited about a story and your brain forgets how to function properly."

"Like how your brain shuts off when you see a stunning man?"

"That's different."

"Semantics, my friend. Don't worry. I'll be careful. This story means too much to me." I grabbed my purse from the couch. "How did you get the info?"

"Mrs. Benedict—one of my favorite clients—called me for an urgent coloring with two of her friends. She just bought a house in Martha's Vineyard. Anyway, the women started talking about some guy selling affordable life insurance. The company doesn't require a physical exam or blood work. Not only that, he's helping them invest in digital currency. You know, stuff like bitcoin."

"Sounds too good to be true."

"That's what I said. But these women have financial advisors guiding them. I'm not too worried about them. Personally, I'd wait to see how everything plays out before putting my life savings into them."

For the past few months, I'd been investigating the deaths of Emmanuel Lopez and his two friends, Bryson Cruz and Mary Chen. They were dedicated church members who often volunteered with my mom at Wild Roots. They were hardworking minorities whose deaths had been ruled as suicide. Bryson had jumped from the top floor of his apartment, and Mary had overdosed on sleeping pills, leaving a cryptic note to her family. Their deaths appeared suspicious to me. I'd met Bryson and Mary before, and they didn't seem depressed. My mom was shocked because she didn't see it either.

"You always get the juicy details. Thanks for letting me know."

"What are best friends for? The insurance guy invited them to his office. When I told them I know someone who's interested in buying life insurance, they gave me an address. Thought it might help you."

"You're the best. Thanks."

"Anytime. I know you love to play detective. Like I said, just be careful."

"I thought you were attending a party with Jake?"

"The party is going on all night. We can be a bit late. Besides, she's one of my favorite clients."

"Thanks again!"

Curiosity was my weakness. This was the case I'd been

working on for Uncover the Truth. It could be dangerous, but if I didn't reveal the truth, who would? I didn't play by the rules at work. Therefore, I wasn't a star reporter who got invited to all the fancy parties. I didn't twist things to suit someone's needs or leave out part of the truth because my superiors feared the backlash from those who supported the news station. Leaving details out was distorting the story.

I slid into my car and turned the key. The engine choked and stalled.

Patting the steering wheel, I spoke to it as though it could understand me. "Please be strong for another year until I can afford to fix you up. *Please.* You've been so good to me. Don't let me down now when I need you the most, okay?" I turned the key again. The engine hiccupped once and roared to life. "Yes! I love you!"

I pulled into a parking spot on the street in front of a coffee shop, got out, and walked toward Apex Insurance and Financial Investments. Something about that name sounded familiar, but I couldn't remember where I'd heard it. The business was closed, but the dry-cleaning place next door was still open. I entered and walked up to the counter to an old woman with her silver hair twisted into a bun.

Smiling, she pushed up her glasses. "Hello. Are you here to pick up something?"

Her warm greeting reminded me of my grandmother with sharp eyes that had seen too much of the world.

"Sorry, no. I'm actually here for Apex Insurance, but it's closed." I gestured to her neighbor. "Maybe you can help me. My mom's friend referred her to Samuel Donatello. But I'm wary about life insurance companies, so I'm trying to gather info before she purchases it. Do you know anything about Mr. Donatello or his business?"

She pushed a pad of paper to the side and considered me with warm eyes. "Your mom's lucky to have you. There are so many scams out there these days."

I nodded. "I want to protect her."

The woman's eyes hardened. "If I were you, I'd stay away from Samuel and his business. He tried selling me life insurance too. When I told him I already have a policy, he kept pushing, saying he'd give me a great discount. I didn't like his aggressiveness or the creepy way he looked at women. Last week I called the cops because he was being aggressive toward a woman in front of my shop. She was crying, calling him a fraud, saying her husband didn't commit suicide. She threatened to tell everyone about his fraudulent company."

Hope sparked in me. "Do you know her name?"

"Sorry, I don't. I only saw her that day."

When a customer entered, I thanked her and headed back to Apex Insurance. The hours on the door said they were open till five in the evening. I was only a few minutes late. Who was the woman? How could I reach her?

I still had a lot to do for Musepaper, so I headed back home. As I drove, my mind wandered. There was definitely a life insurance scam going on. And it involved several companies. Apex Insurance and Financial Investments was the fifth name I'd encountered. How many more were involved?

A pop sounded and a metal noise scraped against the road.

"Shit." I pulled over, got out, and my heart sank at the flat tire. I crouched to see a part of my muffler—or whatever that metal pipe was—hanging on for dear life. "No, not now." I stood up, glanced around at the unfamiliar area.

The house in front of me was hosting a party. Groups of

people hung out on the porch and on the lawn. A couple was making out under a tree.

Two men met my eyes, glanced at each other, smiled, tossed a beer can into the trash can, and walked over to me. The guy with the narrow face wore a Bryant University T-shirt, while the bearded guy had on a University of Rhode Island T-shirt.

"Hey, beautiful." Narrow Face raked a creepy gaze down my body.

"Need help?" Bearded Guy touched my shoulder.

I swatted his hand away. "Keep your hands to yourself."

"We like feisty girls, don't we, Brandon?" Narrow Face laughed, stepping closer to me. I could smell the alcohol on them.

"Looks like you've got a flat, baby. I can give you a *ride* home."

Laughing, Brandon pumped his hips. "All night long!"

Fear twisted in me. Their glassy eyes told me they didn't have any functioning brain cells left. That meant trouble, and I didn't have time for trouble.

Stay calm. Keep your distance.

"No thanks. I've got it." I dug into my purse for my phone, wanting to call the police.

Narrow Face yanked my phone away. "Let us help you."

"Oww!" Brandon held a hand to his head. A rock thudded beside his foot. "What the fuck?" He glanced at the red spot on his hand. "I'm fucking bleeding!"

While Narrow Face was distracted, I grabbed my phone back. He reached for it again, but I backed away. Something smacked into his forehead. Another rock dropped to the ground. Several more rocks pelted him in the face, knocking out a tooth. Then it was Brandon's turn for the rock attack.

I stepped away from them, not wanting to get in the crossfire. Who was whipping rocks at them? Sirens wailed, and a police car pulled up. Someone had called the cops.

The spiky-haired officer exited his car and approached me, glancing at the two men with hands covering their faces. "You okay, miss?"

"Yeah. I have a flat tire."

He called in a tow truck for me, got my version of what had happened, and walked over to the drunken guys to speak with them.

A door slammed, and I looked across the street to see Orion heading toward me with a worried expression. "What are you doing here? Is everything okay?"

Immediately the fear I'd felt subsided.

"I got a flat." I gestured to my car.

"You shouldn't be driving that thing," he said in a tone that sounded like a reprimand.

I wasn't in the mood for this. "That thing is my only mode of transportation."

He didn't know about my financial situation. I didn't have loads of money to toss around like him. His frustration with me from this morning hadn't faded at all.

I was supposed to work with him on Monday. Was this foreshadowing what I could expect? Daily frustration? Just because he was my boss didn't mean he could talk down to me. No one had that right.

He walked over to the police officer and glared at the two men. An ambulance arrived, and two EMTs examined the men. Orion spoke to the police officer and pointed up the street. Then a series of police cars rushed past us, heading somewhere. I saw the Channel 5 and Channel 7 News vans following close behind.

What was happening? I could ask my coworker who was on the late shift tonight.

Orion typed something on his phone, nodded to the officer, and walked back to me.

I had so many questions for him, but all I could focus on was the intense gray eyes boring into me. The power he had over me was unbelievable. I was so attracted to this man and didn't know what to do about it. It was ridiculous that I couldn't control myself even in this terrifying moment. I was just harassed by two men, and some freak was whipping rocks at them. But none of that mattered when Orion was present.

What the hell was wrong with me?

I could almost feel my ovaries jiggle when he stood near me.

Questions sparked in his eyes, but all he said was, "I'll give you a ride home."

Though his voice was calm, I could feel the energy thrumming between us. Maybe it was just me feeling this one-way attraction. But I wondered if he was the slightest bit attracted to me.

He's a handsome, rich man, Elena. You're out of his orbit.

"You don't have to. I can call an Uber."

"You are NOT calling an Uber," he said and brushed a hand over my cheek.

The unexpected contact made me jerk. Tingles cascaded down my body and pooled in my uterus. Yup, I felt it twitch. Scenarios regarding a twitchy uterus would be a great topic for Random Riddles.

He skimmed a finger down my cheek, and my lips parted with a soft gasp. His eyes darted to my lips. I bit my bottom lip to prevent any other embarrassing sounds from escaping.

Was that a slight smirk on his face?

"As my employee," he said, moving his hand away from my face, "I can drive you home. I need you safe so you can start working next week."

Calling an Uber would cost me money, and I didn't want to know how much it would cost to get a new tire and the metal piece replaced. I knew about the old tires, but I had hoped they would last until winter when I could afford new ones. I had to recalculate my budget yet again.

"Okay. Thanks." I buckled myself in his SUV and watched as more people from the home poured out to see their injured friends.

"Where do you live?" Orion asked, driving off.

Like my car, my home needed an update. Nerves squirmed in me. The only people who had been to my home were my mom, my ex, and Elliot. My ex only stayed twice and decided he preferred to hang out at his place. His family had money, and he preferred the luxurious lifestyle, which was why he had moved on to someone who could afford the same.

"So what were you doing here today?" he asked.

I looked over at him, studying his profile. So gorgeous. "If I tell you, then you'll have to tell me why you were in the area too."

CHAPTER FOURTEEN

ELENA

ORION TURNED TO ME, arching an eyebrow. "Okay." He punched my home address into his GPS monitor.

"Okay," I repeated to myself, suddenly feeling flustered.

Being confined to this space with him did so much to my body. I didn't know how to stop it. It was as though there was an entire team of mischievous fairies waving their wands, stirring up trouble and desires at the most awkward time. Images of his naked body, of him kissing me and doing all kinds of wonderful things to me flipped through my mind like a social media post.

My imagination had gone wild, and I had to tone it down before it got out of hand.

It's already out of hand.

How had he become a prominent fixture in my mind?

"Are you okay?" he asked, rounding the corner.

"Yeah." I said, remembering the fear again. "I was just at the wrong place at the wrong time."

"Those guys got what they deserved," he said casually. Too casually.

I stared at him, and the mischievous sparkle in his eyes fascinated the reporter in me. "What do you know about that?"

The corner of his lips tilted. "Enough."

I sucked in a breath. "You did that? How?"

I stared at him, wondering what else was hiding beneath the preppy façade.

"With a slingshot and some rocks. I'm an excellent marksman." He tossed me a serious expression. "They deserved that and more."

More questions bubbled into my brain. "Were you following me? How long were you watching?"

"Is this your house?" He pulled into my driveway that needed repaving.

I was too intrigued by what he'd just admitted to care about what he thought about my home.

"Yeah. I live in a farmhouse-style home that needs some updates."

As soon as he parked the car, something from my house thudded to the ground.

I groaned, got out, and walked across the lawn to pick up the shutter from the living room window. It had been damaged in last week's thunderstorm.

"What are you going to do with that?" he asked, following me to the shed.

I dropped the broken shutter next to the other broken items. "Adding it to the to-do pile." I looked up at the house. "If I weren't afraid of heights, I'd climb the ladder and nail them in myself."

He considered me for a moment. "So you're handy around the house?"

I snorted. "Nope. I just do things to save money. The how-to videos on YouTube are helpful."

"You're an interesting woman."

I crossed my arms. "Why? Because I can secure shutters?"

"That's part of it." He stepped closer, and my breath caught. "But it's your ability to detach from a terrifying event that intrigues me."

I intrigue him? My heart felt like it just grew wings. "What do you mean?"

"Minutes ago, you were harassed by drunken men. But right now, all I see is a woman unbothered by that horrific event. Instead, her attention is on shutters. It's admirable. How do you do it?"

A gust of wind blew by, sending dandelion seeds scattering in every direction. He reached for my hair, plucking out the little white seeds.

I didn't know what got into me, but I closed my eyes, leaning my head into his strong palm. Maybe his nearness had blocked out my logical mind. Maybe it was the dandelion seeds making the warm summer more magical, but I dropped into a quiet space with just him and me. This moment made me believe that anything was possible. That if I made a wish right now, it would be granted.

I was so attracted to this man that I believed in the impossible.

Like the breeze that arrived suddenly, the truth blew out of me softly.

"It's you." The words shocked me, and I opened my eyes to see him staring at me.

"What?" A crease formed between his brows.

Oh. My. God.

Pivot, Elena.

"Oh, nothing." I slapped a hand on my forehead. "I meant to say it's *you* who looks different."

I had no idea what I was saying or if it answered his question.

"Me?" His eyes narrowed on me, revealing no suspicion about my fib.

Well, he did seem different tonight. More dangerous. However, my slip had nothing to do with that.

"Unless you want to be a mosquito snack, come inside and I'll explain."

He followed me inside.

"I leave the debris of the day at the door." I kicked off my designer brown flats I'd gotten on sale at an outlet store two years ago that were both comfy and stylish.

"I like that," he said, and then mimicked my gesture, putting his shoes neatly on the mat next to my toppled shoes.

Staring at our shoes, I pursed my lips. "Look at them. What do you see?"

Amused, he studied his black Armani shoes that cost more than anything I owned in this house and my fifty-dollar flats. "Shoes, Elena. I see shoes."

I didn't know why, but his casual tone made me laugh. "Use your imagination." I bumped my shoulder into his arm because he was like a head taller than me. "They're more than shoes. They represent how different we are." I pointed to his perfectly placed loafers. "You live in luxury. Everything is neat, organized, and shiny." I straightened out the flat that was toppled on its side. "My life is messy, unorganized, and not shiny." I tapped a stain on my shoe with my toe. "We are so different."

"But I like that."

His calm voice pulled my attention to his face. "You're showing me something I never thought of."

What did he mean by that statement? Part of me wanted to know, but another part was afraid, so I switched on my sarcasm.

"Like sarcasm laced with wisdom?" I winked. "You can always depend on me for shoe jokes."

A laugh roared out of him, filling up my home. I could almost imagine the walls and all the furniture blinking awake.

I like that his energy differed from mine. Maybe that was why I was attracted to him. But drastically different couples couldn't last. In the beginning, differences were intriguing, but in the long run those differences could turn them against each other. They'd wear each other out. That was what happened to me and Liam.

"You have an ability that no one else has."

"And what is that?" I walked down the hallway.

"You can yank me out of my anxiety and drop me into another world."

I turned to look at him, his expression serious and vulnerable. I'd never seen him like this. This wasn't the man displayed to the public.

My heart danced because I got to see a side of him that no one else could. "That's a good thing, right?"

Nodding slowly, he stepped closer. Only a few inches separated us.

I swallowed. "What are you doing?"

"Experimenting." He tipped up my chin with his fingers. He was so beautiful.

"With what?"

"With how many abilities you have that affect me."

Something flashed in his eyes, and he stepped back from me. His hands dropped to his sides. What had just happened?

I ambled into the kitchen. "Please excuse the mess."

I had several boxes in the hallway with some winter jackets toppled over them. I hadn't had time to drop them off at the donation center. A box of tools sat on the floor of the family room. Though the house was old, it had character.

I picked up a small cardboard box that had fallen over and placed it on top of the stack of bins and boxes.

"Looks like you're still moving in."

"Not moving in. Been here a while." I gestured to the boxes. "This is from the upstairs guest room where there's a leak in the roof. I had to move everything out of the room for the guys to repair it."

"Is it fixed?" he asked.

"Getting there."

"You've a lot going on."

"That's life, right?" I shrugged.

Tonight confirmed that Orion was attracted to me, but something else had him keeping his distance. I desperately wanted to know, but I didn't think tonight was the night to find out.

Besides, did I want to date him? It was obvious he and I were from different worlds. Why start something that would eventually end badly? I should save myself the heartache.

My stomach growled, and I didn't want to think about that anymore. "I'm making myself a turkey sandwich. Want one?"

"Sure."

We both pretended that the last ten minutes didn't happen and spoke casually. I opened the refrigerator door while he browsed the kitchen.

"Why were you in that area today?" he asked.

I made his sandwich, placing it on a dish and mine on another. Then I boiled hot water for tea.

"I was investigating something."

Besides Elliot, Orion was the only other person who knew about my investigation. I didn't know why I told him. There was this inexplicable connection between us. Maybe he could help me see my investigation differently.

"What were you investigating?" he asked, wandering over to my living room like he was gathering information about me.

CHAPTER FIFTEEN

ORION

AN INDESCRIBABLE SENSE of home and comfort stirred in the air as I studied her house. Like visiting an old home where one could feel the history of it.

The table with pots of herbs and dandelions fascinated me. I understood herbs, but dandelions? What was she doing with them? This woman intrigued me more and more.

A quick scan of the house revealed a mix of styles. There was some traditional furniture sprinkled in with modern decor. I couldn't pinpoint what her style was, eclectic? A little of this and that?

Stacks of newspapers and magazines sat on the coffee table beside an outdated couch. A modern chair with a starry print throw pillow added a homey touch.

Elena Sanchez was buried underneath so much mystery. It was my mission to find out who she really was.

She had a saying framed on her wall.

Impossible.

I'm possible.
Everything is perspective.
-Nadia Han

That quote made me pause. "I like it."

"Like what?"

"The quote you have on the wall. It's profound, yet simple."

"Isn't it? It's from a journal called *Finding Your HeART*. I have the author's new book on preorder. That one's called *Finding Your YOUniverse.*"

"I'll check her out."

She considered me. "I don't know if you'll enjoy her work. She's a romantic suspense author. Most guys are embarrassed to read those books. They prefer books on sports, war, finance, or philosophy, or espionage thrillers."

"I'm not most guys." Was that how she thought of me? Normal? "Do I look like a guy who gives a shit about what others think?"

"You are *definitely* not like most guys."

I was about to ask her to elaborate when her phone rang.

She brought the plates to the kitchen table. "Can you grab the mugs? Be careful. They're hot." Then she answered her phone. "Hi, Mom." She smiled at me, gestured for me to sit, held up a finger, and walked to the family room, speaking in English and Spanish, which I understood.

"*No te preocupes, Mamá. Tengo suficiente dinero,*" Elena said with a laugh. "I'm fine. There's nothing to worry about."

Her mom was worried she didn't have enough food to eat.

"What? You didn't give them your bank information over

the phone, did you?" A pause, then she sighed. "Good. Be wary of scammers."

She went silent for a moment, listening to her mother.

"If you don't recognize the number, don't pick up. Okay, have fun on your trip to Martha's Vineyard. You deserve it. I'll see you when you get back. Also, I have enough dandelions. Don't give me anymore."

Elena walked back looking annoyed. "I swear, the government needs to do something about fraudulent calls. It freaks people out. Especially those who are prone to trust others."

"What would you do to those scammers?"

Fire flashed in her eyes. "Scam them. Call them out. Flip the rug and see who's really hiding under there. I used to work with a girl who worked in the police department. She used to get these calls all the time. People are constantly being scammed. What could they do about a scammer in another country? This was beyond them. Makes me angry and sick." She blew out a frustrated breath, and I could feel the frustration leave her. "Anyway, ready to eat?"

There it was. That easy switch from anxious to calm. How did she do that?

She flicked off the irritation as if it were a little breadcrumb that had fallen into her clothes.

When she sat down, I asked, "So what were you investigating?"

She bit into her sandwich, chewed, and considered me. "Are you sure you want to know?

I want to know everything about you.

"Yes." I bit into the turkey sandwich, and my taste buds swooned. Though the turkey sandwich was simple, the flavor it produced satisfied me more than anything I ever had.

More than those expensive appetizers or meals made by award-winning chefs my parents used to hire.

But I knew it was the company that made everything taste better. Being with her simplified my day, allowing me to just relax. It had always been hard for me to let go and just be, but with her, it was easy.

She placed her sandwich down and sipped her tea.

"One of my mom's friends died a few months ago. It was ruled a suicide. The life insurance wouldn't pay until a year after his death. So they didn't have enough money to pay for the funeral costs. The church helped raise money to help the family. But that's not the suspicious thing." She sat her teacup down and looked at me. "Apparently, he took out a loan and another life insurance policy from a different company that the family didn't know about."

"How did you figure this out?"

"He received several threatening phone calls to pay up. The wife had checked his phone's voicemail. There were hundreds of horrific messages blackmailing him. I heard some of them."

"You think the harassment pushed him to suicide?"

Her eyes brightened. "Yes! But the question is why? If he dies, they wouldn't get their loan payment, right?" She sipped her tea again, thinking. "I've been trying to track down the insurance company. But the name listed on his policy is no longer in business."

I loved watching her in contemplation. The gleam in her eyes. The twitch of her temple, the gentle tapping of her index finger on the side of the cup. But I couldn't steer my eyes away from the slight pout of her luscious lips. I wanted a taste of them.

I grabbed my teacup and glanced at the bag of dried tea leaves. "Do you want to hear my take?"

"Please." She watched me intently. "I'm at a dead end."

"Why are you doing this?"

"Because I want to know the truth. The family deserves that."

"But the truth cost you your job, Elena."

She angled her head, studying me. "So you have researched me."

"You're an interesting woman."

A hint of blush bloomed on her cheeks. I smiled and made her even more flustered.

She shrugged. "It's my job to tell the truth." Her eyes flashed with defiance. "The media is dangerous with its ability to distort. I just want the truth, even if it's bad."

At that moment she appeared even more beautiful to me. A person who valued the truth was someone I admired and respected.

"I agree."

"When I received a tip today, I had to go check it out. What are your thoughts on this?"

"I think you're onto something." I leaned into the table, and her floral scent teased me. "The deceased got a loan and bought a life insurance policy. Sounds counterproductive. If you need a loan, you shouldn't have the extra income to pay for the monthly policy. Do you know if he was experiencing financial issues?"

"Yes. His wife had a medical condition that required surgery and their health insurance wouldn't cover all the costs."

"Do you have a copy of the policy?" he asked. "I'll look and let you know."

"I got a copy from his wife. Why are you helping me?"

"You're working for me, and this seems important to you. I prefer you to focus on what I need. If I can help you, it benefits me too. Besides, I also want to know the truth. Sounds like an elaborate scam, but I need more details."

"Thank you."

I shouldn't have volunteered to help her because I had a full plate already, but I couldn't help it. I should have left her house now. There were things waiting for me to do, but I couldn't get myself to leave.

I should push all inappropriate thoughts about her out of my mind. It was making me unproductive, but being with her relieved my anxiety. It was all the excuse I needed to spend time with her.

The passionate way she spoke about the case made me want to help her. She wasn't doing this for money. She was doing it because it was the right thing to do. If there was ever an injustice done to me, I'd want someone like her to be on my side.

The case intrigued me. I had more thoughts on it, but I didn't want to share them with her until I was certain my suspicion was correct.

"Why were *you* in that area today?" she asked.

How much info should I give her? I'd never shared what I did with anyone.

"I was doing some charity work. Was heading home when I spotted you."

That wasn't a complete lie. I was helping society remove filth. That was my charity, my contribution. What I took from him was going to be sold, and the money would be donated to local charities. I didn't want Elena to be involved in this darkness.

Though she appeared like she enjoyed investigating unsolved cases, the world I dwelled in and the monsters I knew were too dangerous for her.

"Thank you for coming to my rescue," she said.

"You're welcome."

"You carry a slingshot in your car?" She flicked me a curious gaze.

I had a box and several bags of important tools for my escapades. Preparation was key to a successful and quick escape. But she didn't need to know all the details.

I was her boss. If she knew who I truly was, she'd quit before even starting.

I lifted a shoulder. "It's a childhood hobby that I still love."

To my surprise, she smiled. "Can you teach me sometime?"

"You want to learn how to use a slingshot?"

"Why not? Sounds like fun." Mischief gleamed in her eyes.

"That can be arranged depending on how you perform on your first day of work."

She rolled her eyes, a gesture that would have annoyed me if it were from anyone else. "Really?"

"I don't take on slingshot students easily. They need to prove their worth."

The gleam in her eyes disappeared, replaced by an indifference I didn't like. Had I said something wrong?

"I'm very capable." She got up with her teacup and placed it in the sink.

I supposed that was a sign that I should get going. I finished my tea. "What kind of tea is this? I like it."

"Dandelion tea with honey."

I stared at the tea bag. "I've never had dandelion tea. It's pretty good."

"I love it. Do you know there's symbolism behind a dandelion, Slingshot? You're drinking in this cosmic wisdom."

I tucked my hands into my pant pockets, rocked back on my heels, and considered her. "Wanna tell me about it?"

"Let's see how you perform on your first day as my employer. An excellent performance deserves a reward."

I wanted to kiss that smirk on her face.

She got me there, using my method against me. It had been a long time since anyone had fascinated me like that.

But a kiss would be the start of something I wasn't ready for. Elena Sanchez wasn't a woman I could kiss and move on from. For my sake, I had to be careful with her. She could reach into me deeper than anyone I'd known.

My chest hurt as guilt gnawed at me. My fingers went to the ring on my necklace, rubbing it as though that gesture were an apology. For the first time, a woman had touched me more deeply than Kate.

It wasn't Elena's fault, nor was it Kate's. Kate had been gone for a long time. She had been my best friend. But Elena . . . she was becoming something more without even realizing it.

The need to stay longer to chat with her and the need to get out warred inside me. Confusion rose, and I forced myself out of the chair.

"I've got to go. See you tomorrow." My phone buzzed, and I glanced at the screen to see the confirmation I'd been waiting for. "There's going to be a car here for you to use tomorrow morning." I strode toward the door.

"What?" She followed me. "Wait a minute. There's no need to—"

I whirled around and she slammed into me, almost falling backward.

My arm immediately wrapped around her waist, holding her close. *Fuuuck.* This was exactly what I needed, but also what I'd feared. My body desperately wanted her. My cock twitched. I shifted her, creating enough distance so she didn't know what she'd done to me.

"It's a company car, Elena. You can use it as you please while you're working for me. There's no charge. It's safer than the car you're driving. You should sell that old car to the junkyard. It's not safe."

"It just needs some updates." She bit her bottom lip.

"The updates will cost you more than what it's worth. Get a new one."

Her face scrunched. "Says Mr. I Drive A Bugatti Voiture. I don't have money to spend like you do. Some of us have to be frugal."

Was she having financial problems? I almost forgot about her second job.

"How often do you work for FoodHub?"

Embarrassment flushed her face, and I regretted asking her.

"It's an easy job."

Her journalism salary should allow her a comfortable lifestyle. But I'd learned not to assume or judge.

I dropped the subject. "You can use the company car for as long as you like. Use it until you save up for your own."

"But that could be forever."

"Then use it forever."

She tilted her head, eyeing me like I was a crazy alien

that just crashed into her home. If I didn't leave her house right now, I'd probably do something insane that would make her back out of helping me.

"Are you like this to all your employees? Generous? Bossy? Demanding? Confusing?"

The last adjective stood out because it wasn't every day I was emotionally confused. If I told her she was the first person who got a car from me simply because I didn't want her driving that clunker or have a stranger pick her up, would she believe me? No, she wouldn't. She'd probably think I was a psycho. What logical woman would want a psycho near her?

"I care for all my employees, Elena. I want to ensure they get to work safely to do their job. See you soon."

CHAPTER SIXTEEN

ELENA

I WOKE to exhaustion dragging me back to bed. I didn't know why I was so exhausted. Well, actually I did. But I didn't want to admit it. I'd been thinking about him all night.

Then I had a nightmare. It had been a long time since I dreamed about my childhood trauma. But the recent stress had brought up all the crap from the past. Sometimes I wondered if my subconscious mind was teasing me, testing to see how much I'd grown since I was thirteen.

Even now, as I lay awake in bed, the past came back to life fast and furious.

Fear surges in me as I grip the rope on the wobbly bridge for dear life. The bridge is the closest thing that will lead me back to the camp's administration building.

"You should've gotten down on your knees, bitch." JR2 smirks. I don't know his real name. All the kids at the camp call him that. He's only two years older than me, but he thinks he rules the campsite.

I hate him and his group of spoiled brats.

"That would have been a privilege for you." JR2 laughs while standing on the ground, shaking the bridge.

"No! Please stop!" I glance down at the river below me, and my legs wobble even more. The muscles and bones in my body melt into fear.

"You're a filthy slut. You don't belong here. My family sponsors this camp and your scholarship. You need to repay me by doing what I ask." He grabs his crotch and then shakes the bridge even more.

Tears stream down my face. I wish I'd never come here. I didn't know I could get dizzy from fear until today.

I want to crawl over the bridge to the other side, where it's safe. Elliot's probably looking for me.

"If you tell anyone about today, you'll regret it." With all his body weight, he swings the bridge back and forth. I think I'm going to puke.

The force sends the bridge into disarray, and my foot slips through the wooden planks. I topple onto the planks, losing my grip on the rope railing.

I shriek, but he laughs and points at me. Why is he so evil?

Then he takes out his phone and starts recording. I hate him so much. If I die, my ghost will haunt him forever.

Somehow part of my body slips through. But I grab the planks with my arm, holding on for my life. "Please stop!"

I'm going to die. I wet my pants as fear fully consumes me. The river below is going to swallow me.

He continues laughing at me. How can he be so cruel?

I don't know how much longer I can hold on. He might shake me off the bridge. Is that what he wants? He wants me to die because I wouldn't kneel and do—

"There she is!" Elliot rushes onto the bridge. "Elena! Hang on!"

JR2 tucks his phone away and steps away from the bridge. "Thank God you're here! I was so scared for her!"

My phone buzzed, whipping me back to reality.

Elliot: *Don't forget today's hair appointment!*

Elena: *It's on my calendar.*

Elliot: *When do you start your new job again?*

Elena: *Monday.*

Elliot: *Your boss is sizzling hot, girl! He's attracted to you.*

Based on the event at my house, Orion *was* attracted to me.

Elena: *How can you tell?*

Elliot: *From the way he wanted to murder me that day.*

I recalled Orion's agitation. But it wasn't because of me. It was something else. Or someone else.

But Elliot's assumption made me smile.

Elena: *It wasn't toward you. I think he's just a moody guy.*

Elliot: *He was jealous. Do you have an outfit ready for work?*

Elena: *No. I'm just going to wear casual office attire.*

Elliot: *What if his office demands more business style?*

Ugh. I had a pencil skirt and a suit, if that was what he wanted.

After texting for a few more minutes, I told Elliot I had to go. I stared at my closet and didn't like any of the clothes I had. But they'd do. I didn't want to waste money on a new wardrobe for a temporary job.

I had to know and sent him a text.

Elena: *Hi! What's the dress code for your company?*

Orion: *Wear whatever you want.*

Elena: *Really?*

Orion. *Yes.*

Elena: *T-shirt and jeans?*

I teased.

Orion: *If you want.*

Elena: *Okay. Thanks.*

Orion: *Did you see the car yet?*

Shit. I'd forgotten about it after the horrible nightmare and my chat with Elliot. I rushed to the window.

"Holy shit!" I shouted with glee and horror.

Elena: *You got me a Land Rover. Why? (Shock emoji)*

Orion: *Because it reminds me of you. Stylish but also practical.*

I stared at the message as warmth bloomed in my chest. That SUV was out of my price range. I'd always wanted one, but couldn't afford it. Did he know he was lending me a dream?

Elena: *Thank you.*

Orion: *Don't tell me to return it for something simpler.*

How did he know I wanted to say that? There was no use arguing with him. If he provided his employees with a luxury car for work, then I should take advantage of it while I could.

Elena: *I don't start until Monday. Why deliver the car today?*

Orion: *So you have a car for transportation. Yours is dead.*

The repair shop had told me the car wasn't worth the repair, and I sold it to them so they could use it for parts. I guessed Orion already knew this. I was scheduled to work tonight at Let's Ketchup and also had to go get my hair colored.

Elena: *The timing is good. Thanks again.*

I wanted to continue chatting with him, but he was probably busy. So was I. I turned my attention to organizing articles and images for Musepaper and familiarizing myself with Orion's shared folder. Then it was time for my hair appointment. I got my purse and slid into the Land Rover. The inside was like a posh world that was so foreign to me. I'd never driven a luxury car. Did he just buy this one? I inhaled the scent of the new car. Maybe he had several new cars sitting in some garage for his employees.

I sighed at how vastly my life differed from his. Orion was *too* rich. I couldn't comprehend his lifestyle.

I opened his email to get the address for the building location and punched it into the GPS system, preparing for Monday. The Land Rover drove like a dream as I turned into the packed parking lot of Salon Oasis. Elliot was efficient, transforming me with a trim and highlights that gave my hair a boost.

"Beautiful." I stepped back and studied his artwork.

I smiled. "You never disappoint."

With my new trim that added more layers to my long hair, I headed into Let's Ketchup and used the bathroom to change into my restaurant T-shirt. It wasn't so bad working multiple jobs. It allowed me to adjust to an unfamiliar state of mind. The chaos of a busy restaurant kept me on my toes and the stress of my career and financial issues away.

Bruce called in sick because he had to take his wife to the ER, so I offered to do delivery during my last hour of work. The day flew by, and I couldn't wait to get home after this last drop-off. I pulled into a parking spot in front of the apartment building and rushed up the stairs, and rang the doorbell for Ed Nash.

An old man with a warm smile opened the door. "Elena, so good to see you."

"Enjoy your food, Mr. Nash!"

"You want some?"

I laughed. "No thanks. I have dinner waiting for me at home. You have a great evening."

I couldn't believe he gave me a fifty-dollar tip, which was more than the cost of his meal. Grinning, I headed to my car, imagining the dinner and a hot bath waiting for me. It had been an exhausting day, and my shoulders and back begged for a bubble bath.

Someone bumped into me from behind, sending me into the side of a light pole.

"I'm sorry!" A man with a ponytail gripped my arm, preventing me from falling. "You okay?" He turned to his friend. "Yo! Watch your step!"

"It's the damn uneven pavement. Sorry about that!" The guy with the red cap saluted me.

"Don't worry about it." I walked to my car and slid inside.

A second later, a knock sounded on my window, startling me. My heart raced at the sight of Orion. The man had gorgeous eyes that could switch me on instantly.

Why did I keep bumping into him?

He signaled for me to roll down the window.

Oops. I got distracted for a moment.

I pressed a button, and as the window slid down a whiff of his cologne slithered into my nose. Warmth churned in my stomach and the muscles in my inner thighs flexed. I'd never responded to any man like this. But then again, I'd never met anyone as mysterious or intense as him.

"Hi," I said. "Thanks for lending me this car."

"You're welcome." Orion crouched and studied me. "Are you missing anything?"

"Huh? What do you mean?"

He waved a fifty-dollar bill in between his fingers. "Is this your tip?"

I gasped and checked my back pocket. The money was gone. I got out of the car. "I guess I dropped it."

"You didn't." He handed it to me.

I furrowed my eyebrows. "Explain please."

"The guy who bumped into you. He created a distraction while his friend extracted the money from your pocket. They've been watching you."

And so were you.

But I kept that to myself.

"Gosh. I've never been robbed before. I guess that's how professional thieves steal."

His eyes twinkled as though he knew something I didn't. He stood beside me, looking relaxed, like when he'd been at my house enjoying my sandwich.

"They're amateurs." A smirk slid onto his face. "You were busy and weren't paying attention." He turned to look at me, and I almost melted into a pool of goo in my seat. The high sexuality of this man was beyond anything I'd ever experienced. It made me yearn for the intimacy in a relationship.

"And you know that because . . ."

My stomach growled, and I slapped a hand over my stomach.

"Because I stole the money back for you. And I also got this." He pulled out two wallets from his pocket.

"No way!" I grabbed one wallet, flipped it open, and recognized the guy on the driver's license. "I can't believe it."

"Believe that I got your hard-earned money back?"

"More like I can't believe I'm employed by a *thief*."

I didn't know why, but excitement thrummed through me. Orion had so many sides that fascinated me. There was something wrong with me to find theft interesting.

I considered him. "Why?"

"Why what?"

"Why steal?" I leaned in and whispered, "You're filthy rich. You don't need the money."

His stomach growled, and an idea sparked. "I'll treat you to dinner if you let me interview you."

He arched an eyebrow. "What do you want to know?"

"I've always been fascinated by the art heists in history. I want to write an article for Musepaper, but I'll keep your name out."

Amusement gleamed in his eyes. "Okay. You pick a place."

"One more thing. I should have asked this before I agreed to work with you." Though the money we'd agreed to was great, I didn't want the job if I had to commit a crime. "The job you hired me for . . . does it require committing crimes?"

"No," he said. "How many jobs do you have?"

I twisted my lips. "Three. Well, four if I include the free-lance writing for a few magazines. But I'm cutting back on that."

He shifted to stand in front of me, studying me. He wrapped a strand of hair around his fingers. "I like your new look." Then he tipped up my chin. The contact sent a jolt through my body. "That's a lot to manage."

I shrugged. "You do what you have to do. Anyway, let me treat you to some comfort food."

He got into the passenger seat, and I took him to Let's Ketchup.

CHAPTER SEVENTEEN

ELENA

FOR WORK, I wore a summer dress because it made me feel pretty and feminine. Spending too much time on my hair and makeup wasn't my thing until today. After all that, I opted to leave my hair down with big waves. A side clip and some gold earrings finished my summer ensemble.

You look like you're going on a date instead of work.

I didn't care. It had been a long time since I'd dressed up. With all the stress I'd been dealing with, I almost forgot what it felt like to feel pretty. Even if it were just for one day, I wanted to wallow in this joy for as long as I could. It was an escape I desperately needed. The chaotic reality could resume tomorrow.

My mind wandered back to the dinner we shared at Let's Ketchup. He'd enjoyed the food there and told me enough about professional thieves to start my article. Most thefts were committed for money, but some did it for the thrill. I asked too many questions that he'd deflected, answering them in a way that made him more mysterious.

What was he hiding? One day I'd find out who the true Orion was.

Arriving at the parking garage of my workplace, I took a moment to gather myself.

My phone buzzed, and I smiled at the name.

Vivian: *Hey! You busy next week?*

Elena: *I can make time for you. What's up?*

Vivian: *Hosting a gathering on Thursday night. The girls want to see you.*

Elena: *Okay. Sounds like fun.*

Vivian: *We've got events planned that could be great for Musepaper.*

That was true.

Elena: *Want me to bring anything?*

Vivian: *Nope. Just show up. (Smile emoji)*

Elena: *See you soon!*

I should probably sign up for one of her self-defense classes at the Martial Arts Studio in case an incident with drunk men occurred again. But I didn't have any time and the extra income to pay for something that wasn't a necessity.

I got out of the car, entered the building, and pressed the button to the fortieth floor. Glancing at my phone, I shook my head.

"You're five minutes late. Way to make a great impression on your first day, Elena." I shoved the phone back into my purse.

I glanced at the directory poster on the wall, showing several financial firms, law offices, and software companies. The top ten floors belonged to the Reimann Group, but it didn't list what each floor did. From my research into the Reimann Group, it was an umbrella for a vast number of companies throughout the world.

How did he manage them all? Was he stressed? I juggled multiple part-time jobs while working on Musepaper, my dream. Though it wasn't making me any big profits yet, I was happiest when working on what I loved. But anxiety never stopped hounding me.

The door to the elevator opened, and I stepped out into a spacious hallway. No one sat at the front desk. *Maybe she just stepped away.* I approached the desk, waited, and admired the modern furniture, unique three-dimensional art on the wall, and the décor that looked too pricey.

My gaze landed on a breathtaking painting on a wall. It was a night sky with the Orion constellation. I recognized the three stars that made up Orion's Belt, which reminded me of what I dreamed about last night. It was fun yanking off his belt in his office. I read somewhere that there was a hidden meaning behind sexual dreams, but I didn't have time to investigate yet.

See what stress did to my body?

I turned my attention back to the artwork. I could see him in the painting. The darkness blended with the light. What exactly was the hunter aiming at?

"Hey! It's you!" It was the friendly man who had been present on the day of the car accident. He'd told me to leave before the owner found out.

"Hello," I said, studying his cargo vest over a T-shirt and dark khakis.

He glanced down at his attire. "It's a casual dress code for me. How are you?" He extended a hand. "I've been worried about you, Elena."

He knew my name?

"What's your name?" I asked.

"Ralph." His friendly eyes eased the nerves in me.

"Worried about me? Why?"

"Because you damaged my boss's precious car."

"He's *your* boss?"

Why hadn't he said anything that day? I thought he was a random person who'd walked by and witnessed my misfortune.

"Unfortunately, yes," he said with a wink.

"*Unfortunately*, Ralph?" Orion repeated, emerging from the hallway.

Our eyes met, and my stomach flipped. This man could fill the room with intense energy. It was hard not to notice him. A white shirt with sleeves rolled up to his forearms and fitted dark pants, cutting a mysterious figure. Like a decadent and dangerous secret no one could see. My curious nature desperately wanted to know what that was.

Smiling, Ralph walked over and patted Orion's back. "*Unfortunately*, it's time for me to go. I have a long to-do list."

"Apparently, it's not long enough if you're standing here complaining about me. Maybe I should add a few more items to it." He smirked.

I loved the playful relationship between Orion and Ralph. What was their relationship? An employee who had worked for him for a long time?

Ralph laughed. "Go ahead. I'm used to it." He turned to me. "Watch out for him. He can be very sneaky, steering you to do things you didn't think you'd want to do. But then somehow you end up doing it and believing it was *your* idea to begin with. He's *dangerous*." He narrowed his eyes at Orion. "You're just like your mother—cunning and . . . kind."

Kind.

Of all the adjectives I would have used to describe Orion, kind wasn't one. I hadn't met a kind business executive. Orion was wealthier than any wealthy man I'd encountered. From my various encounters with him, I'd concluded he was an intelligent and calculating man who had an active mind. It was easy for a wealthy person to donate a lot of money to charity. Was that the gesture Ralph was referring to?

Regardless, I got to see a glimpse of the mystery inside the Orion conundrum. What else was in there?

"Nice seeing you, Elena. Be gentle with this guy, okay?" He elbowed Orion playfully. "Otherwise, he'll take it out on me. Then my to-do list will be miles long." He winked at me and left the office promptly.

The air in the spacious room suddenly thickened. The walls seemed to shrink as sexual energy swelled around us. I never knew what it meant when I read these kinds of descriptions in romance books. But right now, that tension in the room was palpable. My skin tingled from his gray eyes.

Orion felt the energy too. He swallowed, and his Adam's apple shifted. We stood about four feet from each other, and I could see his vein throbbing on his neck.

His eyes fixated on me, and I should have looked away, but I couldn't. What was he thinking? Why wasn't he saying anything?

Why wasn't *I* saying anything?

Did he think I overdressed for the first day of work? He said I could wear anything, but still. I felt self-conscious underneath that potent stare that probably made most people cower. I tugged at my dress, pretending to straighten out the perfectly fine sweep. Ugh. I'd never been this nervous around a man—a boss.

A boss who was in your sex dream.

Shut up, I scolded myself.

Orion's eyes roamed my body, and I could almost feel the gaze traveling from my face down to my shoes.

Oh, God. My body was overheating, and I was going to combust under his stare. I needed to do something before I leaped onto him, climbing his body like a fool and getting myself fired.

"Good morning," I said, breaking the silence.

"Morning," he replied.

"The floor seems quiet. Where's your receptionist?" I jerked a chin to the front counter.

"He just left." Orion closed the distance, now standing too close to me.

My heart rate increased, but I focused on something else. "Ralph's your receptionist?"

"He's a lot of things to me."

"Ralph is an interesting man. He was there the day I dented your car. He told me to leave so I didn't have to pay for the damages."

"Why didn't you?" His eyes sparkled.

"Trust me, that thought crossed my mind. But in the end, I had to do what was right."

"Which was why I didn't make you pay for the damages."

I pursed my lips in confusion. "What do you mean?"

"I saw you from the multiple cameras I have around the building, the ones in the streets, and the one embedded in my car. I heard your conversation with Ralph."

"So you saw *everything*? Why didn't you show up when it first happened?"

"I was on an important conference call."

"While you watched a video of me?" I didn't know what

to think that he'd been watching me interact with his employee.

"I can multitask." The corners of his mouth rose.

"And you offered me the job because . . .?"

"Because I needed your help. After the accident, you were honest. That's something I respect." He swallowed again. "I need to trust the people I work with."

I understood this statement too well. Chantel had tried to sabotage my career multiple times, and I couldn't trust my manager to help me.

"I completely agree. Are you the only person on this floor?"

"I like my space and solitude." His eyes remained on me.

"I assumed you would have a whole team here helping you."

"My team is working on various projects on the floors below us. This floor is my personal space."

He sounded like a man who had built invisible walls around himself. What was he hiding?

"But there's a lot of space here. Am I the only one working with you on the floor?" Nerves shifted in my stomach. If there were other people here, they could serve as a buffer. But now I was forced into this close space with him.

"Is there a problem with that?" He asked, sounding annoyed.

"No," I said, wondering what triggered the mood change. A part of me thought he was attracted to me. I prayed the rest of the day would be a smooth one without unexpected mood swings. "What do you have on this floor?"

"Your office is this way." He walked beside me. Our arms touched, and I didn't move away, and neither did he. Our arms continued to brush against each other as though a silent understanding passed between our bodies.

This was silly. We were both testing each other's limits. Who would be the first to break?

Orion didn't seem like someone who feared anything. He seemed different around me.

Was he afraid of me?

I couldn't forget the day he'd saved me from those drunk idiots. He looked like he wanted to kill them. This man harbored so many emotions.

Even though he told me the reasons why he'd been at the scene, something told me it wasn't the whole truth. The more I got to know him, the deeper I had to dive in to figure him out.

We rounded the corner and our hands touched. A spontaneous idea popped into my head. I smirked as I tripped on my foot. He reached for my arm, yanking me against his hard body. His other arm wrapped around my waist, holding me tight to him. I inhaled his musky scent and melted into him. His hard cock pressed into my body.

Okay, now I knew for certain Orion wanted me.

"You okay?" he asked, looking down at me. A dangerous yet beautiful storm brewed in his eyes. I wanted to jump into them, swim in all of his secrets.

"Yeah. I'm clumsy today." I straightened up, trying to wriggle free from his grip—from the hand that warmed my lower back. But he held me close.

"Do I make you nervous, Elena?" His voice had a deep, velvety undertone of seduction. Then he released me. Was he playing some game with me?

"No," I lied. "Just first day of work jitters."

"Let me give you a tour." He took me down the hallway,

past several rooms. "Bathroom is over there near the kitchen."

We walked past a room with the door left ajar. The lights were off, but something sparkled inside it.

"What's in there?" I asked.

"My Cosmic Lounge."

"Your what?" Fascination tickled me. "May I see it?"

He hesitated, but kept his gaze on me.

"It's okay if you're uncomfortable—"

Orion took my hand, and the gesture surprised me. My heart galloped as he led me into the dark room. It felt spacious, but I couldn't be sure. When the stars emerged from the ceiling and the walls, all thoughts fell away, leaving me in complete awe.

His hand squeezed mine, and a wonderful sensation rushed through me. Maybe it was because I was standing in the middle of the cosmos with a man I'd been dreaming about. In this moment, the impossible seemed possible. Orion had been out of my reach, dwelling in a different world. But right now, we both stood hand in hand while the stars winked at us. The background changed colors, like the mesmerizing nebula images from NASA.

After a few moments of silence, I looked at him. "It's magical."

"It is." He met my eyes, and stars gleamed in them.

"I've never been in a room like this. It feels so real."

"With the right technology, anything is possible."

"It's easy to do that when you have unlimited money. My dreams have limitations." I broke away from our joined hands to walk around the room. Looking up, I reached for a cluster of stars that gleamed close by. I closed my eyes and imagined clasping them into my grip as though I'd captured my dream. As though I'd captured Orion in my hand.

"Do you know what constellation you just caught?" he asked.

I should lie and tell him I didn't know that I was holding the Orion constellation, but the way he looked at me demanded honesty

"The hunter in the sky," I said.

He sighed and ran a thumb across my cheek. "I like how you reached for me." The slight rumble of his voice and the arrogant smirk made me speechless.

His musky scent overwhelmed me, and his voice was like a drug that numbed all my logic. I rose to my tippy toes so that my lips were a breath away.

"What is the hunter looking for?" I whispered.

Lust smoldered in his eyes, and he cupped my face with both hands. "You." Then his lips crashed into mine.

The embers in me burst into a bonfire, and I kissed him back. I'd been yearning for this, and now I knew he wanted me just as much. My body fell against his broad chest. His cock throbbed against me.

I moaned as his tongue coaxed my lips apart, darting in to greet my tongue. My legs wobbled, so I looped my arms around his neck, wanting to be closer to him. He lifted me up, and I wrapped my legs around his waist. He pushed away the fabric of my dress, cupping and molding my ass. Sensations roared through my body.

"You taste even better than I imagined." He sucked on my tongue and dragged an open mouth down my neck, carrying me somewhere.

I felt the cool surface of the wall on my back while his lips lingered on the junction of my shoulder. The stars sparkled everywhere in the dark room. It felt so magical that he was adoring me underneath the stars.

A hand skimmed up my body, feeling and touching everything. When he cupped a breast, I arched into his hand and moaned.

"You're so beautiful, Elena."

I met his gaze and saw the hunger he had for me.

"So are you, Slingshot."

His eyes sparkled as he kissed me again. He angled his head for a deeper kiss. I wanted to feel him everywhere. Desire leaked out of me, wetting my panties, but I didn't care. His hand squeezed one buttock and found its way under my pantie to cup my sex.

"Fuck. You're so wet."

I gasped when he shoved a finger in me. It was glorious. I loved the feel of his long finger pumping me while his powerful hand secured me against the wall.

"Oh my God." I moaned into his neck, inhaling his scent.

Right now, he smelled of musk and sex, a predator enjoying its prey. I bit into his neck, and he groaned. I dropped kisses along his neck and came to the necklace.

I held it in my hand. "Interesting ring-pendant."

Orion froze. He pulled out his finger and the lustful expression disappeared. He gripped my hand and tore it from the pendant, looking angry. He released me and stepped back.

Saying nothing, he walked to the door and paused. "Your office is two doors down. The assignment is in the folder."

"What just happened?" I asked, feeling confused.

He stopped in his steps for a second, then turned around. "A test."

"A test?" My body was still vibrating from the passion

we'd just shared, so I couldn't thoroughly comprehend what he meant.

"I wanted to see if you were attracted to me. You are." He smiled. "Just like all the other women."

My heart cracked. Shame overwhelmed me. I'd never felt so used and discarded like this.

"So I'm like all the other women you kissed in your office?"

He lifted a shoulder.

"You're an asshole." My heart raced with indignation.

"I never said otherwise. It's best that you don't romanticize me. After all, I'm your boss."

I fumed, anger tightening my chest. If I didn't need the money, I would've just quit on the spot. He'd already given me an advance. If I were to quit, I couldn't pay him back.

Oh, Elena. Why do you always get yourself involved with assholes?

"Don't think about quitting. There's a clause in the agreement that states you'll have to pay for my search for a replacement if you quit during the first week of employment. The fee is costly, Ms. Sanchez."

I couldn't believe this. I'd signed the agreement mere days ago, but I didn't remember that clause. But then again, my stressed brain had overlooked a few things lately.

Orion was friends with people I knew, so I wasn't on guard with him.

Big mistake.

I wish there were a hole in the floor that could suck me in like a Black Hole, taking me anywhere but here.

I was angry, sad, but also determined to see this through.

"Don't worry. I keep my word. I'll do my job and you won't ever see me again. Make sure you clean *that* off, Mr.

Reimann." I gestured to the cum on his pants. "It'd be awkward when your next test subject shows up."

He glanced down at his pants, looked back at me, turned, and disappeared from view.

I almost expected him to toss money my way as a gesture of gratitude for falling into his trap! What had I gotten myself into? I was a fucking test, like some kind of sick game billionaires played with women.

All the feelings of unworthiness surfaced, reminding me of why Liam had broken up with me. Tears blurred my eyes, and as much as I tried to prevent myself from crying, I couldn't. The tears streamed down my face as I made my way to my so-called office and slammed the door shut.

CHAPTER EIGHTEEN

ORION

WHAT THE FUCK had I done? I dropped into my office chair and blew out a breath, and heard her door slam.

Wonderful. Just wonderful.

Tension throbbed in my temple. I stalked over to the minibar, poured myself two fingers of whiskey, and downed it, letting it burn my throat.

Fuck.

This wasn't the outcome I'd envisioned. I'd started the day intending to give her a snapshot of why I'd hired her. But when she was near me, my desire for her rose above everything else. I became a new person beside her.

I didn't like it. Who was this man who wanted a woman so desperately?

A man who hasn't been with a woman in months.

I shouldn't have allowed things to go as far as they did. But dammit, I loved the way her lips molded to mine. The way she kissed me back with the same ferocity.

Needing fresh air, I walked out to the balcony and inhaled a deep breath. I gripped the railing, curling my fingers around it until my knuckles whitened. What should I do with her? She had me in knots. As much as I'd like to blame her for my problem, I couldn't. She was an innocent woman standing in the danger zone of a confused man.

Don't hurt her.

Don't fuck up.

I hated talking to myself, especially when my inner voice reprimanded me. I glanced down at the city street, letting the chaos distract me from my misery.

What do I want?

Elena.

What's stopping me?

Nothing.

So why did I feel like shit?

Let the past go.

I closed my eyes at that statement. How many times had I wanted to do that? And how many times had I failed? Too many.

But I'd never experienced a pull as powerful as I did with Elena. Letting go of the past would mean I'd abandoned Kate, right? I'd failed her. I should've been with her the day she died. But I was elsewhere . . .

It was a mistake to bring Elena here. No employee had been on this floor except Ralph. She did not know the power she held over me.

I could've set up an office for her on any of the other floors below, but I couldn't help myself. I wanted her close to me. Being on my private floor was an invitation I'd never given to any other women. Not even Kate.

I'd kept the dark part of me from her because she had too much going on in her life. With Elena, I didn't even hesitate. Why?

Elena didn't know what was in that Cosmic Lounge. She only saw the night sky. Showing her more would have revealed too much of myself to her.

I thought I knew myself until today when confusion and desire turned me into a sexual predator in the office. The incident made me feel lost . . . and found at the same time.

What the fuck?

It made no sense. My emotions were playing games with my mind and I didn't like it. A man who lost his mind lost control. And Orion Reimann *could not* lose control. There was so much at stake.

My empire needed my vision and dedication. More so, I had to ensure that Reimann Corporation, which my father managed with my cousin, stayed strong. That had been my mother's wish. To watch over my father from afar.

I didn't understand why she kept reminding me of that when I was younger. My father was a capable man who could take care of himself. He made no effort to be part of my life, so why should I?

Had Mom asked him to watch over me from a distance too? Was that her way of trying to keep us close? Why was I thinking about this now?

Despite the tension in my body, I didn't feel the surge of a panic attack like I'd expected. Usually anxiety assaulted me intensely, but not today. I knew it had to do with the woman sitting in the office across the hallway from me.

Elena was the only woman who could ease my panic attack. Admitting that to myself relaxed my stiff shoulders and back. Then a sense of calmness overcame me, and I inhaled and exhaled the fresh air, looking out at the city before me.

I'd bought this property when I began working with the

WaterFyre Rising boys as their PI. The more I worked with each man, the more I admired and respected them. They had become my friends in a world where genuine friends were rare.

My mind wandered back to Elena. Today proved she wanted me. She called to every fiber in my body, and I couldn't resist her. Could I have her? Would she want to be with me if she knew the story behind the ring?

I didn't have these issues with any of the other women I'd been with. They'd been flings with no attachments. No expectations.

Elena wasn't that kind of woman.

I clasped the ring on my necklace, rubbing it with my fingers. Was I ready to let the ring go? I didn't know. Or rather, I was afraid to find out.

My phone rang, and I returned to the office. "Yes, Ralph?"

"How's everything going?" he asked.

"Why? Do you need me to add more things to the list?"

"I'm working, boss. As you requested, I'm sitting at a café monitoring the subject. He's chatting with a man, lawyer type. Will send you pictures later. But I can't help but wonder if you're doing okay."

"Why wouldn't I be?"

Ralph had been my mother's chauffeur and acted like a father to me. When Mom died, he came to work for me and never left. I appreciated his support, loyalty, and honesty.

"Because you brought a woman onto that floor."

"I know, Ralph." I wasn't sharing that she was mad at me. He would ask why, and I didn't want to get into the reason or how it had started.

"You make a good-looking couple," he said, surprising me. "Do you like her?"

"What kind of question is that? If I didn't like her, she wouldn't be on the floor."

"Don't bite my head off. Why do you sound so frustrated talking about the woman you like?"

"Because it's complicated."

"Let Kate go," Ralph said, understanding me more than I realized. "She'd want you to be happy now."

"I just need time."

"Don't take too long because Elena might not want to wait," Ralph said. "The longer you make her wait, the more she'll think you're not serious about her."

"I'm not sure if I should listen to relationship advice from a man who has his own relationship troubles. Someone who's afraid to ask the woman he loves to marry him."

"I'm not afraid," he blurted out.

"Then why haven't you?"

"I've got my reason, and I don't want to talk about it right now. For what it's worth, I think Elena is the one who can save you."

I laughed at the ridiculous concept. "Save me from what?"

"From your destructive self."

I paused at the statement. He knew me as the flawed Orion and The Roc.

"We have to be gentle with her," he said. "She comes from a different background than you. If you're not careful, she's going to run away."

I pondered on his insight, letting several thoughts appear and disappear.

"All the other women you've dated were from your

circle. They had money, status, wealthy families. Elena doesn't have those connections, and I don't believe she wants a temporary thing. So if you don't want to be with her, then you should cut your losses now. Save you both the heartache."

"How do you know so much about her?" I inquired.

"I don't. But from my brief encounter with her, I can see she has something that none of the other women you've dated have—genuine kindness."

There goes that word again. Ralph had always called me kind, but I never saw it.

"Why do you always say that I'm kind? I think that's the furthest thing from the truth."

"You have a kind heart to take in your old chauffeur as your assistant. It takes a kind heart to go after a crime organization that abuses women and children. A kind heart donates billions of dollars anonymously." He paused. "But your kind heart is wrapped in spikes."

I didn't know what to say, so I told him, "Send me the pictures when you can."

CHAPTER NINETEEN

IRRITATION PRICKED my skin as I flipped through the folder on the table. Obviously, I was the only one who was pissed. I heard him on the phone laughing. What was he laughing about?

Was he laughing at that embarrassing scene in his lounge?

He could deny it all he wanted, but I knew he was attracted to me. Maybe he was too afraid to admit it. I didn't want to be with a man who was afraid to acknowledge his own feelings.

Did he think I would cower to his arrogance and quit? Elena Sanchez was not a quitter. I'd stay on this job until it was done.

With a renewed mindset, I focused on the documents inside the folder. It had detailed information about a man who had passed away a month ago. The goal was to find the killer. Possibly hiding in Providence.

I stared at the image on the document. Pablo Toledo, also

known as The Condor. He was sixty-five when he was murdered on the street.

Who was The Condor? Who was he to Orion?

Was this a personal pursuit? Or was Orion helping someone with this case? I searched for the alias The Condor on the internet and nothing came up for him except the bird. A few Pablos appeared, but the images weren't of the man in question.

I didn't know why I bothered searching on the internet. Orion had probably done it already. I opened the shared drive and reviewed the details of The Condor. His birthdate, place of birth, blood type, and a silver Toyota RAV4. He enjoyed traveling. I browsed some pictures and noticed he liked birds. There were various birds from all over the world. Orion noted two wildlife charities that had received Pablo's donations.

Pablo's body was found on the street near his apartment. I knew that area. Orion didn't have a lot of information about Pablo's connection to people in Providence. I'd take that angle and see what I could come up with. He had to have had some friends in the city.

I wondered if his murder was linked to the suicides I'd been investigating. I'd never imagined myself researching murders. But the desire for the truth had always excited me. I'd seen the truth distorted, rewritten, and delivered repeatedly. It became the norm that no one questioned anymore. That bothered me.

I was a victim of that distortion.

If it weren't for people creating false accusations, I wouldn't be sitting here. Just thinking about Chantel made my blood boil. Why would she smear my name like that? She was already an established reporter with a great reputation.

People surprised me every day. The limits they would go to in order to harm another baffled me. Where did they find the time to do that? I'd rather devote the energy to something that made me happy.

I looked at all the information on The Condor. My meticulous boss seemed too organized. It made me want to unsettle him.

He has unsettled you today.

I flicked the thought away like lint stuck to my shirt and looked at the image of The Condor again. "Who are you? What did you do, Pablo?" I tapped his photo. "How many enemies do you have?"

Orion gave me a list of tasks. He must love his to-do lists.

- Review the list of locations The Condor visited.
- Link any connections that they had with each other, if any.
- Who owns the locations?
- Info on them.
- Add everything to the spreadsheet in the shared folder.
- Compile in alphabetical order.
- We'll review updates every few days.
- New tasks will be provided as needed.

Had Orion always lived by a list? It was too structured. Too rigid for me. It would drive me crazy. I made lists too, but nothing like this.

Did he know how to live without structure? A successful man like him had to be disciplined, keeping his eyes on the goal. But if he always had his eyes on one thing, then he'd be missing everything else along the way, right?

Did he ever have any fun? What did he do for fun?

I stared at the list, which was a printout of the document in the shared drive. What would happen if I deviated from his list? Would that annoy him?

I smiled as I envisioned him fuming.

Excellent.

I reviewed the first location on the list and gathered as much information as I could. Then I compiled the data into a document organized by location. I also cropped pictures, creating a collage to give me a quick snapshot of that location. A visual map of all the things connected to this case would be helpful. He didn't ask for any images, but I was a visual person and this would help me do my job.

Next, I made a list of places to visit, hoping to talk to anyone who might have known him. Or might have seen something.

I got lost in the work until someone knocked on my door. There was only one other person on this floor. It had to be him, but I pretended I heard nothing.

I was still mad.

After a third knock, I asked, "Who is it?"

"It's me. The only other person on this floor."

I rolled my eyes. "Come in."

He opened the door and stood in the doorway, looking gorgeous.

I couldn't tell if he was still irritated as I was. Maybe he was pretending everything was fine too.

"I'm ordering lunch. Would you like anything?" He gave me a stack of takeout menus.

I'd planned on heading out to grab something, but at the moment I wasn't even hungry.

"I'm not hungry. But thank you." I handed the menus back to him. He took them and stared at me.

"I'll pay you to have lunch with me."

"What?" I gaped at him. "Why?"

The gaze intensified for a while. I could tell thoughts were racing through his mind. This man perplexed me. Earlier today, he kissed me passionately only to dismiss me, saying it was a test.

Now he wanted to pay me to have lunch with him?

"You can save money and just eat in your office."

"You can make extra money by eating with me. We can discuss the investigation."

He knew I needed money when I took the advance from him to pay my uncle. The extra money would help pay for my mom's massage chair and fix the leaking roof.

"Okay."

The security guard dropped off our food. Orion brought my turkey club and fries and his steak and cheese sandwich into his office, which was four times bigger than mine. Tall windows revealed a gorgeous view of the city, allowing abundant sunlight to stream in. He walked to the furnished balcony, opened the wide doors, and placed the food on the table. Pots of beautiful plants made the balcony welcoming.

My steps slowed as I approached the balcony. Anxiety climbed up my body like snakes. Heat increased and my legs wobbled, remembering the fear that had been instilled in me all those years ago.

Be brave. You're stronger than that.

I paused for a moment, inhaling and exhaling, trying to calm my body.

"Are you okay?" he asked.

I didn't want to appear weak and forced myself to put one foot in front of the other. I kept my focus on his face as I did so, not looking anywhere else. He was the goal. I envisioned him embracing me as I made it to the balcony to safety.

I gripped my hand on the cushioned chair and exhaled. "Yeah. I guess I'm hungrier than I thought." I didn't want to lie, but I didn't want him to think I was a weakling.

He retrieved some plates from inside this office, brought them out to the balcony and sorted the food. He placed his steak and cheese sub and my turkey club on the plates. "What would you like to drink?"

"Just water is fine, thanks."

I was still standing beside the chair when he put down the bottle of water. He walked to the railing and leaned against it.

I gasped and held up my hands. "That's dangerous."

"What?" he asked.

"You leaning against the railing."

He considered me. "Are you afraid of heights?"

"Yup. We're not friends." I sat down on the chair and picked at my fries.

He smiled. "I learned something interesting about you. This lunch was worth it. I'll add another thousand dollars to your paycheck this week."

I gaped at him in disbelief. Guilt gnawed at me. I shouldn't make him pay me to have lunch with him. Taking a break from work to recharge was necessary.

"It's okay. You don't need to pay. The free lunch is good enough."

"I gave you my word, so I'm keeping it." He unwrapped his sub and bit into it.

I wagged a fry at him. "It must be nice to toss money around like that."

"I don't *toss* money. I use it wisely." His eyes gleamed. "It's an investment."

He considered me an investment?

"So you view things as business projects that garner profits."

"I didn't say that, Elena. Just eat. Enjoy the food and the view."

He sat next to me instead of across from me. Our elbows touched slightly. It was so strange sitting here with him, given what had just occurred this morning. I felt like I was in a different movie. How could he completely ignore what happened in the Cosmic Lounge?

I still replayed the scene in my mind over and over again.

We ate in silence, and I admitted it was nice. Simple and casual. No expectations. A much-needed pause. I realized I hadn't sat down to turn off my brain like this in a while. Even when I was home, I was always rushing to get things done. Sometimes I ate while I worked.

"Thank you." I sipped my bottle of water.

"Thank *you* for having lunch with me."

I wanted to ask what was bothering him, but I was afraid he'd say it was none of my business.

"So when are you going to tell me the secrets to dande-lions?" he asked.

He remembered that? I remembered asking him to teach me how to use a slingshot, but I didn't want to bring that up. It was best to keep our distance from now on.

"I guess we'll have to see how the rest of the day plays out. You haven't earned it yet."

He leaned back in the chair and pinned me with those powerful eyes. "Fair enough."

His phone rang, and he picked up. "Hey." He kept his gaze on me while he spoke to whoever was on the other line. "I haven't forgotten. See you tonight."

Did he have a date? Jealousy stirred in me.

Well, I had an event tonight as well. Speaking of which, I had to leave early to get my hair and makeup done at Salon Oasis.

"Is it all right if I leave an hour early? I've got a hair appointment I made a while ago. I'll make up the time tomorrow."

His eyes scanned my face and hair. "That's no problem. Are you cutting your hair again? I like it long."

Joy sprouted in my stomach, but I squashed it. I shouldn't romanticize anything.

"No. Just an updo."

"Do you have a date?" he asked.

"Yes." I had a date with a fashion show.

His jaw tightened, and the veins on his neck throbbed. But his face remained impassive, probably trying to hold back his genuine emotion.

Joy was like the seedlings of a dandelion scattering inside my stomach, flowing all around me. I held back the urge to tell the truth, or even correct his assumption. It wasn't my fault he assumed certain things.

"Who is he?"

I chewed on a fry. "Oh, you don't know Octavius Rollins."

"What does he look like?" His eyes flashed like he was ready to subdue an enemy. "What's his personality?"

Was Orion Reimann feeling insecure? *No . . .*

"Handsome. Arrogant. Mysterious. Moody." I sighed. "He's got a lot of issues."

"And that's *your* type?"

"We've all got issues, Orion. No one is exempt from that."

He considered me for a long moment. I could feel his gaze on my face as though he were tracing my features with those sharp gray eyes.

After what felt like forever, he said, "It won't work out."

I arched an eyebrow. "How do you know?"

"Because you'll be thinking of me." He leaned in and tucked an errant strand of hair behind my ear. I shivered at his touch.

Traitor.

My body should be loyal to *me*. It shouldn't respond to him when I didn't want it to. He had shoved me away.

Orion's eyes sparkled as though he knew what he did to me. He leaned into my ear, his warm breath brushing my heat. "You can't erase me that easily."

"I'll make that my mission then."

His eyes darkened. "Why?"

"What kind of game are you playing, Orion? You don't want me. You said I was an experiment. Why do you care what men I'm dating?"

He didn't answer me. Instead, he rose and ran a thumb over my bottom lip. "I'm trying to figure out what I should do with you."

Then he left.

Why was I attracted to a man with multiple personalities?

CHAPTER TWENTY

ELENA

I PACKED up to leave and walked to his office, wanting to wish him a good evening. But then he was on a conference call. Not wanting to interrupt, I scribbled, *Good night. See you tomorrow.* and added a smiley dandelion drawing on a sticky note and stuck it to his door.

I debated on texting him, but then he'd text back. And I needed a break from him.

As I sat in my car, my phone rang inside my purse. My heart raced, thinking it was Orion. But my heart sank when I saw that it was Reid Lanaro, the owner of Wild Roots.

"Hi, Reid."

"Sorry for the last-minute request, but I was wondering if you could swing by the greenery today? We're giving Anita a surprise paid trip to Bermuda."

"Oh my gosh! That's so generous of you, Reid! My mom will be thrilled!"

My mood immediately lifted. On days when I felt defeated or when the world was too dark, people's generosity surprised me.

"She's been instrumental here. Besides, she plans on volunteering a couple of days a week in the garden. All her coworkers contributed. They'll be joining her in Bermuda too."

"You're just too much. I'll swing by after my hair appointment."

"See you then."

I glanced at my watch and saw I had another hour and a half before the show started. I rushed to the salon and Elliot waved me to a seat. Like always, his salon was packed.

"Darling, let's go. You're late."

"Only five minutes. Sorry."

"You're my last client before I head over to the hotel to work on the other models. They have a few stylists volunteering from other salons."

"But you're the best," I said. "Thanks for making me pretty tonight."

"You're already gorgeous. But I'll make you a knockout tonight."

"Hopefully I can help sell some dresses for the charity."

"Don't worry, you will. Karina just left for the hotel."

Nerves churned in my stomach, but I didn't know why. It was probably from what happened this morning in the Cosmic Lounge. I couldn't wait for the fashion show to be over so I could go home, take a hot shower, and roll into bed.

When Elliot was done, he spun me around so I could look at my makeover in the three-way mirror. "See? Absolutely stunning."

The dramatic eyes, soft blush, and rose lipstick created an elegant yet sexy appeal. I hadn't worn this much makeup in a long time. It had been a long time since I'd worn a fancy dress. I hoped whatever dress they wanted me to wear would fit. Elliot had given them my size, so they had some pieces for me to try on.

"You're a genius, Elliot. I love the makeup. The updo is elegant too."

"You're the perfect canvas. Don't be surprised if men are begging for your number tonight."

I loved getting pampered like this. Elliot made me feel beautiful. I could forget the ugly incident from this morning, my uncle's debt, my unstable job situation, and this feeling for Orion. Tonight, I was free of those things.

Twenty minutes later, I embraced my teary-eyed mom at Wild Roots. Her employer and coworkers loved her.

"You're starting off your retirement with a bang!" I kissed her cheek.

"I can't believe it." She drew back with a beaming smile on her face while waving the folder with her plane ticket and hotel information. "I'm going to Bermuda!"

My mom had worked hard all her life. My grandmother had also worked here before she passed. Dad had worked as a mechanic for a car repair shop. Together, these three people had raised me.

I planned on buying the massage chair for when she returned from her trip. The fashion show tonight would allow me to get her a nice chair.

"It's a new chapter for you. You deserve it." Reid gave her a hug. He wore overalls with his dark hair pulled back in a ponytail. He owned Wild Roots and another landscaping business in the next town over. Business had increased for him and his family. It made me happy to see great things happening to great people.

"I know you have an event tonight. Don't be late." She

kissed my cheek. "You look beautiful, by the way. Elliot is amazing."

"He is." I turned to Reid. "Thanks for doing this."

"You're welcome. I've got some dandelion plants and some vegetables for you. Your mom will be on vacation, so you should take them."

I was going to decline because I had no time to start a garden, but an idea percolated in my head.

"Okay, I'll take them."

"They were watered with shungite-infused crystals. I'll give you a container to bring them home."

"Cool, thank you."

Wild Roots was also looking for innovative ways to improve plant growth for better nutrients.

By the time I got to the hotel conference room, most of the models were already there. The fashion show was held in the restaurant.

I spotted Elliot working on a model's hair, so I didn't bother him.

Monica Mellows, the fashion designer, greeted me. She had curly red hair and a bright smile. She gave me a silky red dress with a low neckline and low back. It had a built-in bra, so I didn't need the extra support.

Slipping the dress on, I glanced at myself in the mirror.

"That dress is gorgeous on you. It makes you look irresistible." Monica beamed, wearing an elegant blue strapless gown.

"You look like Grace Kelly," I said.

She blushed. "Thanks."

The hostess announced a quick rehearsal, showing us the path around the restaurant on a TV screen. The dresses could be made in the donor's desired size. All the money would be distributed between three local charities.

My jaw dropped when I saw the starting bid requirement. The price tag for the dress I was wearing was twenty thousand dollars! I ran my hand over it. My entire wardrobe didn't even add up to half of the price. It was surreal what people spent on clothes these days.

Though the dress was stunning, I couldn't comprehend buying it.

I glanced at the live feed on the screen, showing people entering the restaurant. When Chantel entered the restaurant with her friends, bitterness rose in me. Her family came from wealth, so she could afford to buy these couture clothes. I didn't want her to see me.

Then I saw Orion walking in with Ralph. The nerves in my gut exploded yet again. What was supposed to be a simple evening just took another turn.

CHAPTER TWENTY-ONE

ORION

ELENA STILL LINGERED on my mind as I entered the extravagant silent auction. I couldn't push her away as easily as I'd hoped. Could I abandon what I had with Kate? She was an integral part of my life. Was I ready to move on? I didn't know what to do.

And *that* infuriated me too.

I'd hoped this event would distract me from the embarrassing episode in the Cosmic Lounge. But all it did was make me wish she were here at the auction with me. I could buy her all the clothes she wanted.

You have it bad for her.

Elena left without saying anything to me. She probably saw me on a conference call, but still, she could've interrupted me. I didn't mind.

She left me a sticky note with a drawing of a smiling flower. I'd stared at it for too long.

Elena was like the sunshine to my gloom and doom. Even her reaction to my inexplicable explanation of what had transpired earned my respect. She didn't push me away like I had expected.

More importantly, I hadn't stepped away like I had planned. I'd stepped even closer.

Clearing my head, I headed to the crowded banquet room. I hadn't expected this many people to attend the silent auction, but I supposed the New England elites enjoyed their fashion and food. Arrow had donated some CheckMate Red and CheckMate Black to the hotel for the event.

The host standing in front of the banquet room checked us in, providing Ralph and me each with a bidding tablet and our table number.

"We're over there." Ralph gestured to a table with four chairs and an elegant centerpiece with glowing lights.

I didn't know who was sitting at our table. I glanced around at the conference room, taking in the faces. Unfamiliar faces met my gaze, and I offered a courteous nod. I hadn't planned on attending tonight's event until I learned Samuel Donatello would be here.

He had been roaming freely even after two women were discovered held captive at his home. His lawyer got him released on a two-million-dollar bond awaiting trial. When I discovered Sam had posted bail, I directed Ralph to reach out to those girls' families and offer them the best legal team. Their legal fees would be paid under a company that couldn't be traced back to me.

Ralph had been tailing him upon his release. Who was the judge who'd allowed him to roam freely? I had no doubt he received an irresistible bonus. Ralph had sent me pictures of Sam living life as if he didn't have a trial waiting for him. As if he didn't care who was watching him. A man with this kind of confidence or arrogance confirmed one thing for me:

he had someone backing him. Someone powerful was protecting him.

No one was invincible. He should also know that no one was indispensable. A man like Sam was normally a scapegoat —the man who harbored all the blame and would probably die for it.

So here I was attending a silent auction to observe a man who probably had connections to The Trogyn. Perhaps members of The Trogyn would be here tonight.

I would rather be at home, continuing my research on Octavius Rollins, the man Elena was seeing. What kind of name was that anyway? I spent too much time on her social media pages to see who he was. I couldn't find anyone with that name. This was something I'd never done before, but I had to know her type.

"There he is." Ralph's voice yanked me back to the auction. He jerked his chin to the entrance. "That woman looks underage. What do you think?"

I studied the brunette with her hair piled up onto her head. Her youthful face was dolled in makeup. The black gown and diamond necklace made her appear older. The fucker enjoyed young girls. She looked like she was eighteen. According to my files, Sam was an Italian man in his fifties. He'd never been married and had no kids.

Bringing a date who could be his daughter to this event wasn't a smart idea. "We'll just monitor him and see who he speaks to."

A waiter walked by with a tray of champagne and some hors d'oeuvres. Ralph and I each grabbed a champagne flute and sat down.

"Do you think he's an elite?" Ralph asked.

"Not sure." I sipped the champagne. "But his careless

actions tell me no. An elite would be more careful. But then again, he could be an elite who believes he's untouchable."

But my gut told me he wasn't an elite, he was simply working for one.

"Hello there." A pretty brunette approached our table with her red-headed friend. Both wore fitted dresses that showed off their figures. "You must be Orion Reimann. I'm Chantel Henderson from Channel Seven News. This is my friend, Sabrina Marshall from Hollywood Chitchat."

I didn't want to be sitting at a table with journalists, especially someone specializing in gossip. The only reporter I trusted was the one mad at me right now.

"Are you ladies here to buy dresses?" Ralph smiled at the women.

"How can we resist exceptional designs? We like supporting charity." Chantel sipped her champagne.

"What about you?" Sabrina asked Ralph and looked over to me.

Ralph lifted his champagne flute. "Supporting a good cause."

"It's important to support the community," I added.

"No significant others for you to buy dresses for?" Chantel smiled, revealing perfect teeth.

I liked a confident woman, but this one appeared overly confident. I'd seen her on Channel 7 News. Did Elena get along with Chantel? She reminded me of my cousin, Jasper, a spoiled trust fund kid who believed everyone worked for him.

"He's got too many to buy for." Ralph slapped a playful hand on my shoulder, looking at me with amusement in his eyes. "How do you even remember all their names? I'd be so confused."

Asshole.

But I appreciated him stepping in so I didn't have to reply to Chantel.

Chantel raked a gaze down my body, making her invitation obvious. "The noncommittal type fascinates me."

"They're like a charging bull, focusing only on expanding their empire," Sabrina said.

Chantel studied me. "There haven't been many images of you until recently. What made you step into the spotlight?"

Because I wanted to. Because my presence in Providence benefited the WaterFyre Rising video game and several business ventures I needed to promote.

But that wasn't what Chantel was asking. She believed it had to do with a woman. So I played along.

"I'm redefining the term commitment. It's time to see who's out there that's suitable for me. If I'm in the shadows, she won't see me."

"A fashion show is the perfect place to meet potential partners." Chantel smirked.

Ralph lifted his eyebrows and nibbled on the appetizers.

"What do you know about me?" I asked.

"You're an eligible bachelor with businesses all over the world. Your father and cousin run the largest bank in Europe. You're not married, and you don't have a girlfriend. You're friends with billionaires like Remington Starke, Grayson Wu, Arrow Holt, Forrest Navarro, and Royce Viktorsson."

"I suppose you did your homework."

"I'm a journalist, remember? I like to uncover information about those who interest me." Her eyes gleamed. "You interest me a great deal."

"The audience at Hollywood Chitchat would love to know more about you and the WaterFyre Rising team. All of them have significant others but you." Sabrina got out of her seat. "Can I take a photo of you and Chantel?"

"Take one of me with him first." Chantel leaned close to me.

"Beautiful." Sabrina snapped a few pictures and passed her phone to Ralph, asking him to take a picture of me with the two ladies.

Christ.

"That's enough photos for today," I said.

"But you're so photogenic." Sabrina glanced at her phone.

"Don't I get a picture with you pretty ladies?" Ralph winked.

"Of course." Sabrina passed me the phone. "Please?"

I tossed Ralph an amused look. Unlike me, he didn't mind the attention from the women. Mom told me when Ralph was younger, he was a ladies' man. But his heart was now set on a woman who took care of my home in Sweden. They'd been in love a long time, but he hadn't asked her to marry him.

"Can you send me those pictures?" Chantel asked Sabrina, then turned to me. "Do you want a copy?"

Absolutely not.

"No thanks." I wouldn't offer my phone number. "Where are your boyfriends? They should be here making donations on your behalf."

"I'm recently single," Chantel said.

"My boyfriend is traveling right now." Sabrina sat back down and began a conversation with Ralph.

Chantel whispered, "Feel free to make a donation on *my*

behalf." She placed her hand on my thigh, running it up and down.

I'd dealt with several aggressive women before. They needed to know where I stood before it got out of hand.

I gripped her hand, placing it back onto her thigh. "We should concentrate on the auction."

She pouted, and a slow smile crept onto her lips. "If you want to concentrate on other things later, I've got a room in this hotel for the evening."

"I'm busy tonight."

She was an attractive woman, and a lot of men would want the enticing offer. She had a perfect body, the right curves, a pretty face, and plump lips that promised an exciting evening.

Despite that, my body didn't react to her. Not in the slightest.

Another woman held my interest. This woman not only commanded my body, she also reached into my psyche, shoving away the darkness like no one had done.

A woman dressed in a gold ballgown approached the podium, gave the audience instructions for the bidding process, and announced the beginning of the show. The band in the corner increased their volume, and the waitresses emerged with platters of more hors d'oeuvres.

Chantel slipped a piece of paper with her phone number into the chest pocket of my jacket. Then she placed her palm on my thigh. I'd met a lot of brazen women in my life, but this one was beyond that. Was this how she conducted all her interviews? Or was she testing to see how far she could go?

I gripped her wrist, moving it aside. "You're a very aggressive woman."

"You seem like a guy who prefers a woman who knows what she wants." She licked her bottom lip.

There were several ways a woman could show her desires and confidence. But not any of these ways were admirable to me.

From under the table, Ralph kicked me lightly. I looked at him, but he pretended he was busy eating.

"These are delicious," he said to Sabrina, who nodded in agreement.

Wasn't Chantel covering the banquet for Channel 7 News? Did she choose this table on purpose? Had she targeted *me* tonight? I kicked Ralph back, and he knew what to do.

"So what kind of men do you like to report on?"

Chantel's face beamed as though she'd been waiting for someone to ask her that question. If that question had come from me, it would've given the wrong impression. I'd experienced this kind of situation several times and Ralph had helped me maneuver out of each unscathed.

Though I ran a successful empire, women were a different topic altogether. Some required too much energy from me.

And some women—like Elena—introduced me to a fascinating uncharted terrain. Everywhere I looked, something new intrigued me. She filled in the parts of me I had assumed were already full. I was discovering a lot about myself recently, and it was all because of her.

I wished she were here with me.

As the models emerged from the back, the waitress placed two plates of hors d'oeuvres filled with stuffed mushrooms, smoked trout croquettes, goat cheese and salami stuffed dates, and other delicacies.

A woman wearing a black gown with a section of the dress twisted into a flower shape walked between the tables. She stopped and chatted with potential buyers.

I glanced at the tablet and saw the dress had already had a few bids.

Sabrina kept Chantel busy as she swiped to see more dresses.

My gaze remained on Sam at the far-right table. The young girl walked off with a woman. He chatted with another man, eating and laughing.

Something red caught the corner of my eye, pulling my attention away from Sam. My heart galloped when Elena walked down the carpeted aisle like a powerful goddess who didn't need to say a word or make a single gesture.

Her mere presence demanded all the attention from everyone.

CHAPTER TWENTY-TWO

ELENA

I FELT Orion's eyes on me the moment I stepped into the room. I tried my best to compose myself as I made my way to the tables, showing off the red dress as best I could. Though I tried not to be bothered that Chantel sat with him, disappointment and jealousy surged. Was she the reason he had pushed me away?

How long had they known each other? I had assumed Chantel was dating Alvin.

"What colors does the dress come in, dear?" asked an old woman wearing her silver hair in an elegant French twist.

"It's on the tablet, Grandma," said a girl wearing a beautiful blue dress. She tapped the screen to enlarge the image for her grandmother.

"Wonderful. I'll get this for your birthday. What color would you like, Emma?"

"The emerald, please," Emma said and looked at me. "The dress is gorgeous on you."

"Thank you."

I walked over to another table and spotted the man I'd

seen inside Uncle Carlos's office. I didn't know his name, but he gave off negative vibes I didn't like.

Tonight's event was supposed to be easy. Jealousy and terror had replaced the anxiety I'd felt about modeling. I didn't know which one was worse.

My heart raced as I approached the man. He sat with a couple, who offered me a smile. His eyes fixated on me, and chills raced down my spine.

As I headed off to another table, the man reached for my arm, but I shifted away from him.

"How are you doing, Elena?" A smirk slid onto his face.

"I'm all right."

"You're looking better and better every time I see you." He extended a hand to me. "I don't think we've officially met. I'm Samuel Donatello, a business partner of your uncle's. We should have dinner sometime."

My stomach twisted as I recognized the name. He was the man selling the insurance scams.

"No thanks." I ignored his hand.

Everyone at the table was occupied with another model who had sashayed to a nearby table. She wore a short dress, revealing beautiful legs. Sam's eyes remained on me. People probably assumed he was interested in purchasing the dress I had on.

"Why the dismissal?" He leaned closer and whispered, "I've got ways for you to pay off that debt with your Uncle Carlos. If you behave, I'll even ask him to erase it altogether."

I shifted away, glaring at him. "No thank you. Have a good evening."

Was my uncle involved in the life insurance scam? My gut told me yes.

"We'll meet again, Elena." He smirked and licked his lips. "You'll say yes soon."

I should have just left, but I hated the way he viewed me like an item he could buy.

"It will *never* be a yes."

"I like a feisty woman in bed. If you don't say yes, your debt will increase. Your dad should have said yes to me too. His loan tripled because of his defiance."

Anger and something else sparked in me. Sam knew my father? The thought that my father had been threatened had never crossed my mind until now. I had assumed . . .

Stupid. Just stupid, Elena.

I had assumed my father's debt to his brother was legal—or as legal as it could be. The documents had stated the amount my dad owed. What if the documents had been manipulated or were completely false? I didn't know what to do. I needed proof.

Maybe intuition had been trying to tell me something from the beginning, but I didn't listen because Uncle Carlos was family. He just wanted his money back, and I was a responsible daughter trying to clear my father's debt, keeping the family peace.

Where had I gone wrong? What did I miss?

Those closest to you can hurt you the most. I never understood that statement until now. I'd been blind, seeing half-truths when I should have stepped back to look at the situation objectively. Did Mom know about the threats? No, Dad would've kept them from her and me.

Trying my best not to reveal my emotion, I asked, "Are you threatening me like you threatened my father?" I waited a beat. "Should I hire a private investigator to look into the debt?"

Something flickered in his eyes. Was it regret for letting that slip? It didn't matter what his response was—I'd find out if Sam and my uncle had anything to do with my father's death. Anger surged, making me want to grab the knife on the table and stab him.

He grunted a laugh and smirked. "It was a joke, Elena. I wanted to see you all riled up. You know, see that fire in your eyes."

I pretended to believe him. "Just so you know, it's not a funny joke. I loved my father, and I don't appreciate you smearing his reputation."

He gripped his champagne flute, drank, and placed it down on the table. "I mishandled the situation because I desperately wanted to have dinner with you."

"Enjoy your evening. I hope you choke on your champagne." Irritated, I stalked off to another table, making my way closer to Orion.

CHAPTER TWENTY-THREE

ORION

MY EYES FOLLOWED her every move. I lost my breath at how beautiful she looked in the red dress. It elongated her body, enhanced the dips and curves in all the right places, making me wonder what mesmerizing landscape lay beneath the dress. I'd never been this enthralled by any woman. For a moment it felt like it was just me and her in the room.

Was this the date she was talking about? I scanned the room for any man that resembled an Octavius Rollins. It was hard to tell who the guy was because most men had their eyes trained on her.

"She looks beautiful in that dress," Sabrina whispered to Chantel.

"It's the dress." Chantel retorted. "The color and cut would make anyone stand out. I should get it for myself."

"You should!" Sabrina cheered. "You'd look fabulous in it."

"Elena *is* beautiful." I said, realizing these women must know each other.

Chantel whipped her attention to me. "If I were you, I'd stay away from her. She's *not* your type."

"She's trouble with a capital T," Sabrina added.

I didn't disagree with that comment because Elena had been nothing but trouble for my mind and body. Was there more than just jealousy between these women?

"You don't know my type," I replied.

"You're a man with wealth." Chantel gestured with her hand, and the diamond bracelet glistened from the chandelier above us. "So it makes sense for you to align yourself with wealthy women." She sipped her champagne and placed it down on the table. "Elena isn't that kind of woman."

What Chantel didn't know was that I defined wealth differently than her. I preferred those who didn't walk in my circle. These people showed me a different perspective in life. Too much glitz and glamor blurred the truth. I had to step away, otherwise I might not see myself anymore.

"A bank account doesn't determine someone's worth," I said.

Chantel chewed on her bottom lip, probably weighing my words. "You're absolutely right. I like how you look at things." She smiled.

"I think Elena looks gorgeous too," Ralph said. "And so does the audience. That dress already has a bid of five hundred thousand."

"What?" Sabrina huffed and glanced at the tablet.

I didn't like the way Sam looked at Elena. He said something to her, and her uncomfortable expression told me she wanted to be nowhere near him. How did they know each other?

I didn't like where this was going. Unease settled in me.

Did she know what he did to those girls? Sam reached for her, but she shifted away.

That's my girl.

The fucker had better keep his hands to himself, otherwise I'd have to break his limbs. All the self-defense lessons from my past had been ingrained in me. Right now, my hands itched to use them.

Chantel said something to me, but I didn't hear her. My attention focused on Elena and the intense conversation she was having with Sam. What were they talking about? She looked angry when she left his table.

He kept his gaze on her even after she wandered off. I came here tonight to see who his acquaintances were, but his connection to Elena intrigued me more. Sam Donatello wasn't a good man, and I had to make sure he stayed away from her.

Elena turned to an older woman who admired her dress. Though Elena smiled, the unease—or was it fear—splashed on her face. My fingers curled into a fist. What did Sam say to her?

What was wrong with me? The calm and collected mask I often wore disappeared, replaced by this overwhelming need to protect her. This desire to be with her and make the world know that she was mine coursed through me. Anyone who dared touch her would pay dearly.

I'd never felt this inexplicable surge of protectiveness and possessiveness before. Who was I? Where was Orion?

"Here she comes," Sabrina whispered to Chantel. "You'll look better in that dress. You should get it. By the way, is she returning to work after her vacation? Is it even a vacation? Did you say it's an excuse for her to distance herself from the issues at work?"

"If I were her, I would give my notice and move on. But who knows?" Chantel lifted her shoulder. "She thinks differently. But I don't think she'll return, especially not after what she's been accused of."

What was Elena accused of? A wave of protectiveness billowed in me. "You know Elena?"

Chantel turned and placed a gentle hand on my arm. "She's not your type, Orion."

"You need someone more stylish and with connections." Sabrina smiled at Chantel.

"I have eclectic tastes." My eyes met Elena's as she approached.

I took in her perfect face, the updo that revealed her elegant neck, the low neckline that enticed me, and the lovely figure that had men from other tables fixated on her.

Jealousy spiked in me. "Hello, Elena."

"Hi." Her eyes disconnected from mine and traveled to the hand on my arm.

Something flashed in her eyes, and the event in the Cosmic Lounge sprang to mind. I nudged Chantel's hand off my arm by shifting toward Elena.

She looked at Chantel, Sabrina, and finally at Ralph, where her expression softened. She walked over to him. "It's good seeing you at this event."

"Likewise. You should buy the dress for yourself. It's perfect for you."

She blushed, looking more attractive than I'd ever seen her. The genuine smile and the gleam in her eyes brought the dress to life.

More models in pretty dresses walked by, but my attention was glued to her. Though I loved Ralph like he was family, jealousy still stung me. I envied the ease they shared.

I wanted that with her.

But you ruined it when you pushed her away.

"So this is your part-time job?" Chantel asked Elena.

"I can't say no to charity," Elena said. "Maybe you should buy a few pieces to support this cause."

"I should." She smiled. "I can afford it."

Elena looked away from Chantel, but not before she rolled her eyes, a gesture I loved seeing on her.

The men from a nearby table eyed Elena, waiting for her to come over to their table. Possessiveness overcame me, and I pulled her onto my lap.

People from the nearby tables gasped.

"What are you doing?" she yelped.

I loved the way her ass pressed into my thigh, fitting perfectly on my lap. People stared at us, even Ralph. Chantel and Sabrina exchanged glances.

I slipped an arm around Elena's waist. "Testing to see how stretchy this dress is before I place a bid on it." With my other hand, I brushed the silky fabric on her thigh. Then I leaned into her ear. "I want you to remember this moment and think of me before going to bed." I inhaled her scent. "You smell nice."

Embarrassment flickered on her face.

Then she pushed herself off my lap and whirled around to face me. God, she was so beautiful, even when she was pissed.

"The dress has plenty of movement." She scoffed, yanking gently at the dress. "Whoever you buy this for would be very comfortable in it." Then she stalked over to another table, dismissing me.

Satisfied that the entire room knew she was mine, I sat back against the chair and watched her exchange conversation with an older woman at a table full of women. She twirled and posed for them.

Ralph leaned into me. "What was that all about?"

I flicked him a gaze, and disapproval splashed onto his face. His reaction surprised me more than I expected. Ralph had never reacted this way with any woman I'd been with. But then again, he never cared for them either. How had Elena won him over?

"I'm bidding on the dress," I said.

"Who are you buying it for?" Chantel pursed her lips.

"Can't I buy it just because it's a beautiful dress? I'm a collector of beautiful things."

Ralph snorted, grabbed a fork, and ate his entrée, which the waitress had just placed in front of him.

"You have a lot of luxury apparel at your home?" Chantel arched an inquisitive eyebrow.

"You must have a beautiful collection of things," Sabrina commented, not knowing how accurate she was.

"I'm very proud of my collection."

"Is your collection open for visitors?" Chantel asked.

I submitted my bid and placed the tablet on the table. "Sorry, it's private."

What the fuck got into me tonight?

I looked over at Sam, and our eyes connected.

Stay away from her. She's mine.

Seeing Elena with another man had unhinged me. I was unmoored from everything. At that moment an epiphany struck, and I knew exactly what I had to do. Consequences didn't matter.

The only thing that mattered was Elena. I wanted her.

I oversaw several businesses in finance, communication, technology, and in the science arenas, but failed at relationships. Anxiety had crippled me, but Elena was the cure.

When the auction ended, Ralph went to retrieve the gown while I walked around the room, trying to scan the faces near Sam. I recognized a judge with silver hair. He was probably the one who had approved Sam's bail. Did the city send the police to examine his fucking house? What exactly had they done?

The judge walked off with the young girl, and Sam strode over to a group of people in the lounge.

I texted Ralph to follow the judge in case something inappropriate occurred. Ralph would know what to do.

More people filled the room as I searched for Elena. Then Sam yanked her arm from the crowd and dragged her into the corner. She had changed back into the dress she'd worn to the office this morning.

Fear splashed on her face, and rage boiled in me. Someone called my name, but I didn't hear him or her. With fury coursing through me, I stalked over to Elena.

"Let me go!" She sneered at him, trying to get away from him.

"You do as I say or—"

"Let. Her. Go." My words fell like heavy boulders.

"Who the fuck are you?" Sam glared at me.

"Her boyfriend." I seethed. "Touch her again and you'll die a painful death."

He released her and she rushed over to me.

"Are you okay?" I studied her, and she nodded.

My fist itched to pound his face, to break his arms and legs, but there was a bigger fish to lure out. A dead body was useless to me. Who was watching us? I had to consider all the options and play it safe. Playing the part of a jealous man would suffice in this situation. Though I wasn't pretending at all.

Rage coiled in me, but I contained it.

I wrapped an arm around Elena's waist, pulling her to my side. "It's best that you keep your hands away from my woman. Understand me?"

A muscle twitched in his face as he looked at Elena. "You should've said you were dating someone."

She slipped her arm around me and placed her head on my shoulder, playing along. "You never gave me the chance. When a woman says no, listen to her if she has a man or not." She rose to her toes and placed a gentle kiss on my cheek.

"Apologize," I told him. "A decent man would apologize to a woman he inadvertently disrespected."

He hesitated, but people were now staring at us.

"It's in your best interest. We're all here to support charity. That should be our only mission, correct?"

He flared his nostrils and faced Elena. "Sorry for any disrespect I may have shown you. It wasn't my intention."

Then he stalked off. Sam was probably fuming from the humiliation. A callous man like him would retaliate somehow.

Taking Elena home was all I wanted to focus on tonight.

I sent Ralph a text saying I'd catch up with him later. He replied okay and told me the judge's wife arrived to find him kissing the girl. Ralph said he made an anonymous call to the wife. He also called in a different news station so they could get the scoop rather than alerting Chantel.

I gripped her hand in mine, leading her out to the car. Though she tried to appear calm, I sensed the nerves in her.

"Are you sure you're okay?" I asked once she settled into my car.

"Yeah. Thanks for helping me."

"I have a lot of questions for you."

"I know." She sighed.

"Do you want to talk about it?"

"Not tonight." She looked exhausted.

"Okay. I'll take you home. But I'd like to know what you and Sam Donatello discussed."

"Why?"

"He's not a good man, and I didn't like the way he made you scowl."

A small smile appeared on her face, making me feel better already.

Her phone rang, and she dug into her purse. "Hi, Elliot. I'm okay. What do you mean?" She paused, listened, and then smiled. "Orion was just trying to protect me. I can't believe people are already starting rumors about us." She shifted in her seat. "The guy was an asshole. You were busy. I know you would've helped. Don't worry about it, you goof. I'm fine. Really. Orion's taking me home. You are?"

I'd be lying if I said I weren't jealous of her close relationship with Elliot. I didn't care if he was gay. He was a man, and all men were my enemies now.

Fuck. What was going on with me? At this rate I'd be jealous if I saw her sitting next to a tree. This was getting out of control.

I grunted at this change in me.

Her free hand was on the seat, and I clasped it in mine while I drove to her house. If she didn't want me to take her hand, she would have yanked it away. Her hand relaxed in mine, followed by her body as she leaned into the seat while speaking to Elliot.

Elliot said something to her, and she smiled. "It's exciting news! I'm so happy for you. Have fun in Milan, and don't forget to come back." She laughed and ended the call.

"How did you meet Elliot?" I squeezed her hand.

She glanced at our joined hands and examined them for a moment. "We grew up together. I met him in elementary school. Being minorities, we stood out and were often picked on. So we became friends."

As I turned down the residential street, I tried to put myself in her situation. It must've been hard for her, trying to fit in with her Latina background. I wished I could've been there with her. But I had my own issues growing up. If I had been in the same school as Elena, would I have noticed her? Would we have been friends?

"I bet your life was smooth sailing. Private school all the way? Were there any minority students in your class?"

"Yes, I went to a private school, but there were international kids there. I wouldn't call it smooth sailing."

"No? Wanna tell me about it?"

My mother used to say the people we met were like angels placed on our path to help us grow. Some remained with us, while others disappeared because their purpose had been accomplished.

I met Elena's curious brown eyes. I was at a fork in the road, and she appeared, luring me down this interesting path with an unknown destination.

"How about we exchange curiosities?" I asked. "You tell me what Sam told you, and I'll share my school years with you."

She considered my offer, biting her bottom lip. "Is everything a business negotiation with you?"

"If it were a business negotiation, I would have won

already. This is just me offering a safe space for two people who are curious about each other to talk."

She smirked. "You're good at twisting words around."

I laughed. "You're reading too much into it. But I guess that's something journalists do. Maybe you're right. I'd twist whatever I had to find out everything about you." I lifted her hand to my lips and kissed it.

She sucked in a breath. "You're so confusing."

"So help me unconfuse myself."

"That's not an actual word."

"It's real in my head. As long as you understand me, who cares if it's in the dictionary?"

I pulled into her driveway, parked, and turned off the engine. Today had been a mish-mash of stuff. But somehow everything fell into place as I sat here with her. Despite all that had occurred this morning, starting with us making out in the Cosmic Lounge, to making sure people knew she was mine at the auction, to me wanting to rip Sam to shreds for terrifying her, to finally holding her hand.

She yanked at my hand. "Okay, I'll unconfuse you."

I smiled. "Let's go inside so you can tell me about Sam."

CHAPTER TWENTY-FOUR

ELENA

AFTER A QUICK SHOWER TO wash off Sam's energy, I changed into my cotton shorts and a T-shirt with a riddle: *I rule the night but can trespass into the day. I make anything possible, but can also fade it away. What am I?*

I ambled out into the kitchen and opened the refrigerator. Today had been an interesting day, to say the least. I'd never experienced so many trials in one day. I'd think about them all later. Right now, I just wanted to . . . let go. Free my mind.

I glanced over at Orion, who was observing the dandelion plants on my display table. "Do you want some cold dandelion tea?"

"Sure. Why are you growing dandelions?"

He'd asked me this question before, and I had told him my reply depended on how my first day of work went.

As though he sensed my thoughts, he straightened and walked up to me, staring at my shirt. "What's the answer?"

I looked down at the riddle. "A dream."

"I like it." His eyes beamed. "I hope I earned some dandelion wisdom from you."

I took out two mugs and poured water in. "To be honest, the workday ended badly, but you made up for it by pretending to be my boyfriend at the auction." I offered a mug to him. "By the way, people are starting rumors about us now. Sorry about that."

"Don't apologize for something I did on purpose." He took the cup, sat down, and sipped the cold drink.

"Aren't you worried the rumor might tarnish your reputation or piss off your girlfriend?"

Amusement flashed on his face. "I don't have one."

I snorted. "I don't believe you. A man like you probably has a lot. Or do you mean you don't have anyone serious?"

His expression turned serious. "I don't have anyone serious or non-serious."

"Why?"

"Busy working. What about you? Will Octavius Rollins get mad? I searched for him, but I couldn't find anyone."

"You looked him up?" I burst out laughing, and he looked at me like I was insane. "I was *joking*, Orion." If only he knew I'd used his initials to make up some silly name.

I couldn't believe it. Part of me felt bad that he'd wasted time doing that. But my heart leaped with joy. He was interested in me. But what was holding him back? I had to find out.

"I'll get you back for that." He narrowed his eyes at me. "So Octavius Rollins has my initials. Were you indirectly giving me a sign?"

I twisted my lips, not admitting or denying anything.

He smiled and knew the answer. "Since we're both single, who cares what the media says?"

Something had been bothering me. "How do you know Chantel?"

"I don't know her. She showed up today and sat at our table."

"She likes you."

"I know." He sipped tea, but his gaze never wavered from me. "I'm sure she acts like that with every business executive."

He was right.

"Chantel will probably ask Sabrina to write some crazy story for Hollywood Chitchat."

Orion shrugged. "It's what they do. If it gets out of hand, or you're uncomfortable about it, I'll stop it." He placed his hand over mine. "It's best to pretend you're my girlfriend, so Sam—or any other men—will think twice about getting near you. Now tell me about dandelion tea. It's growing on me."

"Don't you have other things to do tonight? Surely a rich guy like you has more exciting things to do than sit and drink tea with me. We can catch up tomorrow at work."

"Stop stalling." He intertwined his fingers with mine. "Being here with you and talking about strange things is very exciting to me. It's different from what I'm used to."

I didn't know what to say. Warmth simmered in the pit of my stomach. My relationship with him had taken another wild turn. Technically, he was my boss for the duration of my contract, and now he was also my fake boyfriend. The entire situation confused and thrilled me all at once. Anything new carried a fresh and exciting energy. But after a while, that energy fizzled. That was why a lot of relationships failed.

Stop analyzing. It's supposed to fizzle out. You're only his fake girlfriend.

I should just enjoy this *thing* with him while I could.

"Being with you takes me out of my headspace. You may not believe this, but I'm more relaxed when I'm with you."

The statement surprised me. Here was a man who had all the money in the world to escape to any retreat. He could buy an entire country, and yet he just confessed that being with me was his form of relaxation. What was the appropriate reaction to an admission like that? None of the previous men in my life had ever said anything that touching to me.

"I don't know what to say to you. You keep surprising me."

"Likewise, Sunshine." He stared at me, and I could see his eyes studying my face.

No matter how much I tried to prevent myself from blushing, it happened. He noticed, smiled, and didn't comment on it.

"You're like the sunlight that shot through the clouds I've been living in. It's refreshing."

My heart swelled. "You're so poetic—I'm surprised you're not dating."

"You bring out the poet in me." His fingers tightened around mine.

I stared at our joined hands and tried to imagine the pressure Orion faced daily. The demanding businesses, the obscene money that required careful management, the people who needed his guidance, the projects that needed approval. I shivered as I imagined his chaotic workload. Where did he have time for himself?

When he's with you.

I loved knowing I could offer him an escape.

Orion finished his tea, placing the cup on the table. "Thanks for the tea."

I wrestled my fingers with his, and he responded by overcoming mine with his powerful fingers.

A finger war ensued that brought out laughter from both of us. "I'll destroy you!" I said in my most villainous voice.

"Doesn't look like it when your thumb is being crushed by *my* pinky."

"Shut up." I laughed.

I lifted our joined hands and secured my elbow to the table, preparing for a different battle. "Arm wrestle me."

Amusement beamed on his face. "You're going to lose."

That wasn't my goal, but he didn't need to know that.

"We'll see about that, Slingshot."

The nickname suited him. He'd come into my life at the most unexpected time, saving me in more ways than one.

"One, two, three, go!" I pulled his hand down with all my might. But he resisted, and his powerful forearm dragged my arm down, down, and down. I couldn't resist his strength, nor could I resist the charming smile of a man who had just won something extraordinary. I was finally beginning to understand this complicated man. Something in me softened for him even more.

Returning my attention back to arm wrestling, I said, "Was it fun?"

Orion considered me the way a quadrillionaire would eye a project that had taken an unexpected turn. "What's the reason behind that arm wrestling? You do it often?"

"Nope. Just today." I tapped his forearm gently.

"Why?" He arched an eyebrow.

"Because it took you out of your headspace. Guess I'm really good at it." Smiling, I rose from my seat and gestured for him to follow me. "Now that your mindset is in a different space, it's time for some dandelion wisdom."

Pursing lips, he looked at me as though he wanted to punish but also kiss me.

"Besides dandelion and honey, there's a special ingredient in the tea that harmonizes your body, making you more relaxed."

He glanced at the empty cup. "No wonder my body feels fifty percent lighter. I should drink more of it. What's the special ingredient?"

"I can't tell you. It's my secret recipe."

"Okay." He grinned. "I guess I'll just have to come to your house whenever I want dandelion tea."

"I'll start charging you for it."

"I'll pay whatever you want." He stood beside me.

"If you want to know the wisdom of dandelions, then you need to see it."

With hands tucked inside his pockets, he stared at the pots of dandelions. "I've never met a weed collector until you."

"Is that supposed to be a compliment?" I tilted my head. "Actually, don't answer." I turned to the table. "What do you see?"

Laughter gleamed in his eyes, but he didn't show any signs that he thought my question was testing his intelligence.

"I see three pots of dandelions. This one only has leaves, the second pot has bright flowers." He tapped it. "It reminds me of you."

I snorted. "I'm a bright weed?"

"A wildflower with healing properties." His lips tilted

just enough that it made the muscles in my stomach slide, contort, and do all kinds of spectacular things.

I'll show you how wild I can be, was what ran through my head. But I didn't share that with him.

"You're looking at the lifecycle of a dandelion. Most people would dismiss a dandelion because it's a weed that takes over their manicured lawn. Personally, I like them scattered in my yard. Dandelions have a cosmic symbolism." I gestured to each pot. "They represent life and how we're connected to the sun, moon, and stars."

"Tell me more." Intrigue splashed onto his face.

I grabbed the pot with the dandelion puffs. "Follow me." I opened the sliding door to the back deck and stepped out. The motion sensor lights flickered on, revealing the lawn that desperately needed maintenance.

"You need to mow your lawn," he said.

"Been meaning to. Haven't had time."

"I don't mean *you* literally. Do you use a lawn care service?"

"I can do it. Saves time and money. I have a mower."

"You know how to use it?"

I rolled my eyes. "Yes, I do. My dad taught me, and I'm pretty good at it. Time has gotten away from me lately."

He studied me, and I changed the subject before he asked questions that would eventually require me to share my financial predicament. I wasn't ready for that yet.

"So the yellow dandelion represents the sun. The dandelion puff symbolizes the moon." I plucked one stem from the pot and offered it to him.

"It's a full moon on a stem."

"Exactly.

"And the seeds are the stars." I blew at the puffs in the pot, watching them fly out into the night.

He held up his puff, examining it. "After all these years of looking at the stars, I missed the most beautiful symbolism. It's so simple." He twirled it around. "I've been so focused on developing innovative software and finding new ways to expand my business that I've blocked out the beauty that exists in front of me. I missed out on the obvious things." He met my eyes. "Thank you for reminding me to appreciate the simple things." He stared at the dandelion puff for a moment. "I'll never look at a dandelion the same way again."

"You're welcome. I took you out of your headspace again." I beamed. "You're literally holding the moon in your hand. Blow at it and make a wish. Let the seeds take your wish into the sky and give them to the Cosmic Dandelion Goddess."

"You just made that up." He blew at the seeds, scattering them into the night.

Something magical occurred tonight. I felt it in the air stirring between us. It was as though the seeds that floated around us symbolized our relationship and its potential. What were we planting? How would we grow from this moment forward?

"There's power to creating your own magic."

"You're absolutely right."

I didn't know why, but I felt the urge to share a part of my childhood with him. My previous boyfriends were never interested in my dandelion story. They thought it was too weird and hated the dandelion tea. Orion appreciated it all. For that, he deserved a reward: a sliver of me.

"When I was little, my grandmother told me the dandelion story because I enjoyed looking at the stars. It was how I started drinking dandelion tea. It made me believe I was drinking in the magic of the sun, moon, and stars." I turned to see his gray eyes had grown darker, more intense.

In the dark night with just the lights from the deck casting a soft glow around us, his eyes looked like they belonged to a mysterious wolf, watching and waiting.

"That's what I'll be thinking from now on. Drinking in the cosmos."

"My grandmother and my mom got me into eating dandelion leaves too. I'll make some for you to try one day. Grandma was from Peru and into holistic medicine. She said plants hold the key to great health, and the cures for all diseases can be found in nature." I placed the pot down on the wooden table. "I believe she's right. But I think the world isn't ready to acknowledge it yet. People are too caught up on convenience, or how to make more money." A mosquito flew around his face, and I swatted it away.

He gripped my wrist, pulling me close. I didn't resist him.

Couldn't.

He brushed his lips over mine, and I surrendered to him. The kiss was slow, wet, and inviting. It wasn't like the passionate kiss we'd shared in the Cosmic Lounge. This was gentle and special, reminding me of the natural way the dandelion seeds moved with the wind. His tongue sought mine, and I moaned against his mouth. I slid my hand up his chest, shoulders, looping my arms around his neck. Then I felt his necklace and stiffened.

He drew back. "What's wrong?"

"I . . ."

What could I say without sounding jealous?

He held me close, and I could hear his heartbeat. My

eyes landed on the gold band around his necklace. After this morning in the Cosmic Lounge, I promised myself that if a relationship were to happen between me and him, he had to be honest with me. I had to know why he was still wearing that ring. Obviously, she still mattered to him.

Who was she?

I considered myself a generous person, but I wasn't that generous. If he wanted to be with me, he couldn't be wearing a piece of jewelry that belonged to another woman. It was wrong and disrespectful to both parties involved.

I sighed. "It's late. I have to get ready for bed. I have work tomorrow."

"But I'm your boss, and you're allowed to come in a few hours—"

He was about to say something else but his phone rang. A crease formed on his forehead as he took the call, releasing me from him. "What is it, Ed?"

My body yearned for his touch again. I had to train my body not to get used to this. The more he gave, the more I wanted. But what if things ended as quickly as they started? I didn't know if I had the energy to cope with another heartache.

As I brought the mugs back into the kitchen, he let out a curse. "I'll be there tomorrow. Have the authorities been alerted?"

Inside the kitchen, I studied him as he stalked over to the railing, glancing into the darkness. His face had taken on a stern expression, a man detached from emotion and focused on a task that required his objectivity. He just did a one-eighty like it was ingrained in him. I found myself doing that often too. We all needed an outlet, a way to detach from things that bothered us.

After a few more words, he ended the call and walked back into the kitchen. "I won't be in the office tomorrow. The elevator will recognize your facial features and allow you to the top floor. Ralph might stop by, but I'm not sure. Go into my office and look at the research board I've been working on. There's a lot of information there. Text or call me if you have any issues."

I didn't remember seeing a board during lunch, but I hadn't been looking. "Is everything okay?"

"There's a dead body on my island."

"You have an island?" I gaped at him, wondering why he had an island. But then again, why did wealthy people purchase the things they did?

I couldn't ignore our stark differences. The gap between me and him widened every day. I wasn't sure if I could have a relationship with him. We'd be talking about things that didn't exist in each other's world.

He tipped up my chin. "I'll take you there soon. Thank you for today and this evening. See you soon." He kissed my forehead, sending a zing of energy straight to my toes.

CHAPTER TWENTY-FIVE

ORION

I WALKED AROUND THE ISLAND, surveying the area for clues about the dead man. Was he a random person who had fallen off his boat and washed on to my shore? Was he murdered on my island? Had he been lurking and gotten injured by the laser traps I'd placed near my home? But these traps weren't meant to kill anyone, they would only subdue the trespasser. He'd have to be near my home for that to occur. But my security system would have alerted me of his presence. The coroner's report would provide me more details, but that wouldn't happen for another week.

I walked through the wooded area behind my house and glanced at the devices installed in the trees. Nothing seemed out of place. Then I strode around, reviewing the construction of my abstract building and the guest house. They were close to completion. My mom had left this island to me, and I'd taken care of it. For the longest time, I didn't know what to do with it.

Quintile Island was my sanctuary from my chaotic life.

This place possessed a peaceful atmosphere that was

difficult to explain. Anyone who dared desecrate that would pay.

Most people knew Quintile Island was private property owned by one of my many companies. The small circle of people who knew it belonged to me were mostly family and a few business acquaintances.

A thought trickled into my head. Was Jasper behind this? He'd been harassing me about selling it. Maybe he was creating bad press to force me to sell it. Jasper could talk someone to death, but I didn't know if he had the guts to kill anyone.

I looked at the picture of the man on my phone. "What were you doing on my island, Aaron Turner from Massachusetts?"

Records showed he was a lawyer working for a New York law firm and often traveled to Europe.

My legal team didn't work with him or his firm. Aaron owned two boats, but they were docked in Newburyport, Massachusetts. It was possible he was on a boat with friends and drowned. But his family and friends should have looked for him.

Did Aaron Turner know my mentor? Though I'd been close to The Condor, he'd never been to this island.

This private sanctuary wasn't a tourist attraction. Several signs had been posted around the shore to alert people it was private property and cameras were in use. How had Aaron been on the island without the cameras catching him?

Was I being paranoid? Or had someone known where the cameras were positioned and avoided them successfully?

I strode to an area that had been sectioned off for solar panels that my energy company had developed. These advanced panels hadn't reached the market yet. I wanted to test them first. This island ran on solar energy, of which I had enough for the entire year.

The speed with which these panels collected and replicated solar energy excited me. I had so many projects going on that made me proud. I thrived on innovation and inspiration. But it required me to divide my energy in so many different directions. So many areas to manage, which meant I could've gone wrong somewhere.

I had a feeling I was missing something important. But I couldn't pinpoint it.

I'd called off the construction team for the week. The Swedish authorities would visit me tomorrow. I had to make sure everything was squared away before I returned to the States.

Elena's face popped into my vision. I missed her. She'd become more important to me than she realized.

That kiss.

The kiss we'd shared touched me to the core. It was like I remembered something deep within me. The closer I got to her, the more I remembered things about myself—what made me happy.

But then Elena had hesitated, and I knew why. She wanted to know about the ring on my necklace. I'd want to know too if she wore a ring that had belonged to another man.

I walked through the woods back toward my house and stepped on something. As I bent down to pick up a gold button with a mandala in the center, my necklace fell to the ground.

I stood there for a moment, staring at the gold chain and gold ring on the dry leaves. Was the universe helping me? Now I had to put it back or tuck it away in my pants pocket.

Picking up the necklace, I noticed the clasp had broken after so many years of having no issues.

I hadn't met a woman who touched me the way Elena had. My chest constricted as though it knew what I was about to do.

"I'm moving on, Kate. I hope you're happy for me." The necklace and ring warmed in my hand. I imagined the warmth as confirmation from the universe. My body felt lighter as I tucked the necklace into my pocket.

Then I turned my attention to the button. I'd never seen the gold mandala before. It could belong to one of the construction workers or one of my men monitoring the island while I was away.

I'd send it to the DNA lab for them to analyze. In half an hour I'd be meeting with two members of my team. Urgent meetings had come up, requiring me to go to Sweden. I had to call Elena to let her know I wouldn't be back for another week.

What was she doing now? Was she missing me?

CHAPTER TWENTY-SIX

ELENA

WE ALL GATHERED in Vivian's lounge area with comfy couches located beside her massive gym. Her fiancé, Arrow, had renovated his home to suit her needs. I could see the love and joy oozing from her. All the girls here tonight exuded that bliss. All except me.

"Look at these fresh spring rolls. Viv taught me how to make them." Kiera placed a platter down on the coffee table. "There's shrimp and chicken teriyaki." She had gorgeous brown hair, a little darker than mine.

We all dove in, filling our plates with spring rolls and dipping sauce.

I shouldn't compare myself to these girls who had become my friends. But it was hard not to yearn for the same. Would I ever meet a man who put me as his top priority?

My thoughts wandered to Orion. He showed interest in me and we had fantastic chemistry. But he had baggage.

We all do.

He had one foot in the past and one in the present.

Would a man like him drop everything to be with me? In romance books that always happened, and it sounded wonderful. But this was reality.

I didn't want to ruin the evening with the girls with my negative mood, so I pushed him aside.

"So when is your Kindness Fund charity?" I asked Vivian. She and her fiancé had expanded Whiz Kidz to incorporate a dental office that performed affordable dental work for the community. They had a lot of doctors on staff.

Vivian held up her finger as she chewed on a spring roll. "It's in two weeks. If you have time, I'd love for you to cover it before I schedule other media outlets."

I grinned, thinking about Channel 7 News and how Chantel wouldn't like that one bit.

Sitting beside me with her pretty auburn curls, Michelle kicked my foot. "Why are you smiling?"

Kiera jabbed a finger at me from across the table. "I know what that is."

I furrowed my eyebrows and laughed at her facial expression. She looked like she knew a big secret that I was unaware of.

"What?" I asked with a laugh.

Natalie shook her head. "It's your turn, Elena."

I bit into my spring roll, still unsure of the chatter amongst the girls. They were staring at me.

"It's your turn." Audri placed her dish on the table and narrowed her eyes. "Is that why you've been avoiding us?"

"You're all acting strange. I don't know what you're talking about."

We'd become friends after I wrote about them in Musepaper. My readers loved these girls. They kept asking for updates on Audri's jewelry collection, Natalie's new dress collection, Kiera's notecards, Vivian's dental office and her sister's plushie business. Michelle's travel blog had grown with my readers, loving all the excursion sites she promoted.

I had few female friends growing up. They didn't like me. Elliot was the only one who understood me, but he was a guy. So these girls were my first genuine female friends who didn't make me feel unworthy, even though they were all more successful than me.

"Who's your boyfriend? Is he in the media?" Michelle asked.

"I think there's something going on with you and Orion," Vivian said casually.

How did she know?

"Orion?" Amusement gleamed in Audri's eyes. "We don't know much about him."

"How long have you been seeing him?" Kiera inquired.

"He's quite the catch, but is he a good kisser?" Natalie arched an elegant eyebrow.

"When did this happen?" Michelle kicked my foot again.

I put my plate on the coffee table, held up two hands, and laughed at the curious faces gawking at me. "How did talking about your dental event turn into the third degree on my love life?"

"See that?" Kiera wagged her finger. "See how she twists things around with her use of words?"

Audri narrowed her eyes. "Journalists are dangerous."

Everyone laughed, knowing she was just teasing. But there was truth to that. I could and would use my words wisely. However, among family and friends, I only wanted to offer the truth.

"Wait, before I forget!" Audri slapped a hand to her forehead and looked at me. "The girls and I chatted about this at the last gathering, the one you couldn't make." She got up from the couch and retrieved a tray of leather bands from a table. "I'm having a Make Your Own Bracelet event at Natalie's flagship store. Please come! The proceeds will be donated to a local charity and Vivian's Kindness Fund to help low-income families achieve a healthy smile."

Vivian held up a finger. "Part of that will go into a scholarship fund for students who want to study dentistry but can't afford it."

I was in awe of these inspiring women making an enormous difference in the world. They had money and power and used them well.

"I love that. I'll definitely do a write-up on Musepaper."

"Thanks!" Audri beamed. "So tell us about Orion."

They all whipped their attention to me, making me laugh. "It's complicated."

Michelle smiled. "It's always complicated."

"Your reply just confirmed one thing: SSG!" Kiera high-fived all the girls.

"What's that?"

Audri's lips curled into a mischievous pout. "Super Spy Girls. Is there something you'd like to know about Orion? Does he want to be with you? Does he love you? How can you find out?" She gestured to all the women grinning at me like they'd been waiting for this opportunity. "We can assist. With our combined brainpower, nothing is unattainable."

I couldn't help but laugh. "You sound like a female vigilante group."

"Exactly." Audri punched a fist into the air. "We're like the Bond Girls."

"But better," Vivian added.

"I'm starting a SSG fashion collection. Something chic,

cool, and fun." Natalie wiggled her eyebrows. "There's going to be a lingerie line too."

"Oh!" Michelle clasped her hands together. "Send me pics when you have them. I'll blog the hell out of it. If you have postcards or a flyer, give some to me. I'll have Royce place them in all of his excursion offices."

"When I have the samples ready, I'd like all of you to model an outfit for me." Natalie beamed.

Everyone cheered, and somehow all the issues I'd been dealing with fell away. At the moment I felt so inspired that anything was possible.

"We kissed," I blurted out.

The room went quiet.

"And?" Kiera asked.

"How was it?" Michelle grabbed another spring roll.

"Amazing." I bit my bottom lip. "But he has baggage."

"They all do, honey." Audri placed a hand on my shoulder.

"No. This is different." I sighed. "I think he's still hung up on his ex."

Vivian furrowed her eyebrows. "What do you mean?"

"He's wearing a necklace with a gold band that probably belonged to her. Maybe he was married before. I don't know."

"Interesting." Audri twisted her lips, thinking.

Natalie nodded slowly. "Have you asked him about it?"

"Not yet," I said, sorting through the tray of leather bands. "But I plan to."

Kiera lifted a hand in the air. "I've got it. This could be your SSG mission. Make him, or rather, inspire him to remove the necklace. When that happens, it means he's releasing the past to be with *you*."

"That's perfect!" Audri agreed.

"But how do I do that? I mean, I don't want to force him. But I also can't be with a man whose heart is still occupied by someone else."

"We understand, babe." Michelle offered a warm smile. "Women can be generous, but not for this." She narrowed her eyes. "With love we have to be selfish. We can only be with a man who's willing to give his entire heart to us because we give our entire heart to him."

"Too bad we know so little about him or his ex," Vivian said. "I don't think the boys do either."

"Start seducing Orion with little things." Kiera yanked at her wide-neck knit top, revealing a silky bra strap on her shoulder. "Sexy lingerie always works."

Laughing, I blurted out the truth before I could stop it. "I can't afford it."

What is wrong with me?

The girls looked at me, and heat bloomed on my face.

"Natalie, my love," Audri said. "What do you think about preparing a self-care package for our friend?"

"Absolutely!" Natalie raked a gaze over me. "I've got the perfect styles for you. When he sees you in these—" she purred and moved her shoulders seductively "—he might lose his breath and collapse into a heap on the floor. You'll probably need a defibrillator to bring him back to life."

"Oh, I've got that covered." Kiera lifted a hand. "I'll steal one from Forrest's clinic."

"Why don't you just ask him?" Audri wondered.

"Because he'll ask me why. Then I'll have to explain that we're trying to make his boy pass out for a Super Spy Girl mission. He'd be too interested and wouldn't leave me alone." Kiera stared at us with a serious expression. "This needs to remain as a girls-only meeting, okay?" She winked at us. "I'll ask the office to buy a new defibrillator to replace the old one. Forrest is too busy to notice what's missing in his supply closet."

"You're getting a gigantic bag of luxury beauty products from Iceland." Michelle patted her cheeks. "The lava masks are the best."

I'd always wanted to try them. Tears welled in my eyes, but I forced them to stay put.

"I have this new mouthwash that creates a tingle in your mouth . . . and on his cock. It's the best," Vivian said.

All the girls hounded her with questions why she hadn't told them.

"I had to test it out first! It's been proven successful, and everything's been approved. Mint Sensations will be on the market within the next six months. All of you will get a case for free." Vivian narrowed her eyes at me. "But I'll give you the *only* bottle I have left at home."

The tears came slowly but eventually turned into a full-on cry. I loved these girls so much.

"I demand a full report." Kiera grinned and gave me a tissue.

"Give it to Kiera. It might expire by the time I get to use it." I beamed. "And she can report her findings to us."

"Gimme gimme!" She gestured with her fingers.

Everyone laughed, and I'd never blushed as much as I did tonight. But it was good embarrassment amongst friends. I was the only one in this room with financial debt and an unstable career, and yet they didn't make me feel less than them.

"Your SSG mission needs a name. What do you want to call it?" Audri asked.

My mind whirled with ideas as the girls threw out some silly names that made me tear up even more.

Michelle placed a box of tissues on my lap. "We're here for you."

I took a tissue and dabbed my eyes. "Thank you." I looked at the girls. "And thank you for not asking me to explain."

Though I loved my friends. I wasn't ready to share my financial problems.

"We got you," Kiera said. "*Moonraker, Never Say Never Again, Dr. No, and The Spy Who Loved Me* are some James Bond movie titles to inspire your SSG mission. Do you like any of them?

One title stood out to me. "How about The Thief Who Loved Me?"

"There's a lovely ring to that." Michelle's eyes gleamed. "Wanna tell us why you chose that?"

I didn't want to disclose anything personal, so I improvised. "Since he's stealing my heart, he's considered a thief."

Kiera laughed. "I love it!"

"Please keep us posted," Vivian added.

"Want to make a bracelet for him?" Audri asked, gesturing to the tray.

"Yes, please. What should I start with for a masculine bracelet?"

"Here's a version I made for Remi." Audri gave me a leather bracelet that was about half an inch wide with some gunmetal accents.

We spent the next hour making bracelets, and I was happy to set the SSG mission aside. When it was time for me to go home, I had a beautiful bracelet for Orion. I'd chosen dark leather with a cord running through the middle with some topaz beads and a matte gunmetal clasp. It was masculine, stylish, and sturdy.

I placed it on my nightstand, unsure when I'd give it to him.

What was he doing now?

We'd chatted on the phone for the past few nights as well as texted several times a day. Based on the number of texts I'd gotten from him, it appeared like he had a lot of free time. But I knew he was busy. Perhaps he made time for me? Maybe, maybe not.

We also discussed the investigation, and I gave him my perspective on places I'd visited. It made me feel accomplished that I could offer something useful to him. Somehow this research felt different from other stories I'd researched. Maybe it was because I didn't want to disappoint Orion. The Condor seemed like an important person in his life, a family member who had been murdered. Personal matters often blinded a person from seeing things objectively, and I offered that point of view for him.

After showering, I got into bed and turned on my computer and opened the email from Cathy Lindbergh, the Human Resources Manager of Channel 7 News. Something sharp twisted in my gut.

Dear Elena,

Effective immediately, your position has been eliminated. We discovered drugs in your desk and inside your locker at the office gym. Having drugs on the premises violates company policy.

. . .

The letter described how they could bring criminal charges against me, but given my contribution to the news station, they saved me the stress. So they fired me instead. I wouldn't be able to collect unemployment because I was fired for misconduct.

A massive wave of anxiety pummeled me as my list of unpaid bills and responsibilities grew. How would I repair my house now? When would I emerge from this financial sinkhole that was dragging me deeper into debt? Why was this happening to me? It seemed like no matter how much I tried to overcome obstacles, more were tossed my way. I could only take so much.

Anger and exhaustion spiked as my financial burden formed into a monster. The only well-paying job I had now was working for Orion until my contract ended. My part-time gigs at FoodHub and Let's Ketchup helped with some expenses, but I needed more income. Would I be working multiple jobs for the rest of my life? The tension in my body snapped, and I sagged into my bed, surrendering to life. Tears broke free, sliding down my face.

Breathe.

It's just a phase.

After the tears released the mounting stress from my body, I took a few moments to gather myself. I wasn't going to surrender to these bullies. I didn't do drugs. I was framed. But by whom? Chantel? Why? They didn't even give me a chance to defend myself. The company wanted me out. I had to get to the bottom of this.

I could get a lawyer to fight this accusation. But I didn't have the money. It was odd how things played out. After the girls' night out, I had already decided to look for a new job. I had come home tonight preparing to draft my resignation letter. I needed to do something that could provide the capital for me to take Musepaper to the next level.

But I didn't have to resign now. The letter asked me to call security to set up a time to retrieve my belongings.

No thanks. I didn't want to bring home anything from that place.

Leaning back into the pillow, I stared up at the ceiling. I was going to chat with Orion, but now I just wanted to be left alone. My health insurance would end soon. I needed this contract job with Orion. If an unexpected bill came up, I could ask him for another advance. He would be okay with that, right?

I should start looking for a new job soon, but I didn't have the energy or the motivation to.

Expecting me to be a saint when I was being wronged and vilified was just too much.

Be strong. Conserve your energy and fight back.

Don't surrender.

My inner voice was trying really hard to motivate me. I just had to let the self-doubt phase run its course. Bills flashed through my mind followed by horrific images of rain flooding my house, which made me tremble.

I wished Orion were with me, having dandelion tea and talking about random things. He made me feel safe. Like he was the eye of the storm—the force that kept me protected from the chaos of the world.

What was he doing? I stared at my phone. Should I text him? He was in Europe, so he was probably sleeping.

Thoughts swirled in my head, and I stepped away from them. Unlike someone who was terminally ill or trapped in a war zone, my financial dilemma was something that could be resolved over time. Little by little, I could chip away at it. That was all I could do. Sitting around moping wasn't going to erase my debt. I needed to recalculate my budget again.

Feeling restless, I got out of bed, dragged an ottoman over to the window, and sat down, shoving the curtains aside. The dark night greeted me as I looked out at the clear sky. A sense of peace blanketed me like a soft throw. Insecurity was raw tonight, and I did what I'd always done in the past: look elsewhere for motivation. I escaped to a different world that made me feel better, even if it was temporary.

Wasn't that why I'd chosen to be a writer? To be elsewhere. To deliver news and truth.

"Must be nice to gaze at everyone, huh?" I asked the seven stars blinking in the night sky as though they could hear me. I was certain there were more stars hidden from my view.

If I lived outside the city, I could see more stars. The night sky was magical. It always made me wonder what lay beyond the visible.

"Since you see everything from up there, what should I do?" I asked the stars. "What's waiting for me around the corner?"

I imagined the stars beaming at each other, probably giggling at my ridiculous imagination.

An image popped into my head, making me smirk. "Am I in Orion's orbit? Or way out of his league?"

I was probably some unknown space object that didn't belong anywhere. How sad was that?

I didn't know why, but more silly thoughts appeared in my head. "Are you friends with the moon? If so, why is it so moody?"

Everyone knew a woman's mood was often associated with the moon.

"You don't know? Seriously?" I asked, shifting on my ottoman. "Well, let me tell you. The moon is always moody because it's going through phases!" I beamed at it and knew I was going crazy for having a conversation with the sky.

But the sarcasm and silliness distracted me enough from the horrible news I'd received. I missed those days where I used to blog about silly things.

I knew someone out there was experiencing something worse than me. War and famine were constant issues somewhere in the world. The long list of missing children grew every day. Homelessness was a major issue in most cities. Some single mother or father was trying their best to take care of their children while working multiple jobs. I saw and reported on these stories daily. At least I had a roof over my head, money for necessities, and family and close friends who loved and supported me.

You're okay, Elena.

Feeling better, I slid back into bed and released a long sigh. Tomorrow was another day. The moon was transitioning into another phase, and I had a job to do that required my rest. I had a couple of places to investigate and needed to look into Sam's comment about my father. If he thought I'd let it slide, he was wrong.

And whoever had framed me would soon find out they'd underestimated me. Staying down wasn't my nature.

CHAPTER TWENTY-SEVEN

ORION

INSIDE THE CONFERENCE room of the Reimann Sienna Bank in Stockholm, Sweden, I stood beside my father, looking out at the lush courtyard.

"Did you know your mother designed that courtyard?" Rex Reimann gestured to the intricate shape of the landscape. He had aged significantly since the last time I saw him at his brother's funeral. He had more creases on his forehead and lines around his eyes.

I looked down at the courtyard. From above, the mandala was more noticeable. Those wandering on the ground would miss the pattern, but they could enjoy the flowers and plants.

The silence hung between us. It wasn't awkward because I was used to it, but I just didn't know what to say. Too much distance had grown between my father and me. Our relationship wasn't salvageable.

Guilt twisted in my gut, remembering how many times my mom had asked me to give my father a chance.

He loves you very much.

She was trying her best to keep the family together.

I studied my father, whose dark brown hair and cold gray eyes reflected mine. When I was younger, I'd wished for my mother's blonde hair, inviting blue eyes, and her ability to dissolve anxiety the way sugar melted into warm tea. There had been moments when I'd yearned for my father's attention, but he'd turned me away for meetings. I could never forget what it felt like to be dismissed like that.

How had my mom dealt with his coldness?

Rex Reimann was a powerful man in the business arena. I wondered if he ever spoke about me to his colleagues. He kept his family private, and when my mom passed, it became even more private.

"I didn't know that." I broke the silence. "Mom was very talented."

"She was indeed." Sadness tinged his voice.

I should forgive him for all the suffering I'd endured, shouldn't I? I'd been a child working like an adult. My anxiety had become my weakness. A weakness that had pushed me to become a thief. Thievery was the only remedy that had helped me.

I never dreamed I'd become a thief, but life often took us down interesting paths that redefined many things for us.

A thief was someone who stole. But to me, a thief stole to patch up parts of his broken self. We were all thieves in some aspects. If someone took away your happiness or sanity without your consent, was he a thief too? How about all the corrupt politicians who stole from the common people by approving laws that only benefited them? Wasn't that thievery as well?

"Helen was a very intelligent woman who saw things most didn't," my father said, still staring at the courtyard.

"She was," I agreed.

My father turned, studying me. "I see her in you. I miss her."

After my mother died, I hired someone to monitor my father. I was curious if he'd taken on a mistress like my uncle. My uncle had several mistresses, but his wife had her own men on the side too.

But my father didn't disrespect my mother. He loved her and only her. For that reason I remained cordial . . . and hopeful that one day he and I could reconcile.

Life was hard and lonely after she died. The Condor and Ralph became my family, my father figures. Resentment stirred in my gut, and I just wanted to attend the banquet to celebrate Reimann Corporation having acquired another bank and head back to Providence.

The urge to be with Elena had grown during the past week. I needed to see her, touch her, and tell her I was ready to date.

"What did you want to talk to me about?" I turned to him. He'd left me a voicemail asking to talk, which surprised me.

"Jasper has been asking to buy Quintile Island."

"And you told him persistence pays off."

He chuckled. "He has selective hearing. I told him there are other islands for sale."

"I'm not selling it."

"Good." A smirk slid onto my father's lips, followed by a relaxed expression I had never seen on him.

For a moment I thought I saw pride gleam in his eyes. Or had that been my imagination? My dad had never shown any sign he was proud of me. Not when I aced all my exams, won top prizes at all the tournaments, or graduated top of my class.

"That's what I have left of Mom. Nothing is going to make me sell it. Not even a dead body."

My dad's face hardened. "Who died?"

"A lawyer named Aaron Turner from New York. Do you know him?"

"Doesn't ring a bell. Do you need me to ask around?"

My eyebrows furrowed at the offer. "I've got it. But thank you."

He nodded slowly. "Don't let anyone on there that you don't know."

"Why?" What did he know that I didn't?

"Because that's your mother's sacred place—our sacred place. It was where she told me she loved me. She left something for you on the island, but I don't know what or where it is. She was going to tell me the day she died."

What did she leave for me? Was it in the house I was living in?

"She enjoys patterns like the mandala in the courtyard. Maybe she designed something like that for you. Let me know when you find it."

"How do you know I'll find it?"

His eyes sparked, and for a moment, I thought he knew I was a thief. But then he said, "Your mom used to say that things reveal themselves when they're meant to."

A knock sounded on the door, and my dad straightened his posture. "Who is it?"

"Jonah."

"Come in." Dad's face transformed into the stony expression I remembered so well.

Jonah entered wearing his custom Italian suit, his dark hair slicked back, looking tired. I could only imagine the stress he was dealing with. Losing both parents and now having a pivotal role in the Reimann Sienna Bank.

Smiling, he walked up to me, offering a brotherly embrace. "Orion. I didn't know you'd be here at the banquet."

"It was a last-minute decision. How are you?"

"Same old. Working hard and trying to not let Jasper ruin things. I know he's been asking you about your island. Ignore him."

"You should give him a job to keep him busy," I said.

"Don't have time." Jonah turned to my father. "Uncle Rex, we need your input on a potential acquisition."

Nodding, Dad turned to me. "We'll catch up later."

Something shifted between my father and me today. It actually seemed like he cared and was proud of me.

After the banquet, I needed air and distance from all the business executives and conversations about investments. What was Elena doing? She hadn't texted me in a few days. I'd been busy and hadn't texted her either. I wandered to the courtyard, sat down on a bench, and studied the trees and flowers. Did my mom choose the shrubbery? A monarch butterfly flew by and landed on a red rose.

"Fancy meeting you here." Chantel sashayed over with her black dress. I'd seen her earlier with the media crowd, interviewing my father and other members of his board.

I didn't know why Providence Channel 7 News would cover a bank acquisition in Europe. Maybe she knew some executives who had invited her.

"Good evening, Chantel." I offered a casual nod.

She sat down on the bench beside me, and I rose to my feet, creating distance. I wasn't in the mood for company.

The only person I wanted to see right now was back in Providence.

She got up, stepped closer to me, and placed a gentle hand on my arm. "It seems like the Reimann Corporation is expanding to Asia and Africa as well. What does it feel like to be part of such a successful conglomerate?"

"I don't do interviews without it being scheduled ahead of time." I smiled. "You can call my office to arrange a meeting."

"You look tense. Do you need help to unwind?" She flicked me a seductive look. "I haven't stopped thinking about you."

"Not interested, Chantel." I gestured to the banquet hall. "But there are plenty of men in there who would take that offer."

She grinned and leaned in my ear. "This could be our secret. What happens in Stockholm stays in Stockholm. I want to taste your cock."

"Like I said, I'm not interested." I made my way out of the courtyard.

"It's her, isn't it?" Chantel's tone changed as she caught up with me. "What do you see in her? Do you know that she recently got fired?"

I paused. "What happened?"

A sly smile stretched. "She didn't tell you? If I were her, I'd share everything with you, babe."

She gripped my arm, and I extracted it. "Please keep your hands to yourself. Why was Elena fired?"

Looking annoyed, Chantel kept her hands at her sides. "She's dealing drugs. They found them in her desk and in her gym locker at work. Stupid. I always knew something was off with her. Always creating more work for herself.

Anyway, Channel Seven has canceled her show. They're starting my show in a couple of weeks." Her eyes beamed. "I'd like for you to be my first guest."

How was Elena taking the news? Why hadn't she said anything to me?

Why should she, you moron? You're not her boyfriend.

"No thanks."

"My interview could boost your family's business."

"My family's business doesn't need a boost." I walked out to the courtyard, wanting to get back to my hotel so I could text Elena.

CHAPTER TWENTY-EIGHT

ELENA

AFTER GETTING DRESSED, I slid into the Land Rover and drove to work. I'd gotten used to this car now and didn't want to think about having to return it when this project was over. I'd look for another car soon, but not right now.

I didn't realize just how bad Channel 7 had gotten. How could anyone work in a place full of snakes? I couldn't trust anyone except for two staff assistants who were looking for new jobs as well.

Jill and Brett had texted me this morning, asking how I was doing. I told them the truth. I was angrier that I couldn't defend myself than not having a job. It was ironic that something so twisted occurred at a news station that should have delivered truthful news. From what they told me, a new company had bought over NewsCom Group, which owned Channel 7 News. The reorganization was already happening with more layoffs on the way.

Everyone was nervous except Chantel Henderson because the Henderson Family had shares in NewsCom. Her family probably secured a safe position for her.

I was too tired to entertain the anger that bubbled every time her name came up. She was probably the one who framed me. Who else had a reason? I needed time for things to settle before I could find proof.

Today was reserved for work, the only job I had now. The next debt payment to my uncle was due by next week, so I'd need to drop it off in a few days. My mom would return from her Bermuda trip soon, and I had to look for a massage chair for her as well.

I dreamed of a bird last night, and I took that as a sign that The Condor's murder needed my full attention. When I stepped off the elevator, I didn't see Ralph. The lights automatically flicked on for me as I walked down the hallway toward Orion's office. It was strange to be the only person on this massive floor. What did he have on the other side of the office? Was it storage for all the businesses below?

I entered his office, and his masculine scent embraced me. I could've gone back to my office after reviewing the board he displayed in the corner, but I wanted to be in his office. His things reminded me of him. The office definitely needed a woman's touch. It needed more color, something to soften the masculine table, chairs, bookcases and such. All the books and files on his bookshelves were too neat. I wanted to move them a little. His desk needed a plant. Actually, a few plants in the office would bring the room to life.

I could swing by Wild Roots to pick up a few things.

Turning my attention to the board, I stared at the images of The Condor, places he'd visited, and people he knew around the New England area. I narrowed my focus to the businesses in Providence.

I was familiar with two of the locations on the list. It was a small coffee shop that I hadn't visited since high school.

They sold delicious Colombian and Peruvian pastries. The other place was a laundromat my mom and I had used when our washer and dryer broke.

I walked back and forth in front of the board, imagining Orion doing the same as he pondered the details. The Condor was a thief, making me wonder about Orion's involvement in that world. He had the skills but had refused to give me details when I'd inquired.

Was Orion a professional thief? What should I do if he was?

Focus on The Condor's death, Elena.

The more I read the files and studied The Condor, or rather, Pablo, the more he fascinated me. What prompted him to become a thief? Based on his financial report, he didn't need to. He had half a billion dollars in his several bank accounts.

Perhaps he had this money when he first started out. Still, I wanted to know what made someone choose thievery. Did he steal people's money? Were they his enemies?

Orion's words appeared in my mind. *He was my teacher.*

I had thought he meant a teacher in the business arena. But now I wondered if Orion was his protégé. But why? How?

Orion was the wealthiest man I knew. He didn't need to steal. He didn't even need to work. There was so much I didn't know about him. If Orion wanted my help, he had to be honest with me. I had to know the entire story. Most of all, I wanted to understand him.

I'd ask when he returned. I smiled as I remembered waking up to his text.

Orion: *Are you working hard, Sunshine? I miss my dandelion tea.*

I had to get used to this sunshine thing. No man had called me that, and I'd never considered myself to be the light for anyone.

Elena: *Sunshine is always working hard to brighten your day.*

That had been cheesy, but I didn't care. He'd heard about Channel 7 letting me go and asked how I was doing. Apparently, Chantel told him I'd been fired. Why was she there with him? That bothered me even more than me losing my job. I didn't want to continue the conversation and told him we could talk when he returned.

To make myself feel better, I concentrated on The Condor's case. I grabbed my purse and headed to the laundromat. The answering machine from the café informed me of the shop's hours. I'd swing by there if I had time today.

Tumble Dry had grown in size since I last visited with my mom. I entered, walked up to the counter, and smiled at a man I recognized. But he wore glasses and had a white beard now.

"Hi, Mr. Wong! Do you remember me?"

He stared at me for a while, then grinned. "Elena!" He rounded the counter and offered me a hug.

Though I'd only visited his laundromat a few times, Mom and him became good friends, exchanging traditional food recipes. He used to let me watch TV in his office while I waited for my laundry.

"How are you doing? I miss watching you on Channel 7."

"I'm doing other things now. How's everything? You well? How are your kids?" I asked.

I'd never met his wife. She'd died from an illness when she first came to America.

"Thomas lives in California with his family, and Stacey lives in Boston. She visits often."

"I'm so happy to hear that." I held up a picture of Pablo. "Do you know him? He lived in an apartment not too far from here. He was murdered."

Willam Wong took the photo and his eyes warmed. "Of course, I know Pablo. All the regulars who come into this laundromat know him. Kind man. Very generous. It's sad what happened to him." He gave the photo back to me. "Are you working for a PI?"

"A close friend of Pablo asked for my help."

"Come." He waved me to the back of his office, which also had a TV screen showing various angles of the laundromat. Two people sat in the corner glued to their tablets.

I sat down at a couch with a coffee table.

"Want some jasmine tea?" he asked.

"No, thank you."

He sat across from me, sipped his tea, and placed the cup down. "Pablo used to come here whenever he was in town. He had his own washer and dryer, but he liked coming here to talk to people. People loved him. He's helped a lot in the community."

"How did he help them?" I took out my little notebook, preparing to take down notes.

"Paying their rent, their utility bills, buying them food, and making sure their little ones had money for school supplies." He sighed, looking sad. "I remember how the Browns, the Smiths, and the Nguyens were so grateful for his assistance. Winter months in New England are difficult, and paying for heat is always a challenge. Oil and gas prices are horrendous."

"Pablo sounds like he was a good man."

"He was." Mr. Wong placed a hand to his heart. "When we found out he was murdered, the community did a small memorial in the community garden for him. They planted an apple tree in his honor."

My heart warmed. These were the kind of stories that belonged in Musepaper. Stories that inspired people; stories that showed the positive side of humanity.

By the time I left Tumble Dry, I felt like I'd gotten to know Pablo. He would be someone I admired, respected, and wanted to be friends with. Mr. Wong even called up a few customers so they could give me details about Pablo. I appreciated that everyone wanted to find his killer. The info I'd gathered today didn't give me any clues to why someone wanted him dead. No one saw anything suspicious in the days prior to his death.

As I headed to my car, I planned on adding a folder to the shared drive for Orion's review. He probably didn't know the effect Pablo had on the community. I drove to the community garden and studied the apple tree that stood tall and proud. Perhaps next year, it would bear fruits for the people to enjoy. Even in death, he would continue to give to those who mattered to him.

I didn't know why, but I started to cry. I didn't know this man, but his deeds had touched me. I took a photo of the tree and the boulder with his name engraved on it. No one was in the garden, so I took my time studying the herbs and flowers.

I slid into my car, getting ready to head to Mona's Café when my phone rang.

I answered with a grin. "Hi, Elliot. About time you called. How's Milan?"

"Incredible, darling. Everything is finalized. The previous owner will stay for the next month to help me transition. All the stylists here are talented! The salon is so chic, and my list of clients has doubled in the last week alone. The move is official. You must come visit."

I could hear the joy in his voice. Elliot had talked about opening a salon in Europe, and this opportunity appeared at the right moment.

"Oh, I will. Is Jake excited too?" I asked.

"He's very excited. He'll be helping with the business side of things for the salon. Anything new with your sling-shot?" he purred.

"It's going okay."

"Why do you sound sad?"

"I'm not sad. Just stressed."

"When are you not stressed? But you can deal with it better than most people."

"I do?"

"Yes, you do. You feel the pressure, you see the problem, you find a solution, and you move toward it. Most people get stuck in one place."

I thought about his comment. "I analyze, but I don't spend days lingering on the issues. Mostly because they don't solve themselves."

"I've learned a lot from you."

"Are you keeping Salon Oasis or selling it?" I asked.

"Not sure yet. What's gotten you stressed?"

"Channel Seven News fired me." I briefed him on it.

"It had to be Chantel," he huffed. "If she ever comes into my salon, I'm turning her hair pink. Use this time to find a new job. At least you're working for Slingshot. Are you dating him yet?"

"No." But I imagined what it would be like to be his girlfriend.

"You're his fake girlfriend, remember? This could be a fun thing to continue."

I had forgotten. "It was a temporary thing during a crisis moment, Elliot. That event is over and there's no need to pretend anymore."

"Did he say that?" Elliot inquired.

I could imagine the wheels turning in his head. He was always coming up with creative plans to find me the perfect man.

"No." I remembered Orion's comment. "Actually, he said to keep pretending so men won't bother me."

"See?" Excitement filled his voice. "He wants you. I think this fake dating thing could be exciting. Have fun! Explore! You've got no limits. Show Slingshot how to step outside of his comfort zone. He's got those immaculate looks, so your job is to get him dirty."

I laughed. "Maybe."

Would Orion agree to get dirty for me? I tried to imagine him covered in dirt and couldn't. Plus he was still wearing the ring on his necklace . . .

"Gotta go now, darling. We're heading to a party. Talk soon. *Ciao!*"

I tucked my phone into my purse and drove to Mona's Café. I found parking along the street, got out, and glanced around. The café was in the corner of a residential area with a community park that was well cared for. It had changed so much since high school. More shops had crowded the retail strip.

I entered the small café and inhaled the lovely aroma. A bench had been added for extra seating by the window. Two customers were at the counter paying for something. I walked up and glanced at the pastry assortment, and my mouth watered. There was no way I'd leave this place without buying something.

They had everything my grandmother used to make. I used to love *picarones,* which were sweet, dripping donuts.

When the two customers left, I smiled at the sales associate. The woman wearing a pink apron had curly hair and a friendly face. "How can I help you?"

I pointed to the display case. "I'd like two *picarones,* two *alfajores,* and one *pionono,* please."

"Where are you from?" she asked. "You grew up in America?"

"I was born here. My grandmother was from Peru. She used to make these. But she's not with us anymore."

"Life is too short. Enjoy it while you can."

"I agree. I had a friend who used to come in here often. Do you know him? Pablo."

She studied me for a moment as sadness washed over her face. "Yes. He was a regular at the shop. Traveled a lot though. It's sad what happened to him. We'll miss him."

I nodded. "The police haven't caught the murderer yet. They're taking a long time."

"They always do." She rubbed her thumb and finger together. "If you want results, you need to know someone. Or have money or pay for a private investigator."

"I run an independent online newspaper. I'm not getting paid by anyone. No company owns me. I just want to find out who killed him. If you're comfortable, I'd love to hear your thoughts. I can keep you anonymous."

She considered me for a moment. "What's your name?"

"Elena Sanchez. What's yours?"

Recognition splashed across her face. "I remember you.

Uncover the Truth! What happened to that show? My name is Mona."

I sighed. "I don't work there anymore. The company is taking a new direction."

With a pout, Mona rubbed her thumb and fingers together again. "Money talks."

"Unfortunately, yes."

Then Mona looked past me, and her expression changed to surprise and something else. She glanced around the shop. When she didn't see anyone, she turned toward the back. "Pedro, can you man the counter? I need to help a customer with something."

A man with a beard wearing a pink apron emerged from the back room. He looked at me and nodded.

"Elena is trying to find Pablo's killer."

Pedro gave me a thumbs up. "A good man. Helped us out many times."

Mona sat down on the bench, and I sat beside her. "Pablo helped us open this shop. He lent us the money, but when we paid him back, he wouldn't take it. Instead, he told us to donate it to a local charity that assisted immigrants. That's what we did."

Why couldn't my uncle be like Pablo? Here was a stranger helping others and not asking for anything back. But I had an uncle who not only wanted the money, he also slapped on huge fines just because he could.

"That's very nice of him," I said, making sure I was careful not to reveal too much. Though Mona seemed like a nice person, I had to be cautious. Deception and fraud reigned supreme these days.

"I have to tell you something," she said. "It's strange, and don't be afraid, okay? But I have to tell you before he disappears."

The hair on the back of my neck rose. How could I not be scared after hearing something like that?

Mona held my hand. "I see Pablo's spirit. He appeared when you were at the counter. Then he disappeared when Pedro emerged. But he's here again."

My heart raced. "What?" My eyes widened, gazing around and not seeing anything.

I'd heard about mediums connecting to people who have passed, even pets. But I'd never experienced it. It spooked me.

"I have the sixth sense, a gift passed down by Mother," Mona said. "I'd never seen Pablo around until now. He knows you're investigating his case."

"What's he saying? You can hear him?"

"Not really. It's an innate knowing. I know him, so I sensed his familiar energy. He's showing me flashes of images." She reached for my hand and closed her eyes. A second later, she opened them. "I see a box. It's like a treasure box. There are a lot of papers in it."

Then customers entered the shop, disrupting the quiet.

She sighed, releasing my hand. "I lost the connection."

"If he contacts you again, please let me know. If you remember anything, call me."

Mona nodded and went to assist her customers.

I didn't know what to think about the experience, but I noted what she said in my notebook.

CHAPTER TWENTY-NINE

ELENA

I'D JUST FINISHED my shift at Let's Ketchup and walked to my car when I spotted Orion leaning against a truck I didn't recognize. I'd been fuming most of the day about him attending a banquet with Chantel. She'd posted pictures on her social media. Didn't he know she was my nemesis? Did he know she tried to ruin my reputation?

He walked up to me. "You've been ignoring me."

"I'm not," I lied. "Just busy working."

"Can we talk?" He eyed me.

"Go ahead." I crossed my arms, irritation mounting inside me. "I'm listening."

"Not here."

I inhaled a breath. "Fine. Then you can follow me home."

When I arrived home, I stalked into the house, and he was right behind me.

"Make yourself at home," I said. "I need a shower."

"Take your time. You seem to need it."

I scoffed. "What does that mean?"

He shrugged, looking innocent. "That you need a shower to cool off. Water is healing. You've been running around delivering food and running tables. I'm sure you want to wash the day's stress off, right?"

Jealousy of Chantel and of his ex swarmed my thoughts, and frustration clouded my judgment.

A small smile crept onto his lips. "Are you okay? You're not acting like yourself."

I locked the door to my bedroom because somehow that act created the space I needed from Orion. Leaning against the door, I closed my eyes, taking in a deep breath. When I exhaled, I imagined the frustration leaving my body. Then I opened my eyes and pushed myself off the door, thinking about the compelling man overwhelming me.

He was a thief. A thrill skipped along my body. Why did I find that attractive? What was wrong with me?

I was a reporter who tried her best to stay on the right side of the law. But my body betrayed me when he was around.

Stripping off my clothes, I walked into the bathroom, turned on the shower, and hopped in. I lifted my face to the cool water, letting it beat against my face. The frustration subsided.

I needed answers tonight. It was the only way for me to further my investigation. Someone had killed The Condor, and that meant someone could be after Orion too. He had to know this. What was he doing about it?

Was he prepared? I didn't know why this overwhelming need to make sure he was safe seized me. He'd made me feel safe, and I wanted the same for him.

But jealousy was making everything worse. As I toweled

off and lathered lotion onto my skin, mischief sneaked into my thoughts.

Lingerie.

Seduce him.

Have fun.

This was probably from the conversation with Elliot and the girls about having fun. Mona's words about life being too short increased my desire to take what I wanted.

I'd gotten more cautious with every heartbreak. What if I never got to experience the very thing I'd been dreaming about? What if the world ended tomorrow? Where would that leave me?

Was a dream effective if it was tucked away safely? I was trying my best to make excuses.

I had to know if he wanted me. This was the first step in my mission of The Thief Who Loved Me. We weren't anywhere close to love, but it gave me hope. It sounded better than The Thief Who Liked Me.

The girls had sent me a fabulous self-care package that sat in my closet. The lingerie was still in the lovely box. I hadn't had time to think of an occasion to wear it until tonight. I walked into my closet and pulled out the large bag, bringing it out to my bed.

My hand trembled as it slid out of the box. What was wrong with me? I'd never been this nervous with a man. I didn't want to compare myself to the previous women he'd been with. They probably wore luxurious clothing for him all the time.

Most of all, I didn't want to compare myself to his ex. What was she like?

I noticed he wasn't wearing the necklace. Did he take it

off to be cleaned? There was no way I could seduce him if he were still wearing that.

Stop the negative thoughts right now. Stop being too cautious. A courageous heart can conquer anything.

Courage dared me. "I'm going to have fun."

With excitement, I lifted the lid to the box, and several lingerie sets were neatly folded in the box. I pulled out a black lacy thong with a matching bra. Nerves spiked in me at how tiny it was. Would my breasts fit into this bra?

Only one way to find out.

I slid on the bra and the thong, glanced at myself, and blinked. I'd never worn anything so revealing. The small patch covering my sex was sheer, with a single flower embroidered on it. The lacy edge along the upper cup just barely covered my nipples. If I bent over, he'd see *everything*. I'd never been this risqué. This was *way* out of my comfort zone.

Elliot had told me to lure Orion out of his element. But *I* was the one standing in an uncomfortable terrain right now.

Despite that, a thrill coursed through me. I looked at myself, twisting my body from side to side, admiring my curves. The lingerie hugged my body beautifully, accentuating my ass and breasts, making me feel feminine, sensual, and desirable.

I had the power to *command* him. But of course, this entire scenario was just in my head. I smiled as my imagination spiraled out of control. Just pretending that this intimate evening could happen brought a smile to my face.

I sprayed some perfume on because I felt like it. I wasn't doing this for him. It was all for *me*. It was an exhausting day. No, it had been an exhausting couple of years. Tonight was just a reward for me for surviving and chugging forward.

Tonight, I want to feel . . . wanted.

I pulled on a pair of cotton shorts and threw on a T-shirt that read: *I'm hot and I'm cold. Some call me bold when I make them jitter. What am I?*

There had been a time when I had my riddles printed on T-shirts. I couldn't afford that now. There was another time when I enjoyed blogging just for fun. But now I was too busy trying to make money.

I blow-dried my hair and walked out to the kitchen. I didn't see him and assumed he'd left because I'd taken a while prepping myself. But then I heard a creaking sound from the back deck. I walked toward the deck as he was coming in.

"Hey . . ." He studied me. "Feeling better?"

"Yeah. Sorry I took longer than expected. What were you doing outside?"

"I kept busy." He glanced at my shirt and arched an eyebrow. "Is it a fever or the flu?"

I smirked. "Nope. It's coffee."

He stepped closer, and my heart raced. The smoldering look in his eyes told me he was reading something provocative. "It could also be *you.* Hot and cold. You can be bold, and you certainly make my heart jitter."

"You're good at manipulating words." I looked toward the back deck. "What were you doing outside?"

What was wrong with my voice?

"I found a dandelion puff and made a wish." His fingers brushed across my cheek and traveled down to my chin, tipping it up.

The admission surprised and delighted me. I didn't know any man who would admit to making a wish like that. Most would probably think it was cheesy. But this man standing in front of me didn't care what others thought of him. He was a man in a world of his own, and I wanted an invitation to explore it.

"Do you want to know what I wished for?" He pressed his thumb on my bottom lip.

I swallowed as the scenario that had played out in my head flashed through my mind.

Unable to speak, I nodded.

"I want to kiss you . . . and *have* you tonight."

My eyes immediately darted to his necklace. Still gone.

He noticed where I was looking and said, "I'm ready to move forward with you."

He couldn't have said anything better than that tonight.

"I'm a high-maintenance woman with several demands." My arms looped around him.

"And I'm an even higher-maintenance man who can meet those demands." His hands wrapped around my waist, then lowered to cup my ass. "Are you going to be the bold coffee that'll keep me up all night?"

I laughed. "Maybe."

His lips hovered over mine. Hot breath. A nip of my bottom lip. Then a moan escaped me.

He gripped the hem of my T-shirt. "I want to see all of you."

This was really happening. I lifted my arms. "Be my guest."

Lust sparked in his eyes as he lifted the T-shirt, whipping it aside. His eyes wandered all over me, making my body tingle.

"Are you trying to kill me with this bra?" His voice grew husky, and I loved it.

"I wouldn't do that to a decent man." Could he hear my heart pounding?

"There's nothing decent about what I want to do to you." He nudged the cup of my bra down, revealing my pebbled nipple. He groaned and rubbed it back and forth with his thumb, giving it too much attention. Then he captured one with his mouth and suckled.

I moaned as heat shot straight to my core. He reached to my back, removing my bra and whipping it aside. My breasts were now exposed to his mouth. My hands gripped his hair, loving the wet tongue all over me.

"Shorts off too," he crooned.

I dropped my shorts, standing in front of him with just a teeny tiny thong barely covering anything. This captivating man explored my body with his eyes, making me shiver. Then his hands and mouth adored my breasts. I saw the erotic image of us reflected in the glass pantry cabinet. Muscles tightened in my core.

An idea sparked. "Let's play a game, shall we?"

CHAPTER THIRTY

MY HANDS SLID to his fine ass and squeezed. "I've been wondering about this. So firm and perfect."

"You've been checking out my ass?" He released my breast, looking at me with darkened eyes.

"I have." I went on my tippy toes. "You're so handsome, you know that?"

"I do now."

"Haven't other women told you that?"

"They have." He smirked, and butterflies emerged in my stomach. He was arrogance and magnetism personified.

Who could stand next to him and not feel the pull?

"But only your opinion matters to me." He tugged on my thong. "What kind of game are we playing?"

I surprised myself too. Orion liked a disciplined schedule. I wanted to have fun with him tonight, make him detour.

We were so different, like two roads—one winding and one straight—heading to separate destinations. Somehow our roads intersected, and this was the moment of contact. Where would we go from now? I didn't know, and I didn't care. Right now, being here with him, was the only thing that mattered to me.

"Do you dare, Slingshot?" I asked with hands on my hips, not caring that my chest was bare to him. Not caring that I had a tiny patch covering my most private part. The sight must be ridiculous, but I loved how he was looking at me.

He wanted me desperately. If eyes could talk, his told me things that made my panties wet.

"Rules," he said, his tone guttural and desperate.

I loved that I could affect him like this.

"The more answers you get right, the more you can ask to remove something." I palmed his cock, and he sucked in a breath. "And the more you can touch."

"Vixen. I like this version of you." He swallowed, and I watched the way his Adam's apple shifted on his neck. It was sexy as hell. "You're not just any sunshine, you're sexy and sassy sunshine. The kind that can burn me to cinders."

"Then you should be afraid of me."

"I am." A seriousness swam across his face.

Was he afraid of me? Why?

The concern must have been obvious on my face because he said, "I lose control when you're around. I'm not my usual self."

My body relaxed. "It's okay to let go, Slingshot. That's how you hit your target."

"I love your puns and riddles." He reached for my breast, but I stopped him.

"You sampled me earlier. But starting now, no touching unless you answer a riddle."

He looked adorably frustrated. "What kind of game is this?"

"Don't pout. I'm struggling too because I want to touch you as well."

"Then why don't you just touch me and forget the damn game?" he panted.

"Don't you want to get to know me? This game will allow that."

"You've played this game with other men?" he asked.

"Nope. You inspired it. I'll tell you the reason later." I pointed to the chair. "You need to sit on the chair while I'll sit on the kitchen table."

He pulled out a chair as I hopped onto the table.

"Since I have my shirt off, you need to take yours off. But keep the jeans on."

"But you have your shorts off."

"That was a mistake," I replied.

Pursing his lips, he took off his shirt. "I'll be sampling every inch of you, Sunshine. You're not getting out of this."

He had no idea how much I wanted his mouth on me. I'd dreamed about it.

But I was doing this for him. I bit my bottom lip as I absorbed the gorgeous specimen of a man in front of me. Those firm abs. The broad shoulders were perfect for tailored suits. No wonder he looked delicious in them. Those biceps I wanted to bite and squeeze. My stomach churned with desire. Orion had sex appeal like no man I knew.

I could practically smell sex in the air. Everything about him was *more*. More intense. More stunning. More complex.

I wanted to dive into the mystery of him—into his mind, his soul.

"I might break a rule if you don't hurry with the riddle," he said, his eyes trained on me.

"I thought you were a patient man."

"Not today." His gaze met mine, and I could see the restraint in them. He looked like a beast ready to pounce on me.

"All right. Here's the first riddle." I opened my thighs a little, just for a tease. Then I shimmied my shoulders, shifting my breasts seductively. His eyes followed their every movement.

"Fuck, Elena. You're definitely trying to kill me," he muttered. "If I have a heart attack, it's your fault."

"Don't know what you're talking about." I lifted a shoulder, enjoying the hungry expression on his face. "Why does the sun enjoy working at the bakery?"

"What? You're so random." Amusement flickered in his eyes. "And strange."

"Thanks for the compliment. Now, answer the question." I held up a finger. "You have one minute to think about it."

Orion stared at my lacy thong as though it could tell him the answer.

"You won't find the answer there." I leveled my head.

"You're wrong. Just looking at it has given me some ideas." His lips quirked. "The sun likes working at the bakery because it likes to rise."

My jaw dropped. "How do you know that?"

"Because your pussy told me." Orion leaned in. "I answered correctly, so now I get to remove one thing, right?"

There wasn't much to remove on me, but that wasn't the point of this game.

He must have read the riddle somewhere. I had a collection of weird riddles from when I had my blog.

"One thing." I straightened my posture, still trying to figure out how he knew the answer.

"I want your thong off." With finesse, he slid off my panties and pressed them to his nose, inhaling. "You smell so good."

The image of him with that intimate gesture was etched into my mind. I'd never watched a man do that before. It was hot as hell.

"My turn now." He scrunched up my underwear in his hand and leaned back in the chair, looking like a decorated general who had won a battle. "Why did the book go to the police?" He met my gaze, but then his eyes slid to my sex.

I crossed my legs and folded my arms over my chest, wondering if he had a weird collection of riddles too.

"Why did you do that?" he asked.

"Do what?"

"Cross your legs. The whole reason for me taking off your thong was for me to admire it, along with your gorgeous breasts. You're like the perfect piece of art for me to study. You know I collect art and other fine things, right?"

"I want to see them one day," I said, then glanced over at the sliding door with the bug net. "Well, there's a breeze, and I could catch a cold, so I need to cross my legs." The summer humidity had lessened compared to the last few days.

He didn't call me out on the ridiculous excuse.

I didn't have to think long to reply to his riddle. "The book went to the police station because it had to report evidence of an indescribable plot twist."

Something flashed in his eyes. It wasn't surprise, but something else. A recognition? An epiphany of some sort? Had my silly answer helped him figure something out?

"Did I answer it correctly?" I pursed my lips.

"You did." He tucked my thong into his pants pocket.

"I want your pants off," I said.

Without hesitation, he rose from the chair.

"No. Let me do it." I hopped off the kitchen table—which had never been kissed by my ass until today—and gripped his dark jeans. I removed his belt, dropped it to the floor, and tugged down his pants. A massive bulge tented under his boxers.

Orion was so gorgeous, so masculine. He stood like an inexplicable monument in my kitchen. He possessed the face of a sex god while radiating irresistible power. Though he called me Sunshine, he was the one who emanated power like the sun. I couldn't look away.

I wanted to touch him, but I couldn't until I answered another riddle. It was my rule, and no matter how I wanted to break it, I had to see this through.

How long would it take for him to lose control? How long would it take me?

As though he understood my need, he smiled and sat down. Unlike me, he opened his thighs so I could see his massive bulge in its glory.

"What's next, Sunshine?"

"What?" My gaze was fixated on his cock, and I heard nothing. I was in a world of my own, playing this unique story in my head where I could converse with his cock. I imagined it breaking free of his boxers to come out to say hello to me. Something was really wrong with me.

His smile expanded. "The next riddle?"

My gaze met his. "You'll find this interesting because you're into the stars and stuff." I cleared my throat. "Imagine you're an insignificant asteroid floating aimlessly in space. Then you see a cluster of stars close to Earth. What would you do?"

Orion's expression immediately transformed from casual

entertainment to shock, and then something I couldn't pinpoint. He leaned forward, staring at me. Did he like my question? Was he that into it?

He stood up from his seat and stepped toward me. The power that radiated from him made me suck in a breath. His chest rose and fell as though he were trying his best to control his emotions.

What was happening? Had my question triggered something? Or had he finally lost control?

A few inches separated us. "What's your answer?"

"May I please join your cluster?" He breathed, lips parted, as his gaze bored into me. "The asteroid's name is Sassteroid. Now I get to do what I want."

No way.

My heart skipped and twirled at this realization that Orion had been one of my blog readers. He'd stood out from the others because of his odd question. And because he was the last inquiry I'd responded to.

Orion ushered my thighs apart. He positioned himself between my thighs and placed his hands on either side of my hips, pulling me closer to the edge. I wrapped my legs around his waist so my sex kissed his abdomen.

He crooned, looked down at the contact, and pressed his body into me. Then he slid his finger between us, stroking my bud. "Nice to finally meet you, Madame Sarcasm."

Pleasure raced through me. "It *is* you. Wow."

He cupped my face with both hands and kissed me. The kiss was fueled with desperation and urgency. He devoured me with teeth, tongue, and lips. Arousal pumped through me, firing up all my nerve endings.

He broke for breath, dropping kisses to my neck. Then his lips traveled down to my breasts, nipping one gently with his teeth before giving the other the same attention. When he fluttered his tongue, I moaned. "More."

Oh my God. He was so good. Exceptionally skilled. He continued fluttering his tongue with just the right tempo, and I thought I was going to come right then.

But then he cupped my breasts, pushed them together, and buried his face in them. "I can't believe it's actually you."

"You're the asteroid inquirer." I watched as he kissed the side of my breasts and under them. He seemed to enjoy his exploration. It turned me on even more to see him taking his time.

He'd been my last blog post. His inquiry had been strange and creative, and perfect for me to end the blog. I had so many questions for him, but I couldn't focus on anything except the way he feasted on my breasts. He suckled hard, drawing out my nipples, all while keeping his gaze on me.

A ravenous and unapologetic wolf.

Moaning, I arched into him, offering him more.

"I had a crush on you, you know," he said.

Laughing, I placed my hands on his firm chest. "Madame Sarcasm was a sixty-year-old woman with three dogs, five cats, a pig, a goat, two parrots, and a ferret. That bio, plus the picture of an eccentric woman with catlike eyes, intrigued you?"

"What can I say?" A smile curled onto his lips. "I'm interested in a witty woman who can multitask."

I'd never laughed this much during sex. It was so easy with him.

He nudged me down onto the kitchen table. "I love your sexy, sassy sarcasm."

The coolness of the surface shocked my skin. But heat

spiked when his hands spread my thighs wider. He stared at me, and embarrassment flushed. No one had looked at me like that. The stretch marks . . . the cellulite . . . I hadn't worked out in a while . . .

I closed my thighs, but he held them firmly in place. "Don't move, Sunshine. I'm admiring fine art here."

"Orion . . .," I said, my voice not sounding like myself.

"Yes?" He blew at me and growled. "You're fucking beautiful."

His words calmed my erratic nerves. I heard the chair screech closer to the table. He sat down between my thighs, pressing in his face. His warm breath breathed life into my skin. Nerves woke in places I hadn't considered until now. My thighs quivered as anticipation thrummed.

When he licked me, I bucked in pleasure.

"Fuck. You taste so good, Elena." He repeated the gesture over and over as liquid heat poured out of my core. "You're so beautiful." He licked me up, and my vision blurred.

My arms flew out to grip the edge of the kitchen table. Sensation soared, and the inner muscles of my vagina tightened. I needed him inside me.

"Now." I looked at him. "Please."

"One second, baby." He rose, stripped out of his boxers, and rushed to where his pants had dropped. When he came back, he wagged a condom in front of his face, looking adorable.

I couldn't stop looking at his gloriously massive cock. Would it fit inside me? I'd never seen anything so beautiful and terrifying at the same time.

He pulled on the condom swiftly and held his cock at my entrance. "I'm going to fuck your brains out."

"Please." I braced my hands on the table.

He lifted my ass, and I wrapped my legs around his waist. Holding my gaze, he slid into me, one inch at a time. He felt so good. So unbelievably good. My inner muscles expanded to welcome his thickness.

"You okay?" he breathed.

I nodded and challenged him. "More."

He grinned and increased his speed. Our wet skin slapped against each other, loud in the otherwise quiet night.

"How about now?" he asked.

"More!" I cried.

"You're a fucking goddess."

CHAPTER THIRTY-ONE

ORION

I COULDN'T GET ENOUGH of her. I hammered into her, driving hard and fast. With each thrust, she cried out my name in pleasure. There was nothing more beautiful than the sound of her voice crying for me.

"You're a sex maniac, Orion!" She looped her arms around my neck and kissed me while I fucked her.

Blood pounded in my ears as our mouths sought each other in desperation. She tasted like everything I'd ever wanted, but didn't know until this moment. On one hand, it didn't make any sense. But on the other, it made perfect sense. My logical and intuitive minds were blending together.

"You're so fucking hot." I gasped and absorbed her wild look. The messy hair, the darkened brown eyes gleaming with desire for me, and the swollen lips that begged for more kisses. She was a gorgeous wildflower, and she was mine.

Primal need surged in me as I extracted myself from her.

She pouted with disappointment, so I said, "Turn around. I want you from behind."

Smiling, she turned and bent over, her arms stretching out on the kitchen table. I spanked her behind gently. "I've wanted to do that for a long time."

"Oh really? Since when?" She arched her back, and her fine ass greeted me.

"The car accident." I bent down and dropped kisses on her glistening skin.

She released a moan and turned her head sideways toward the glass cabinet. Our eyes met in the reflection, and a mutual understanding passed between us. I loved that I could read her.

She enjoyed watching me adore her.

"Watch me feast on your fine ass." I gave her butt another slap, then dropped to my knees, spread her legs wider, and swiped my tongue over her wetness.

"Oh my God," she whimpered.

Her moan echoed in the house. Her decadent scent was the oxygen I needed to survive. I stroked her bud once, and her body thrashed. I repeated the action, loving how my tongue detonated her. Her body trembled.

I smiled as I sucked on her bud and pushed two fingers into her, pumping hard.

"Orion!" she screamed with delight.

An image of a dandelion puff bursting free into the air popped into my head.

"Yes, Sunshine." I sucked on her swollen bud again.

"You're a sex god!" She squirmed, trying to escape my tongue's assault.

I turned to meet her eyes on the glass panel. "I enjoy being your sex god, the one who'll savor you all night."

"You're also a fine thief," she breathed.

When I'd first hired her, I had no intention of sharing this part of me. Only three people knew about my extracurricular activity: The Condor, The Raven, and Ralph. Now Elena—the first woman to see this side of me. Kate didn't even know.

Elena only knew a facet of me, not about The Roc yet.

But Elena got me to share private details about my life so quickly. I'd delve into that matter another time.

Then I slammed into her, pumping hard and fast. Heat soared in me as a surge of ecstasy pushed me closer to the edge. I sensed her inner muscles tightening, preparing for her release.

"Elena!" I roared her name as the orgasm ricocheted through me.

"Oh my God!" Her body trembled, and I loved how her muscles squeezed my cock even tighter.

I rested my body on top of hers. Sweat slicked between us, and I heard her racing heartbeat.

After a moment I yanked her up to a standing position and turned her to face me. "That was extraordinary." I brushed the wet strands of hair from her face.

"It was indeed." She smirked and kissed me.

I released her to go wash myself and brought back a towel. "Want me to clean you up?"

"I can do it." She took the towel from me.

Now that my mind had settled a little, I asked, "Does it bother you that I'm a thief?"

"Maybe." Tossing the towel on one of the kitchen chairs, she looped her arms around my neck and smiled. "You just stole my brain cells and all the insecurities I had leading up to this moment."

I tapped her forehead. "I think your brain reproduces

brain cells too quickly for me. You had insecurities about being with me?"

She shrugged. "I live in a different world than you, Orion. We're on opposite sides of society. Your privileged lifestyle opens a lot of doors. But where I come from, it takes a lot to even get near that door."

She had to know those differences didn't matter to me. But I understood her concern. It was a practical analysis and response to a world that had been conditioned in a certain way.

"I don't care about those things. Remember this, Sunshine. Your self-worth isn't defined by your bank account or your status in the world." I gave her a soft kiss. "You offer me what my privileged life could never give me."

"And what's that?" she choked.

"A deep connection. This inexplicable friendship. This ability to let go and relax."

She smiled. "Most people don't have trouble relaxing."

"Anxiety has been my weakness . . ."

She did it again. She could bait out the truth like no one else. But she didn't do it intentionally like a therapist would. It was simply how I reacted to everything she did and said.

"I can help you with that . . ." She gave me a wicked grin and drew something on my chest with her finger.

"You sure can. We can call it Sunshine Therapy."

She snorted. "They have light therapy where you sit under this special lamp that beams a light onto your body for healing purposes."

"Not my kind of thing. I prefer *you.*"

I gathered her up into my arms and carried her into the bedroom. "Let's get some rest in your bed. Then we can have round two and three later? I'm up for four and five too."

Her chuckle grew into a laugh. "You've got quite the stamina." She pressed a kiss to my chest. "Not normal."

I laughed. "You've no idea what I have when I'm with you. An inner power comes to life, a surge of imminent power." I dropped her onto the bed, crawled in next to her, studying how beautiful she was.

All mine.

She stretched out like a cat, looking at me with a satisfied expression that did something to my chest. I'd never had a long conversation during sex. But with her, it seemed normal.

She curled up beside me and threw a leg over mine, trapping my cock beneath her soft skin.

"My body is deliciously limp and relaxed. Thank you." She rested her head on my shoulders. These little things reminded me of the past, but those memories weren't as clear as they had once been.

Elena had somehow blurred those memories, allowing me to move forward with hope and ease. For the first time in my life, I felt like I had control of my emotions. It sounded strange to a man who had control of so many materialistic things. A man who stole precious items as easily as pressing a button on a remote control. When it came to my anxiety, I skimmed the edge of a complete breakdown. It had happened once before, and I had my mother to help me overcome it. But she wasn't here anymore, and I was no longer a teenager.

I could easily become a different person when I stepped over that thin line separating me from right and wrong. Mental health was this dark place that distorted everything you believed to be true. It could end a man simply for saying the wrong word or being two seconds late.

When I'd been chasing after a sex trafficking ring, I'd interrogated many people, using methods I'd rather not discuss. But they were necessary techniques I used for the scum of society who only responded to those techniques. To dwell in a dark world, leniency would be a weakness I couldn't afford.

Why the fuck was I thinking of this darkness with Elena beside me?

I grunted, and she looked at me with concern in her brown eyes. "You okay?"

"Perfectly fine."

"You smell nice." She inhaled my neck. "Sweat and sex."

A tightness formed in my heart, but I ignored it.

"You smell nice too." I sniffed her hair, inhaling her shampoo mixed with her unique scent, and it aroused me all over again.

"We sound like two silly teenagers." She nibbled on my neck and gave me a hickey.

CHAPTER THIRTY-TWO

ELENA

"MY TURN." He rolled over me and nuzzled my neck, giving me a hickey.

A series of giggles burst from me and him. I loved this version of him. Tonight changed everything for us.

I escaped from his attack to lie beside him. "When did you follow my blog?"

"Two years ago."

"Really? How did you find out about it? I didn't advertise or anything. That blog was something I did for fun."

He kissed my nose, then my mouth. It was a slow and seductive kiss that made me want to stay in bed with him forever. His cock hardened under my thigh. "Someone's perky again."

"He's always perky around you. Horny bastard." He kissed my forehead.

Laughing, I wondered about us. Where would this relationship be next week? A month from now? What exactly were these feelings blossoming between us?

Though I enjoyed being with him, I had to know if this

relationship was going anywhere. My life has been one obstacle after another. I needed something hopeful. I supposed a causal relationship could work. We could meet up for amazing sex and that would be it.

But I knew myself. I couldn't be casual with Orion. I'd get attached to him emotionally. That was already happening. He was constantly in my thoughts. The attraction between us was indescribable. It ran deeper than what I could explain. There was something special here, and I wanted to find out.

Sitting up, I reached for a sheet to cover myself. I couldn't have a serious conversation with him staring at my bare chest.

"Can you confirm something for me?" I tightened the sheet around me as though it could protect me. "What's going to happen tomorrow?"

"What do you mean?"

I rolled my eyes. Here was this intelligent man who managed a successful empire, and yet he was clueless about what I was hinting at.

He smirked. "You know, your eye roll was one of the irresistible traits I noticed about you. It's sexy."

I rolled my eyes again, but a small smile formed on my lips.

I loved his facial expression when he looked at me. The warmth in his eyes was sunlight, giving me life, a reminder of the wonderful things that existed around me. The world didn't seem so dangerous anymore, and the burden didn't seem so heavy. Anything was possible.

When I was a kid, it was easy to believe that anything was possible. But adult responsibilities made that difficult. The cruelty I'd seen in the world as a reporter jaded me.

Despite that, I remembered that spark again because of him.

"I was in a hotel lobby in New York for a conference and heard a woman raving about your blog. She said the writer answers odd questions." He pushed himself up, tossed a pillow behind him for support. "I was curious and had time to kill while waiting for a colleague to show up."

"Are you ever late?"

"Not if I can help it. The day you hit my car I was five minutes late."

"Maybe the Universe wanted you to be late so I could hit your car." I grinned.

"Then I have to thank him for that." He pointed to the ceiling. "I'd been following your blog and reading the strange submissions you received. There are some weirdos out there. I loved how you replied to them. With sarcasm and sass." He pulled me close. "It was fun for me. So that's what I did after a rough day or when I needed a break from something."

He didn't know what that comment did to me. The blog had been my heart, and to know that it had connected us years ago made it more special.

"It was fun for me too."

"Why did you stop? I was disappointed."

"When my show started, it took up a lot of time. I also started Musepaper and began a new relationship. I didn't have time for the blog."

"What happened to your relationship?" he asked.

I shrugged. "It ended a year ago. He was a reporter too. More popular now that he's in New York."

"What's his name?"

"Why?"

"Why not?"

"He's not important," I said.

He looked at me for a moment. "I enjoyed reading your articles on Musepaper too."

"Sounds like you've been stalking me." I smirked.

"Aren't you stalking me? Isn't that what people do when they're interested in someone?"

"In my book, it's called *research*."

His smile widened. "Tell me about Musepaper. Why don't you have more articles? From the comments I've read, people love what you've done."

Liam was never interested in my work. Elliot had listened to me, but he was my best friend. Still, it was different to have Orion ask me.

"I enjoy sharing stories that inspire and motivate people. Right now, it's just local stuff. I hope to expand on it someday."

"Musepaper." He repeated to himself. "I love the sound of it. It's so you."

"I'm covering a few events for Vivian and Audri."

"You should bring Madame Sarcasm back." His eyes sparked. "I have a crush on her."

"I should be jealous." I pinched his cheek playfully. "That idea has crossed my mind, but I'm already struggling to keep Musepaper afloat. I have two interns helping me part time. It's a lot of work. I don't have the team or the funds—"

"I'll invest in Musepaper. But the catch is you have to bring back Madame Sarcasm. Her comeback should be extravagant."

I laughed. "Why? Don't you have other things to work on?"

"Part of being successful is having the eye to spot a precious opportunity. You've got to grasp it before it disappears. It's like seeing a shooting star. You have one second to make a wish before it's gone." He gripped my chin with his fingers, looking at me with those intense eyes that sent a flurry of nerves dancing in my stomach. "I invest in things with potential for growth. Madame Sarcasm helped me at a time when even therapists couldn't. She deserves a second chance."

I'd never had a man believe in me this much. My internal recycling bin tipped over, and all the self-doubts, fears, and negative thoughts I'd collected over the years poured out, leaving me empty. In that emptiness, I could see how they had weighed me down, blocking my joy and self-worth.

"You can incorporate her into Musepaper. A weekly column for Madame Sarcasm. All her followers will flood to Musepaper, which will become your one stop for all the things you've ever wanted. I also enjoy Random Riddles. You can expand on that. Reach out to get sponsors to tag along with the riddles. It has the potential to make you a lot of money."

Excitement whirled through me as several ideas popped into my head.

"I saw the passion in you from your show, Uncover the Truth. The truth matters, and Musepaper could be the place where people come for the truth." He reached for a lock of my hair and wrapped it around his finger, twirling. "There are several media companies in the world, but they're all owned by a few communication giants. These giants have agendas, and those agendas sometimes require them to twist the truth."

"Why?"

He tapped my forehead. "Control. Money. Power. You know, all those things that have created wars in history."

"You could be a very interesting villain."

"What makes you think I'm not? I'm a thief, after all."

"But a different thief." I retorted. "I think you find it more fun playing against the bad guys. You're a hot and dangerous vigilante."

He smiled. "You're not wrong. The WaterFyre Rising boys and I are part of a group called VATV—Vigilantes Against the Villains."

"We girls have our SSG—Super Spy Girls."

"Oh yeah? What do you do?"

I couldn't tell him about my mission, The Thief Who Loved Me. I didn't want him to be influenced by it. He needed to show me that on his own accord. It was the only way I knew it was true.

The mission had morphed from its original purpose. I didn't want to know if he liked me. He'd opened my heart, and now I wanted more. Could he *love* me? I might reach too far there. I might fall off the cliff, but I wanted to know anyway.

The more I talked to him, the more I fell for him. It scared and thrilled me. I had to be careful though because this thief could steal my heart and run away with it, leaving me shattered—heartless.

"We all have our missions," I said. "I'll tell you about mine later."

He eyed me suspiciously but didn't press on. "Okay."

Changing the subject, I said, "I'll do it. I'll bring Madame Sarcasm back with your help."

"Good girl. We can work out the details later. I'll have my financial and tech teams help you with whatever you need. I'll look at Musepaper and give you my feedback on where improvements are necessary. You'll get paid weekly too. Separate from the contract job."

"Are you sure?" My heart raced because he'd just solved my financial predicament.

"Of course. The contract job is just temporary. Musepaper is your dream job." His eyes leveled on me. "Quit FoodHub and Let's Ketchup. I want you to focus on your dream."

I'd already planned on giving my notice but knowing he thought about it sent joy soaring through me. My heart bloomed as I looked at him, amazed at how he formulated a successful action plan in seconds. I supposed when you had limitless money, there was nothing holding you back. For someone like me with restrictions, my thought process had been limited.

"So you want to be my business partner with Musepaper?" I asked, needing a clear answer.

"Absolutely," he said.

"Draft up a contract for me to review, and I'll take a look."

"One more thing." He kissed me gently. "You're my girlfriend now. We're dating."

"Is that how you always ask women on dates?"

"You had hinted at it earlier. I'm just providing you with an answer." He rolled over, pinning me to the bed. "But if you need more clarification, I'm willing to provide it." His hard cock pressed into me, rubbing against my skin.

My phone rang, startling me. The bird song ringtone belonged to my mother.

"Sorry, it's my mom."

"No worries." He shifted his body from mine, and I

yearned for his heat. "This horny bastard will always wait for you."

Smiling, I shook my head and refrained from rolling my eyes.

"Hi, Mom," I said, sitting up, but this time I didn't bother pulling the sheets up to cover myself. An extra layer of comfort had developed between me and him.

"Elena! I *love* the massage chair."

"I'm so happy to hear that, *Mamá*. The delivery was supposed to arrive today. I guess it came early. How did you get it in the house?" I imagined an enormous box and my mom trying to push it with her knees. She shouldn't be putting weight on her weak knees.

"No, Reid stopped by to help. He called to see how the trip was, and I mentioned there was a big box on my porch."

Relief settled. "Reid is a good man."

"Which is why I won't stop volunteering there. What are you doing?"

I looked at Orion, who wore a smirk and pointed at his hard cock.

"Just hanging out with a friend."

Orion narrowed his eyes at me, placed a hand on his chest, pretending to look hurt.

"My *boyfriend*."

"Oh, you have a boyfriend?" Excitement filled her voice. "Since when? Why didn't you tell me? What's his name?"

"Orion." I met his gleeful eyes.

"That's an interesting name. When do I get to meet him?" Mom asked.

"I'll bring him by in a few days. I have some work to get done first." I hadn't told my mom about my unemployment.

She'd be worried. Technically, I was employed, but not by Channel 7 News.

"Great. That gives me time to make a traditional meal. Bring him to dinner. See if he passes the test."

My heart warmed at the thought. Liam didn't like my mom's Peruvian meals, and he made it known gently. According to my mother, Liam lacked decency and the ability to be open-minded. She didn't like him. Maybe she saw something in him I didn't.

I was nervous about her opinion about Orion.

"*Mamá*, I can just pick up dinner. You don't have to go through all the work."

"My baby is dating again. It's an important occasion, and I need to know."

"It's nothing serious," I said, then realized how that must have sounded.

A grunt sounded from Orion, and I covered the phone with a hand, mouthing, *Sorry. Not what I meant.* But it was too late.

I shrieked when Orion grabbed me, pushing me onto my back, sinking into the bed.

"You okay there, honey? What's going on?"

"Yeah, I'm fine. I just dropped something," I said, trying my best not to laugh.

Orion narrowed his eyes at me, probably punishing me for the comment. He scooted down, nudged my thighs wide apart, and buried his face against me, licking and sucking.

"Do you think the relationship has the potential to grow?" Mom asked. "I hope he's not materialistic like Liam. I don't want you to get hurt, sweetie."

Orion swiped at me with slow, seductive strokes. I clamped a hand over my mouth to prevent a moan.

"Yes," I said in my best voice.

Arousal surged in me. His wicked mouth was too much. I didn't want to come while my mom was on the phone. That was just too weird.

"Good. I'm going to make a list of ingredients to fill the refrigerator and ask Betty to go on a grocery trip with me."

"Okay. See you on Wednesday evening." The phone dropped on the bed, and I moaned. "I didn't mean it that way."

"No?" He opened my legs wider, sucking on my bud harder.

The orgasm burst, blinding and beautiful. My body absorbed the powerful bliss, and the quivering ebbed. He kissed my thighs, making his way up to my mouth. "Remember this: when you're with me, it's *serious*." Then he kissed me deeply.

Now it was my turn. I pushed him back onto the bed.

"Let me show you how *serious* I am." I gripped his pulsing cock, stroking its glorious length. Things had happened quickly tonight, and I didn't get a chance to thoroughly examine him.

A masterpiece. An extraordinary weapon that throbbed for me. I pressed kisses up and down, tasting him. He was so male and so perfect.

My lips hovered over his crown. Then I licked around him. "Am I being *serious* enough?"

"Not yet." He growled, daring me with his eyes.

Pleasure strained his face, and I loved that I had the power to do that to him.

He bent an arm behind his back, watching me with darkened eyes. "Show me the power of that seductive mouth and curious tongue." He swallowed. "I've dreamed about them too many times."

Knowing he'd envisioned me pleasuring him made me want to give him everything.

I took him into my mouth, his flavor overwhelming me. Dark, dangerous, and delicious.

He let out a loud curse, followed by a growl and heavy breathing.

"My Madame Sarcasm and Sunshine all in one." His eyes rolled back, and I quickened my pace.

After round six of our sexcapade, we finally drifted off to sleep . . .

CHAPTER THIRTY-THREE

ELENA

ORION DROVE to the shopping center in his Rivian SUV, an electric truck I hadn't seen or heard of until now. Apparently, he had stock in this brand of high-tech cars that were better for the environment, and they gave him a prototype to drive.

He pulled into the shopping center, parked, and squeezed my hand. "What kind of flowers does your mom like? What about pastries? Cookies? Macaroons?"

"You don't have to bring her anything," I said.

He scrunched up his face. "First impressions matter. I'm dating her daughter, so I want to make sure she approves. Besides, my mother would be disappointed if I brought nothing. She taught me manners, you know."

"Are you saying I should buy your family flowers and pastries when I meet them?"

He let out a laugh. "My father wouldn't appreciate them. But if you offer him finance or political books, he'd appreciate those."

"You and your father are different."

"I like those too." He lifted my hand to his lips. "But I like you more, so I'll take whatever you give me."

We browsed the plant section, and I helped him choose the right gift.

"Are you sure she'll like this hibiscus plant more than a bouquet?" he asked, putting it in the trunk. He'd gotten a decorative ivory pot for it as well.

"Yes, because the plant will keep growing, unlike a bouquet that will last about a week."

"What about you? Do you prefer plants over bouquets?"

"That depends. Sometimes I don't mind a beautiful bouquet. But I can see why a long-lasting flower or plant would be more practical."

After picking up a box filled with a variety of pastries, we drove over to my mother's house. I checked my phone, and the reminder to pay Uncle Carlos popped.

I huffed out a stressed sigh. "Almost done," I muttered to myself.

"What's almost done?" Orion turned to me.

"Debt to my uncle," I said, not wanting to discuss it.

"You never sent me the contract to review."

"You have a lot going on. It can wait."

"I'll always have a lot going on. Send it." He reached for my hand and intertwined his fingers with mine. "I'll make time for my girlfriend."

"Okay, I'll send it later today." My lips twisted into a smile. I had to inform the girls of what had transpired. They'd want details.

Though we were now an official couple, it still felt strange to me. Fear settled in the back of my mind, thinking that this relationship would end soon. I wasn't being negative. I was being practical, seeing things from all sides. Orion and I didn't live in the same world. Our differences would catch up to us eventually. When that day arrived, would he still choose me?

Like those dandelion seeds you send out into the world, you need to give them a chance to grow. See what happens.

Orion approached my mom's cape-style home, and nerves wrenched in my stomach as I spotted the black Mercedes.

"Oh no." Sweat formed on my palms.

"What's wrong?" Orion stared at me.

"He's here." I inhaled deeply.

"Who?"

"Uncle Carlos," I muttered. Orion already knew Sam was my uncle's business partner.

"Why is he here?"

"My mom doesn't know about the debt. I hope he's not coming to collect. The news would devastate her. The payment isn't due until next week."

"How much do you owe him?"

"I don't want to burden you."

"You're not." He touched my chin.

"It's a lot."

"How much, Elena?" His jaw tightened. "You're my girlfriend now and if someone is cheating you out of money, I need to know." His eyes flickered. "Most loan sharks will slap on a heavy fine just because they can. That's deception. That's playing with someone's vulnerability."

"I have three hundred thousand dollars left," I muttered. "But my dad only borrowed one hundred thousand on the initial contract. He was late on several payments, and the fees piled up."

He scoffed, and ice formed in his eyes. "Sounds like a classic case of a ruthless loan shark."

I sat in the seat, feeling ashamed that I couldn't do anything about my situation. "I had a feeling he was ripping me off, but I didn't have the funds to get a lawyer." He squeezed my hand, and I looked at him. "What if he sent someone to hurt me or my mom? He'd do it." My shoulders sagged. "I thought if I could pay off the debt, he'd leave me and my mom alone."

"Getting a lawyer won't help. These people need to be dealt with differently. You're not doing this alone now. Let's go." He got out of the car.

"This is *my* issue. I don't want it to burden you."

"Elena, part of being in a relationship is making sure the other person is safe and happy. I'm happy to take on your burden. Besides, I can't stand people like your uncle." He smiled. "It's fun for me to toy with them."

His comment about being a vigilante against the villains came to mind. Was this what he meant?

I tried my best to contain the nerves inside me. Uncle Carlos probably possessed an energy my body didn't like. Grandma used to tell me to pay attention to my intuition and my body's reaction to things. That they always told the truth.

The unease my body felt could be from all the negative energy Uncle Carlos had collected over the years from screwing other people. How many lives had he ruined?

I forgot to mention to Orion about my suspicion of Uncle Carlos and Sam regarding the life insurance scam.

Orion carried the hibiscus plant, and I held the box of pastries. I used my key to open the door. Kicking off my shoes, I placed them on the mat and didn't see Uncle Carlos's shoes. He had removed his shoes when my father was alive, but now he didn't even bother. Orion placed his shoes next to mine.

"*Mamá*, we're here," I said, walking into the living room where Mom sat in her new massage chair.

Uncle Carlos turned to me and his gaze slid over to Orion, where it remained.

I prayed my mom didn't know about the debt. She didn't need the burden. I wanted her to have wonderful memories of my father. Not of a man who gambled and got into immense debt.

"Elena!" Mom pushed herself out of the massage chair, which seemed almost too large for her now that I could see her in it. She embraced me and gave me a kiss on the cheek.

"You must be Orion." She studied him with curious brown eyes, holding back her friendliness. Mom was a friendly person, but after Liam had shoved me aside, she was careful of who deserved her affection.

"I am. It's very nice to meet you." He placed the plant on the floor. "I hope you like hibiscus."

She walked to the plant and smiled. "I do. Thank you." She turned to my uncle, who continued to study Orion. "This is Carlos, my brother-in-law. He's here visiting. This is Elena's boyfriend, Orion," she told Uncle Carlos.

"Nice to meet you," he said.

"Likewise," Orion replied.

Uncle Carlos never visited us unless he wanted something.

"*Mamá*, Orion also got this for you." I placed the box in her hand. "He insisted, even when I told him he didn't have to."

"Thank you. Let me get some plates for us. Have a seat. Make yourself at home. Would you like anything to drink?"

"No thank you." Orion sat on the loveseat.

"I'm good too," I said.

When my mother walked into the kitchen, I turned to my uncle. "What's the special occasion, Uncle Carlos?"

"I was in the neighborhood and just wanted to see how my sister-in-law is doing. Checking in on family, you know?"

I wanted to roll my eyes, but I didn't want him to have a reason to add another fine to my debt.

"I'll stop by to pay you next week before the due date."

"I know you will." Uncle Carlos smiled.

"Why do you need to drop it off?" Orion asked. "You can wire directly to his account. That's more efficient for everyone." He looked at Uncle Carlos. "Every legitimate business understands this, correct?"

Orion's comment surprised me.

"We have our way of keeping data," Uncle Carlos replied.

"I'm helping Elena with the payment because the late fees are extraordinarily high. It makes me question the legality of it. But since you're her uncle, I'll dismiss that." Orion looked at me. "You're going to wire it to his account. If he doesn't want that, you write a check and use a certified mail service. Okay?"

I nodded and looked over at Uncle Carlos. "What would you like? Wire transfer or certified mail?"

I could see the anger behind his eyes, but I also saw the restraint. Orion made an excellent case. Uncle Carlos knew Orion saw his scam and would call him out on it. He had two options to get his money.

For a moment I considered what he'd do if I stopped payment all together. He'd probably send someone to kill me, my mom, and Orion when we least expected it.

"Certified mail is fine," said Uncle Carlos, who turned to Orion. "Who are you?'

"A business executive who understands an insubstantial business contract."

When my mom brought out plates for the pastries, the conversation changed to mundane things. Uncle Carlos didn't stay long after eating one pastry.

"What did Uncle Carlos want?" I asked my mom when he left.

"He asked if I needed a new washer and dryer." She shrugged. "I guess someone gave him a new set, and he didn't have a place for them. He offered to install the new machines, but I declined."

Orion and I exchanged a suspicious look.

Generosity wasn't in his vocabulary. I'd believe that he wanted to sell my mom a new washer and dryer for double its price rather than him offering it to her for free.

What was the real reason Uncle Carlos visited my mom?

Before we left my mom's house, she pulled me into her bedroom and gave me a thumbs up. "He passed the test, sweetie. I really like him."

On our way home, I relayed the message to Orion and he replied, "What's there not to like?"

That earned an eye roll and a grin from me.

ORION

I SPENT the next few days following up with my team regarding the drone development, AI software, and the water project I was working on. When I was satisfied with the updates, I researched Elena's uncle and Sam. I passed some information to my research team to help me get through the clutter of information. While they worked on that, I turned my attention to why Elena had been fired from Channel 7 News and examined the updates on Pablo's investigation.

She had gotten a lot of priceless information about The Condor for me. I felt privileged to be his student. I didn't know he'd been immersed in the community. The common people loved him. I appreciated the photos she'd taken of the apple tree and the community garden. I'd be donating money and assigning a team to ensure that garden continued to flourish.

When Elena worked in the office, she left me alone to attend my virtual meetings. When I didn't have any meetings, she'd come in and work at the desk in the lounge area where I stared at her. I loved the ease of working with her.

Some nights I stayed over at her place, while other nights she stayed in my apartment below this office.

Today, she stayed home to work so she could water and organize her dandelion garden.

I held the blue canteen she'd prepared for me. "Who knew dandelion tea could fix my most troublesome issue?" I sipped and placed it down.

When I asked her for the name of the special ingredient, she said it was hard to pronounce. She called it a magical leaf. To my surprise, the tea had made me more relaxed. I had more clarity in my mind, and my body felt more invigorated. Most of all, I was happy.

Feeling inspired, I worked on Level Six. I created new characters, changed up the plot, and added more details to my little fantasy world. I grinned when a beautiful Madame Sarcasm character came to life, holding a pot of powerful dandelions that could grant extra lives to the players.

A thrill rushed through me, confirming this was what the video game had been missing. Elena had inspired this new character that would take Level Six to where it needed to be. The work flowed effortlessly, and before I knew it, the demo was uploaded to the shared drive for the boys to review.

Immense relief overcame me as I checked off a big accomplishment. Now I just had to wait for their feedback.

A text buzzed on my phone, and I grinned like a fool.

Elena: *Want to join me on an obstacle course?*

Orion: *Are you asking me on a date?*

Elena: *Yes.*

Orion: *Okay. (Smile emoji) Where are we going?*

Elena: *The Mudstacle Course. We can get dirty together.*

Christ. This wasn't what I expected. I didn't mind a

challenging obstacle course, but a mud race? I'd seen some of them. Mud could creep up into your ass.

Elena: You still there?

I guess I'd taken too long to reply.

Orion: Here. Just trying to see the fun in it.

Elena: You'd be with me. That's fun enough, right?

She knew what buttons to push with me.

Orion: Always. But we can get dirty without the nasty mud.

Elena: They have an area that teaches me how to shoot a slingshot.

Orion: You did fine the other day. Just keep practicing.

I'd shown her how to shoot it in her backyard. She was pretty good at it.

Elena: We've been working hard. Need a break to de-stress. Come with me.

Orion: I always love cumming for you. (Wink emoji)

Elena: (Eye roll emoji) If you prefer to stay home, I can ask the girls to go with me.

Orion: No, I'll go. (Heart emoji)

This seemed important to her, so I'd face the gross mud for her.

Elena: You're the best. (Heart emoji) (Kiss emoji)

Orion: Kiss here. (Cucumber emoji)

Elena: Who's dirty now? (Laugh emoji) See you at home.

CHAPTER THIRTY-FIVE

ELENA

I LOOKED FORWARD to the mud obstacle course with Orion. It was an opportunity for us to forget about our responsibilities and just play.

I'd never participated in a mud race before, but I'd wanted to. This would be the first time for me and Orion. I was more excited about it than he was.

Inside our lodge room, we got ready to prepare to head down to the obstacle course. Orion stood by the window, talking to someone on the phone, wearing his polo shirt and khaki slacks, looking handsome and way too preppy for this event.

I wore my black tank top and shorts I'd ordered online for this event. When he finished, he turned around, and I held up his outfit. A lightweight T-shirt and knit shorts that matched my outfit.

"Let's go, Slingshot. We've got an obstacle course to overcome."

"I watched the videos on YouTube." He took the clothes and placed them on the bed. "How is this fun? Getting all dirty? Running in the mud and swimming in the muddy river?" Disgust flashed on his face, along with a little anxiety.

"Don't think of it like that." I walked over and gave him a peck on the cheek. "Think of it as spending time with me—your favorite girl."

He pulled me close. "That's the only reason I'm here. I have to make sure no man is getting dirty with you."

"Thanks for giving it a shot." I smiled. "We're creating dirty memories together."

"There are other ways of creating dirty memories without having to be here, you know. My office, my house or your house, a lovely retreat in the Bahamas, the Maldives, or even on my island. Lots of places."

"Those places are wonderful, and I'd love to visit your island one day. But this is an unforgettable adventure. This is us trying new things. You're stepping into my world by doing this. It's not an extravagant retreat like what you're used to. Or what you can afford." I removed his shirt, rubbing my hands across the firm and muscular chest. "This is something I can afford because a friend got me discounted tickets. And because it looked fun. Besides, we'll get a good workout out of it." I stripped his shorts and admired how endowed he was.

"Keep going with your little speech, Sunshine. It's turning me on."

Smirking, I palmed him. "None of my previous boyfriends wanted to do this."

"No?"

"Like you, they weren't interested in running through the mud." I took off his boxers, releasing his cock. "But you did, even though you're uncomfortable with it." I stroked him, loving the heat in my palm.

He moaned. "If this is how you ease me into an uncomfortable situation, I'll let you know every time I stumble into one."

"Don't worry about anything. Have fun. If you slip in the mud, I'll get you out." I met his eyes, and there was so much emotion in them.

"You'll run through the muck to save me?"

"I'll get down and dirty for you." I dropped to my knees and took him in my mouth, loving every inch.

He groaned and placed his hands on my head, watching me watch him. There was something special between us, a connection that was beyond this physical attraction.

"Feels so good, baby."

Then I released him, got up, and placed two hands on his chest. "That's just a taste of what's to come *after* you finish the race with me."

He narrowed his eyes at me. "You're evil."

"A teaser isn't evil." I tapped his cheek. "You've been working late the past few days. You need a break."

I tossed him his clothes, "C'mon, Slingshot. Let's have some fun!"

As we headed out to the obstacle course, a weird sensation overcame me. Then I heard her voice.

"Orion!" Chantel strutted up to us with Sabrina. "Nice seeing you again." She brushed a hand down his arm, ignoring me.

I glared at her, wishing my eyes could send out a beam of light to burn off her hand. I didn't want her touching him. Though he was my boyfriend now, the surge of jealousy still surprised me.

Chantel flicked a glance at me and back at him. Sabrina

met my eyes and looked elsewhere. I knew she had helped Chantel spread the drug rumors about me.

"Hello." Orion slung an arm around my shoulders, pulling me close. "You're here for the obstacle course?"

I wrapped my arm around his waist as well. "Nice seeing you and Sabrina here. I didn't think you'd like rolling around in the mud."

Arching an eyebrow, Chantel stared at Orion's arm on my shoulder. Then she slid her disapproving gaze to me. "You get around fast."

I blinked at the rudeness. I guess I shouldn't have given her the benefit of the doubt. Indignation soared in me as I extracted myself from Orion's arm.

"If you think my dating someone new after a year is fast, then how do you describe yourself when you date a new guy *every* month?" I paused as Chantel's mouth dropped open, looking embarrassed. She stepped on my toes when all I wanted was a calm vacation. I continued my tirade. "We all know you screwed those guys from the lighting crew."

She flared her nostrils, sending darts into my chest with her eyes.

I sent my own darts back at her. "And let's not forget Mr. Gallini's son, who had just turned nineteen." I shook my head. "Seriously, he's still a kid." A kid who was big and tall like his father, who owned the gym she attended. Maybe she slept with the father too, but I hadn't heard anyone whisper that.

Sabrina whipped her head at Chantel, whose face was beet red with anger.

Orion stood with his arms crossed over his chest, looking intrigued.

"Someone's spreading rumors about me," Chantel spat.

"It must be because you did that to them. What goes around comes around."

Sabrina glanced at the floor, probably trying to escape the embarrassing situation but afraid of Chantel's wrath afterward.

"Stay out of my business," Chantel seethed.

"Then you stay out of mine." I whirled around, walked to Orion, gripped his hand in mine, and stalked off.

Anger pulsed through my veins. This was my mini vacation with Orion. Our first actual date and Chantel had to ruin it.

Orion swung my hand back and forth. "That was admirable."

I flicked an annoyed look at him, even though he had nothing to do with it. Actually, he did. Chantel wanted *him*. Had he given her any indication that he was interested? Doubts swarmed in my mind like annoying ants.

I stopped in my steps and narrowed my eyes at him.

"What's wrong?" he asked.

"Chantel said it was nice seeing you *again*. What didn't you tell me about seeing her on your last business trip?"

He considered me for a moment, studying my face with amusement. Then a smile appeared on his face as he leaned in and whispered, "Are you jealous?"

I rolled my eyes, not admitting to anything. This entire situation was already ridiculous and my behavior baffled me. Still, I couldn't help it.

"Answer my question," I scoffed.

His smile widened. "I saw her at an event, but nothing happened." He touched my face tenderly. "I was too busy thinking about dandelion tea and a sexy eye roll from someone else."

I twisted my lips, feeling better. But also feeling annoyed at myself for letting Chantel push my buttons. I knew without a doubt she'd been badmouthing me to all my colleagues. Her family had influence at Channel 7 News, so I wasn't surprised if they chose her over me.

Those with privilege had an upper hand at everything.

Feeling drained, I sighed. "Okay."

"Come here, Sunshine." He pulled me flush to him for a warm embrace. "I love that you're jealous, but never doubt how I feel about you. Okay?" He kissed my forehead. "That was the most interesting spat I'd ever witnessed. She stepped on your toes, but you twisted her arms."

Grinning, I imagined the image, and it made me feel a little better. "Sometimes you have to draw a clear line for the bully. I'm not dismissing her attack. Let's stop talking about her. I need to release some tension."

His eyes sparked, thinking about something entirely different. However, I wasn't in the mood for anything sexual.

I needed to sweat off this irritation.

CHAPTER THIRTY-SIX

ORION

WE BELONGED to a group of twenty competitors, including Chantel and Sabrina. It was a five-mile course with obstacles like the Crazy Block Maze, Pyramid Net, Cage Crawl, and Cry Baby. The ten-mile course was on the other end of The Mudstacle Course. Thank God, Elena chose the smaller course.

"You think you can make it?" Elena looked up at me. The tight tank and shorts were like a second skin on her fabulous body.

I was grateful she'd gotten me shorts that kept the mud from attacking my dick.

"It's a team effort. Everyone's supposed to help each other finish the race. Water and snacks are available at various posts along the way. You good?"

"Never been better." I glared at the mud. "What's in the mud?"

Laughing, she shrugged. "Dirt and water? I don't know."

"Gross." I winced.

"Just get dirty this once for me, okay, preppy boy? Think

of mud as a luxury. Soil is crucial for life. Without it, plant life won't exist. Think of it that way."

I snorted. "I can't see mud like that, Sunshine. Not gonna happen."

As we approached the Crazy Block Maze, Chantel and Sabrina did too, but they stood on the opposite end.

I didn't know how much Elena had to deal with until today. Not only was she carrying the weight of her father's debt, she was also dealing with toxic people at work. Despite that, she didn't stop researching a family friend's death or helping me with The Condor's investigation. She did all of this with a smile. However, underneath that smile were layers of anxiety. Unlike me, she wasn't trapped by it. At least not in the same way.

Perhaps this was why I was attracted to her from the beginning. She wasn't affected by the monster who had gripped me for so long. What was her secret?

"Mud race!" Elena cheered with everyone.

I flicked a glance at the bright sky, wondering if God was being sarcastic. I'd watched several videos on mud racing from around the country. Why would people want to get dirty like this? How long would it take me to clean myself? My dick would be covered with mud, reminding me of chocolate sauce hardening over ice cream. Why the fuck was I even comparing my dick to that?

Obviously, I was out of my element. I didn't know how to act at this event. My initial reaction was staring at the pool of mud and trying to calm my nerves. My skin trembled from the impending grossness.

Over the years I'd taken all kinds of extracurricular activities that had gotten me dirty and sweaty, but none of them had gotten me this dirty.

Elena had lured me here. She wanted to do this with *me*, and even though I'd prefer any other physical activity like fencing, archery, or even the slingshot, I came here for her. To learn more about her.

I turned to look at her, and excitement and irritation splashed on her expression. Determination gleamed through her eyes.

James, the announcer, gave a brief speech about the rules. This race differed from others in that everybody won as long as they finished the race. There was no gold medal waiting for us at the finish line.

"You'll earn the magnificent feeling of accomplishment—of working together," James said. "To get through the muck is a victory worth celebrating."

I wrapped an arm around her. "Ready for victory?"

"Always." She smiled.

When the horn blew, we all ran into the pool of mud. I was right behind Elena as the mud engulfed us. It was fucking gross. The cool mud covered my legs as we tried our best to trudge to the next obstacle. When we finally emerged from the nasty pool, I slipped once, got up, and saw Elena had fallen on her ass.

I bent down to help her up and slipped again. She roared with laughter, pulling me up.

The guy in front of me also slipped, but when he got up, his mud-strewn shorts were halfway down his ass. Fuck, I didn't need to see that horror of a butt crack.

As we continued, Butt Crack lost his footing and slipped again. When he stood up, his shorts fell to his knees.

Elena gasped, and I cursed, blocking her vision with my hand. Butt Crack let out a series of curses too. But his girl came to the rescue and helped him along.

I stood there shaking my head, while Elena tried her best to suppress her laugh.

"If that happens to you, I'll help you," she said.

"You know you can pull down my shorts anytime. Just not here." I wiped the mud off my face and arm, but that only made it worse.

"If there's anyone I want to be nasty with, it's you, Slingshot." She embraced me, smearing more mud on me.

But I didn't mind it. I'd try my best to achieve victory with her.

We climbed over wooden barrels, hopped into rows of tires, zigzagged our way over cones. Then we arrived at the Pyramid Net, a forty-foot climb up and down a net structure. Unlike the other obstacles where she dove ahead immediately, this one had her feet rooted to the ground.

Chantel and Sabrina approached, flicked us a bitter look, and moved on. They jumped onto the net and climbed.

Elena didn't see them or her mind was too focused on the pyramid net. Anxiety strained her face, and she inhaled and exhaled slowly.

"You okay?" I asked.

Her hand trembled. "Not a fan of heights."

I remembered her hesitation on the balcony of my office and gripped her hand. "I've got you. One step at a time. There's no rush."

"There *is* a rush. We're part of a huge team. I don't want to be the last couple."

"Who cares?" Even though I hated losing, I'd rather she be safe. "This is for fun. We'll be losers together."

A smile fought its way to her lips. "You don't seem like a guy who likes to lose."

"This course is to promote teamwork, comradery. There are only winners."

"Okay. We'll be the last winners together." She wiped the patch of mud on her chin, smearing her face even more and looking adorable.

Ten people had already climbed to the middle. We gripped the rope and pulled ourselves up. Elena looked scared, but also brave.

Not too far away, Chantel looked at Elena moving slowly on the rope. She exchanged a glance with Sabrina and they jumped on the net, making it more unstable for everyone, but especially for Elena.

Another contestant shouted to Chantel. "What the hell is wrong with you?"

But Chantel and Sabrina ignored her.

Elena yelped as she lost her footing. She tried to find it and got one foot on the rope again, but Chantel shook the net even more.

"Stop it!" I told Chantel.

But she arched a defiant eyebrow and continued. Anger soared in me.

I reached for Elena just as her other foot slipped. She screamed and gripped the rope with both hands. The fear in her eyes was . . . unforgettable. Her fear pierced through me. It was worse today than what I'd witnessed on my office balcony.

I stepped to the next grid, reached out, and wrapped my arm around her waist, pulling her to me.

With her feet balanced on the rope, she tightened her arm around me and held on tight. Her face was in my muddy shirt.

"I've got you, baby," I whispered.

"You guys need help?" asked an older man who stopped climbing with his wife to check on us.

"We just need a minute. Thank you, though."

"Take your time. Don't rush. This is our fifth time here." The friendly woman smiled. "Just have fun. No one will care if you're the last to finish."

"Thank you," I said.

Elena's heart pounded against my body, and tears filled her eyes.

Chantel and Sabrina just earned themselves the top spots on my shit list.

"Yo! Stop that shit!" shouted another team as Chantel kept jumping on the rope.

A guy yelled at them. "We're on the same team. What the fuck?"

"Kick them off the course!" a woman with red hair barked at them. "They're making it dangerous for everyone!"

I wanted to go over to Chantel and Sabrina and toss them out, but I needed to keep Elena safe with me.

Chantel and Sabrina shrugged, grinned, and climbed over to the other side and down.

Then Elena looked up at me. "I'm okay now. Let's finish this. If I don't, they'll win." She jerked her chin toward Chantel and Sabrina, who were already onto the next obstacle.

"We're doing this our way." I gripped her hand, lifted it into the air. "Victory is ours."

She rolled her eyes, and I had my Elena back.

"You go ahead, I'll be right beside you." With each climb, she looked over at me and smiled. Finally, we made it to the other side and down to the ground.

She leaped into my arms, slipped from my muddy shirt, but I gripped her ass, holding her tight. "We did it!"

The next obstacle required us to crawl under this mesh, which she accomplished with ease.

When we arrived at the finish line, to our surprise, Butt Crack was limping along with the help of his friends. A crew member emerged with an ATV to help him. His friend told the group that he'd sprained his ankle.

"Poor guy," Elena said. "We were second to last place, but that was because we didn't train."

"You're supposed to train?"

She nodded. "Some do, to help their bodies adjust. Especially those who prefer the ten-mile obstacle course."

"Excellent job!" The girl who had shouted at Chantel and Sabrina high-fived us. "You okay? I made a complaint about those bitches. I mean, seriously. This is a teamwork course, and they wanted to hinder people's progress. You could've gotten hurt."

"I don't know why they're here," said another woman. "Getting their hair done and shopping is more their style."

"Oh, the manager said one of the girl's fathers had placed a bid to purchase this place. Maybe she came here to check it out. If she's going to be a regular attendee, then I won't be coming back. There are other places I can support." The lady with the ponytail placed two hands on her hips, looking toward Chantel and Sabrina talking to the crew. "She has spoiled brat written all over her."

"The world of privilege differs from ours, Terri," said a woman with mud all over her blonde hair.

"Glad we made it to the end." Elena forced a smile. "I'm going to be so sore tomorrow."

"Make that a few days." Terri straightened her back,

stretching out her arms and legs. "Nice meeting you both. Hopefully we'll see you again."

"Have a good evening." I waved to the women.

I turned to Elena, trying to wipe the mud from her forehead, cheek, and chin. "Need a massage?"

"You give massages?" She reached up, removing the mud from my face.

"No. But I'll make an exception for you," I said, wanting to ask her more questions about the source of her fear of heights. But I held back, seeing how tired she looked.

After spraying mud off our bodies, we went back to our hotel, washed up, and spent the rest of the evening in bed, watching a random science show on television.

Elena snuggled into me, looking drowsy.

"I can't believe we spent four hours on the uphill terrain," I said.

"It would have taken us nine hours if we had done the ten-mile course." She looked up at me. "Did you enjoy your time in the mud with me?"

"You're the highlight of it all." I kissed her gently.

"I've always wanted to do it, but didn't have anyone to go with."

"Why did you want to go through this mud course?" I asked.

She looked at the TV screen, which was showing abnormal weather around the world.

Sighing, she sat up and looked at me with weary eyes. "The obstacle course reminds me of life. The ups and downs, the difficult sections that make you want to give up, but you don't because you see people in front of you succeeding." She paused, tugging at the bedsheets. "I agree the mud is gross, but there are so many things in life that are worse. The evil things people do to one another are worse than mud. I can wash the mud off, but some things don't come off that easy, you know?"

I also sat up and shifted to face her, letting her words flow into my heart.

"You're right. See? This right here—" I tapped her forehead "—is why I love Madame Sarcasm. Not only does she possess sarcasm, she also possesses innate wisdom."

She blushed and looked at my shirt. Curious, I glanced down at my black V-neck shirt, not seeing anything strange about it.

"What are you looking at?" I asked.

She met my eyes. "What did you do with your necklace?"

I knew this moment would come, and she had a right to know.

Her shoulders slouched. "Today is one of those days that makes me wonder about a lot of things. I want to know what's going on in here." She placed a hand over my heart. "Were you married to her?"

I gripped Elena's hand and kissed it, wanting to remove her vulnerability and self-doubt.

"No. We were engaged for a week before she died," I said, and finally described the dark memory that had made me feel guilty all these years.

Excitement rushes through me as I stop by Tasty Thai and place an order for shrimp pad thai and tom yum soup. Kate loves Thai food and I'm hoping she'll forgive me for missing our lunch date today. I stared at the text messages we had exchanged earlier today.

Kate: Can't wait for our date. Love you so much!

Me: Sorry, babe. I'm stuck in a meeting. Can we reschedule, please?

Kate: You're always in meetings. Can't you just leave earlier? I have something to tell you.

Me: I can't today. Sorry. Please don't be mad. We'll chat when I get home.

Kate hasn't responded yet. It's been hours. I sit in the chair and wait for my order, watching the cars rush by. I check my phone again, but no messages from her. She must be furious at me. Or she's busy working. Kate works for her mother's real estate company, so her hours are flexible.

She wants a small wedding, and I'm fine with whatever she wants. We've been together for three years, and I'm excited to start our future together.

She doesn't know about my extracurricular activity, and I don't plan on sharing it with her. Her father works for INTERPOL, the International Criminal Police Organization. If he finds out what I do as a hobby, he won't let her marry me. No father wants his daughter to be with a criminal—a thief. Right now, he knows I'm a successful entrepreneur and heir to my father's wealth. I don't want Kate to be in a difficult position.

We're similar in so many ways. Both of us suffer from extreme anxiety. On top of her depression, she also has to deal with thyroid issues, which have made her hair thin over the years.

But we love each other, and that's all that matters.

My order arrives, and I head home. I walk into her apartment, place the takeout bag on the kitchen counter. The stack of cardboard boxes is pushed against the wall. She has one box open, but there is nothing in it. We're supposed to pack her stuff and move it into my new house next month. This is my first house in Sweden. I've always stayed in a luxurious apartment, but Kate wants a backyard, so I'm giving her a big house with a big yard.

"I'm home, baby." I walk into the living room, but she's not in the comfy chair I got her last Christmas.

The house is exceptionally quiet. She has to be home. Her car is parked in the spot next to mine. A sick feeling clenches my stomach. I walk into her bedroom, but I don't see her. The closet door is ajar. I open it and my heart collapses.

"Kate!" I cry, rushing to her limp body, dangling from a rope that was secured to a steel bar.

I know she's gone from the look of her pale skin. With trembling hands, I remove the rope from her neck, carry her out to the bedroom, and gather her into my arms. I cry like when my mother died.

Why is this happening to me? Why are the people I love dying? Am I cursed?

Call the authorities, I hear an inner voice call out.

I wipe the tears from my eyes so I can look at the numbers on my phone to call the authorities, giving them my address. They ask more questions, but I don't hear them. I don't have the energy to think. I just want to hold on to Kate for as long as I can.

"Please hurry," I say to them and hang up, turning to my fiancée. "I'm sorry I wasn't here for you. I'm so sorry."

While I wait for the police to show up, I intertwine my fingers with hers. The simple engagement ring gleams from her finger.

Why, Kate? I know it's a stupid question, but I can't help but ask it. She must have been devastated that I missed our lunch date. Her depression has gotten worse in the last few weeks.

What kind of fiancé am I?

I glance at the opened bottles of medicine on her night-stand. I've seen her moody, but didn't know it was this bad.

My chest feels like it caves in, and I know that a part of me has died with her.

"I'll never forget that day," I said, feeling lighter by sharing this memory with Elena. "I shouldn't have cancelled our date. She tried her best to fight the internal monsters, but they were too much for her. I wish I could've helped her."

Elena threw her arms over me. "I'm sorry to hear that." She drew back, her eyes full of emotion. "I think she knows how much you wanted to help."

"I always wondered what if I hadn't been out that day. Would she still be alive? The guilt ate at me. The toxicology report showed high levels of antidepressants."

I saw a part of me in my father, who had always placed work before his family. I had done that to Kate on that awful day.

Elena's hand rubbed the area below my neck where my necklace had been. "It's hard to know what goes on in some-one's thoughts. I've seen people who always wear a smile, and yet they're suffering inside. I know this is hard, but you shouldn't blame yourself."

"Thank you for listening."

An understanding smile slid onto her lips. "You've worn the necklace for so long. Seems too bare around here." She brushed her fingers around my neck and collarbone.

"Seven years." I took her hand and interlaced my fingers with hers. "But it's time I give myself permission to heal and move forward." I kissed her fingers. "You inspired me to do that."

Surprise and honesty gleamed in her eyes. "I tried to be

understanding, but it's hard to see your boyfriend wearing another woman's ring, you know? I don't mean to sound petty. I'm just being honest."

My heart swelled. "I appreciate your honesty. I wouldn't want you wearing another man's jewelry either."

Her eyes brightened. "Oh, I almost forgot this." She got out of bed and rushed to her purse, searching for something. She found it and brought over a gray box in her hand. "For you." She placed the box in my hand.

"You proposing to me or something?" I teased.

"Nope. I'm not that kind of girl. Though I'm all about empowering women and all, I prefer a man to get on his knees for me." She wiggled her eyes, and I knew the horrible event she'd experienced had faded from her mind. "Open it. I made it for you."

I removed the lid, dropped it to the bed, and held up a masculine bracelet in my hand. It had small leather straps intertwined together, creating an exceptional texture along with the metal accents and a unique clasp. "It's perfect. Thank you."

Joy burst in me as I watched her put it on. No woman had made me a gift like this. My mother had made me wonderful things, but that was different. I couldn't explain this happiness enrapturing my entire body. It was like watching a new life form in the dark universe, where a new star just emerged revealing itself to the world.

"What did I do to deserve this special gift?"

She shrugged. "Because you braved the dirty obstacle course with me. I knew it wasn't your thing, but you did it anyway. That deserves a reward."

A thought occurred to me. Though I wasn't thrilled about the mud course, after reaching the end, a sense of accomplishment overcame me. But being with her made it more special.

"I'd do the course again with you," I said.

"Okay." She smiled.

Then I asked, "Do you want to talk about it? Your fears?"

She kissed my jawline. "Another day, okay? Right now, I just want you to touch me."

"I'm always happy to comply." I pushed her down onto the bed.

CHAPTER THIRTY-SEVEN

ELENA

FOR THE NEXT WEEK, Orion busied himself at work. I knew he'd shifted his schedule around to join me at The Mudstacle Course, so now his workload had tripled. Every time I walked by his office, he was on a conference call. Ralph had popped in and out of Orion's office, dropping off documents for him. The two men had a rhythm going where all they did was nod at each other, and they both understood. I supposed that was what happened when you've been with someone for so long.

My relationship with Orion had deepened after the mud race in New Hampshire.

Stop meandering around the truth. Just face it.

I closed my eyes and released a sigh. I was falling in love with Orion, and it was terrifying. Even more than the fear of heights. With that phobia, I could avoid high elevations and feel safe. But my feelings for him lived inside of me. They followed me everywhere.

What if he doesn't feel the same way?

For now, I'd keep this secret safe. Sharing it was like

exposing my vulnerable heart to him. I'd never felt this connection with anyone. And no one had shown me affection the way he did. So I knew he cared about me.

But I wanted more. This was something I had to be selfish about.

Our relationship took a wonderful turn after he'd shared about his ex-fiancée. My heart went out to her and him. Mental health was an enormous problem that was difficult to treat. I'd seen too many stories during my time as a reporter.

Everyone dealt with some form of depression growing up. But I could only imagine the extremity of it where the darkness consumed all your hope and purpose.

Sitting in my chair, I twirled the pen around my finger, thinking. *Don't be jealous. Don't be ridiculous. Don't be petty.*

No matter how many times I reminded myself that Kate was gone, I couldn't help the fangs of jealousy sinking into my skin. Last night Orion had called out her name during his sleep. I didn't mention it to him.

Had he truly moved on? Could anyone move on after witnessing his fiancée commit suicide? Did he still love her?

He hadn't said those three words to me. But then again, I hadn't said it to him either. Could I continue this relationship knowing that Kate was always lingering in the background?

What the hell was wrong with me for being jealous of a dead woman?

I zoned in and out. Then I glanced at the knock on the opened door.

"Do you have a minute?" Ralph smiled and walked in.

"Of course." I gestured to the chair in front of my desk. "Please have a seat. What's up?"

"Oh, I need your opinion on something. But first, how are you doing? Is he keeping you busy?"

"I'm good, thank you. Yeah, he's keeping me occupied for sure. You?"

"Always." With gleaming eyes, he held up a finger. "But I'm officially on vacation starting now. He *forced* me to take it."

Laughing, I crossed my arms. "When was the last time you had a vacation?"

"Years ago."

"What?" I gawked at him. "That's wild! Why haven't you taken one?"

He gestured to Orion. "Been watching over that kid since his mom died. He hardly takes a vacation, so I didn't either. But he just threatened to fire me if I don't do it now. I guess it makes sense to take it, right?"

"Gotta listen to that man. He pays you, and he runs the world," I teased.

His eyes beamed. "You have no idea, Elena. He's truly one of a kind. If I had to pick one person to run the world, it would be him."

"Maybe that's why his anxiety is insurmountable." I glanced over at his office.

Ralph looked at me. "But he has you. I've never seen him happier than he is when he's with you."

Joy surged in me, and curiosity rose to the surface. "He told me about Kate. Did you know her?"

His expression softened. "Yes, I did. She was a sweet girl." Then he changed the subject. "I need your opinion on something."

"What is it?"

He showed me two images on his phone. A rose bouquet and one with a variety of flowers. "Which do you like?"

"Who's this for?"

"Evelyn, the woman I love. She's been mad at me for a while."

"Why?" I asked. "What did you do?"

"I work too much. I haven't told her I love her. She wants to settle down." He shrugged. "You know, all the things that a woman wants from a man."

I smiled and studied him. Ralph appeared to be at retiring age. "Why don't you settle down? Life is short."

"Thinking about it. Orion seems happy now, so that's a possibility."

"I suggest you choose both bouquets. Send her the rose bouquet with a message that says *I love you*. Then the other bouquet can say something like, *I want our life to bloom like these flowers. Give me time.*"

His eyes lit up. "Excellent idea. I knew you'd be able to help me."

"The bouquets will make her happy and buy you some more time to decide. Orion will be fine. You can retire and help him on a case-by-case basis. You should discuss it with him."

Ralph rose from the chair, beaming. "Thank you, Elena. I have a lot to think about. Do you mind if I ask you for more bouquet questions later?"

"Anytime."

When he left, I returned my attention to The Condor's murder. My phone rang, and I picked it up.

"Hi, Mona. How are you?"

"Elena, I just remembered something. I forgot about it until a man came into the shop earlier today."

"Who came in?"

"A man who sells life insurance policies. I remembered seeing Pablo meeting him here in the shop."

How was Samuel Donatello connected to The Condor? Pablo didn't need life insurance from Sam's financial firm. It had to be something else. But what?

CHAPTER THIRTY-EIGHT

ORION

"THANKS, AJ," I said to my team leader, who had worked on my special projects team for several years. "Excellent work. Please let the team know I appreciate their efficiency."

"Do you need anything else? If not, I'll return to AI software development for SIGMA."

"Do that. That needs priority because I have a feeling something's about to happen." I lifted my wrist, admiring the bracelet on my hand, wondering what Elena was thinking when she created this for me.

"I'll give you a status update soon," AJ said.

"Thanks."

I tucked my phone into my pants pocket and ran a hand over the bracelet's texture. I'd never worn a bracelet before. The only other accessory on me was the Rolex or the special edition Bugatti watch.

A surge of nerves rose in me as I acknowledged what was happening to me. I was in love with Elena. We had exceptional chemistry, but this love I felt for her was indescribable.

Unmatched. Like a life force that made the universe come alive—limitless.

I looked up at the sky where clouds took on the shape of a flower. It could be a dandelion or some strange-looking animal. Everywhere I looked, I saw aspects of her.

"What do you think about Elena, Mom?"

I believed my mom had orchestrated this from up there. It was something she'd do. She wanted me to be happy.

Despite this acknowledgment, it was still new. I needed time to settle before I could determine my next step. There was danger around me. The Trogyn, and those associated with it, would no doubt target her. She was too important to me.

All the projects I'd set into motion years ago under SIGMA ensured my life and the lives of others would remain free. The Trogyn was one crime organization amongst many others. With money came power, and powerful people wanted to control everything.

Everyone had their agendas, and my agenda was to protect my free will and those I loved. No one liked to be controlled, especially me. There were those who wanted control so desperately they'd do anything to achieve that.

Locating The Condor's killer and destroying as many members of the Trogyn as possible were on the top of my to-do list. With the new information I just acquired, I was able to track down a man named Javier Ortiz. He had been hired by a Trogyn member to kill my teacher. He was an assassin whom I'd interrogated last night, and whose body had been fed to Calvin Wong's animal farm.

Sam had hired Javier to kill The Condor. I'd dug into Sam's several bank accounts connecting him to a sex trafficking ring that I had eliminated last year. Javier got his money, did the deed, and rushed off to the Bahamas. It had taken my team a long time to hack into people's phones for images of Pablo. They had gotten a match this week when Javier played a recording of him in Providence, watching Pablo walk down the street. My SIGMA software had picked it up, and Javier had paid for his part in The Condor's death.

As I turned around to my desk, I saw a flash of color in the corner of my eye. I looked into the sky, where a little rainbow appeared between two clouds.

My chest constricted. "Thank you, Mom."

I didn't always believe in these signs from another world, but my mom had taught me to keep an open mind. And right now, that was her answer.

I wished she were still around to meet Elena, the first person who eased my anxiety after my mom passed. Kate was too much like me, so she couldn't help me. I didn't blame her. I only wished I could've helped her.

Elena was healing me just by being with me. She showed me how thoughts were like birds. Sometimes you just have to let them go and see where they take you.

I walked over to Elena's office and found her eyebrows furrowed while looking at a folder.

I knocked, and she looked up and smiled. Warmth spread all over my chest.

"All done with all your conferences?" she asked.

"For now. How are you doing?"

"I think I found a link between Sam and The Condor and all the people who committed suicide."

I already knew what she was going to tell me. I hadn't told her about Javier or what I'd done to him. Keeping her safe was always my top priority.

"Excellent. Tell me later. Right now, I want to show you something." I reached out my hand to her.

She got off her chair and took my hand. "You look suspicious. What's going on?"

I smiled. "Not suspicious at all . . . just appreciative of life. Of what I have."

She glanced around the room, pretending to look for something. Then she turned back to me. "What have you done to my Orion? This is unlike him."

"There are many versions of Orion," I smirked. "Consider yourself lucky you get to have all of him." I led her back into the Cosmic Lounge. "Let me show you The Roc."

It was time for her to see this other side of me.

"Is it a thing or a person?"

"Both."

CHAPTER THIRTY-NINE

ELENA

I HADN'T STEPPED into this room since that last time. It held both negative and positive memories. It was strange how the body remembered the negative experiences more.

Orion looked at me. "What's wrong?"

I glanced at the wall where he'd kissed me, but also dismissed me. "Just trying to forget a memory."

He wrapped his arms around me. "Don't erase it. Think of it as a critical moment for our relationship. That day was the day I wanted you so badly, but didn't have the courage to face it." He drew back. "I'm sorry I hurt you that day. I was a mess too. It was all because I wanted you."

His confession completely shifted the energy in the room. How could I not feel better with that admission?

Orion was a conundrum that surprised and intrigued me more each second.

I smiled. "So who or what is The Roc?"

"You're talking to him." He smiled. "He's your boyfriend. Other than Ralph, you're the only person who gets to see this room."

My heartbeat quickened. I'd never felt so important to a man until now.

Orion took my hand, leading me to a wall with a dark forest mural. The soft sensor lights illuminated the area and the painting. I hadn't noticed how beautiful it was during my first visit. I'd been too occupied with the starry ceiling. But now I could see and sense the peacefulness that emanated from the forest painting.

With his index finger, he tapped different points on the mural—a red leaf, a green leaf, an orange leaf, a butterfly that blended into the trees until his finger pointed to it. Then his finger moved to a bird perched on a tree branch, a squiggly vine, and a blooming flower on a floral tree. Then he placed his palm onto the trunk of a maple tree. Light radiated around his hand as though reading his palm print.

Something clicked from behind the wall, and the forest painting shifted, looking different. A part of the wall slid to the side, revealing another wall that also moved aside as he stepped in.

I didn't dare blink or move, fearing I'd miss something important. Orion was showing me his secret room—he was showing me his other self.

As we stepped in, a hallway opened and lights illuminated, revealing a cozy room fully furnished with comfy couches.

Stone statues, marble figurines, and unique abstract art were displayed all over the massive room. I walked around the room and examined the intricate art pieces.

I'd always wondered what was on the rest of the floor because the office only occupied a small portion of the entire floor.

"Is this your collection of fine things?"

"It's one of them."

"You've stolen these things?"

"Some of them," he said.

"How many rooms like this do you have?"

He lifted a shoulder. "One or two on every continent."

"You don't have one on Antarctica. There's nothing there." I laughed.

His serious expression had my mouth dropping.

"You've got to be kidding me." My eyes widened with intrigue.

"That could be one of our future trips." He touched my face gently.

I didn't know why I was so fascinated that he had something in Antarctica.

"Why there? It's freezing."

"There's an office that nobody knows about. Just because you don't read about it in the news doesn't mean it doesn't exist. For safety reasons, it's kept from the media." He tipped my chin up and brushed his lips against mine. "A lot of things are kept from the world, and some of them belong to people who have ill intentions."

"Do you have those intentions?" I asked, trying to piece together this profound man who had captured my heart.

"My intention is to stop the people who are trying to harm us."

"I don't understand what you mean."

"There are things you don't know, Elena." He pointed to a black rock on a pedestal. "This is shungite crystal originally from Russia. I took it from a man who's developing a system to manipulate the properties of water. When ingested, it changes the brainwaves—making it more susceptible to control. The changes are subtle, but over time, the brain gets used to it."

I made a disbelieving face. "Is that even possible?"

"Of course it is. This crystal is pure, and the frequency it emits is potent. If used in the right way, this crystal can maintain the purity of water, heal the body in miraculous ways." He looked at me. "But if it's being used in the wrong way, our society will become mindless, falling prey to those who want to control us. What we eat and drink. How we live our lives."

"Wow." I didn't know what else to say.

He placed a hand on the crystal that was the size of my fist. "My mother told me about it because she read the man's natal chart and saw his intentions. The man leads one of the largest energy companies in the world and had asked her to delineate a good time frame to announce the new project. She told him the wrong dates."

When my grandmother was alive, she told me that astrologers and even psychics could predict a good day to get married or start a business.

"This man is also part of a dangerous organization called The Trogyn, with members all over the world."

"You should take everything that belongs to them."

"I try, but the elite members aren't easily traceable. They have other members like Samuel Donatello to do the work and take the fall."

The wheels in my brain turned and turned, making a connection. "So you're in Antarctica because there's water there and no one's around. What exactly are you doing there?"

Orion smiled. "I admire your brain, Madame Sarcasm. You can connect things easily." He went over to a refrigerator and pulled out two containers. One had a black crystal inside it, the other didn't.

He offered me the container with the black crystal. "Try it. This water has been purified by the shungite crystal and energized by sunlight." He pointed to a table with light beaming down into an indoor pool. "You'll taste the difference."

I sipped the crystal-infused water. "Wow. I can taste the freshness. My body also feels more energized." Then I tried the container without the crystal. "It's tasteless. I didn't feel anything."

"I'm trying to preserve the true healing powers of water. Because if I don't, there are people who will start charging a lot of money for water, which should be free. Before you know it, they'll start charging you for grass, trees, and for the air that you breathe, which should always be free to everyone."

"Can people do that?"

"Of course they can."

"How?" I was trying my best to understand everything, but having a tough time.

"By creating a circumstance where you *will* need their products or services."

I still didn't understand.

"If you want to sell clean air, then you must first pollute it. If you want to sell clean water, then you must first contaminate it. And you need to do this slowly by creating catastrophic scenarios that seem natural. There's equipment that can alter weather. And Mother Nature is a powerful force."

I stood there, speechless.

"How can you alter weather?"

"Operation Popeye. You can read about it online, but most people dismiss it as irrelevant." He looked at me. "Weather manipulation is real. Arrow was in the military. He knew about it and the other programs they had. Operation Popeye extended the monsoon season for Northern Vietnam during the Vietnam War. They created more rainfall, flooded rivers, disrupting supplies to soldiers, and so on. There are machines that can create extreme moisture in the sky. Militaries around the world have this equipment. It's just not talked about."

I couldn't fathom what he was telling me. People had time for that shit? I should know better from all the inhuman stories I'd encountered over the years. Despite that, I believed there was goodness in the world. I wanted to believe that.

Perhaps he was being paranoid? There were shows on the internet about conspiracy theories and other weird stuff, but I'd never paid any attention to them.

"I'm not trying to dismiss anything. It's just hard for me to grasp what you're saying." I looked at him. "Is there proof?"

"I have that equipment, Elena. But I choose not to use it. Not in those ways. My company, SIGMA, is more advanced than NASA and NOAA. I have the technology because I want to understand it, learn its complexities and capabilities. This way I can plan and anticipate the enemy's next step and how to stop them."

"You have enemies?"

"Of course I do. People who disagree with what I do are enemies. There are a few of them, and they're extremely wealthy. Wealthier than me. You don't hear about them, but they run the show behind the scenes."

Who could be wealthier than Orion, who was a quadrillionaire? Amazed, I glanced around the room, pondering on the eclectic collection.

He knew what I was wondering and said, "Yes. Everything in this room—and all the other rooms around the world—is stolen from those who have hurt people and plan to do worse. Sometimes I take things that aren't tangible—ideas, formulas—and make them better. My version. Does that make me a bad person?"

I waited a beat, letting the question hang between us. Did he believe I saw him that way? Did he see himself that way?

"No," I said with conviction, touching his face. "It makes you an *extraordinary* person. You care in your own way. I understand you better now."

His anxiety had stemmed from so much more than what he'd told me. It wasn't just the stressful childhood crammed with tough classes and strenuous activities. It was also his innate ability to foresee dangerous things and gathering all the data to create an action plan to *protect* and *defend* what he believed in. He had a good heart.

"That was the intention." He smiled, looking more relieved. "I have more to share with you, but I think this is enough for now."

Orion had resources most of us didn't, and I was so proud he was using them to better the world. I'd always considered those with privilege didn't do enough. Or care enough. But today, this man who filled my heart with love proved me wrong.

He was so brilliant, shedding light on things I had never even considered. It blew me away.

With emotions filling me, I embraced him, hugging him

so tightly, he muttered, "I think my liver just moved to the other side of my body."

Loosening my embrace, I laughed. "Can I come into this room whenever I want?"

"Yes, I'll give you the code."

A light bulb flashed, reminding me of the question I'd wanted to ask earlier, but had forgotten when all this wonder took over.

"You were tapping at little bits on the wall. What were you tapping? Was that the code?"

He nodded. "The seven major stars that outline the hunter in the Orion constellation." He tallied them with his fingers. "Alnitak, Alnilam, Mintaka—those are the three stars that make up his belt—Meissa, Betelgeuse, Bellatrix, Saiph, and Rigel."

Amused, I stared at him. "You're such a nerd. No one is going to decode that."

"Good. That's the idea."

There was no way I'd remember the code. I'd need him to sketch out a map for me to enter this room. I spun and studied the room, realizing I could spend all day here and not get bored.

"There's so much to explore here," I said. "Unique and magical things that could make this world better. Inspiration, innovation, new technology, and concepts that haven't been introduced yet." I looked at him. "It's like I'm wandering inside your mind. It's beautiful and scary. Thank you for inviting me."

"You're welcome." He took my hand—a gesture I loved— and swung it back and forth as we wandered around the room some more.

I'd held hands with my previous partners, but it didn't

seem as intimate as it did with Orion. Everything done with him was amplified tenfold. His presence alone heightened my senses.

We walked by sculptures, a dagger with various gems on the handle, a necklace that looked really expensive, a book encased in a glass display, and so much more. It was like a curated Orion museum, and I was a child in awe.

"Don't tell me those are ancient scriptures." I stopped at a stone tablet with hieroglyphics etched on the surface.

"From the Great Pyramid of Giza," he said casually, as if it was normal to have something that had been inside a pyramid.

"From the Great Pyramid of Giza," I repeated, gawking at him. "I can't believe it. You're lying."

"I don't lie." He eyed me. "Not to those who matter to me."

I was going to ask why he had the tablet and how he had retrieved it, but it didn't matter. I was in love with the best thief who ever existed. If he showed me a royal crown from some dynasty from the seventeenth century, I'd shrug it off as though he'd just told me the weather for the day.

My goodness. I'd come a long way. I'd always wanted to uncover the truth to a mystery, and Orion Reimann was the biggest mystery in this lifetime for me.

"What's the gemstone?" I walked over to a purple gemstone sitting by itself inside a glass display. I saw it sparkle from afar.

"It's the purple taaffeite gemstone, rarer than diamonds."

"It's so pretty." The light purple with a flicker of pink called to me. "And who did you steal this from?"

"I actually bought this at an auction years ago."

"Oh." At least I got to see one item he'd purchased. "It's

going to take me some time to absorb all of this, okay? I have a lot of questions."

"Take all the time you need." He smiled, looking as though he knew I'd react this way. "Ask away."

"What's the significance of The Roc? Who gave you that name?"

"It's a mythical bird that represents power, freedom, and transcendence. Stories link it to myths from the Middle East and Madagascar. The giant bird has powerful claws large enough to fly away with an elephant. The Condor had a fascination with birds. He thought I had qualities of The Roc." He shrugged. "He was an interesting man who saved me from myself. I think thievery saved him too."

The sadness in his voice pricked at me. I kissed him on the cheek. "We're getting close to finding his killer. He'll get the justice he deserves."

"Sam hired an assassin to kill The Condor. But I want the man who directed Sam to do it."

He knew so much more than me. "When did you find this out?"

"Just recently. You can focus your research on the life insurance scam. I'll cover The Condor."

"Okay," I said, then teased him, "so it was just you and The Condor taking over the world back then?"

"The Raven is my brother-in-arms, but he's been retired for a while."

"When do you plan on retiring?"

He considered me, and his pupils darkened. "Not sure yet. But I haven't felt the urge to steal anything lately. I've got what I need and want with me." He squeezed my hand.

We arrived at a wooden coffee table with a leather

loveseat facing it. The table had intricate etchings around it. A gunmetal box sat on the table.

"Have a seat." He nudged me down, sitting beside me. He reached for the box the size of a shoebox and slid it in front of me. "Of all the things I've stolen, there's one thing that's the most precious to me. You can't forget your first." He tapped the box. "I've never shown this to anyone but The Condor. I want to show you how it all began. How The Roc was born."

Orion didn't know what this moment meant to me. To see the very thing that created him was . . . sacred and indescribable. I didn't know why but tears filled my eyes. I did my best to hold them back.

He typed in a code into the lock. When it clicked, he nodded for me to lift the lid.

I placed a hand on the lid, and my hand trembled for no reason. Meeting his eyes, I smiled. "I feel like a thief looking into another thief's treasure chest."

"You're no thief." A chuckle escaped him. "Not yet anyway."

Inhaling a breath, I lifted the box to see a black velvet box inside of it. I took the box out, removed the top lid that didn't have a lock, and gasped. For a moment my heart stopped—and then it galloped.

"Isn't it beautiful? That leaf brooch was my first steal when I was a teenager. I accompanied my mom to Providence that year."

Tears streamed down my face. I couldn't believe what I was seeing. I met his eyes. "It's not a leaf. It's an abstract wing." I choked. "It's *my* brooch."

"What?" His eyebrows furrowed, looking perplexed.

CHAPTER FORTY

ORION

I'D BEEN SHOCKED many times in my life, but this was the most beautiful surprise that could ever happen to me. I'd met Elena all those years ago and didn't know it. It was before I even connected with Madame Sarcasm.

"You were at the park with another kid. I didn't see your face clearly. Everything happened so quickly that day. I targeted you because you weren't with a crowd of people. I was so nervous."

"Can I take it back? I'm gonna steal it if you say no." She tucked it behind her back.

I grinned. "You're not stealing it—it's yours. Take it. Thank you for letting me borrow it all these years."

Elena held the brooch to her chest, smiling and looking so beautiful my heart almost burst. "I can't wait to show my mom this. She'd be thrilled to see this again."

"I should say I'm sorry, but I'm not." I cupped her face and kissed her gently. "It brought us together."

She nodded. "You never know what life has in store for you just around the corner. Just when I thought I'd lost it forever, it's returned to me in the most profound way." She paused and studied me.

I could see the wheels in her head turning. She wanted to say something to me, but settled on something else. The emotions in her eyes revealed a lot about her. I respected her space and didn't question it. Eventually she'd tell me.

"I was with Elliot that day," she said. "We were going to attend a citywide ping-pong tournament. I didn't realize I'd lost it until I got home."

My phone rang, and I pulled it out of my pants pocket, glancing at the number.

"Hi, Ralph. Aren't you supposed to be on vacation?"

"I'm packing up. But I thought you'd want to know Sam is dead. His body was found floating in the Providence. A boater discovered him. Do you need me to do anything?"

"There's nothing more important than for you to go back to Sweden and make Evelyn happy. She loves you. Show her. We have other trusted members on our team. Go home."

"Okay. Okay. All the info I have on him is on the shared drive."

"Thanks." I tucked the phone away.

"Is everything okay?"

"Yes and no," I said. "Sam is dead."

I'd planned on speaking to him and Carlos separately. But now I had to shift to Plan B.

"Oh my God." Elena clamped a hand over her mouth. "Who do you think killed him?"

"A man like him has a lot of enemies. Could be anyone."

But I had a feeling it was The Trogyn.

"Let's go back to my office. I found some things that linked Sam to the life insurance scam with several banks."

Inside her office, I pulled the chair beside her so I could

look at her computer screen. She slid the manila folder over to me. "The interviews I did with people who live within the vicinity of The Condor's apartment are in there. One acquaintance was very helpful. She called me earlier today."

Elena briefed me on the info from her conversation with Mona.

"Sam works for Apex Insurance and Financial Investments, which is part of Orange Leaf Investments, which is part of Norwell Bank, which falls under Stockholm Bank."

"From Stockholm, Sweden?"

The Reimann Sienna Bank owns Stockholm Bank. I needed to have a meeting with my father before I called a board meeting.

"Yes." She nodded. "It appears the people who died were coerced into suicide. I interviewed a family who wants to remain anonymous. The son recorded a conversation his father had with a banker. The banker blackmailed him with some embarrassing information. The man said he didn't have money to continue paying for his life insurance. He was told to pay the early termination fee or they'd release personal information about him on the web. He didn't have money to pay them." Sadness strained her face. "His family—his children—didn't know he was gay. And he'd rather die than face their judgment. It's really sad."

I'd never met a journalist who cared as much as she did. If more people cared like her, this world would be a better place.

"And the banker cashed in the life insurance."

"Exactly." She pressed her lips into a thin line. "The car accidents I'd been investigating were connected to the scams too."

I remembered spotting Elena on the day an SUV had smashed into an eight-wheeler.

"But I don't really understand how it works," she said. "Does the banker route the money to his own account?"

"There are many ways to hide it so that it doesn't seem like the bank is behind it. They need to keep it safe from probing eyes like tax audits, the media, and such. It's not that hard to hide money if you know how to do it."

"You know how?" she asked, but then lifted a hand. "Never mind. I'm talking to the King of Thievery here." She leveled her brown eyes at me. "My thief knows all the secrets, right?"

I smiled, loving that she accepted all of me.

"I can share some of those secrets with you." Leaning in, I nuzzled her neck, inhaling her delicious scent. "For a price."

Laughing, she squirmed away. "I don't think I can afford your asking price, *sir*."

"Keep calling me sir, and I'll give you a freebie."

"Stop it." Elena shoved me away. "We're having a serious conversation here. We need to sort this out before more people die. I want to give the family the justice they deserve." She rattled off several bank names. "Stockholm Bank is from Sweden. Have you heard of it?"

"Yeah. I'll look into it," I said. "Why don't you start the article for Musepaper? Call it *Bank Forcing People to Suicide* or *Life Insurance Scam from Banks Around the World*. Make this article be the next breaking news before any other news outlet."

"But Musepaper is just an online newspaper," she said.

"That's okay. Show the world that a small company can

achieve something the giants can't. Don't forget to introduce Madame Sarcasm to the Musepaper."

She stared at me in wonder. "I'm amazed at how fast your mind works."

"I've had a lot of practice. I want you to focus on Musepaper going forward. You've done enough for The Condor. Thanks for your help."

"You're welcome." She twisted her lips. "I guess this means my contract is up. We won't be working together anymore."

"Says who?" I spun her chair to face me. "I'm an investor in Musepaper, remember? Starting tomorrow, you're getting paid to work on your article."

Her eyes brightened. "But nothing's been confirmed yet."

"The terms of my interest will be in your inbox by the end of the day tomorrow. Review them. Let me know if you want anything revised."

"I suppose I don't need to send out my resume now."

"No, you don't. Do what you love and don't worry about the financial portion of it. Has your uncle reached out to you after that day at your mother's house?"

She shook her head. "No."

"Good. If he does, I want to know. I'm taking care of your debt—which shouldn't have been a debt to begin with."

She sighed. "You don't have to take on my burden. It makes me feel guilty. I don't want you to think I'm taking advantage of you."

"If I don't take care of the woman I love, then who should I take care of?" The words came out easily, naturally. I'd debated on when I should tell her, but I realized life was too short, and I didn't want to miss the chance to let her know how I felt. This moment was as good as any other moment. The sooner she knew, the sooner she didn't have to question my actions.

Elena sucked in a breath, stared at me for a long moment, and then she smiled. I could see a variety of emotions churning in her eyes, starting with surprise, hope, excitement, confusion on how to respond, and the relief of settling on sarcasm.

"What did you say, *Sir Slingshot?*" Her eyes sparkled with mischief as she got off her seat to settle onto my lap. "Say it again."

"I love you." I cupped her behind, shifting her so she could feel my cock pulsing for her. "You're like a nebula, bright and colorful in my dark sky. On my darkest days, all I have to do is think of you and I see a way out. You make the darkness seem insignificant because you exist. You remind me of the wonders of the universe—that there's something sacred, mystical, and inexpressible. I feel so much in my heart, but I can't fully express it in words."

"Orion . . ." A stream of tears slid down her beautiful face. "You're doing a fine job expressing your feelings. When did you get so poetic?"

I caught the gleaming stream with my knuckle. "When you lured me with your brooch."

"I guess I know the way to a thief's heart." She laughed, moving her hips to taunt me. "I love you too."

CHAPTER FORTY-ONE

ORION HAD a meeting with his friends to talk about Samuel Donatello's death and his connection to The Trogyn. There were a lot of moving pieces. He didn't want me too involved with the crime organization and told me to focus on Musepaper.

After organizing all the information I had regarding the bank schemes, I took a break.

I sat in my kitchen and opened a recipe book that hadn't been touched in years. I wasn't a good cook. I didn't really like doing it, but mostly I didn't have time. But today, love and hope rose in me. I wanted to cook a traditional meal for him. *Lomo saltado* was a stir-fry dish with seasoned meat, french fries, onions, tomatoes, and peppers served with rice. I'd learned it from my mom a while ago.

Orion said he loved me, and I told him I loved him. Smiling, I looked around my home, appreciating what I had. Love truly changed the energy around a person, and I felt the bliss in my heart and everywhere I looked. I had to notify the girls that the mission The Thief Who Loved Me was completed!

I loved my messy home, but I should clean it up a bit. Orion preferred order and organization. I could find everything I needed in his office. His suite was just as neat. I sorted through a pile of old mail and discarded things I didn't need.

Satisfied with my cleaning job, I looked in the refrigerator for ingredients, but there was nothing. Orion and I had been ordering out most nights. Not wasting any time, I drove to the grocery store two blocks away, grabbed a cart, and searched for my ingredients.

Thoughts swirled in my head about the bank scheme, recipe ingredients, Musepaper, and the anticipation of telling the girls about my successful mission. I crashed my cart into a man with a cast on his arm. He stood beside his wife, who was driving the cart full of groceries.

"Oh my God!" I cried. "Are you okay? I'm so sorry. I should've paid more attention."

"Don't worry about it," he said.

I turned to the red-haired woman. "So sorry."

"It's okay." Her eyes warmed. "Life gets busy." She placed a hand on his back. "He's a strong man. A shopping cart won't hurt him."

The guy looked at me. "Have a good day."

"You too." When they disappeared from the aisle, I blew out a breath and muttered to myself, "Need to pay attention. Don't let happiness blind you."

As I wandered down the meat section, I spotted two of my nosy neighbors. One was recently divorced, and the other had broken up with her boyfriend. I heard all this from a neighbor I'd bumped into when I stopped by the post office to mail the check to Uncle Carlos.

I didn't hang out with my neighbors, but they knew I'd

worked for the news station. Right now, I didn't want to have a conversation with them.

As I swerved my cart around, I heard, "Elena."

Shit.

Splashing fake surprise on my face, I turned around to see Melissa, who had cropped brown hair, and Brittany, with her bleached-blonde hair worn in a ponytail.

"How are you both?"

"Good," said Melissa.

"Sorry to hear there's no more Uncover the Truth," Brittany said. "Beauty Secrets Galore has taken its slot. Chantel is okay, but she can be annoying."

"There are so many changes to Channel Seven News. What have you been up to?" Melissa asked.

This was the perfect opportunity for me to promote my Musepaper and address any rumors that had already started to circulate.

"Oh, I've moved on." I smiled. "I'm working for this online newspaper called the Musepaper. It's an up-and-coming news outlet that tells the truth. There's a juicy article coming out soon. You should check it out."

"Let me look." Brittany scrolled on her phone.

"Who's the guy that's been coming to your house?" Melissa asked.

I thought gossip only occurred in a small town, but I was wrong. I lived on a dead-end street, and there were only six homes there. These women often took walks together in the neighborhood. I wasn't surprised they'd noticed Orion.

"He's my boyfriend."

"He's cute." Melissa pursed her lips. "Does he have any siblings?"

I laughed and told them no. We chatted for a few more

minutes, then I excused myself to get ingredients. It felt good to declare I was with Orion.

Rushing back home, I made rice, prepared the ingredients, and stir-fried the strips of beef and pork sirloin and vegetables. The house smelled delicious. Then I cleaned up some more.

I needed to remodel this home when I had more time and money. A bigger office space, expand the back deck to include an indoor greenhouse so I could cultivate dandelions all year round. I could even start a section about gardening for healthy living on Musepaper. Ideas popped into my head, making me smile. *One thing at a time, Elena.*

I'd need an interior designer to help me make this home more suitable for work and living. The girls could give me a recommendation.

Elena: *Hey, do you have an interior designer you can recommend?*

Audri: *I have a couple. Sending their links to your email.*

Michelle: *I've used Audri's interior designer too.*

Kiera: *How's the mission going?*

I beamed and shared the good news.

Bursting with pride and joy, I got out supplies to make something special for Orion. I giggled like a foolish girl in love as I wrote on the tiny strips of paper and folded them.

CHAPTER FORTY-TWO

ORION

I MET with an acquaintance at the Providence Police Precinct to gather some details about Samuel Donatello. I didn't trust my acquaintance, but he was useful. Now that his bank account was a few thousand dollars richer, I could see Sam's dead body. It had contusions around his neck and wrists. He was hanged to death, his body tossed into the river.

I got to my car and reviewed the file Ralph had sent me. Then I opened the recordings I'd initiated on the day I broke into Sam's house and saved those two girls. The girls had moved to another state with a nice settlement. I wondered if the settlement had escalated Sam's death. The asshole should've been in jail, but I supposed this outcome was karmic enough.

I had planted a tiny camera on the cat's collar. It was just intuition that had me wondering what Sam knew.

I searched for a clip where I could see Carlos in Sam's home. Most of the recordings picked up strange sounds and voices. But there was a recording where the cat jumped on the couch and captured Carlos clearly. I didn't need to know what he talked about. All I needed was a clip as proof of what I planned to do.

I drove to a convenience store just outside of Providence. The shop was a front for drugs and money laundering. On a late Friday afternoon, Carlos occupied a joint he owned and ran. The shop was financed through Stockholm Bank, which Elena discovered to be connected.

I parked my black SUV a block away in the parking lot of a plaza with a family restaurant, laundromat, and a hair salon. I walked to the convenience store and entered. A woman was at the register paying for bread and milk. Three men sitting at the table in the far corner stopped chatting when they saw me.

A man with long dark hair wearing a black shirt and dark pants strode up to me. Up close, I saw a tattoo of a cross on his neck and wondered if he had that to protect himself from all the sins he'd committed?

"How can I help you, *amigo?*" He smirked, sizing me up.

I wore a dark suit made of Kevlar materials. At a glance it looked like a regular Armani suit. My closet was filled with a variety of Kevlar apparel. I had a team developing a more advanced version that incorporated elasticity within the fabric for better ease and movement. During a battle, those qualities secured safety and victory.

"I'm here to see Carlos. We have business to discuss. Tell him The Condor is here with a proposal."

"He didn't tell us he was expecting anyone," said Cross Tattoo.

"Are you his wife? Does he always share his agenda with you?" I asked with a straight face.

He dismissed me with a laugh, and his two buddies approached.

The bald guy wearing a T-shirt promoting an alcohol brand stepped up to me. "If you want bread or milk, go down the street. We're closed for business."

Then he placed his hand on my arm, trying to nudge me out. I gripped his wrist and twisted it, cracking bones.

"Don't put your dirty hands on my expensive suit unless you can afford two hundred thousand dollars. Got that?" I seethed and released him, adjusting my suit. Then I looked up at the camera perched in the top corner of the room.

I knew Carlos was watching me from the camera. *Bastard.* If he wanted a show, I'd give him one.

The third man charged at me with a fist, which I blocked. Then I pounded three punches into his face. A tooth flew out of his mouth and clanked to the floor. He reached for a knife on the counter by his plate and came at me. I blocked it with my forearm, grabbed his other arm, twisted it, and yanked the knife into my hand. Then I stabbed the knife into his thigh.

A scream erupted, and the other men stood back.

"Don't fuck with me." I shoved him away, and his comrades caught him.

Cross Tattoo tossed a towel to the injured guy to stop the bleeding.

"*¡Mata el jodido pendejo!*" the wounded guy shouted to his friends in Spanish. He extracted the knife from his thigh.

Kill the fucking asshole!

"*Debes cuidarte esa herida antes te que mueras desangrando, cabrón,*" I replied and was grateful for all those years spent learning multiple languages.

He should take care of that wound before he bled to death, fucker.

The men appeared shocked that I could speak their tongue. I didn't want to waste time and walked up to the camera, looking right into it.

"I'm not here to fight. I'm here for a decent proposal, but if you're not interested, that's fine. Sam's body was found recently. I doubt he fell off a boat. Perhaps The Trogyn have something similar planned for you."

Then I turned my attention to the men, glaring at me with violence. "Do you think I came here alone? If anything happens to me, or if I don't inform them of my safety, there will be a swarm of armed men charging in here for bread and milk."

It wasn't a lie. I'd alerted my team of my whereabouts. But I had exaggerated on swarming in for food. This visit should have gone smoothly, but Carlos was probably too terrified of people looking for him now.

As I headed to the door, Carlos appeared from an aisle. "Let's go to the back and talk."

He wore a gray suit looking like a man in charge, but his face was strained with anxiety. The fatigue in his eyes told me he hadn't slept much.

Inside a room that smelled of leather and cigars, Carlos gestured me to a brown leather chair. I sat back, watching him at the mini bar counter.

"What do you want to drink?" he asked.

"I'll pass, thanks."

He walked over with the bottle of whiskey and a glass, settled on the couch, and poured two fingers, gulping it down.

"I apologize for my men's behavior. They've been on edge lately."

"Seems like you are too."

He flicked me an annoyed look. "Why are you here?"

Leaning forward, I held up two fingers. "One, Elena no longer owes you anything. That debt is void. I looked at your contract, which was signed by her father. Nowhere on it does it say the debt must be paid by his family."

He opened his mouth to reply, but I held up my hand. "Your lawyer can argue the clause on the contract, but no judge will agree with you. Especially the ridiculous late fees. If I were you, I wouldn't want the spotlight on your illegal business right now."

A muscle twitched in his jaw.

"The debt is a minor issue compared to what's troubling you. Am I right?"

He flared his nostrils.

"The second reason I'm here is because you and Samuel Donatello concocted a life insurance scheme to steal money from a bank."

I didn't go into details that Stockholm Bank was owned by my family.

"Sam did it all on his own."

"Is that why his body was floating in the Providence River?"

I turned on my phone, clicked on the saved video, and slid it over to the coffee table.

"Isn't that you and Sam discussing the scheme? You were part of it."

Shock splashed onto his face. "What do you know?"

"I know you and Sam killed many people. You used their vulnerability and made money from their deaths, which you coerced. Who else is part of this scheme? I want all the names."

I left the meeting feeling satisfied because Carlos agreed to give me the names. In an exchange, I'd help him leave this country anonymously.

I gave him forty-eight hours to provide the names of those he'd worked with, including the names of his victims. He'd be paying them all back with interest.

At first, he'd hesitated, but what was the point in having all this money if he were going to be killed by The Trogyn? Who was the elite member inside the Reimann Corporation?

When I'd alerted my father about the life insurance scam, he said he'd look into it. I hadn't heard from him yet.

Anxiety increased in me, but I thought about Elena and it subsided. I couldn't wait to tell her that she owed nothing to Carlos. She'd be getting all her money back with interest.

On the drive home, I pressed the button on my car to call her.

"I'm heading home. Do you need me to pick up anything for dinner?"

"Nope, I'm good. I've made dinner for you, so hurry and get home."

"What did you make?"

"A Peruvian dish called *lomo saltado*."

It had been a long time since I had a home-cooked meal. I'd never driven home so fast in my life.

CHAPTER FORTY-THREE

ORION

AFTER FINISHING my second plate of *lomo saltado*, I felt like the luckiest man alive. "You should cook for me every day."

She smiled. "It's gonna cost you."

"Name your price."

"Well, if you consider lunch and dinner, that's two meals a day, five days a week." She ticked off each finger. "Weekends, we order out. So the cost of the food plus my labor. If you add love to it, it'll be around a hundred thousand dollars a week."

I choked on my tea. "Wow, you're some negotiator, Sunshine. That's a hefty price."

"I forgot to add in the dandelion tea with my special ingredient. That's gonna be an additional twenty thousand dollars." She lifted a shoulder. "I guess I learned from experience—how to inflate money to benefit me."

I sensed a tinge of sarcasm and sadness in her voice.

"For you, I'll allow the scam. Know that I intend to get my money's worth. These meals must come with happy endings." Smiling, I wiggled my eyebrows, which earned me a sexy eye roll.

I reached for her hand. "I have good news to tell you, but let's clean up first."

"There should be more good news in the world. I've got some ideas lined up for Musepaper. Wanna hear about them?"

"Absolutely." I brought the plates over to the sink, loving this casual dinner with her.

I could do this every day with Elena—coming home to her after a long day of work. Her presence was like a calming bath after a strenuous workout, or the gentle breath the body takes during a peaceful sleep. But she was also a powerful jolt that invigorated me. When I lost all hope or energy, I just had to think of her.

The more I fell in love with her, the more terrified I became. My enemies were everywhere, and they'd figure out how important she was to me sooner or later.

I needed to take action to protect her. But right now, all I wanted was to spend a peaceful evening without thinking about danger or death.

"Wanna watch a movie with me later?" she asked while washing the plates, after sharing all the ideas she had planned for Musepaper.

I helped her dry the dishes, noticed a rotting wooden plank on her back deck, and remembered she wanted to update things around the house. "When are you going to hire the contractors to repair the back deck?"

"I'll call them tomorrow and see if they're available."

"I know someone perfect for it."

"Great, thank you!" she said and then gasped as she looked out the window. "Oh my gosh, look!" She toweled off her hands, dragging me out to the porch. "I've never seen the Aurora Borealis. I thought I had to go to Iceland or Alaska, but it's right here in my backyard!" Her face beamed with wonder and love. "How's that possible?"

"There's been a lot of geomagnetic storms lately. It changes the magnetic field around the Earth. Things that were once impossible are now possible."

She turned to me and smiled. "I like achieving the impossible. It makes me think that I've accomplished some-thing magical."

"My team has been reading the Schumann resonance from the powerful solar flares bursting from the sun."

"What does that mean?"

"The Earth is changing, and so are we. Everything is energy, and with this continual bursting, we have to adapt to a massive energy influx. But there are those who would use it to carry out their agenda."

"How?"

I loved how curious she was. "Potent geomagnetic storms have the power to disrupt or even wipe out the electricity on the Earth, which means people could lose power instantly. Think of it this way. If you have gigantic lightning bolts hitting the Earth all at once, what do you think will happen?"

"Everything we depend on will be obsolete. No more social media, no more TV, no phones, hospitals, banking . . ."

Fear swam in her eyes, and I didn't like it. "Why would people do that?"

"To prey on fears and to instill control." I embraced her. "But I have ways to counter that. My team is working hard to develop several energy sources that could sustain a pandemic like this."

"Seems like there are many people with control issues." She drew back and stared at me. "There's so much going on that I don't know about."

"You don't need to know. It's a . . . different playing field —a long game that requires careful steps."

"Which adds more anxiety to your already stressful life."

"But I have the most powerful source of energy with me —you. Sunshine is all I'll ever need."

Smiling, she looped her arms around me and offered me the most beautiful smile. "Guess what, thief?" She rubbed the back of my neck, loosening the tension in my muscles.

Her smile stole my heart while her sneaky hands tucked it away safely.

"What?"

"Empty your pockets, sir. You've stolen something from me." She narrowed her eyes at me.

I lifted my arms, loving how she could switch my mood instantly. "Not sure what you mean, Madame Sarcasm. You plan on interrogating me?"

"Indeed." She lifted my T-shirt and ran her hands over my shoulders, biceps, and abdomen. "You've taken my sanity." She dug a hand into my pants pocket and yanked out a fist of air. "Thief, you've stolen my heart and now you must pay for it."

I chuckled. "What's the punishment?"

"Teach me how you do it." Her eyes gleamed with mischief. "How you steal. The process intrigues me."

"Are you serious?" I arched an eyebrow. "You want to be my protégé?"

"The best way to write about something is to experience it, correct?"

If only she knew what I had planned for her tomorrow.

"I want to learn from the best. I'm an outstanding student." She tugged at the button on my pants. "You said there was something you wanted to tell me."

"You're now a millionaire."

She paused, then gasped, and finally grinned as I told her about Carlos's agreement.

Her eyes gleamed with gratitude. "I should ask how you managed that, but I won't tonight. Right now, I just want to love you for turning an awful situation into something incredibly wonderful."

It was best she didn't ask. I didn't want to describe the violence in the convenience store. Violence and danger had to stay away from her.

"It's best you don't ask, Sunshine."

She looked at me, and understanding gleamed in her eyes. I was truly the luckiest man alive to have a partner who could read me.

"I know what kind of world you dwell in, Orion." She touched my face. "Your success demands certain things I won't understand. This world is a cruel place, and sometimes you have to be worse so you can protect yourself."

"How do you know me so well?"

"From paying attention to everything about you. Most of all, it's because I love you." She palmed me, and I lost my breath. "When you love someone or something, you have this invisible connection to them."

Then she dropped my pants and boxers. It felt strange and sexy as hell, standing naked in her house while she was fully clothed.

"If you want to be my protégé, then you must pass the test first," I breathed.

"Okay." She offered a sly smile. "I've got some ideas. You

let me know how many points I get. I plan on scoring well tonight." She dropped to her knees and loved me with her mouth, tongue, and hands.

Holy fuuuck.

I swore our lovemaking lured in the Northern Lights because I'd never seen colors and stars flickering in the kitchen like I just did.

CHAPTER FORTY-FOUR

ELENA

ORION GAVE me a long blonde wig to wear with a baseball cap. I wore jeans and a Harvard business school T-shirt. And he wore a Boston Red Sox cap and a Red Sox T-shirt with jeans as well. We both had dark sunglasses. He tossed a black backpack into the back seat and got into the driver's side of my Land Rover.

"I understand we're in disguise, but for what?" I asked him, buckling into my seat.

"You're going to solve your case today."

"My case? You need to give me some more details, Slingshot. I don't know what you're talking about."

"You'll see."

"You know you can't just tell me that and expect me not to ask. It's torture."

He smiled. "I like it when you pout. It reminds me of your sexy swollen lips from last night." He took my hand in his. "By the way, you passed the test with flying colors. You're a magnificent student."

Heat blossomed onto my face, and I looked out the

window, smiling. We branded every room in my house. The man had incredible stamina.

Orion pulled into a small street with a hair salon and a convenience store on the corner. We got out, and I glanced around, not familiar with this place. It seemed like a residential area with a couple of local shops.

He slung a backpack on his shoulder and took my hand in his. "If anyone asks, we're college students in love, researching a project."

We walked to the corner store parking lot, cut through the wooded section, and ended up in the backyard of someone's house.

Then I realized what was happening. "I can't believe this."

"You wanted to be my protégé. I'm showing you how it's done. This is the beginner's level."

My heart raced, knowing I was about to commit a crime. It seemed wrong, and yet I couldn't stop myself.

"Whose house is this?" I whispered. "Are there any cameras around? Have you checked out the area already?"

"You make an exceptional thief. You're asking all the right questions." He smiled at me. "We're at Chantel's second house."

"What?" I gasped.

Chantel had created a horrific workplace for me and others.

"She's behind all the rumors about you."

I'd had a feeling, but I didn't have any proof.

He headed to the back deck. "I hacked into her security alarm this morning, so we're good."

These criminal confessions had become the norm to my

ears. I should've been surprised, but I asked, "How do I manipulate this lock?"

He arched an eyebrow. "That kind of question tells me you've been researching techniques?"

I twisted my lips. "I had to get a head start somewhere."

The smirk grew into a grin. "Show me what you learned."

I glanced around. "We have to be fast. What if she comes home?"

"She's on a flight to California this morning."

"Take your time," he said casually, as though he were breaking into his own home. There was no sense of urgency.

However, I was trying my best to tame the nerves wreaking havoc in my body. Fear slid down my spine like an icy finger. I was out of my comfort zone. But this experience would allow me to see and feel all the things Orion had undergone. It was one way of getting to know my thief better.

The heightened excitement and fear overwhelmed me. I could see how they numbed other sensations—numbed his anxiety—bringing the mind to focus on the pivotal moment.

Orion opened his backpack and pulled out a box of tools. "Help yourself."

I opened the plastic box and found a razor, various knives, scissors, pliers, wires, a container of bobby pins, paperclips, and other lock-picking tools.

"I heard a bra wire can pick a lock too."

"Anything that can be bent into a tension lever will work." He gestured to the lock on the door. "That's a pin tumbler lock, which is common in most houses."

"How long did it take you to pick your first lock?"

"Two minutes. The second time was faster."

I gaped at him. "They need to make better locks."

"A lock only provides an illusion of security, Sunshine. If someone really wants to get into your house, they can easily do it. You always need extra security."

"So I'm going to need a security system for my house now?"

"I've already got that covered. Your new system arrives next week."

I scrunched up my face. "Were you going to ask me?"

"May I please buy a security system to make sure my beautiful girlfriend is safe when I'm not around?" he asked with a serious expression that made me annoyed and also warm inside.

"Okay, fine. But please ask me next time. I like to know what's going on in my home."

"Noted."

Of all the tools he had available, I chose the bobby pins because of the video I'd seen.

Smiling, he arched an eyebrow. "Interesting."

"I'm an amateur, so I need an amateur tool." I wagged the two bobby pins in front of him. "The bobby pin is a woman's accessory—not that men can't use it in their hair—and I want to acknowledge that it can get things done efficiently without all the bells and whistles."

He laughed. "More power to the bobby pin."

I spread the wavy and straight ends to a ninety-degree angle and used his razor to remove the rubber tip. I bent the other pin to look like a coffee mug handle, turning it into a tension lever. That was what the guy on the video called it.

I stuck the flat end of one pin into the top of the lock and began my process.

I could feel his eyes on me. "Stop looking at me. You're disrupting my concentration."

He kissed my cheek. "You're the best partner in crime a thief could ever ask for."

After a few minutes of struggling to get the two pins to work properly, I heard the five clicks of the lock pins settling into the barrel. Excitement swelled in me as I turned, beaming at him.

"I did it!" I said, trying my best to keep my tone down. Something was wrong with me for being excited about breaking into someone's house. But I shoved that guilt aside for now.

Pride gleamed in his eyes. "You've got the thief blood in you. You're a natural criminal."

"Shut up." I laughed. "If there is such a thing, it's because I'm spending way too much time with a professional thief."

"You're allowed to rob me of anything, Sunshine."

I rolled my eyes. "Let's hurry before someone comes by."

Inside Chantel's house, Orion led me to the living room.

"How do you know where to go?"

He pointed to the cameras in her house. "After the event at the fashion show, I was curious."

"You were curious about her?"

"No." He smirked. "I was curious about why she hated you so much." He brushed a finger down my face. "But the mudstacle incident was the turning point for me. There's more than jealousy behind the hatred. I hacked into her security system. It didn't take long for me to review the recent recordings to see where she hid the information."

Orion pulled on a pair of gloves and gave me a pair as

well. Then he walked over to the wooden coffee table and pulled a folder from the drawer and gave it to me.

I sat down on the couch and reviewed the bank statements and email printouts. I didn't recognize the man's name on the documents.

"Jason Dudek works for a small bank in Providence. That bank is under the Reimann Sienna Bank. She's letting them use her warehouse to store drugs." She scoffed. "And she accused me of working with the cartels?"

"Sometimes people accuse others of the very crimes they commit. It's a defense mechanism, I guess to distract the attention from themselves."

"Do you think her family knows?"

"Doesn't matter. What matters is this information is already sent to the media. It'll be her downfall."

My chest warmed at the incredible man who was always steps ahead of me. He already had this information, but wanted me to experience the break-in while also discovering Chantel's crimes.

"She targeted me because my show was investigating bank scams." I looked at him, grateful for the information. "Thank you. This means a lot to me."

"This can be another story for Musepaper."

I sighed. "Musepaper will be the talk of New England."

"Of the world," he said. "These banks have international ties."

"Will your family's bank be okay?"

"Yes." His eyes softened. "We're closing in on the corrupt people."

After snapping images of the documents onto my phone, we left the house the way we found it and rushed back to the car.

"I just realized something profound." I traced his chin with my fingers.

"What is it?"

"That you're a complex lock with many intricate parts that somehow work together beautifully."

He smiled at me. "I found the perfect key. It's you. From the very first moment I met you, something clicked in me. The rest is history."

I blushed, and my phone rang.

"It's Rebecca Wright, the HR Manager from Channel Seven News," I told Orion.

"Elena, do you have time to meet tomorrow?"

"Hold on. I have to put you on speaker. My hands are tied up." I winked at Orion. "What's this about?"

"About you returning to Channel Seven. We value your work. The station has been bombarded with viewers demanding your return. We miss you."

Intrigued, I said, "I can be there tomorrow around ten. Does that work for you?"

"It's perfect. See you then."

CHAPTER FORTY-FIVE

IT FELT strange to sit inside the Human Resources conference room of Channel 7 News talking to two members of the HR team who had refused to speak to me when I'd first complained about Chantel.

Rebecca Wright wore a beige suit with dark-rimmed glasses. She sat beside Zoey Stern, her assistant, who had on a bright lipstick that hurt my eyes. The two women smiled, thinking they were giving me a lucrative offer. They weren't, but I let them finish their sentence.

"We plan on making Uncover the Truth even better," Rebecca said. "Moving it to prime time."

Though it sounded nice, I couldn't trust the people here. They didn't have my back when I needed them. The only reason they called me was because news of Chantel had spread like wildfire.

"You never gave me a chance to defend myself regarding the false accusations. Chantel put those drugs in my locker, and you just fired me without an investigation." I looked at each of them. "I don't have faith in Channel Seven anymore. Seems like you're fond of illegal acts, so I'll have to pass."

Coming back to work here was never an option for me. I just wanted an opportunity to tell them how I felt.

Before I left, I went to look for two coworkers I liked, but I learned they were laid off last week. In my car, I drafted an email to both asking them if they were interested in working with me at Musepaper. With Orion's support, I could build a fabulous team to help me succeed.

After stopping by a sandwich shop to pick up lunch, I headed home. When I pulled up to the driveway, I saw two familiar cars. Why were my neighbors here?

I could hear voices in the backyard, but entered through the front door. Then I ambled to the kitchen and leaned against the wall, watching my handsome boyfriend entertaining Melissa and Brittany. Orion was shirtless and sweat gleamed on his body, enhancing his taut muscles. The two women stood nearby as he hammered a plank on my deck.

"You're so handy," Melissa said. "Do you have time to repair my back steps?"

"Sorry, I don't have time."

"Where's Elena?" Brittany asked.

"At work." He smiled as he reached for a towel draped over a chair and wiped his face.

"Do you have any friends that look like you?"

"Unfortunately, no."

I smiled and bit my lip at his arrogance.

The ladies laughed. "So confident."

To save my boyfriend from the ogling women, I called him on his phone, which was sticking out of his back pocket.

A smile beamed on his face as he picked up my call.

"Hey! How are you?" Then he turned to my neighbors. "Sorry, ladies, I've got to go now. Thank you for visiting."

Melissa and Brittany waved at him and walked off the deck.

Orion entered the kitchen, and I walked into his arms. He smelled of hard work, male, sweat. "Thanks for rescuing me."

"I think we need to put up an electric fence. What do you think?" I teased.

"Whatever you want." He smiled and looked at the kitchen counter. "You brought me lunch?"

"Let's sit and have lunch." I poured iced dandelion tea into two cups and briefed him on my conversation with HR and how I'd made two employment offers to two former coworkers.

"I designated two people from my office to assist you with the hiring process." He wolfed down his steak and cheese sub. "They should reach out to you soon."

"Thanks. I thought you were hiring someone to work on my back deck?"

"It's me." He sipped his iced tea, sitting back in the chair and looking masculine and relaxed.

"I didn't know you were handy," I said. He was beautiful, and I wanted to bite him.

"The Condor and Ralph taught me these skills." He finished his sub and wiped his mouth with a napkin. "My father was too busy traveling for work, and he wasn't handy. Your porch is all set."

"Thank you. I've got the best boyfriend."

"Also, I have roofers scheduled for next week."

My eyebrows furrowed. "How do you know I have a leaking roof?"

"You mentioned it the first time I visited your home."

I loved how he remembered those little things. Rising from my chair, I walked over and straddled him, dropping kisses to his cheeks, his lips, and his neck, eventually nipping at the pulse on his skin.

"I just want to bite you."

"Why?" Amusement gleamed in his eyes.

"Because you're absolutely adorable and hot. I can't stop imagining all the scenarios we could roleplay in bed with you as the thief, carpenter, and business entrepreneur."

"And your teacher." He smirked and slapped my ass.

"Yes, Mr. Reimann. How could I forget? Please don't deduct points from my grade."

His phone rang, and he glanced at the number, then picked it up. "What's happened?"

He listened to the person and looked at me. Something twisted in my stomach.

"Send me the details of what you have. Okay. Thank you." He hung up, tapped his phone to check something, and placed it down on the table.

"What happened?" I asked.

"Carlos was found dead in an alley downtown."

"Like The Condor?"

Orion nodded. "Carlos was supposed to give me a list of people's names, but someone got to him quickly."

My phone rang, and my body jerked. A knot formed in my stomach. "Hi, *Mamá*."

"Elena, there's been a fire at the house."

Nausea rose in me. "Are you okay? Are you hurt?"

"Shaken, but I'm okay. Don't worry."

How could I not worry? With Uncle Carlos's recent death, I wondered if the fire was related to his death. What if the people who had killed him went after my mom, thinking she was important to him? Thinking she had what they wanted?

My mind raced with a hundred awful scenarios.

Mom's house was old, but everything was to code. She was usually careful with the stove, so what could have caused the fire?

I looked over at Orion, who wore an impassive expression.

"I'll be on my way," I said, trying not to let fear blind me from thinking clearly. "You can stay here with me."

"No, sweetie. Reid has a furnished apartment I can use until the house is repaired. It's on the same street as Wild Roots, which will make it easier to volunteer. I'll stay there until repairs are done. The entire back porch and storage are gone. The family albums in storage are gone . . .," she choked.

"I have copies of some pictures stored on my computer. Don't worry, I'll make you new albums." I could only imagine the fear and sense of loss my mother was experiencing.

"Okay. Thank you, sweetie. I've got to go now. The detective wants to speak to me."

"I'm heading over." I rose from the chair and looked at Orion who was already standing beside me.

"Everything okay?" His calm voice comforted me immediately.

"There's been a fire at my mom's house."

CHAPTER FORTY-SIX

ORION

WE PARKED on the street and walked over to Mrs. Sanchez's house. Two fire trucks, an ambulance, and three police cars occupied the street in front of the house. Smoke still lingered in the air, but the danger had already been subdued.

I tightened the grip on Elena's hand. "Your mom is fine."

Nodding, she looked at me with tears brimming in her eyes.

I wished I hadn't told her about Carlos's death because it made the situation worse. A wary person like her would assume there was a connection.

Anita Sanchez stood with a group of friends. When she spotted her daughter, she rushed over and embraced her. "I'm okay."

I glanced around, taking in the people that stood nearby. Then I saw him, and the entire situation changed. What the hell was The Raven doing here? I thought he'd retired? Was he responsible for the fire? It made no sense.

He wore denim overalls, a completely different look than

the man who had sat with me at the Wellness Center. That man I'd encountered had danger written all over him, but this man . . . this man was a fucking farmer. The Raven had some explaining to do.

"So glad you're here," Mrs. Sanchez said.

"I'm glad you're okay, Mrs. Sanchez." I smiled. "Who's the guy in overalls?"

"That's Reid Lanaro. I've been working for him for years at Wild Roots. The best boss I've had. He offered to let me stay at his apartment until the damages are repaired."

I turned to Elena. "I'm going to speak to the officers."

She nodded and joined her mom's group of friends.

Who the fuck was Reid Lanaro? To be fair, I hadn't researched my brother-in-arms because I'd never dealt with him. I'd only heard about him through my teacher. Apparently, I missed an important detail.

He met my eyes and walked over. "Hey."

"We need to talk."

Reid and I walked across the street and stood by his truck that was filled with garden tools and three shrubberies.

"Is Reid your real name or another alias?" I studied him with the grown beard. The dark hair was still there, but was loose and messy.

Tucking his hands into his overalls' pockets, he smiled. "It's my real name. When I retired, I tried to make life as normal as possible for Charlotte and the kids."

"How many kids do you have?"

"Two."

"Does she know about your history?"

"Oh, she sure does." His eyes warmed with love. "She was an assassin sent to kill me, but I charmed her instead."

I laughed. "I should've researched you. Are you completely off the grid?"

"Eighty percent of my life is off the grid. The other twenty percent is a promise to The Condor."

"What do you mean?" I envied him for knowing something about my mentor that I didn't. But then again, Reid was his first student.

"Did you know The Condor had a lover?"

"No. We never spoke about his personal relationships. He told me his family had passed away in Peru."

"His parents and siblings did. He fell in love in the States, and her name is Anita Sanchez."

We both looked over at Anita and Elena as they spoke to the police officer and firefighter.

Revelation hit me. "Is Elena his daughter?"

Reid nodded. "Anita thought Pablo had died in an ambush. He didn't know she was pregnant. Pablo was injured and took several months to heal. When he discovered he had a child, he feared Anita and Elena would be endangered if he were near them." He kicked a pebble across the sidewalk. "Our teacher has been watching over them all these years. Which is why he had an apartment in Providence. Keeping an eye on them from a distance."

I couldn't believe what I was hearing. All the tiny pieces were falling into place. Now I knew why I'd been attracted to her on a different level. We had a unique connection. Her biological father had been my teacher. Now I was in love with his daughter.

The Condor saved me back then, and now his daughter healed me.

"Did he ever contact Anita? Does she know he was alive?"

"He visited her once when Elena was born. Anita had remarried, thinking Pablo was dead. Her husband treated her and Elena well, so Pablo stayed in the shadows. He didn't want his enemies hurting them because of him. But then her husband developed a gambling addiction, and Carlos was an asshole. I'm glad he's dead."

I had to inform Elena of this new revelation. How would she react? The father she'd known wasn't her biological father. Regardless, today wasn't the day for that. She was already an emotional mess.

"Do you know who caused the fire?"

He took out his phone and showed me a dead body. I recognized the man who had attacked me at Carlos's convenience store, the one with the cross tattoo.

"He was sent to torch the house. I stopped by to drop off some plants for her and saw him light up a trash can and place it on the back porch. We got into a scuffle. I retrieved information from him before I killed him."

"What info?"

"He had orders to kill Carlos and torch this house."

My eyebrows climbed. "Why the house?"

"Apparently, Carlos's brother hid evidence of him working with an elite member of The Trogyn. Not sure how he got it. But the drive is destroyed." He dug into his pocket and waved a melted flash drive. "It was inside the wall of the back room."

"The laundry room?" I asked.

Reid nodded.

That was why Carlos had stopped by to visit Anita, trying to give her a washer and dryer.

"Carlos also killed his brother because he wouldn't use his wife's savings to pay off his debt."

"What a loving family," I said.

I had to be careful in how I delivered this news to Elena. She'd be crushed.

"You can let her know when you think the time is right."

"Do you enjoy working at Wild Roots? Or is it just a ploy?"

"I love it. It wouldn't have succeeded if I didn't love it. You should stop by sometime. I'll introduce you to my wife Charlotte and my kids, Ava and Logan. She's going to work in the office soon. Our business is growing."

"Is there anything else you'd like me to know?" I eyed him.

"No. The Condor only asked me to watch over his ex-wife and daughter to make sure they're safe." He placed the hand on my shoulder. "They're in excellent hands because of you. You love her."

It wasn't a question.

"I can tell," he said. "Because I had that look when I met Charlotte."

"I wondered if Pablo knew I had a connection with his daughter early on."

"Not sure." Reid shrugged. "But I remember him being thrilled when you showed him the first item you'd stolen. He said he knew the item and the person it belonged to. What did you take?"

"A brooch that belonged to Elena."

I wasn't comfortable about having Elena's mom stay at Reid's apartment. It was best for her to be away for at least a month or until things settled down. What if The Trogyn sent more because they thought there was still evidence hidden in the house? I didn't want to risk it.

After discussing it with Reid, we both agreed she'd be

safer in my condo in Cancun. She could go with two friends. "There's a nursery there that teaches about bonsai and other exotic plants. We can use that as an excuse for her to stay there to learn and bring back to Wild Roots."

"I'll send two of my workers to join her. The ladies will be thrilled."

"Excellent," I said.

By the time we got back to Elena's house, she was exhausted. My mind was crammed with so many things. Danger was here, and I had to shift gears to ensure the woman I love was safe.

She dropped onto the couch, closed her eyes, and released a slow sigh.

"You need a break." I sat beside her, gathering her into my arms. "There's a restaurant that just opened up in town. Let's go on a date."

She opened her eyes and smiled. "Sounds good."

"Your mom is going to be in Cancun at my place, learning about new plants. She'll be safe. I'll have a team renovate her house. No need to worry about that."

After she fell asleep, I had an urgent conference call with the boys and updated them on the recent events, my suspicion of the banks being tied to The Trogyn, and what I planned to do about it.

They agreed to help with whatever I needed.

CHAPTER FORTY-SEVEN

ELENA

AFTER CHATTING with my former coworkers, Amelia Chen and Ruby Anderson, excitement swirled in me. Their enthusiasm inspired a few new ideas. My plan was to have Musepaper up and running by November with some room for fluctuations.

Orion had gone over to Remi's home to meet up with Arrow and Forrest. I had a lunch date with Kiera, Audri, and Vivian at the Krazee Tavern. Michelle and Natalie weren't available.

"So how's your mission going?" Kiera asked.

"We have so much to catch up on." I sipped my iced tea, shoving away all the stress from the past few days to enjoy time with my friends. "The Thief Who Loved Me is complete with success."

The girls stopped drinking and eating, gawking at me.

"Details please." Audri stared at me.

"I've been wondering since our last chat." Vivian grinned.

"C'mon. Tell us!" Kiera exclaimed.

"Trust me, I wanted to tell you. But so much has happened lately." I briefed them on the fire at my mom's house, the bank scam investigation, how I was fired but now working full-time on Musepaper. But I left a lot out as well, like how I'd broken into Chantel's home. That was a secret shared only with my thief.

"That's a lot to deal with. Do you need us to help with anything?" Audri asked.

"I'm okay for now. Oh, I do need images of your upcoming events. I'll have a section for future events so people can mark them on their calendars."

"Will do," they all said.

"So . . . is he excellent in bed?" Vivian wiggled her eyebrows.

"The best." I smiled, thinking of his hands on me. I needed his touch tonight.

Perhaps after our dinner date, I could seduce him . . . rob him of his clothes and sanity.

"Earth to Elena." Kiera waved her hands in front of me. "She's in horny land."

Audri laughed. "Do you love him?"

A sense of warmth cloaked me. "I do. It scares me. Seems like when things become important to me, something awful happens."

"It's natural to feel that way." Kiera picked up a french fry. "Don't overthink it."

"Just enjoy it," said Vivian.

"What's new?" I asked them.

"I'm going to an art show by Nessa Lambert." Vivian swiped on her phone and showed us an image. "She's my new favorite artist. I bought the pink waterlily painting from her."

"Oh, I love that one," Audri said.

"We should all go. Take your men with you. She has a new collection she's debuting." Vivian typed on her phone. "I'll send you the invite now."

My house could use a new painting. I could also get one for Orion's suite. If only these girls knew about his little collection.

My phone buzzed with a reminder of my date with Orion. I was supposed to meet up with him at Eclectic Taste, a new hotspot in town with gorgeous outdoor seating. I swiped the reminder away and checked for Vivian's invite. After registering me and Orion for the event, I continued my conversation with them.

I leaned into the table. "What do you guys know about The Trogyn?"

The cheerful expressions on their faces turned serious.

"I know the boys are trying to destroy their organization," Audri said. "Remi doesn't want me to ask much about them, but I'm worried about him and the others."

"Me too," Kiera added. "The Trogyn's sex trafficking ring is massive and elusive. Did something happen to you?"

I sighed. "My uncle was connected to them, and he just died."

"My uncle worked for them too," Audri added. "He kidnapped me, demanding money."

My mouth dropped open at what family would do to each other for money.

"I know Orion is trying to protect me by not sharing a lot of information."

"Maybe we can help them on the side," Audri said.

"My thoughts exactly." I beamed. "But I don't know where to begin."

"We'll take our time and think of something. If women ran the world, it would be a different place, right?" Vivian asked.

"That's for sure." Kiera agreed.

Gosh, I loved these girls.

"We'll wait until Michelle and Natalie are free, and we can all brainstorm. Think of this as another level of the Super Spy Girls." Audri smirked. "We're more than what meets the eye."

"It's not just about relationships with complicated men." I laughed. "We're upgrading to world events now."

We clanked our iced teas and chatted for another hour until I had to leave to get some more work done before meeting with Orion. I started several articles for Musepaper regarding the events for Audri and Vivian and began organizing notes for the article that would shed light on the worldly bank scams. Feeling the need for something more uplifting, I started brainstorming about Madame Sarcasm's return.

An hour later, I was sitting in the outdoor seating of the Eclectic Taste. I texted Orion that I'd arrived and where I sat so he could easily find me. A band played in the corner. Couples of various ages sat nearby. Pretty vines draped down along the pergola like curtains. The orange and purple hues of the sky made a lovely backdrop to the cityscape.

The waitress came by twice, and I felt bad so I ordered a lemonade. I glanced at my phone, but Orion hadn't replied to me. He'd never been late. The one time he was late was the day I crashed into his car.

I didn't know why, but I couldn't shake off this unease.

"You look so lonely. Are you waiting for your boyfriend?"

I glanced up to see Chantel wearing a summer dress. Shouldn't she be in prison?

"I'm fine, thanks. But you look like a criminal who paid off someone so you can have dinner." Irritation clawed at me. "Are *you* waiting for the police to arrive?"

She smirked and irritated me even more.

"Are you waiting for the police to discover other crimes you were involved with?" I asked with a straight face. "Who did you pay off to keep you out of jail? Or rather, who did you sleep with?"

I hit the spot when indignation splashed across her face. "Did you enjoy my creative endeavor?"

"How many know the Henderson household has a drug dealer in their house? Is that how you make your money? Is that your family's legacy?"

Pissed, she pulled out a chair and sat down without asking for my permission.

"That seat is taken," I said calmly.

"Well, your man is fucking somebody right now." She smirked as though she knew something I didn't. "If I were you, I'd back away now because shit is going down."

I had no idea what she was talking about. And I couldn't trust her. Based on past experiences, she lied about everything. Was she trying to get on my nerves?

"Are you done? You're ruining my evening."

"You should pay more attention to your boyfriend." She made a face. "He's not a one-woman kind of guy. You'll see."

With that, she rose and walked over to a table with a group of women.

Was she trying to annoy me? Or was there some truth in there?

Frustration clawed at me for not being able to shake off her words. She'd planted self-doubts in my head.

A text from Orion popped onto my screen. And it wasn't what I expected.

Orion: *Can't make it. See you at home.*

The self-doubt grew as I drove home.

CHAPTER FORTY-EIGHT

ORION

I HUNG up the phone with Dr. Karl Cederholm and waited for Elena to arrive. My chest ached from the news of my father's dire situation and my missed date with Elena. The guilt tore at me, but I had to deal with an emergency.

I had to maintain composure and clarity to deal with it, otherwise I'd make a mistake.

My hands trembled as I wondered what had happened to my father. As far as I knew, he'd always been a healthy man. Earlier today, he had a horrible allergic reaction to seafood that collapsed his body into a coma. Everyone knew he was allergic to seafood. Like me, Rex Reimann had enemies as well. Probably more because he'd been in the business arena much longer than I had.

My chest tightened again. I didn't realize how much I wanted him to be proud of me until this moment. What if there would never be an opportunity? What if he never woke up from his coma?

Had I been too stubborn to forgive him? To make amends like my mother had always wanted? The emotional instability overwhelmed me, and my mind wandered back to Elena for comfort.

I loved her more than she could ever know. A powerful storm had arrived, placing me in the middle of it. I was trying my best to deal with each issue carefully and cautiously.

In the unpredictable business arena, I was used to instability. The only difference now was that I had more at stake. I was in love. Before Elena, I didn't need to worry about anyone. But now, my world and hers had blended. I'd never wanted the darkness from my world touching hers. But it appeared we were fated. I still needed to tell her about The Condor.

I heard Elena's car pull up to the driveway. A sense of relief swept over me.

Elena entered the house, looking sad and tired. I hated the crease on her forehead, the tight lips and the sagging shoulders. She kicked off her shoes and met my gaze.

I probably didn't look any better because her facial expression changed.

She dropped her purse on the side table and walked up to me. "What's wrong?"

I wrapped my arms around her, inhaling her scent. The familiar floral scent comforted me.

I drew back. "My father's in a coma. Ralph called me earlier. I've been on calls with the doctors, lawyers, and board members of the Reimann Corporation most of the day."

"Oh my God." She placed a gentle hand on my arm, soothing me. "What happened? Do you need to go see him?"

"Yes, I do," I said, noticing the fatigue in her eyes being replaced with concern for me. "Sorry about our dinner date. I didn't get a chance—"

"Don't worry about it." She kissed me. "Do you need me to come with you?

"I would appreciate that." More than she could ever know.

"I'll go pack now."

Hours later we arrived at Central Care Hospital in Sweden. I'd purchased this hospital years ago when it was about to close because of a lack of funding. The doctors and nurses here had treated me and Ralph many years ago when we'd gotten into a car accident. They were efficient, thorough, and not a single detail about a Reimann family member being at the hospital was leaked to the media. I appreciated that. The media liked to put their spin on things, and I preferred my privacy.

I'd made urgent arrangements to have my father transported to Central Care Hospital for his safety and the best care in the world. My father's health situation made me question too many things. I needed time to investigate while the best doctors cared for him.

Elena interlaced her fingers with mine as we walked down the hallway, heading toward his room. Nurse Nancy exited the room with her clipboard and headed toward us. She was part of Dr. Karl Cederholm's team. My parents were familiar with his team.

Two undercover guards stood nearby, while four other men wandered this floor. More were stationed throughout the hospital. This was a precaution for a suspicion that had percolated my mind since the news broke. I'd rather be wrong than sorry. Though my relationship with my father wasn't the best, he was still my father. Whoever was responsible for this would answer to me.

"How is he? Any improvements?" I asked Nancy, who wore her blonde hair in a bun.

"He's stable," she said. "Don't worry. We have a close eye on him. I'll keep you posted."

"Thank you, Nancy. This is Elena, my girlfriend."

"Nice to meet you, Nancy." Elena smiled.

"Likewise," she said. "You can visit him."

I entered the room with warm-colored walls. My father lay on the bed looking peaceful. This was probably the most relaxed state he'd ever been in.

How fucking pathetic was that?

If you keep going at your pace, you might end up like him too.

My father was a workaholic, and so was I.

"He looks comfortable." Elena rubbed circles on my back. "What caused the coma?"

"He's allergic to seafood," I said. "But there was shrimp paste in his dinner at a restaurant."

"Do people know about his allergies?"

"Everyone knew. It wasn't a secret."

"You think someone did it on purpose?"

I loved how she could read me. "Yes, but everything is just speculation right now. The chef swore he didn't know there was shrimp paste in the food. My father frequented the restaurant often, so this was a shock to the owner and the workers. I'm trying my best to view everything objectively."

"But it's hard when it's your family." She squeezed my hand tighter. "You're too close to see clearly. You need a bird's-eye view. That's when The Roc emerges, right?" She offered me a smirk, trying to add a little humor to the dreadful situation.

I lifted her hand and kissed it gently. "Thanks for making me smile."

My dad was the CEO of the Reimann Corporation, which oversaw several financial firms, including the Reimann Sienna Bank, which was tied to the life insurance scam Elena recently discovered. He told me he'd look into it. I knew he'd stumbled on something that triggered someone trying to kill him.

I'd called a board meeting to demand a thorough investigation. My father had appointed me the power of attorney, so I'd be overseeing his projects from now on.

Had he known something like this would happen? Though I was his only son, I'd assumed he would have someone else take over for him. Did he always trust me? But he'd made it obvious he was disappointed in me.

A headache bloomed, and I turned to Elena. "I have a meeting with the board members this week. I want you to stay on Quintile Island."

"Okay. Let me know how I can help." She embraced me.

Her presence was all I needed.

She drew back. "I need to use the restroom. I've been holding it in since we got off the plane. Drank too much coffee."

"Bathroom is right there." I smiled, pointing to the door at the other end of the room.

When Elena entered the bathroom, I stepped closer to my father's bed, looking down at him.

"Who did this to you?" Anger thrummed inside me. If my mom were watching us now, she'd be devastated. She loved him so much.

"I know I've disappointed you by not following in your footsteps. You probably don't know this, but I tried my best to make you proud. Eventually it was too much. The pressure to be good at everything broke me." Inhaling a breath, I dropped into the chair beside the bed. "I resented you, and that's created a wedge between us." I looked at his hand, still wearing his wedding ring. "Get well. I'll get to the bottom of this."

Things were happening too fast. I felt like I was missing something important.

"Maybe we could start over when you recover." I didn't know if that was possible, but I was trying my best to sound positive. Mom used to say kindness cost you nothing.

When Elena returned, I flew a small plane to Quintile Island.

CHAPTER FORTY-NINE

ELENA

IT WAS five in the morning, and I couldn't sleep. I turned to my side, staring at Orion. Stress had creased between his brows, and I used my finger to soften it.

Stress radiated from Orion, and I wanted to erase it from him. Last night, I got to experience the most wonderful shower with him. The high-tech showerheads and wall sprays with their own heat and pressure adjustments were heavenly.

I'd never made love in a shower that high-tech or that spacious. Orion said he could replicate the shower in his suite or in the house he'd just bought in Providence. It was currently undergoing renovations. I'd leaped with joy to hear about the purchase because it meant he wanted to stay longer in Providence.

We loved each other, but I also knew his empire demanded him to be in different parts of the world at various times. I'd wondered if he ever wanted to move back to Sweden or to any of the other homes he had around the world. I couldn't live like that, ping-ponging all over the place.

Though he told me he had an estranged relationship with his father, I saw the love underneath layers of anger and resentment. Sometimes it took a catastrophe like this to make everyone realize what was important.

I stared at him, brushing away a few strands of hair that had fallen over his forehead. This beautiful, brilliant, and complex man was mine.

Danger lurked around him, but I wanted to protect him just as much as he wanted to protect me.

He shifted and a new crease formed on his forehead, making him look stressed. What was he dreaming about?

Kate.

Kate.

Kate.

My heart cracked. I'd be lying if I said it didn't bother me to hear him calling out his ex-fiancée's name again. How many more times could I stand this? Would I appear selfish if I told him about it?

But I had to tell him. It bothered me. What was the dream about? Did he miss her?

People said dreams were often the result of the person thinking too much about someone or something. Was this the case?

Then his features softened, and his breathing leveled.

He was probably just stressed. I didn't want to think about anything that would make me unhappy, so I got out of bed, brushed up, and walked out to the front porch that gave me a view of the bright blue sea.

My mood immediately changed. How could anyone feel bad staring at something as beautiful as this? This was like a secret cocoon where Orion and I could enjoy our time together, despite what else happened in the world.

Closing my eyes, I inhaled the fresh clean air of the sea and understood how nature could truly heal the body, heart, and soul. Just being here made me feel more relaxed. The temperature was cooler in Sweden, but a long-sleeve knit top with cotton pants suited me fine.

Two arms slipped around my waist and his lips nibbled the crook of my shoulder. "Good morning, Sunshine."

"Morning." I lifted my face for a kiss. He looked handsome and perfectly disheveled. "How did you sleep?"

"I had a nightmare."

Intrigued, I turned around. "What was it about?"

"I think the stress from the past few months took its toll last night. I dreamed of Kate." He paused and gray eyes bore into mine. "In the dream she just smiled at me, then waved and walked off. I wanted to call her back. To say that I was sorry that I wasn't able to help her. But she didn't turn around. She kept going and eventually faded away."

He called after her because he wanted to say he was sorry. And here I was, being a jealous girlfriend. I felt so ashamed.

"You called her name when you were asleep."

"I did?" He looked at me. "Was this the first time?"

"No." I swallowed. "To be honest, I was jealous the first time I heard it. No woman likes hearing her man call out another woman's name in bed." I ran my fingers over the five o'clock shadow on his chin. "But I understand now. I shouldn't have felt that way."

"I love you." He cupped my face. "And I don't want you to ever doubt that. Okay?"

"Okay." I kissed him.

Even though he was going through so much, he still wanted to make sure I was all right. I loved this man so much. He could resolve whatever issue that fell on him.

I changed to a lighter topic. "So what's the significance of Quintile Island? Does the name have meaning?"

"When my mother bought the island, she changed the name from Perry Island to Quintile Island. Quintile is an astrological aspect in astrology. It's when two planets are seventy-two degrees apart. The aspect represents talent, the urge to create order, and a fascination with patterns and structures. It's associated with creativity, innovation, and finding unique solutions."

"She's describing *you*."

He smiled. "She told me she bought the island for me. I didn't know the significance of the name until I got older and studied astrology along with her. But yeah, she saw all of that in me." Love emanated from his face.

"She was a smart woman."

"And so are you." He tapped my chin. "You're very intelligent for being with me, you know."

I laughed. "Most people would question my choices if they knew I was with a thief."

Amusement gleamed in his eyes. "Not just any thief—the most extraordinary thief to ever exist."

"Who's blessed with the most extraordinary protégé to ever exist," I countered.

His smile widened, and he kissed me. "I feel so much better already. Let me put some long pants on and I'll give you a tour." He'd worn shorts to bed.

As we walked, I fell in love with the island. Orion said it would take about three hours to walk from one end of the island to the next. He showed me the new guest house that was recently built. There was also a small house that served as temporary housing for his employees, who came to maintain the island twice a month. He had advanced solar panels that weren't available commercially, collecting energy for the island.

"Even if the world had a blackout, we'd be fine here," he said. "We can sustain ourselves."

I loved his independence and innovative ways of living. Orion also had a machine that turned seawater into drinkable water. I literally tasted the healing of the sea in that cup. Quintile Island was like a hidden sanctuary. He could also monitor his massive home via his phone. His company, SIGMA, had a satellite aiming at the island for a close-up view if he ever needed access to it. I was in awe of what was on the island.

I also learned he'd added new cameras all around the island in discreet locations.

"So that's how you found the guy who died on the island. Did you find out why he was here?"

"Yes." His jaw tightened. "But he's just a pawn. I don't want to talk about him. Let's just focus on cheerful things." He cupped my face. "I have something spectacular to show you."

He brought me to an abstractly shaped building and led me inside to a room where giant glass panels took up three quarters of the room.

I gasped when I saw all the equipment in the room, along the walls, and on the ceiling.

"This looks like something that belongs in a spaceship or NASA." I walked up to an abstract thing suspended in the air. The ceiling was made of glass.

He laughed. "You're not wrong. This is where I like to look at the stars."

"Orion, my love." I placed a hand on my hip while the

other hand gestured to the room. "Most people look at the stars with a normal telescope that can be transported out to the back yard. What you have is . . . an enormous machine that looks complicated and intimidating."

He placed a hand on each side of my shoulders with his eyes settling directly on mine. "This is the most advanced telescope you'll ever find, Sunshine. The Webb Telescope by James Webb from NASA is currently the most powerful. But what I have is the Reimann Telescope. No one has this yet. You can see stars from the next galaxy clearer than the infrared that the Webb instrument delivers. I've seen things that NASA hasn't even discovered."

I blinked at him. "Wow." Just when I thought I'd heard everything, Orion surprised me again. He could see into the next galaxy?

Sometimes when I looked at the night sky, I wondered what was beyond the Earth, beyond the Milky Way. The universe was vast, and it made my problems seem insignificant. That there were more important things to consider than my issues. "I want to see."

"I'll give you the stars tonight." Warmth radiated from his eyes, but there was something else there.

"I see something in your eyes."

"I have something to tell you." He took my hand in his warm palm. "Let's have a seat."

CHAPTER FIFTY

ELENA

THE DREAD in my stomach churned. I should be used to surprises by now.

Orion took me out to a beautiful patio with comfortable outdoor furniture and décor. The breathtaking view of the beach relaxed me, making me think the night sky would look spectacular from here.

He walked over to the outdoor kitchen area and opened the refrigerator that looked high tech. "Would you like some lemonade?"

"Sure." I hoped the drink would settle the erratic nerves.

What did he need to tell me?

Orion brought over two glasses of lemonade and sat down on the cushioned couch beside me. "What do you know about Reid?"

"He's the owner of Wild Roots. Great person to work with. He treats his employees with respect. My mom has worked for him for years. Reid is a big reason why she continues to volunteer there after retirement. Why do you ask?"

"Reid is my brother-in-arms, also known as The Raven. He's retired now from the art. I didn't know he knew you or your mom until the day of the fire."

Nerves rippled low in my stomach. Being with Orion had allowed me to see the multiple layers within everything. Nothing was as simple as it seemed to be.

"Is it a coincidence that we know him? Or is there something else behind the scenes?"

"Reid was asked to watch over you and your mom."

"By whom?" I placed a hand over my stomach as nerves fluttered.

"Your biological father Pablo Toledo, The Condor."

The statement dropped into my lap like a boulder, and I sucked in a breath from the power of it. My heart stopped beating. My world and everything I knew about my life tipped over, pouring out like water from a bottle.

I didn't know what to say or ask. Confusion and questions bubbled in my head.

When I finally allowed my body to calm, two questions came out on their own accord. "How is this possible? Why didn't she say anything to me?"

"I believe she wanted to protect you," Orion said. "Pablo's enemies were after him when your mom was pregnant. She thought he'd died. In a way he had. When he escaped, he lived life under the radar. He didn't want his enemies knowing he had a family. Your mom married Mateo, who didn't mind that she was pregnant with another man's baby. He loved you both."

I needed to talk to my mother. I didn't know how to respond to all this. She could've told me, right? But I knew myself. If she'd told me I'd have wanted to know more details, then investigate, turning over things that could've brought on trouble for the family.

I understood this, but still, I wished I'd known earlier.

Silence hung between us for a while, and Orion didn't interrupt my thoughts as I tried to process all of this.

"Who were Pablo's enemies? The Trogyn?"

Orion nodded.

When I was born, I was already roped into this dangerous world. I couldn't know my parents' exact emotions and concerns, but I knew they loved me. And Pablo—my father—loved me and my mom in his own way.

That was enough, right?

He'd chosen to live beside us, watching over us. That was a sacrifice that deserved gratitude and respect. Had he been happy? Were there lonely moments he'd wished he had a family with him?

Thoughts flowed across my mind, and one came to the forefront. "I think his spirit visited me when I was investigating his case."

"Tell me," Orion said.

"Perhaps he wanted to help me uncover the truth that day when I visited Mona at the café. She saw his ghost near me. Now I understand why."

"He was guiding his daughter." Orion dropped an arm around me. "He has a treasure box that you should have. It's in his apartment in Providence. I haven't been there, but I have a key."

My eyes flicked to his. "Did you steal the key?"

A smirk curved on his lips. "I wouldn't do that to my teacher. I've always had access to his apartment, but never needed to go there."

"Okay," I said. I had so many questions for my mother.

Orion also mentioned that The Condor was happy when he saw the stolen brooch. My father had been watching over me all these years. Part of me was angry that he didn't come to say hello. But then what would've happened to the father I grew up with?

My head hurt just thinking about all the what-ifs.

I got to know The Condor—his character, his intentions, his compassion—because I'd been investigating his case. He wasn't estranged from me.

I looked up at the sky, wondering if he was there watching over me.

Life was so complicated with all the little details and detours. Of all the people I could fall in love with, I fell for my father's protégé.

My thoughts ebbed and flowed as I looked out to the sea. "I understand now."

"Understand what?"

"That someone could easily snap under this kind of pressure. It's like a massive earthquake that just turned your life inside out. The life you once knew has a completely different landscape now." I slouched against the cushion.

"But you have an awareness that most people don't." He hugged me tighter. "You're already steps ahead, Sunshine."

Silence blanketed us as we sat there just appreciating each other's presence. I didn't know how much time had passed, but when I looked over, Orion was staring at the sand in contemplation.

"What are you thinking about?" I asked him.

He looked down at me with a warm smile. "Thinking about you. About how you're absorbing the news."

I just fell into a deep chasm of myself and was trying to

find the energy to crawl back up. But I didn't want him to worry about me. He had plenty on his mind.

"I'm going to need some time to let things settle, you know?"

"It's understandable. Your life just completely changed. It's going to take time to adjust and adapt. I know that you'll find your solution." Gray eyes settled onto mine. "Pablo was a fantastic man. I was lucky to have him as my mentor. I believe what he did was done out of love."

"The investigation showed me his character." I let out a laugh. "I guess I'm surrounded by thieves—The Roc, The Condor, and The Raven."

He grinned. "Now there's also The Robin. That's *you*. You've learned from me, so I can give you an alias." He kissed the top of my head. "You're one of us now."

I sat up. "I only broke into *one* house, and I have no intention of breaking into any more. What's the significance of The Robin?"

"The robin symbolizes change, hope, happiness, renewal, and good luck. You're all of those things for me."

"Do you always know the right things to say?" I pinched his cheek playfully.

"It's easy to speak the truth." He pinched my cheek back. "I'm being honest."

"Thank you." I hugged him, appreciating everything he'd done for me.

I wasn't angry at anyone, just sad that life had to happen this way. The unexpected turns that shocked a person. I never got to meet my biological father, and I wondered what our relationship would've been like if we had known each other.

He pulled me into his arms. "Let's take a walk along the

shore. The exercise and the fresh air will make you feel better."

It would make Orion feel better too. The more I got to know him, the more I realized he was so thoughtful. We walked to an area with three big rocks surrounded by pretty grass. Each rock had abstract etchings on it.

"The rocks are interesting."

"My mother gave them to me. She said they're blessed rocks to protect the island."

By the time we got back from the walk, I felt fifty percent better. Orion had prepared an eclectic selection of fancy food I'd never dared to eat before. Way beyond my budget.

"When did you get all this made?" I asked, since there was no one on the island except us.

"Someone came and set this up while we took a walk around the island."

"Oh." I glanced around. "How did they arrive?"

"By boat. I have a team stationed on the shore."

I saw several boats in the far distance during the walk, but heard nothing close by. But then again, I wasn't paying attention.

"Come." He took my hand, leading me to the table with several dishes. "You should try them all."

I glanced at the fancy plates with gold trimmings and pursed my lips. "I don't know what these things are. They're all so pretty, though." I didn't want to appear rude, but those portions were tiny.

"This is caviar from the Iranian Beluga. Very expensive." He gestured to a porcelain bowl.

"Like how expensive?" I'd eaten caviar before, but this looked pricier.

"Two pounds could go over forty thousand dollars."

My jaw dropped at the obscene price. That amount of money could feed a family of four for the entire year.

"I'd feel bad eating it," I told him.

He squeezed my hand. "If you try some of everything, I'll make a huge donation to your chosen charity."

I blinked at him. "Why?"

"Because I want you to step into my world, see what's available to you."

I considered him for a moment. He wanted me to immerse myself into his ritzy lifestyle. I didn't think I fit. The people in his circle bought things with their black American Express cards. They spoke about food that sounded like a foreign language to me. But the honesty in his eyes made me want to try it.

"Okay. But you have to try my food too."

"I love your *lomo saltado*. If you make it, I'll eat it."

I walked over to a square plate with pasta topped with mushroom shavings. "What kind of mushroom is this?"

"White truffle."

I gasped, remembering my interview with a chef once. "The kind that's a few hundred bucks for a few shavings?"

He nodded, and I rubbed his firm abs. "You've got all the fancy food in you."

After trying a little of everything, including Kobe beef, Orion showed me some incredible drones that were like the size of a dragonfly.

"What are these for?"

"A security prototype my company has been working on."

He flew it around by tapping on his phone. Then he showed me on the phone what the dragonfly saw with its eyes. The clarity of the videos was amazing, like a real high-definition movie. The images could also zoom in and out.

"You have a lot of companies," I said.

He smiled. "I have a lot of interests. You being the most interesting one."

"Here you go again, flattering me."

"What's wrong with a man flattering his woman?"

"Absolutely nothing. I just didn't expect this from you. When we first met, you seemed extremely private and intense."

"You've inspired me to open up." His eyes gleamed. "I'll give you the stars tonight."

CHAPTER FIFTY-ONE

ORION

I'D NEVER BROUGHT a woman to Quintile Island, and I'd never shared the Reimann Telescope with anyone until today. Elena didn't know she was seeing so much of me.

I saw how much the news about The Condor had affected her. I'd feel the same way. But I also saw the wisdom she possessed. She was aware of her situation and understood she needed time to adjust. I'd met many people who couldn't see the obvious. Or maybe they refused to because change was difficult to accept.

If I'd had her wisdom back then, I wouldn't have had so much anxiety. I opened the glass ceiling, prepared the telescope, and let it ascend, shifting it toward the sky.

"This is so magical." She tilted her head up, looking through the ceiling at the starry night. "It's breathtaking."

"I have a portable telescope we can take out to the beach. You can still see a lot, but this is the king of all telescopes."

"Can we take the portable telescope tomorrow?" Her eyes widened with wonder.

"You can do whatever you want."

"Really?" She angled her head. "I'm going to hold you to that."

Curious about what she'd do, I said, "Yeah."

She narrowed her eyes at me, half-believing me.

"Look." I stepped aside for her to look into the telescope.

"Oh my God, Orion," she muttered. "It's a whole new world out there. Oh! Is that the Orion constellation?" She stepped back, her eyes beaming at me.

"It is."

My heart swelled at the bewilderment in her eyes and the joy on her face. Loving Elena had softened my edges. Was that a good thing? My time with Kate had been different. She couldn't soften my edges. It wasn't her fault. I just didn't respond to her in the same way.

Elena and I had a deep connection that was like the mysteries surrounding the universe. Certain things weren't meant to be explained or understood. The beauty was the quiet mystery that whispered beyond space and time.

"I'm speechless, Orion. I know this sounds weird, but it feels as though the stars are speaking to me, or to us, through the silence."

"That's what my mom said too. Did you know the connection between the Orion constellation and the three pyramids of Giza?"

"Do tell, Mr. Know-It-All." She peered in, but turned to me. "How do I zoom in and out?"

I took her hand and placed it on a knob. "Here."

"Oh, thanks." She returned her attention to the telescope. "So what's the significance with the pyramids?"

"Whoever built the three pyramids of Giza aligned their positions to the three stars on Orion's Belt."

"Really? How?" She lifted a brow. "They didn't have the

technology to know the exactitude of their locations back then, did they?"

"There are several speculations. Most people don't know about this alignment until they look at it from a bird's-eye view. Some say the pyramids represent portals to another world. Some say it's just a mathematical coincidence."

"What do you think?" she asked.

"I like to keep an open mind. My technology and designs allow me to see and do things that are inexplicable. Those inexplicable things are beautiful to me." I touched her face. "I don't believe in coincidences. But I also understand that there are certain things better left untouched. How about you?"

"I think someone created magic on Earth. I imagine some beautiful aliens, angels, dragons or otherworldly creatures from far away coming here with their entourage and building these architectural pieces for humans to appreciate. Maybe they're having a party in these pyramids when no one's watching." She smiled, her eyes gleaming with mischief. "Because denial of these masterpieces would be a denial of the imagination. Aren't you glad you asked me?"

I laughed, admiring her humor. "Always, Madame Sarcasm. I'm sure the Nile River appreciates the plug."

"Oh!" With delight, she held up a finger. "I just realized something."

"What?"

"The three rocks your mom gave you . . . They kind of look like the Orion's belt placement, don't you think?"

She left something for you on the island, but I don't know what or where it is. She was going to tell me the day she died.

My heart raced as I remembered my conversation with my father.

How the hell did I miss that? I knew the rocks meant something. They were precious gifts from my mother, and I didn't want to disturb them. Each rock represented a family member. I didn't look at them as anything other than tokens of love.

I cupped her face. "You're a genius. Thank you."

"Takes one to know one."

After gazing at the stars for hours, Elena went to bed. I waited until she was sound asleep before I snuck out with my flashlight and equipment to move the rocks aside. I found a metal box filled with information and knew my mother had been murdered because of it.

CHAPTER FIFTY-TWO

ELENA

ORION FLEW his plane to the board meeting. He looked more stressed and angrier this morning. When I inquired, he told me he had a lot on his mind regarding the meeting.

I could only imagine the pressure he was dealing with. His father was in a coma, and now he had to deal with the aftermath. I wanted to ease the tension when he returned.

An idea formed in my head, but first I had to call my mother. I didn't want to wait until she returned from Cancun. I needed to know now.

"Hi, *Mamá*." I opened the sliding door, letting the cool breeze enter. "Are you enjoying Cancun?"

"I am, sweetie. Orion's place is beautiful."

I could imagine. "Are you busy?"

"No. My bonsai class starts in a few days. Is everything okay?"

"Everything's fine. I just discovered something important about my father."

She sucked in a breath. "What do you know, Elena?"

I told her what I knew, and she cried.

"I'm sorry I never told you. Pablo didn't know I was pregnant. When he visited me later, I was already married. He was involved with some dangerous people, and he wanted us safe. I knew he watched over you."

"Did Dad know I'm not his biological daughter?"

"Yes. He was a good man. The brooch you have is from Pablo. It's a set of wings from a bird statue he had."

"Did you know he died recently?"

"Yes. I received a letter from someone named The Raven. He said he was Pablo's friend."

I had to thank Reid for alerting my mother. I remembered she'd been sad months ago, saying a good friend had passed. After asking her a few more questions, I realized she didn't know what Pablo did for a living.

She didn't need to know any of that. After an hour of chatting, Mom suggested we continue when she returned. She had more things to share about my father. I felt blessed to have two fathers who loved me.

Feeling hopeful, I worked on Musepaper. When I finished what I had to do, I focused on making Orion happy today. I wanted to make him dinner while wearing something provocative. Because of the urgent trip, I grabbed some baby pink lingerie that wasn't as provocative as the black set. If I had known I'd be in the mood to seduce him, I would've brought more options.

I put on the baby pink bra and panties. Then I found one of Orion's T-shirts and threw it over me, making me look like I was wearing an oversized nightshirt.

Orion told me he'd be home for dinner, but he wasn't sure what time. I grabbed the apron from the hook, turned on the music on my phone, and went to look in his fancy refrigerator to see what was available. He still had containers of those lavish foods from yesterday, but I didn't want any of it.

I wanted to make him something simple that reflected my kind of lifestyle. Our lives were blending. I was getting used to his, and I wanted him to get used to mine. A salad with some sautéed chicken strips that were already marinated in a sealed bag. Something simple and healthy.

When I finished making the chicken, I took out the container of salad mix. As I filled two bowls with the mix, I danced to a Taylor Swift song, shifting my hips back and forth.

"Well, hello there," said a male voice, startling me.

I whirred to a face I never thought I'd see again. Terror trickled down my spine like a block of ice. Over the years, whenever that horrific memory surfaced, my body would tremble. He was the reason I feared heights. But something had changed in me today. Though the fear was there, my body didn't tremble.

JR2 turned off the music on my phone, which was on the marble counter.

"Where's Orion?" he asked, studying me.

Nerves had me ready to vomit, but I didn't want to show it. JR2 didn't appear to recognize me.

"He's at a meeting," I said calmly. "He'll be back soon."

"I'll wait for him then. Get me a glass of wine." He jerked his chin to the wine cabinet.

How could I forget the privileged attitude that had protected him and his fucking club? A club that had tormented people who didn't measure up to their wealth or bowed to their demands. I was so sick of people like him. He must be friends with Chantel.

I stared at JR2, not making a move.

"Did you hear what I said?" he barked. "Why are you still standing there? Get me my wine." His creepy eyes raked down my body. "I didn't know Orion had such a hot maid working for him." He crossed his arms, analyzing me like he was about to buy me. "How much does he pay you? I'll pay you double if you work for me."

JR2 stepped closer, and I stepped back.

Nausea still bubbled in me. I didn't want to be close to this asshole, but I wasn't a frightened thirteen-year-old girl any longer. I'd had plenty of experiences with people like them. My armor had strengthened over the years.

Right now, I wished I'd signed up for Vivian's martial arts class.

"Not interested." I moved the bowls of salad aside, trying to look busy. "I think you should leave. I'll inform Orion you stopped by."

"You're kicking me out? How dare you tell me to leave." Annoyance splashed over his face as he walked closer. "Do we know each other? You look very familiar."

No.

He studied me as I wiped the counter with a towel.

"No fucking way!" he said. "You're that bitch from summer camp!" Laughter erupted from him. "I still have that video of you. Wanna see? Wanna see how pathetic you were? Wetting yourself on that bridge?"

In that moment I wanted to *kill* him.

JR2 rushed toward me, but I dodged him, rushed to the other side of the counter to grab my phone. But he reached me, wrapping his thick arm around my waist. I fought him, and my phone dropped to the floor, cracking.

I kicked, screamed, and did everything I could to get away.

"You bitch!" He slapped me, pinning me to the floor.

The urge to gouge his eyes out soared in me. "Get the fuck off of me!"

I curled my knee, hitting him in the balls. He winced and released his grip on my wrists. I scratched his face, and my nails caught one of his eyes.

Even better.

JR2 shrieked in pain, and I pushed myself up. Adrenaline pumped through me as I rushed to the kitchen counter for a knife—for anything that could be used as a weapon. I knew he'd rape me and then kill me. I'd never killed anyone, but I'd do it right now without hesitation.

I rounded the counter, but he caught up to me. "You can't escape me this time! I'm going to fuck you, bitch! Then I'm going to bury you alive!"

"Help me!" I shouted, even though I knew there was no one on the island.

He gripped my legs, and I fell to the floor. He dragged me back toward him, flipped me over. Then he threw his weight on top of me.

CHAPTER FIFTY-THREE

ORION

MY MEETING ENDED EARLY, and I flew the plane home, desperately missing Elena. I needed her presence— her comfort. Everyone on the Reimann Corporation board, including Jonah, didn't object to my plans and the thorough investigation of every single bank under our umbrella.

We all wanted what was best for the company. Even if some of them had objected, there wasn't anything they could do. I'd gotten the majority vote. Those who had showed displeasure were on my list to investigate. A separate team— that no one knew about—had been designated for that.

From what my mother had left me under the rock, the game had completely changed. I'd alerted my friends for help because there were too many moving pieces, too many angles to oversee. If I wanted to succeed—which I would— I'd need help from those I trusted.

I didn't realize how much my father had to endure until I sat in his seat. He was dwelling in a poisonous snake pit. How did he manage it?

Frustration threatened to overwhelm me as I thought

about the damaging information that had gotten my mother murdered. She wasn't killed in a car accident. My father had also paid a price when he started investigating the bank scams.

I wanted to eliminate every single person responsible for hurting my family. Eradicate them like cockroaches. But that would be too easy. Too quick.

I tried my best to shove the thrumming vengeance aside. I didn't want to bring it back to see Elena. If she weren't in my life right now, I could have easily spiraled out of control.

When I landed the plane, I noticed Jasper's boat on the pier. What the hell was he doing here? I'd already told him I had no interest in selling my island. I wasn't in the mood to entertain him right now.

Getting off the plane, I hopped into the car and drove to the house. Arriving, I heard Elena's scream and rushed in.

Blood roared in my ears as I saw Jasper on top of her, trying to rape her. Fury blinded me and I stalked over, yanked the fucker off her, and threw two punches into his face. I dragged his ass to the counter, reached for the knife, and stabbed it into each of his thighs.

He shrieked. "What the fuck, Orion?!"

I shoved him against the counter, placing the blade to his throat. A red stream trickled down his neck, and I didn't give a fuck.

"Don't. Ever. Touch. Her. Again. Do you understand me?" I seethed.

"She's just a fucking *maid*." Jasper looked at me. For the first time, I saw fear in his eyes. He'd never seen me this way. Well, he'd been blind.

I shoved the blade closer. "Do you want me to slit your throat or cut off your dick?"

I wanted to cut off his family jewels, but I needed him cognizant enough to deliver a message. There were bigger fish to fry than him.

"I'm okay." Elena placed a gentle hand on my arm. I could hear the tremble in her voice. When I looked at her, I saw a flushed palm print on her cheek. I stabbed the knife into his hand and yanked it out.

"The fuck! What is wrong with you?" Jasper shouted.

"It's about time you realize there are consequences to your actions. How dare you come into my home and assault *my* girlfriend!"

I examined Elena, who looked frightened and disheveled.

My eyes met hers, and she nodded. "I'm fine."

Jasper eyed Elena while blood poured out of his hand and thighs. "I thought you had better taste than some scholarship funded bitch who doesn't know her place."

Jasper really had a death wish today.

I charged at him, but Elena held me back. "He's not worth it."

The desire to kill him surged in me.

Jasper limped toward the door, took off his shirt to bind the wound in his hand. "You should've learned your lesson with Kate."

"What did you say?" I stalked over to him.

He smirked. "Nothing important. Only that I don't know what you did to her to make her take so many pills."

How did he know that detail that had been scrubbed from the medical reports? I'd paid a lot of money to protect her and her family.

Something dark rose in me. I walked over to a wall and

slapped a hand on it. It recognized my palm, and the door slid opened. I grabbed a gun, cocked it, aiming it at Jasper.

"I can kill you right now and feed you to the sharks. Or I can transport your body and dump it in your back yard just like that lawyer you killed when he didn't want to help you create a fake contract for one of your business endeavors."

The cockiness on his face changed. "I don't know what you're talking about."

The DNA test for the gold button had come back. It was more complicated than I'd realized. But I didn't have the capacity to deal with that right now.

Elena came up beside me, sliding an arm around my waist, trying to comfort me. I didn't want to kill this fucker in front of her.

Jasper was vermin I could use.

"You have five minutes to get off my island. If you ever come near Elena again, or if I ever see you on my island or near any of my properties, you will die a spectacular death. Those are orders my men will abide by. Don't give me a reason to kill you. Get the fuck out!"

He flared his nostrils. "How can you treat family like this?"

"We all know you're really not part of this family," I snarled.

I hit the bullseye. A muscle twitched in his jaw. I could tell he wanted to say something and make a threat to me and Elena, but that truth stopped him.

He knew that I knew what he had done. There was nothing he could do about it.

"You can call the authorities." I gestured to his injured thighs and hand. "Just know you'll be sitting in jail for assault, attempted rape, and trespassing on private property."

When his boat roared away, Elena pushed my hand down, took the gun away, and placed it on the table.

She had tears in her eyes. "Are you okay?"

I gathered her into my arms. "That should be me asking you. Are you hurt anywhere? What did he do to you? Tell me everything."

Usually, I had cameras active when I was away. But I didn't want them on because she was here. I wanted to give her the privacy of being in my home.

If I had the cameras active, I would have seen everything. I would have been here sooner or sent someone to help her.

"I'm sorry," I said, tightening my arms around her.

"It's not your fault."

I cupped her face. "I shouldn't have left you alone."

She shook her head. "I'm not a kid, Orion. You can't be with me all the time. Plus, it's time I face the past."

"How do you know him?" I led her to the couch and ushered her beside.

"From a summer camp. Elliot and I got scholarships to attend."

Memory resurfaced, and my fingers curled as I remembered Jasper laughing at a video from his camp.

That fucker.

"What did he do to you back then?"

CHAPTER FIFTY-FOUR

ELENA

I'D NEVER SEEN Orion like this. It was beyond unhinged, especially when Jasper mentioned Kate.

A darkness rose in him. His face, his eyes, they all transformed.

I could see the love he still had for her. And it sickened me that I was jealous. Maybe all of my insecurities rose to the surface because of what had just happened. Or what would have happened if Orion hadn't arrived home on time.

My body shivered, and Orion took my hand into his. "I want to know every detail."

I pushed away my insecurities and squeezed his hand. "It happened a long time ago."

I wake to someone touching my face and yanking at my T-shirt. I blink to see JR2 with another boy. I don't know his name. But he hangs with the JR brothers.

I sit up, scooting away from them.

"You're a newbie here. That means you need to strip and abide by our rules."

Fear skitters up my spine. Where's my cabinmate?

I hear giggling outside the cabin and know Gina is probably out there. She likes one of the boys.

I wish Elliot were here. But he's two cabins down the path in the boys' cabins.

"You're not supposed to be here. I'm telling the cabin director."

JR2 laughs and slaps his friend on the back. "Hear that, Connor? She's threatening me."

"That means she deserves the punishment." He smiled and dropped his pants. "Suck it."

JR2 grinned. "Do it."

I looked away from Connor's penis.

What's wrong with these boys? I'm so scared.

JR2 takes out his phone and starts recording. Fear overwhelms me, and I vomit.

"Fuck no. I don't want her mouth on me."

"Go rinse!" JR2 barks.

I get out of bed, trying to figure out a way to get out of the room. I sense there's someone else in the room other than JR2 and Connor. He must be standing in the shadows on the other side of the room where it's dark.

I don't have time to think about who else is there. Maybe it's just my imagination scaring me. I walk towards the bathroom, but instead of going in there, I run out the door and scream. "Help me!" Then I run.

They chase after me down the path. I run toward the main camp center. The quickest way there is to cross a rope bridge. I usually have trouble crossing it unless Elliot's with me. I don't know if I can do it now.

You have to.

Be strong.

Plucking up my courage, I step onto the wooden planks

and keep my face forward.

"Let's have some fun!" JR2 grips the rope and starts shaking it.

I almost fall but hold on tight. Fear spikes in me as my body loses control of itself . . .

I didn't have to finish the sentence. Orion understood what I meant. I told him the rest of the story and how terror had seeped into my bones that day. And how Elliot had arrived with the director, who didn't punish the boys at all.

"I'm going to fucking kill him." His jaw twitched with murder in his eyes.

"It's in the past, Orion. He's not worth your time. I don't want to cause any more trouble for you. You have so much on your plate already." I leaned into him. "Plus, I'm not afraid of heights anymore. What came from the horrific event today is that Jasper—that old trauma—doesn't control me anymore. I've overcome the fear."

He released a stressed sigh. I knew he was trying his best to calm the rage in him. It was weird how I could sense his emotions.

"You've helped me find my stability again. I don't think the fear of heights was the issue. It was that event that triggered the trauma and the fear. I don't feel it anymore. At least not to that crippling extent."

He nodded and kept me in his arms for the rest of the night.

CHAPTER FIFTY-FIVE

ORION

THERE WAS SO MUCH at play that my brain was going to explode. My desire to kill Jasper had never been so prominent. I knew the fucker had issues, but I didn't know it ran this deep. The people who let him get away with those crimes at the camp were just as responsible.

Elena didn't want me to waste my energy on him. But my love was wrong. It wasn't a waste of my time to punish those who had hurt her. I couldn't let this go.

"Can you help me with that?" I asked the boys on the screen. I'd called an urgent conference call as soon as Elena went to bed.

She went through hell today, and I would make sure Jasper experienced hell too.

"You got it," Remi said. "We'll deal with them, catch them unexpectedly."

"Is Elena okay?" Arrow asked.

"She's doing better than I thought. Sleeping now."

I'd hacked into the fucker's phone and extracted his video. The fear on her face—and the shame they'd made her feel—made me want to kill him a thousand times over. Still, that wouldn't be enough. I needed Jasper, Connor, the director, and whoever else was in the room that day to pay for Elena's trauma.

I briefed the boys on the information and didn't tell them about her personal experience with Jasper at camp. They knew Jasper had assaulted her, and that was enough. I gave the boys the list of names and some recordings of Jasper and his friends harassing other girls at the camp. Those recordings would be sent to the media and to the camp organization.

Then there was Jasper's admission about Kate's pills that required a separate investigation, which I would carry out myself. What the hell did he do to her?

After I'd finalized the plan with the boys, I hung up and dug into Jasper's past.

CHAPTER FIFTY-SIX

ELENA

A WEEK later we went back to Providence. On the flight, Orion told me Carlos had killed my father—his own brother —because he wouldn't use my mom's savings to pay for his debt. A series of emotions ranging from anger to sadness and betrayal warred within me. But I supposed karma had gotten Carlos.

I prayed to God that this would be the last horrible news I'd hear about this year. There was only so much a person could endure.

For the next few days, I threw myself into work, and Orion did too. Something was happening behind the scenes, but Orion shared nothing with me. I could feel the tension pulsing off of him.

I'd been working harder than usual. Most nights he'd stay at my house. Other nights he'd stay in his apartment. I couldn't shake off this horrible feeling that something awful was going to happen.

My article regarding the financial scam would release soon. I showed Orion what I'd written and made the changes he'd suggested. I'd also written the column for Madame Sarcasm, but I didn't show that to him yet. He was so busy that I only wanted to show him the important things first. He could read about Madame Sarcasm later.

Orion texted me, asking me to get ready to visit my father's apartment. I'd given myself enough time to accept this, and I was ready to discover more about him.

With amusement in his eyes, Orion gestured to the lock on the door. "Wanna try to break in with the skills you've learned? I know you've been watching all the videos on the shared drive."

"What kind of person would I be if I broke into my father's apartment? I'll pass."

I supposed he'd been keeping his eye on me even though he'd been busy. When I needed a break from working or researching for my articles, I watched his videos on various locks and how to pick them.

I'd never imagined myself doing this, but since I was in love with a thief, and my father was also a thief, I figured I should get to know them well.

Something else was going on with Orion. He seemed distant. Or was it me? Had I become distant because I couldn't forget his expression when Jasper had insulted his ex-fiancée?

Was I being paranoid? I hated this feeling.

Let it go.

I entered the apartment decorated in various shades of brown and traditional wooden furniture. Two dark brown couches, sage throw pillows, and a black rug offered a masculine appeal. The sturdy coffee table looked like it would last a lifetime. The craftsmanship was exceptional. He had boxes scattered on the floor and stacked in corners.

His bookshelf was crammed with books. Random art decorated the walls, and I wondered if it had been stolen or bought.

"Are those paintings originals?" I asked.

"No. Unlike me, he kept very little of what he stole. We have distinct taste in art. He sold his art for money and used it to help others. Pablo didn't live a lavish lifestyle."

"You help people too," I said, remembering how he'd bought me the car and donated money to several charities anonymously. Ralph had let that slip.

I walked over and noticed my high school yearbook. I removed it from the shelf and opened it. A newspaper clipping of me holding a certificate fell out from between the pages. I'd won a writing contest in ninth grade about what I wanted to do when I got older. Back then, I wanted to own a media company. Such big dreams for a little girl.

"You look cute." Orion looked over my shoulder.

Had my father wished he could've congratulated me? I could only imagine the pain and regret he'd felt. He probably didn't want to interrupt my life. A part of me wished he had attempted to reach out. There were so many what-ifs in life. What if I died tomorrow and didn't have time to do the things I wanted to do or say what was on my mind?

I looked over at Orion, who was browsing the apartment. I knew he loved me. But to what extent? If Kate came back to life right now and stood beside me, whom would he choose? I knew I shouldn't feel this way. But that emotion was burning inside me.

I had to deal with it. I didn't want to waste precious time.

Returning the book to its position, I browsed through the one-bedroom apartment. Wooden figurines, boxes, chairs, and wooden bookcases adorned the quaint apartment. The disarray in his living space mimicked mine.

"I guess I took after him, huh?" I gestured to the disorder.

"It's organized chaos." Smiling, he tapped my forehead. "I've always admired those who know how to navigate a mess. I don't function that way, but others thrive in that environment."

"That's one way to look at it."

"Come." He took my hand, leading me to the couch.

I sat down and ran a hand over the coffee table with pretty etchings. "The craftsmanship is extraordinary."

"He's a great woodworker. Very handy. He taught me how to fix things around the house, like your back deck."

"But you don't need to do those things. You can afford to hire people."

"Sometimes it's not about the money, but the reason you're doing something." He looked at me. "I repaired your deck because I wanted to put in the effort. The process gave me time to think and clear my head."

"And to attract all the single women in the neighborhood."

"I'm not interested in being anyone's handyman but yours."

I smiled. "I'll put you to work."

Orion reached for a wooden box from under the coffee table and gave it to me. It was about nine inches long and six inches wide, with intricate carvings all around. A card attached to the top of the lid read: Old Receipts.

"A distraction?" I arched an eyebrow.

A proud smirk curved onto his lips. "Only a true thief would know that."

"What can I say? I'm learning from the best. Distraction

is an interesting art form." I placed my hand on the box, trying to absorb all that was my father. "Do all thieves have a treasure box?"

He lifted a shoulder. "I suppose. It's like a journal of our adventure. All the things we want to remember are in there."

I remembered Mona saying my father's spirit had shown her a treasure box. What did he want me to know?

"Have you seen what's in the box?"

"No."

Nodding, I lifted the lid, and my heart galloped at the first item in the box. I reached for the abstract wing, the twin to my brooch. "Look. This is a set."

"It's exquisite." Orion examined the wing.

I glanced back in the box and took out the body of a beautiful hummingbird with its studded head.

Orion connected the wing to the bird and something clicked. He flicked a gaze at me. "It's a lock. I think it needs the other wing to unlock."

I unzipped my purse and pulled out a velvet box. "I've been carrying it around ever since I found out he's my father. Just trying to connect to him." I handed him my brooch.

Orion attached the second wing, and another sound clicked. The tail of the bird detached and a rolled-up piece of paper fell out. He unrolled it, revealing a bank's name and a few account numbers. One line said it all: *For my daughter, Elena.*

Love filled my heart as I held the little paper in my hand. It grew warm as tears flowed down my cheek. Orion got me a box of tissues from the side table and offered me one.

"Thank you."

"He had a savings account for you," Orion said.

I leaned into the couch, letting the cushion support my

back as I looked around the apartment. "Did he tell you what he wanted to do with the apartment?"

"No." He shook his head. "It's yours. His will is stored in one of those bank accounts. What do you want to do with it?"

"I don't know yet. For now, we'll leave it as is." I got up and looked outside the window. "I can see the park where I used to hang out as a kid. You stole my brooch at that park."

"Then you should keep this apartment. This building is like a telescope, showing us moments of our lives. If you want, I'll buy this entire building."

Feeling loved, I placed a hand on his arm. "Don't do that. I only need this one apartment." Then courage crawled up my spine. "I have something to say."

"Okay."

"Thank you for bringing me here today. And thank you for doing so much for me." I inhaled a breath. "I know you love me, but I also know that you still love Kate."

Orion opened his mouth to say something, but I held up a hand. "It's okay. You have a past with her that's rooted deep inside you. I think you need time to work it out. You may think that you love me, but maybe it's something else."

A crease formed between his eyebrows as he looked at me. "Elena, you're confused. I love you."

I didn't know why that comment rubbed me the wrong way. How could he dismiss what I was telling him?

"Maybe you're confused. I know it sounds petty, and I know I shouldn't feel this way. Hypothetically, if Kate appeared before you right now, would you choose her or me? Don't answer yet. Take your time." I looked at him, wanting him to know I meant it sincerely. "So much has happened to both of us in the last few months. Maybe we just need time apart for things to settle so we know what we really want. Okay?"

"You're breaking up with me?" he asked, looking stunned and sad.

"No." I placed a hand on his heart. "I just want to make sure you know what you want. So we can both move forward with no doubts. I guess I just need some time and space."

He sat in silence, staring at me.

"I don't know what your relationship with Kate was like. But I know her death affected you deeply, and you haven't healed from it yet. You might not notice the little things you do or say, but I have. You're still hung up on her. Maybe all of this is just my imagination. Like I said, time will tell."

He embraced me and kissed the top of my head.

I didn't know why I felt so sad and tired. This conversation sounded like a farewell. But it felt right to express my honest feelings. What was the point of a relationship if I couldn't express them genuinely?

"Take all the time you need," he said.

I knew what he meant, but I wished he'd said a little more.

Why didn't he try to explain some more? Why didn't he ask the reason for my insecurity? I wanted him to ask me.

You're being ridiculous, Elena.

A woman's mind was structured like a mudstacle course. There were so many things to overcome that sometimes the individual falls into her own traps. I knew I'd created my own internal mud race. But I had to get through it to the end. I had to know that Orion loved me more than anything. *Anyone.*

Why? Because I love him more than anything, anyone.

I deserved the same in return. No more settling for less.

CHAPTER FIFTY-SEVEN

ORION

INSIDE MY OFFICE, I stared out at the city's nightscape. Elena's comments rang in my ears.

I understood her concern, but it confused me. Hadn't I shown her how much I loved her? What else did she want? What else did she need? Why the sudden insecurity?

I raked a hand through my hair, trying to figure out where I had gone wrong. Women confused me. Maybe all she needed was just time to think about things. She had been through a lot lately, and I didn't blame her for feeling emotionally unstable.

Hell, I admired her strength dealing with the news about her father, people sabotaging her career, the financial stress she'd been coping with, and the trauma Jasper had inflicted on her.

I replayed the video of Jasper harassing Elena and zoomed in on the third person hiding in the shadows. It was too pixelated. So I uploaded the video to my advanced software and zoomed in.

Rage boiled in me.

CHAPTER FIFTY-EIGHT

ELENA

FOR THE NEXT WEEK, Orion only texted me three times. Each time, the conversation was brief. He hadn't stopped by to see me, and I hadn't been into the office to see him. I'd been working from home.

Sadness overwhelmed me, and I made more paper stars for him. I'd started this project a while ago. I wrote little sayings on small strips of paper to make me feel better. Then I rolled the paper strip into a three-dimensional star. I had filled up half of a glass jar already. The making of the tiny paper stars soothed me more than I realized. It was like being in the garden, plucking dandelions to dry. The process made me feel free and happy.

Every time I looked at the stars, I thought of him.

Why did it seem like our relationship was ending? Why did it seem like there was a huge wedge between us now? Was it my doing? Was I wrong to request time and space?

The girls had called me asking about Jasper's assault on the island. Orion had mentioned it to his boys, and they had told their women. I told them I was fine, and I was more worried about my relationship with Orion. After my conversation with the girls, I felt better.

My article regarding the bank scams had released two days ago, making Musepaper the most talked-about online newspaper. I hadn't expected so much exposure, but Orion did. All the other news outlets had reached out to me, which I deferred to the PR team Orion had hired. So many sponsor negotiations were underway. I was thrilled Musepaper was getting the exposure it deserved.

I still had a lot to do, and the marketing campaign for Musepaper was only beginning. From that bank scam article, a series of events occurred, which Orion had to deal with. I saw him addressing the press regarding the Reimann Corporation, which owned the Reimann Sienna Bank and several other institutions. He'd looked handsome and powerful, but also tired. I wanted to hug him.

His father's condition had improved, and he'd fired many people within the corporation. Some were even arrested because of newly released harassment recordings that led to people's suicides. I knew Orion had found those recordings.

Now the lawsuits would come. I was worried about him. Was this ordeal affecting his family's company?

I called Ralph.

"Elena, my dear. It's so good to hear from you. I was just going to call you later."

"You were? Is everything okay? Is Orion okay? He's been stressed lately."

Ralph sighed. "That's why I'm calling you. Can you tell me what happened between you two? He's closed himself off. I know he's dealing with some family and business drama, but I wonder if something else is concerning him."

Guilt tore at me, and my heart ached. So I poured out my

concern to Ralph. "I told him I needed time. But I don't think he really understood where I was coming from."

"Ah . . . I understand now."

"Do you?"

"Of course. I've learned that relationships are like puzzles. It took me a long time to understand what the woman I love wanted from me. She gave me time, and I took too long. Years have gone by, and I could've been with her."

"I don't know if I did the right thing. Is he hurting? Is he even more confused? I should be with him right now, right?"

"You're good where you are. If you were near him right now, his attention would be divided. He needs to focus on his family drama playing out."

"Is Jasper creating trouble for Orion?" I asked.

"Jasper is a spoiled asshole. He'll get what he deserves. But there's so much more you haven't heard. I'll let Orion tell you when he's ready."

"I saw on the news about the lawsuits. Are people suing the Reimann Corporation? But they weren't responsible, right?" I didn't want my investigation to be the reason for his family's financial downfall.

"The Reimann Corporation will be okay. The company will probably eliminate the corrupt banks. Getting rid of negative energy is a good thing. But you know Orion; he's cunning and meticulous, so he can endure this financial hit."

"I'm so happy to hear that." Relief settled, and I blew out a loud breath. "Is there something I can do to help him?"

"Just know that he loves you. If he had to choose between you and Kate, it would be you a hundred percent. Without a doubt."

Joy leaped into my heart, and the insecurities that had

settled in my stomach disappeared. Ralph knew Orion better than anyone.

"How can you be sure?"

"Because I've never seen him as happy as he is when he's with you. There's a joy in him that's unspeakable. Even I can feel it when I'm around him." He sighed. "He tried to help Kate, but couldn't. She didn't understand Orion the way you do, and she couldn't love him the way he needed it. But you can, and you have."

"Do you think he knows this?"

"He will."

After a few more minutes, Ralph had to go. I'd learned he was retiring in two months and would stay in Sweden with his wife Evelyn. Apparently, he'd gotten married during his vacation using the two bouquets he'd shown me. He said he'd continue to assist Orion with whatever he needed on a part time basis. I knew Orion would leave Ralph to retire in peace.

Feeling better, I was going to shower when my phone buzzed with a message from an unfamiliar number.

I clicked on it, and my heart shattered. It was a video of Orion with Chantel at the fashion show auction. They were in an empty room, making out. Then the scene changed to another banquet. I saw a Swedish flag on the hotel wall. They were snuggling and kissing too. When the video showed him fucking her, I lost it.

I whipped the phone across my desk, and it clattered to the floor. I gasped as my chest caved in. My world collapsed as hot tears burned my eyes. Anger, shock, sadness, and betrayal broke me into a million pieces.

After I stopped heaving, I walked over to pick up my

phone. The screen had cracked, but the video was still playing. I turned it off. I'd seen enough.

A second text came in.

Told you he can't be with one woman.

This had to be Chantel. I desperately wanted to reply. But what could I say? She knew she had the upper hand now. I wouldn't give her the satisfaction.

Instead, I buried myself in work so I didn't have to think about them. I texted Reid to let him know I'd be over at Wild Roots tomorrow to pluck more dandelions before the season ended. I didn't want the flowers to wait for my mom to return from Cancun. Plus, I needed to do something different to keep my mind busy.

Working on Musepaper made me think about Orion, and right now I needed all thoughts of him out of my mind.

That night I lay in bed debating whether I should confront Orion about the videos, but I simply didn't have the energy. I didn't want to hear excuses. I saw his face clearly. Unless he had a twin, that was HIM.

Move on.

You're worthy of an honest man who loves you.

With that thought flashing in my mind, I blocked his phone number.

I had to think of a way to sever ties with Orion regarding Musepaper. He was an investor, so I needed legal advice. I wanted to buy the Land Rover from him too. It was the right thing to do. Even though he was unfaithful to me, I couldn't screw people over the way he did.

As my head hit the pillow, the pressure of the day snapped, flowing out of me in hot tears. I fell asleep on a wet pillow and dreamed I was lost in hell.

CHAPTER FIFTY-NINE

ORION

STRESS HAD WORN me ragged the past week, and it was giving me a headache. I realized I hadn't been drinking my dandelion tea. Elena had given me a box of tea bags and a bottle of honey for me to make at work.

God, I miss her so much.

I just needed one more week to complete things, and I could return to her. Then we could deal with whatever hung between us. There was a barrier wedged between us, and I needed to remove it.

I added a little honey like she always did, stirred, and sipped the tea. My body immediately relaxed. It was like I was drinking in happiness. I didn't know what she had in the tea bag, but it always worked for me. I sat back in my office chair and enjoyed this quiet moment. Her face splashed into my vision and released the tension that had wrung my body.

I'd received confirmation that the summer camp—which my parents had funded for a long time—was now closed because of an ongoing international investigation involving sex crimes. All the directors and staff assistants who had disregarded the complaints of former victims were being questioned. Jasper, Connor, and his other buddies were also on the list.

He'd posted bail and was now missing. I was fucking pissed at the incompetence and oversight of the authorities. I knew he'd paid one officer. Jasper wouldn't be hiding for long. He'd been involved in murdering Kate, and now her father knew this. As an INTERPOL authority, he'd make sure Jasper paid for killing his daughter. I didn't need to worry about Jasper. But I also sent out an alert to my team to help locate him.

Jasper was a member of The Trogyn, but he was just a minor player in this dangerous game. There was one more character who had lurked under the radar. A man who had stood in the shadows to instigate and watch the crimes unfold. He was the worst of them all.

I had a meeting scheduled with him tomorrow when I arrived home in Providence. The plan was already set in motion, and I couldn't wait for this ordeal to be over with.

I checked my computer for new emails and saw the response from the boys regarding my Level Six demo. They enjoyed the recent updates to Madame Sarcasm, who grew magical dandelions. Yellow ones could heal wounds and extend the player's life force, while black dandelions were poisonous weapons that were used to kill the enemies. She whipped them out like darts and teamed up with a master thief. Together, they battled their enemies, trying to level up. Level Six of WaterFyre Rising was now complete. In the multiple levels created by the other boys, the WaterFyre was the sacred life force—produced by water and fire—that linked all the games together.

I finished my dandelion tea, then packed my things to

prepare for my flight home in a few hours. I was about to send Elena a text when my phone rang.

"What can I do for you, Ralph?" I asked. "Are you ready to retire earlier, like I had suggested?"

"You sound like you're in a good mood," he said, sounding too serious for my liking. Ralph always had put an amusing spin on things.

"What's up?"

"Do you know that Elena's been suffering?"

My heart cracked. "What do you mean?"

"Do you love her?"

"Yes." What kind of question was that?

"Who do you love more? Kate or Elena?"

I had been thinking about this. My answer had always been the same.

"Elena. I don't understand why it's not obvious."

"Maybe it's obvious to you, but not to Elena. She heard you call out Kate's name while you were sleeping. And your reaction to Jasper mentioning Kate's pills threw Elena off. She saw something that made her question your relationship with her. She believes you're still hung up on Kate."

Fuck. The revelation hit me.

"For someone so intelligent, you're dense about relationships."

I was going to retort that he wasn't great at relationships either, but I dropped it. He wasn't wrong. I'd been so blind that I'd hurt Elena unintentionally.

"What do you suggest I do, Smarty Pants?"

"Show her she's the one. Show her she matters the *most.* Be creative, idiot."

I smiled at his insult. He usually whipped them out when he was angry.

"I've seen you with Kate, and I've seen you with Elena. I can tell who holds your heart. Make her understand this before it's too late. Listen to this old man who's made a lot of mistakes." He sighed. "She gave you time to think about things, but you're taking too damn long. Even for my old ass."

"Okay," I said.

"That's it? Just okay? No smart comeback?"

"You're right about everything."

I'd been blinded by anger and vengeance. I didn't see how my reaction would have appeared from Elena's perspective. She'd been assaulted by Jasper that day, and I'd been furious with him. But his comment about Kate's pills ignited a wrath I didn't see coming. Kate's death had been ruled a suicide, but no one knew about the pills except me and Ralph.

Jasper's comment confirmed he was present the day she died. They'd killed her and made it appear like a suicide. That was the darkness that rose in me.

I mentioned this to Ralph, and he replied, "I know they'll pay for it."

"I'll make it up to Elena," I said. "Thank you for the reminder."

Ralph continued reprimanding me for another five minutes until he had to leave for a date with Evelyn.

I imagined Elena feeling miserable and thinking she held a second place in my heart. It was my fault for failing to make her understand she was the most important person to me. I loved her with everything I had. She dominated my heart and soul. I had to let her know.

Even though it was late, I sent her a text message so she could see it tomorrow.

Orion: *We need to talk. I love you. I'm sorry for taking too long to think.*

Then my phone buzzed with a message. But the text came from an unfamiliar number. Unease wormed into my stomach. Normally, I wouldn't click on unknown numbers, but something urged me to check this one out.

I clicked on the image.

Unknown: *Step down as CEO of Reimann Corporation or this will be all over the news.*

A video of me kissing and fucking Chantel appeared on the screen. Fury spiked in me. Who had created this video? They'd used all the events where Chantel and I had appeared together. The video was fake. The man looked like me, but I could tell it was AI manipulation. I owned a company that specialized in this kind of technology.

Who was behind this?

Unknown: *Elena already has a copy of this. I can send her more. RESIGN NOW.*

Rage rose in my blood, making my fingers tremble. But I closed my eyes for a moment to gather myself. These people wanted to unsettle me so they could attack when I least expected it.

Though I wanted to reply, I stopped myself.

Elena. The video must have devastated her. She had to know the person in the video wasn't me.

I sent the video to my tech team and asked them to look into the source. I also gave them the unknown phone number that was used to contact me and Elena.

Someone from the Reimann Corporation was desperate because I was getting close to him.

Tomorrow, I'd settle this family matter once and for all.

CHAPTER SIXTY

ELENA

IT HAD BEEN two days since I received that video of
Orion. My heart had died and my body seemed to have gone
with it. Sleeping had been tough, even though I tried to tire
myself out by keeping busy. But he was everywhere.

I looked at the jars of stars, and my heart ached. I'd put
so much time and effort into the jars—into the relationship.
A part of me wanted to smash them and destroy everything
we had.

But I didn't have the energy to do that. If they broke, I'd
have to clean up the mess. I'd rather conserve the energy for
something better. So I left them on the windowsill to collect
dust. Perhaps they would collect enough dust to cover the
stars so I wouldn't remember what I'd written in each of
those paper stars.

I was so stupid. How could I be so stupid? I should've
known. How could a wealthy man like him—who had everything at his whim—love one person? Women were like gems
to a thief. How could he resist?

Why hadn't I seen that?

Because you love him.

I closed my eyes, praying that my feelings for him would disappear sooner rather than later. The longer they stayed with me, the more I'd suffer.

I didn't even have the energy to pack up his clothes and toiletries at my house. I could do that tomorrow or the day after. Today, I wanted to do a good workout that used up my entire body.

Wild Roots was packed with customers because of a bonsai class that was being taught by some bonsai specialist. My mom would probably hold these classes when she returned with the knowledge. If I were in a better mindset, I'd take it and learn how to care for one. The last bonsai plant I had survived a whole month.

But I didn't have the energy to learn anything. I just wanted to quiet my mind and work on things that were second nature to me. I helped Reid water the plants. Then I clipped dandelion flowers from my mom's dandelion beds. I collected the flowers in a basket and transferred them to a mesh tray to dry. There wasn't enough room for the abundant flowers, so I dumped them into a paper bag to take home. I had some room in my house to dry them.

I didn't realize I was crying until tears dripped onto the paper bag. I wiped them away with the back of my hand. My heart hurt so much. I was trying my best to hold it together, but failing miserably. I felt stupid for believing Orion loved me. Apparently, he loved too many women.

I hadn't slept well the night before and was too tired to make coffee this morning. I was paying for it now. My head throbbed, needing caffeine. Wiping my hands of dirt, I told Cathy, one of the garden workers, that I was heading out for a coffee run.

"Do you want anything at Coffee Hut? My treat."

"Yes, please! I'd like a chai latte." Cathy grinned.

"You got it." I added her order to the Coffee Hut app.

I went around taking orders. Reid passed on the coffee because he was delivering several trees.

I hadn't gone out to get a new phone yet. It still worked, even though there was a fat crack on it. I needed to charge the battery too. I couldn't help see the phone as a reflection of me—broken and in need of a recharge.

Once I placed the order, a garden worker brought me a new tray of dandelions from a bed I'd missed. I shoved the dandelions into my fanny pack, not wanting them to go to waste. I'd dry those at home too. I tucked my phone into my cargo capris and hopped into my car. With no makeup on, I probably looked like a zombie. But I didn't care.

On my way to Coffee Hut, I saw a couple on the side of the road with a flat. I recognized the man and his wife from the grocery store. I'd accidentally hit him with my shopping cart that day.

I pulled over, got out, and walked to them.

"Are you okay? Do you need me to call a tow truck or something?"

The man smiled. "That would be great. My phone doesn't have any battery."

"I forgot my phone at my mother's," said the woman.

"No worries." I pulled out my phone and made the call. "Someone should come in fifteen minutes."

"Thank you for your help," said the woman. "You don't need to stay here with us. I'm sure you have places to go."

"All right. Have a good day!" I walked back to my car and drove off.

Music blasted in the car, removing thoughts from my mind. Then something cold pressed against my neck.

"Take a right down the next street, bitch." Jasper moved the cold device to my ribcage. "Or I'll shoot you right now."

My heart jumped as I looked in the rearview mirror. Jasper had grown a beard. I saw on the news that he'd escaped during the transfer to the prison while awaiting his trial.

He reeked of alcohol. What was he doing here? My hands trembled as I turned down a street full of industrial warehouses and wooded areas.

"What do you want?" I asked.

"You're going to pay for messing everything up!" He snarled. "Go into that lot!"

He seemed too erratic for any logic, but maybe my chatter would delay his plan to hurt me. Terror tightened my tummy, but I tried my best to stay calm.

"I'm not sure what you mean. I'm sorry if I offended you."

"You're going to be my ticket to two billion dollars and a new identity."

I snorted, trying to sound calm. "No one will pay that price for me."

"Your fucking boyfriend will."

The video of Orion and Chantel flashed across my mind. "Sorry to inform you, but we're no longer together."

He looked at me. "You think I'm going to believe your lies?"

I drove into the parking lot empty of cars except for one black sedan and a silver truck.

"Get out. If you scream, I'll shoot you in the leg."

Even if I were to scream, would anyone hear me? The

street was remote, and the buildings appeared more like storage units.

How had he gotten into my car?

"Was that couple with the flat tire part of your group?"

He laughed. "They've been watching you."

"If you want money, I can give it to you."

"You got billions for me?" He barked. "Besides, I want Orion to suffer. Then I'm going to kill him."

The evil in his eyes confirmed it wasn't a threat, but a firm statement.

My heart stopped as I tried to figure out a way to warn Orion. Even if he had hurt me, I didn't want him killed. And I'd learned a lot about myself during my time with him.

"Why do you hate him?"

"He took what belonged to me and my family. Now shut up!"

Jasper nudged me to the black sedan. Fear escalated as he opened the trunk, took out duct tape, and used it to tie my hands and legs together. Then he pushed me into the trunk. My phone slid out from my pocket, and he took it.

"You're wasting your time, Jasper. Orion won't pay that much money for me!"

"He will." He ripped off a piece of tape. "If you don't shut up, you'll die just like Kate!"

He killed Orion's ex-fiancée?

Jasper needed me alive to get the money.

"Help me!" I shouted.

Jasper slapped a piece of tape over my mouth and slammed the trunk closed.

The piece of tape hung loosely on my mouth. Jasper was drunk, and I could die from a car accident or from him shooting me. I shifted my arms and nudged off the duct tape from my mouth. Jasper was talking to someone on the phone.

"I got her. Now you go do your part," Jasper said.

He laughed at whatever the other person had replied.

"Let me know when the money's been transferred. I'm gonna finish what I should have done at the camp! Don't worry. Her body and the car will go into a lake."

He slammed the door and drove away. "Heading to the cabin now. Chantel there?"

My heart hammered as fear escalated. Inside the trunk, darkness surrounded me except for a sliver of light filtering in. Panic rose as I tried to figure out a way to escape.

With my teeth, I chewed on the duct tape as best I could until a small tear appeared. Hope sparked as I broke free of the restraints on my hands and legs. How could I get out of here?

Unlock it.

I wriggled my bra off and broke out the underwire. I'd never imagine I'd be grateful for my thieving skills, but right now I needed them to break out.

With nerves increasing every second, I reminded myself to remain calm.

Breathe, Elena. You can do this. Warn Orion about Jasper.

Tapping into my memory, I bent the wire and fidgeted with the lock in the trunk. It differed from a door lock, but I kept going, and when I heard the click, my heart jumped with joy.

The car slowed down and eventually stopped.

Jasper slammed the door, and I waited a beat until I didn't hear him nearby. I pushed up the trunk and climbed out. Then I closed the trunk gently, trying my best to not make a sound. He was facing the woods to relieve himself on a remote road.

I prayed for an oncoming car to help me. I didn't see anyone. But could I trust the next car that arrived? What if they were part of Jasper's crew?

A set of woods greeted me on the other side of the street, and hope burst in my chest. The woods were better than dying in the trunk, so I rushed into the woods.

CHAPTER SIXTY-ONE

ORION

I HEADED TO COSMIC BISTRO, the restaurant where my mom had been killed all those years ago. I was tired and needed to go see Elena soon.

There weren't many customers present in the restaurant today. I entered and walked by a table with three men and nodded to them. Two women and two men dressed in dark suits occupied another table.

As a businessman, I scanned the horizon for interesting things. Details mattered. But they mattered even more to a thief.

Right now, I was confronting a man who had stolen more than money from me and my family. Jonah Reimann had cunningly misled me. He'd always been the more studious of the two brothers. Respectable to others, with good grades, and good manners, he displayed himself as an admirable citizen of society. But underneath those pretty layers lay a monster.

I hated myself for not seeing any of this sooner.

Jonah had created a chaotic financial mess for the

Reimann Corporation. I was dealing with it as best I could. Jonah and Jasper would pay for hurting my mother, my father, The Condor, Kate, and Elena.

"Hey." I walked up to the table, pulled out a chair, and folded myself into it.

"Want anything to drink?" Jonah asked. He wore a lightweight jacket over a polo shirt with dark khakis, looking polished as always.

"I'm good. Thank you."

"So what did you want to talk about?" He looked at his watch and then at his phone.

"Thanks for making a detour to Providence before you head back to Sweden."

"Anytime. I like this city. It's good to catch up with my cousin."

"There are some things that need to be resolved today." I didn't want to waste time. "Did you send me this text message?"

I pushed my phone over for him to see the threat, forcing me to resign.

"I don't know what you're talking about," Jonah said calmly. He was prepared for this meeting. What did he have up his sleeve for this confidence?

Leaning in, I grabbed the pepper shaker and twirled it around before placing it back on the table. "I don't have time for your games, Jonah. I want the truth."

His friendly expression changed to dark and impassive, transforming into an unrecognizable person. A menacing smile curved onto his lips.

"I didn't know you enjoyed raping girls at the campground and recording it with Jasper. You guys are sick." I flicked him a look. "Are there more recent videos of you and women? Be honest, Jonah. Unless you're afraid of me."

A muscle ticked in his jaw. "I'm not afraid of you, Orion. But you should be afraid of me."

"Why?"

He glanced around the restaurant. There was no one close to our table. No new customers had entered since I came in.

"Because I killed your mother. I killed Kate." He smiled through narrowed eyes. "And your father is recovering from a coma because of me. The old man should've just died. Lucky bastard."

My fingers clenched, and I gathered every ounce of will to not pummel him right now. But everything he told me I already knew. Still, to hear his confession enraged me even more. He dismissed people's lives as though they didn't matter.

He had information I needed, and I was just getting started.

"Why?" I seethed. "Sounds like you're a trained dog killing for them—"

"You don't know what they're capable of!" He interrupted with a loud voice. "You don't know who I am to them."

"Actually, I do, Jonah Lance Rotherfield—the illegitimate son of Benedict Rotherfield, also known as the Duke of Cambridge, who's an elite member of The Trogyn."

Jonah flared his nostrils, surprised that I knew about his real identity.

"You're not part of the Reimann family. You have no right to anything. You killed Uncle Ray because he discovered you weren't his biological son. And neither is Jasper.

Were you angry at your mother for telling my uncle the truth?"

Jonah could deny it all he wanted, but I had evidence and the motive for his crimes.

He clenched his fist. "How long have you known this?"

Jonah had killed my mother because she found out he and Jasper weren't my uncle's sons. She had copies of their birth certificates hidden under the rocks on Quintile Island. This crucial information, along with names of other corrupt wealthy people within our family circle, was the reason Jonah and Jasper wanted to buy my island.

He probably knew something was hidden on the island, but didn't know its location. The DNA from the gold button belonged to Jonah, which meant he'd been on my island. I found a recording of a figure diving into the water during the night. It had to be him.

The information my mother had left me proved The Trogyn had planted a spy in my family—the most powerful banking family in the world. It had started with my uncle's wife, who bore him children so they could inherit a portion of the Reimann fortune. My mother and father feared for my safety. For that reason, my father believed it was best he kept his distance, showing he had no emotion for his son—his heir. They believed my father didn't love me and wouldn't leave his fortune to the son who disappointed him.

"You're being used by people who don't care about you. You think that poisoning my father would give you the upper hand?"

"He should have died," he barked. "You had no interest in the Reimann Corporation."

"You're wrong." I smiled. "Let's just say I wanted my enemies to believe I wasn't interested. The Reimann Corporation is my family's legacy, and I'll protect it to the day I die."

"Your father hates you, and you hate him."

What I'd shared with him during our teen years resulted from teenage angst that needed venting.

"I lied." I watched as the evil in his eyes intensified on me. "Why Kate?"

"She was at a café and overheard my conversation with Jasper about your mother's death. She threatened to tell you. So I followed her home, forced her to take pills, and displayed her in the closet for you."

I wanted to rip him to shreds, but I was reminded of the bigger picture. "The people who created that video of me and Chantel are being arrested as we speak." I glanced at my watch and knew the boys were already on it.

Chantel and Jonah had been dating, and he probably told her to get close to me.

"Give me all the names of the elite members and I'll let you go," I demanded. "Who's sitting at the top?"

"Fuck you! I'm not telling you shit. You can't do anything to me." Arrogance gleamed in his eyes.

"You're being used by The Trogyn, Jonah. They'll kill you right after they use you. Do you think they'll let you live after this mess you've caused? Being the son of a prominent member means nothing to them. You're just one piece of the puzzle." I pointed at him. "Like everyone before you, you're disposable. And so is your biological father."

"If you don't hand over all the evidence," he spoke through gritted teeth, "I'll kill her."

An iceberg formed in my stomach, completely interrupting my flow.

Jonah saw my weakness, grinned, turned on his phone, and showed me a picture of Elena stuffed in a car trunk.

A wave of wrath broke through the iceberg, hot and destructive. I charged at him, threw a powerful fist into his face, and gripped his neck, squeezing.

"Where is she?" I seethed, not recognizing the voice that escaped my mouth.

I could kill him right now, break his trachea, and watch his eyes roll back as life drained out of him.

Elena needs you to be calm and collected.

Jonah kicked me, but the rage had solidified me into an immovable boulder. I threw another punch at him and shoved him away. If my hands stayed on him, he'd die right now. Jonah had already given me enough to work with. I needed to pivot.

I turned my head to the table with the three men on my team who had risen after seeing me punch Jonah. They nodded, understanding my command. The salt and pepper shakers had recorded our conversation.

They approached him. "Jonah Reimann, you're under arrest for the murders of Helen Reimann, Pablo Toledo, Samuel Donatello, Carlos Sanchez, and Kate Sinclair."

"Who the fuck are you?" Jonah stepped away from them, looking around the café where the women and men from the other tables approached, surrounding him.

"FBI and INTERPOL," said the men and women.

Jonah darted away from them, but was caught by an officer, who read him his Miranda rights.

He glared at me. "You set me up!"

"You set yourself up," I seethed. "Enjoy your prison stay. But I have a feeling you'll have a visit from The Trogyn soon."

Satisfied with the fear on his face, I turned on my phone and looked at Elena's phone tracker. I had her phone tracked because of the mounting danger swirling around us. The phone showed she was in the woods by an industrial park.

An incoming call from Reid flashed across my screen. He wouldn't have called me unless something had emerged.

"What do you know?" I asked him.

"Elena never returned from her coffee run. I hacked into Coffee Hut's ordering system, and the app showed she never made it to the store to pick up her order."

"They have her." Every fiber of my being blazed with fury and concern.

Stay calm. The tracker shows she's moving. Maybe she's escaped.

I clung onto hope for dear life as I gave Reid the location of where her phone had pinged. "I'm on my way."

As I made my way out of the restaurant, I called the boys. "Release the drones."

CHAPTER SIXTY-TWO

ELENA

I MADE it halfway into the woods when I heard. "You can't run from me, bitch!"

Terror escalated as I forced my legs to move faster. I tripped on a branch, fell to the ground. Something sharp poked my leg, but I didn't have time to look. I pushed myself up and ran out of the woods into a parking lot full of delivery trucks. No one was around.

I ran toward the building, but it was closed. So I moved onto the next building. One of them had to be open. My leg hurt so much. I glanced down and blood had stained my pants. My fanny pack had ripped too. Dandelions had poured out of it.

"Where are you, Elena?" A gunshot rang out.

My heart gave a nervous jolt. I ran toward a building with several cars parked in the lot, rushing into the lobby. A security guard rose from the desk. "Are you all right, miss?

"There's a crazy guy with a gun!"

"Come inside!" He buzzed me in and pointed to the back. As I ran down the hallway, I heard him call the police.

Then I heard gunshots.

Two men and a woman exited from a room.

"Go hide!" I shouted at them. "There's a gunman out there!"

I ran to a storage room and limped toward the back by the window. If he came in, maybe I could break the window. I crouched behind the stacked boxes with my heart beating erratically and pain shooting up my leg.

What if I died today? I didn't want to die like this. My mom needed me. I had so many things I wanted to do. I had things to say to Orion so I could officially close out this chapter in my life.

Sirens shrieked in the distance, and I prayed the police arrested Jasper. Something caught my eye from the window. I looked out and a dragonfly drone hovered by the window-pane, looking at me.

CHAPTER SIXTY-THREE

ORION

REMI, Royce, Grayson, Forrest, and Arrow each navigated their drones, helping me locate Elena.

I could see what they saw from my dashboard. My heart leaped with hope when I spotted a pile of dandelion flowers in the parking lot. It had to be Elena. I also saw drops of blood. Was she injured?

I parked my car and rushed toward the commotion. Police cars had arrived, and I rushed up to a group of officers.

I recognized one police officer I'd worked with. "Tim, where's the gunman?"

"He's dead." He jerked his head toward the building. "But his body is still inside for CSI. They should be here soon."

"I need to check on my girlfriend. Can you get me in the building?"

I entered through the back door and headed to the room where I'd seen her with Arrow's drone. Based on the video, she was in a storage room on this floor. My team had pulled blueprints for all the buildings on this street.

I knocked on the door. "Elena? It's Orion."

"I'm here!"

I yanked the door open, and she stood at the other end of the room. A storm of emotions stirred in me: joy, worry, regret, and so many others. I rushed over to her, gathering her into my arms. "Are you okay?"

"I think so. But my leg is bleeding a lot." I glanced down and cursed at the huge stain. "Let me help you out."

"It's okay, I can walk." She limped out of the door, using the wall to brace herself.

She had no idea how much her rejection hurt. But I'd deal with that later. Right now, I just wanted her safe.

I couldn't stand seeing her limp down the hallway and scooped her into my arms. "Don't be stubborn. I know you're mad at me. Let's get the injury taken care of, and then we can talk."

CHAPTER SIXTY-FOUR

ELENA

IT HAD BEEN three weeks since the incident, and I'd been working nonstop from home. Orion wanted to talk, but I told him I needed a little more time.

The ordeal regarding the sex video and the kidnapping took a toll on me. But I also wanted him to have time to deal with his family crisis. After learning his cousins were behind the horrendous crimes, I knew his father needed him.

My new phone buzzed with a message from Orion:

Orion: *Can I stop by on Saturday? Please?*

Elena: *Okay.*

Orion: *I'll bring dinner.*

Elena: *Okay. See you then.*

When he'd brought me home from the hospital, he told me the video was fake. Chantel and Jonah had used AI software to create a deepfake of him. But we never had time to talk about what had broken my heart.

I'd asked Orion and Reid to keep the kidnapping from my mother. I didn't want her to worry.

Nerves churned in my stomach.

What now?

After having gone through what felt like an entire soul makeover, I was afraid of the signs from my body.

The past few times I was nervous foreshadowed horrific events. But I remembered my grandmother saying that a warning was just preparation. So I prepared my mind for whatever was to come.

I knew Orion still had feelings for me. But what if he suddenly decided to live in Sweden or somewhere in Europe to be closer to his father? I heard their relationship had improved, which made me extremely happy.

My phone buzzed again, and I grinned at the text message from the girls.

Vivian: *I have an impromptu charity event at the top of the Skyline Building. Can you attend to do a write up? It'll be great for Musepaper.*

Audri: *I'll come! What's the event?*

Kiera: *Dress code?*

Vivian: *Black tie with a dinner from the recent winner of Best World Chef.*

Audri: *I won't miss that!*

Michelle: *Sorry, Viv. I'm in Iceland right now.*

Natalie: *I'll be there.*

I smiled as I watched the messages pop up one after another.

Vivian: *Where's Elena?*

Elena: *I'll be happy to attend. Just give me the time and date.*

Vivian: *This Friday at 7pm. Thanks, babe!*

Kiera: *So how are things with you and Orion?*

Elena: *I'm meeting him on Saturday.*

I still loved Orion, but my insecurity had gotten the best

of me. If I didn't tell him what was bothering me, it would linger like a dormant virus. Better to face the issue now and heal once and for all.

At a glance it seemed stupid and silly. But for someone in love, these little things mattered.

Natalie: *He loves you.*

Michelle: *We can tell.*

Elena: *How can you tell?*

Audri: *Orion made a character of you in his video game! Remi showed me.*

Natalie: *Yeah. Grayson was playing the demo.*

Michelle: *A man who makes his woman a main character in his video game is a keeper.*

Kiera: *Madame Sarcasm kicks ass!*

I laughed, wondering exactly what I looked like in his game. I'd forgotten he was working on it, along with everything else.

Vivian: *Do you love him?*

Wasn't it obvious?

Elena: *Yes.*

Vivian: *Then there's nothing to worry about. You'll move past this bump.*

CHAPTER SIXTY-FIVE

ELENA

FRIDAY ARRIVED IN A BLINK. I'd been so busy with Musepaper and trying to organize the next few months' articles that I almost forgot about Vivian's charity event. The article I'd written about the bank scam blew up even more after Jonah's arrest, which led to the apprehension of the Duke of Cambridge. I was grateful for my PR team, who handled that side of the business for me.

Because Orion was an investor, I kept him updated even though he didn't ask to be. He always had wonderful suggestions and guidance to help me choose the right candidate or vendor. But he left the final decision on Musepaper up to me. I appreciated that more than he knew.

Sabrina was arrested for helping Chantel launder money. Both of them had already posted bail, awaiting trial.

With everything squared away, I planned on taking next week off just to rest. I got dressed for Vivian's event in the red dress that Orion had bought for me at the silent auction. This would be my first time wearing it after the fashion show.

I arrived at the Skyline Building, a tall business building in downtown Providence. I heard they had a great restaurant on the ground floor, but hadn't visited it.

When I got to the restaurant, there were no customers inside. The waiter in a black suit smiled at me. "You must be Elena. Please come with me."

I glanced around. "Where's everyone?"

"The restaurant is closed today."

"Oh." What was going on here?

My phone buzzed with a text message.

Vivian: *We won't be able to make it today, babe. (Smile emoji)*

Tell him how you feel. (Heart emoji)

Audri: *A man who asks his girls' besties for help is a man deeply in love.*

Kiera: *We want to know all the deets!*

Michelle: *Forgive the man for his obliviousness. (Heart emoji)*

Audri: *All men are oblivious. (Eye roll emoji)*

Natalie: *Some men need to hear the EXACT words to understand.*

Vivian: *We love you! Gonna go light candles now.*

Kiera: *LOL. Me too!*

Audri, Michelle, and Natalie all said the same thing.

Candles? The mystery deepened.

Orion: *I see you, Sunshine.*

I looked up from my phone, and my heart twirled at the most compelling thief who had stolen my heart. Orion walked toward me from the other end of the restaurant. He wore a tailored black suit that rendered him stunning, powerful, and mysterious—all the things that had captivated me from the beginning. But now I knew there was more to the

man beneath that irresistible façade. I knew his vulnerabili-
ties, and he knew mine.

At that moment a quiet answer slipped into my heart. He was the key to my lock, and I was the key to his—we were intricate parts of each other.

"Hello." His eyes sparked as he raked a gaze down my body. "You're beautiful. I'm glad to see you wearing this dress." He touched the strap on my shoulder, and I shivered when his fingers grazed my skin.

"Thank you," I said. "You look like you're ready to take over the world."

"I'm only interested in making my love happy tonight." He brushed a finger down my cheek. "Ready for dinner?"

"Yup. Wanna tell me how you coerced my friends into tricking me to be here? Why didn't you just ask me and save all the trouble?"

He took my hand in his. "Would you have agreed to meet me? It took me a long time for you to agree to have dinner with me tomorrow. I didn't think you'd agree to meet me on Friday and Saturday."

"You never know until you try," I said, knowing he was right. "What's so special about Friday?"

He kissed my hand. "I needed you to be here for tonight."

"Why?"

"Because the sky's clear tonight. But first, let's enjoy dinner."

Impatience and curiosity overcame everything else.

"What if I want to see that special thing now?"

"You need to wait another two hours. Let's eat first, and you can tell me why you've been hesitant with me. I need you to be honest with me."

CHAPTER SIXTY-SIX

ORION

SEEING Elena wearing the dress I'd bought her made the evening even more special. I'd paid the chef handsomely to fly out here to make us dinner tonight. His salmon specialty earned him the Best World Chef title for a reason.

Elena finished her meal and looked at me. "Thank you for this dinner."

"You're welcome."

"I was jealous of Kate," she said.

I wanted to say something, but she held up her hand.

"I was in a vulnerable state on that day. Jasper had just assaulted me, and then I saw your extreme reaction when he insulted Kate. It did something to me." Elena looked embarrassed, and regretful.

I swallowed, watching the emotion displayed on her face. I wanted to gather her up, but I knew she needed to let it all out, and I needed to hear it.

"In my mind, *I* should have been the one to receive that extreme reaction from you. No one should have mattered more than me. But during that weak moment, I felt like I stood second place." She drew in her bottom lip between her teeth. "I felt like my assault was pushed aside for something more important."

Her eyes gleamed with tears, and a sharp pain stabbed at my chest. I wanted to say something, but I didn't want to interrupt her thoughts.

"The entire ordeal made me feel small. On the one hand I knew it was wrong of me to envy her. On the other hand, I questioned my boyfriend's true feelings for me. I was just a mess." She released a sigh. "I know it sounds stupid."

"Being honest with yourself isn't stupid, Elena. It's courageous. I would rather know the truth than assume something that isn't true. If more people were honest with their feelings, more relationships would last. Keeping your feelings hidden wouldn't help me or you. Thank you for telling me, and I'm sorry for not seeing how my actions affected you. It wasn't my intention." I got up from the table, pulled my chair beside her, sat down, and wiped her tears with my handkerchief.

"It's okay. You didn't know."

"You are *everything* to me, Elena. Always remember that, okay?" I touched her chin and waited for her to respond. When she nodded, I continued, "I reacted that way because I realized Kate didn't commit suicide like I had thought all these years. My cousins—not by blood—killed her. The shock and guilt of it blinded me."

Elena sucked in a breath, and regret swam in her eyes. "I'm so sorry to hear that."

I told Elena that Kate got her justice. Jonah was now dead. The Trogyn had gotten to Jonah on his way to court. His biological father, who was an elite member of the crime organization, was discovered in his swimming pool. The news stations reported that he'd drowned, but the boys and I knew the truth. This was The Trogyn's MO—eliminate all threats.

As for Chantel, she was found dead in her car from a self-inflicted wound. The Trogyn had also gotten to her, making it seem like a suicide. Sabrina was still awaiting trial because she wasn't part of The Trogyn. I knew she feared for her life.

Though Elena already knew who was behind the fake videos of me, I had to show her the power of AI. I turned on my phone and gave it to her. "Watch this."

The video showed me and her taking a stroll downtown Boston yesterday during a charity event that truly occurred. But we weren't there physically. We were also on the fake evening news with an AI reporter that looked just like the current anchor for Channel 7 News.

"Wow. That's all AI?"

I nodded. "A picture says a thousand words. With the rise in AI, those words can become dangerous. If the technology is used improperly, you'll believe things that aren't real."

"You can frame people for crimes or create fake alibis." Her brows furrowed.

"The world is becoming more dangerous, which is why my company is a few steps ahead to counter this artificial intelligence. Computers do what we tell them to."

"You're the most brilliant man I know, and I know you'll do your best to stop them." She smiled. "The world is a better place because of you."

At one point in time, I didn't believe it. But now Elena had made it easy for me to believe in that and more.

With the help of Attikus, Forrest, Remi, Grayson, Royce,

and Arrow, The Trogyn had taken a big hit. Two Hollywood producers involved in a sex trafficking ring had been arrested; a pharmaceutical company selling dangerous diet pills had been exposed; and a hotel hosting illegal gambling as well as several elite clubs around the world just closed down. All the bank scam accounts had led to a bank in Switzerland, which was where all the lawsuits were going to. I had no doubt that the bank belonged to The Trogyn.

"I know that fake video of me and Chantel shattered your heart. The company that created that video no longer exists."

"Excellent."

"Are we good now?" I asked her.

I could almost see the stress on her face dissolve, making her smile softer and brighter.

"Yes." She cupped my face. "I'm sorry you had to deal with so much stress."

"You did too. But anxiety doesn't cripple me like it used to. All I have to do is think of you and the stress is reduced exponentially. You're a miracle."

"We're essential parts of each other." She smiled. "Like a complex lock that requires a unique key. I used to fear that our relationship wouldn't work out."

"Why?" I pouted.

"Because we come from different worlds. You're organized, and I'm not. You grew up with wealth, I didn't. You're used to that posh lifestyle, and I'm more comfortable in jeans and old T-shirts."

"You're wealthy now too. Pablo left you millions."

"But I'm giving half of that to my mom so she can enjoy her life. She can go on vacation whenever and wherever she wants. I know she'll donate to charities too. I'll need your help to invest the rest. But I won't splurge because I'm still me. I know what it's like to have nothing, so I'm careful with finances."

"It works for us because we're different. Opposites aren't a bad thing. We complement each other like an inhale and an exhale. Night and day. Sun and Moon." I grinned. "Right foot and left foot. I can't walk with two left feet."

"Why are you so adorable?" She pinched my cheek.

"Because loving you has transformed me." I grasped her hand. "Come with me."

"Where are we going?"

"To prove that *you* are the center of my universe. That you're the brightest constellation in my galaxy." I winked with a smile. My woman didn't know what I'd orchestrated for her tonight.

"You know that sounds cheesy and nerdy, right?"

"Yes, but you love it." I kissed her hand.

I laughed as he led me up to an elevator. "How much did it cost you to reserve the entire restaurant and hire the extraordinary chef?"

"The price isn't important. I recently purchased this building along with the Mudstacle Course. You can enjoy all the mud races you want."

I beamed at him. "It's only fun with you."

"Then I'll be there." I smiled. "We're creating unforgettable memories tonight."

When we arrived on the top floor, Elena gasped. "Oh my gosh." She placed a hand over her heart. "The view is spectacular. I've never seen the city skyline through glass walls. It's mesmerizing at night. I can see parts of the Providence River over here." She walked up to a glass wall and placed her hand on it, while the other hand still gripped mine.

She'd made tremendous progress compared to the first time I'd seen her tremble on the balcony of my office.

"You okay?" I squeezed her hand.

Nodding, she smiled. "Being with you has helped me heal that phobia. My legs don't wobble like they used to. All I feel are gentle nerves swirling in my stomach. I can deal with that." She rose and kissed me on the lips. "No matter what goes wrong in the world, you make me feel safe—my perfect lock. My irresistible thief." She embraced me. "I love you, Orion."

My stomach tightened at her confession. She'd said those words before. But right now, those words seemed more colorful, more powerful because they had survived a turbulence that almost destroyed us.

I tightened my arms around her, kissing the top of her head. "I love you too, Elena."

She broke free from the embrace, walked around the room, and browsed the lounge area. Her fingers grazed the couches, side tables, lamps and plants, and then she ambled around to the other side of the wall and exclaimed, "Orion! There's a telescope here!"

Her excitement was like a beam of sunlight into my heart. I watched as she walked around the compact telescope, which was around six feet tall.

"Watch this." I pointed at the skyline. "Three, two, one."

All the lights in the city went out.

CHAPTER SIXTY-SEVEN

ELENA

I STOOD there speechless as I stared out into the pitch blackness of the city with a sea of stars twinkling at me.

"Have a seat." Orion ushered me to a stool and swiveled the telescope to align with my position. "See what you discover."

I looked at him, a man who had completely changed my life and my heart. "You shut off the lights to the entire city for me?" Tears welled in my eyes, sliding down to my face.

I couldn't stop them from coming. No one had ever done anything of this magnitude for me. I could only imagine the work that had gone into this evening.

"I'd shut off the entire world for you, Sunshine."

I would never ask him to do that. I would never *want* him to do that. But to know he'd do anything for me made me love him even more.

A surge of emotion swirled in me, taking my joy to new heights. As I floated back to Earth, practicality and concern rose on me.

I gripped his arm. "What about the hospitals? What if someone's having emergency surgery? What if someone's giving birth?" My eyes widened. "What about the nursing homes that need constant energy to support their residents? People need the pharmacy, don't they? What about the police force? Crimes could increase. Slingshot, you *need* to turn the lights back on!"

He laughed. "I'm sure the city will be fine for the next half-hour. Or even an hour. I've made arrangements. Don't worry."

"You have?" I couldn't stop all the scenarios spinning in my head.

He tipped up my chin. "This is why I love you so much. You care about people. I knew you'd react this way, so I've made certain the hospitals were well aware and provided them with extra generators for tonight. The elderly homes, homeless shelters, and any place that needed extra attention for this mini blackout would be fine. Nothing is going to stop me from shutting down the city for you. I want you to see the stars at their best brilliance."

"This is why I love you even more. You understand me." Love filled my heart, and I reveled in it. "I'll be selfish for thirty minutes." I didn't sit, but stood while looking into the telescope. "Wow. The vastness of space is extraordinary. What constellation is this? And what's that space object? Is it a planet?" She veered back with curiosity gleaming in her eyes.

"It's an undiscovered constellation from the Andromeda Galaxy. Let's name it together."

"What? Are you sure?" I looked into the telescope again and then back at him with furrowed eyebrows. "Is that possible? I mean, I know it's possible to discover new constellations, but is it that easy?"

He kissed my head. "It is with the right equipment. I told you I have the best technology to see into space. There are so many things out there we haven't even touched upon. It's something I'd like to dedicate more time to explore. I'd love to do it with you."

I embraced him. "That would be amazing. Then I can share that knowledge with the world. Musepaper readers can be the first to see it. What's the process to name a constellation?"

"We have to submit it to the International Astronomical Union in France. I know some people there. There won't be a problem. Besides, when they see what we've discovered, they'll want to know about my telescope."

"I don't really know what to name it." Excitement coursed through me.

"What are your thoughts on Taraxacum for the constellation name? The English will be Dandelion. It's like Canis Major and Greater Dog, Corvus and Crow, and Cygnus and Swan."

I looked at him, understanding what he was doing. "The dandelion means that much to you?"

"It's *you*—my sun, moon, and stars. You taught me that."

I didn't know how much happiness I could feel in one day, but it overflowed in me.

"Do we get to name the stars that make up the Dandelion constellation?"

"Absolutely. We can take our time with those." He walked me over to the window and pointed to the starry sky. "Constellations are merely Earth-based interpretations of a two-dimensional star pattern in a celestial sphere. They're just perspective." He took my hand, lifted my index finger, and traced a heart-shaped pattern of stars from the glittering display. "That could be Orion's Heart for Elena."

"Or Elena's Heart for Orion." I looked at him, my heart wanting to burst. "I can almost hear the stars cheer for us."

"The stars speak to a heart that's open to listen." He kissed me on the forehead. "When you're with me, I hear the stars speak in a love language no one can understand but us."

I pressed the side of my face to his chest, listening to his heartbeat. "I can hear your heart. And I love its voice."

His eyes gleamed at my imagination. "Madame Sarcasm has her own asteroid now."

"What do you mean?"

"That space object you saw earlier? That's an asteroid I recently named, dedicated to an amazing woman who has captured my heart and soul."

Amused, I asked, "Don't they have to be cool names? Like ancient gods, goddesses, or something?"

"No. It can be anything. There are over twenty-thousand asteroids already named. Some have people's last names, some are countries. Mine is Madame Sarcasm, and she exists in a galaxy beyond the Milky Way. I love her with all my heart and soul."

My heart palpitated when he showed me a website with all the asteroid names on it. Madame Sarcasm was listed amongst the letter M section. He gave me the sun, moon, and stars.

Emotions overwhelmed me. "This is the best gift I've ever received. Thank you."

"You're welcome. Now you have to tell me something. What's the special ingredient in your dandelion tea? It's been bugging me. I can't seem to have enough of it."

I laughed. "The special ingredient has been keeping you up at night?"

"It has." He pouted. "No other tea has helped keep me calm. There's something about this tea that just makes me feel good."

I placed a hand on his arm. "Slingshot, have you heard of the placebo effect?"

A slow smirk crept onto his face as his eyes pinned me. "You're kidding me."

"The only thing in the tea is a dried dandelion flower with added honey. I told you about a special ingredient because I wanted you to *believe* there was something more in it." I chewed on my bottom lip. "You're not mad, are you?"

He shook his head. "I'm not mad, Sunshine. I'm in awe that you tricked me."

"My grandmother used that trick on me when I was younger. I hated taking this herbal liquid for colds. She used to tell me it had a special ingredient from a magical plant. It would make me healthy and strong. No other kid had it but me. I believed her, and I hardly got sick during the winter months."

"The placebo effect is powerful. It shows the potential of our mind and the mystery within it." He tipped up my chin. "I fell into your trap."

"Because you love me."

"I'd fall into every trap you set for me." He kissed me lightly on the lips.

"I didn't mean to keep the truth from you. But I noticed the dandelion tea was helping you relieve stress, so I said nothing." I tapped his head. "Your brilliant mind made the tea more powerful."

"There's still a magical ingredient in it. It's called Elena's love. Your dandelion tea is my sugar pill."

"You'll have an endless supply of it."

"Dandelion tea is my favorite tea." He wrapped me into his arms, looking down at me. "Your heart is like a dandelion puff—it seeds the world with love and hope."

"I love it when you're so poetic."

"You inspire all the poetry that comes from me." He tapped on my nose. "I've become a better man because of you. Whenever I see a dandelion, I think of you. I had my landscapers use dandelions in their floral arrangements around the island. And we won't be using weed killers anymore. I'm letting the dandelions loose. Wild and free, just like my Sunshine."

I couldn't help but kiss him.

"By the way, my father would like to meet you. I'm thinking of having a gathering on the island before it gets cold. You can bring your mom too."

"That sounds wonderful. How is your father feeling?"

"I didn't get a chance to tell you, but he knew someone was trying to poison him. And so he played along and *pretended* to be in a coma. He gave me control of the company to lure out all the players who wanted to hurt him and me."

"That's wonderful to hear. I guess your father is just as cunning as you. Is your relationship with him better?"

"It's getting there." He touched my face. "He told me he'd always loved me. In order to protect me—his only son— he had to make it seem like he was disappointed in me. Get this: he knew The Condor was teaching me how to be a thief. My mom did too. Your father was friends with my parents."

Wow. We were intertwined in a complex web with so many connections.

"They knew about you stealing?"

"Yes." He beamed. "They knew my targets, and why I was stealing from them."

"Your parents loved you in their own way. They were trying to love and protect you, but also ensure you're well prepared for the cruel world."

"Everything makes sense now." He smiled.

I had something for him at home. "The city lights will turn back on soon. Want to come home with me tonight?"

"Is that an invitation, Madame Sarcasm?" His eyes twinkled in the dim light.

"It is. Since you gave me the stars today, I have some to give you as well."

"Oh yeah? I'm intrigued." He arched an eyebrow.

"I've bottled up some stars for you."

"So you were busy catching falling stars for me?" he asked.

"Just like how you were busy exploring other galaxies to find our constellation."

"It all started with Sassteroid, the name you gave yourself when you replied to my query."

"It just popped into my head." I patted his notch lapel, loving how he looked in a suit.

"You know what's in Sassteroid?"

"What?" I looked up at him.

"Ass." Smiling, he gripped my behind with his hands. "You were mine from the beginning. I was going to name the asteroid Sassteroid, but I didn't want to share that with the world." He squeezed my buttocks.

"I'm gonna make you see stars tonight, figuratively and literally."

"I can't wait. Let's go." He gripped my hand, and at that moment the lights returned to the city as though nothing had happened.

"Also, I heard I'm a character in your video game." I grinned up at him. "When can I play it?"

"Let's get home and we'll play it, Sunshine."

EPILOGUE

SIX MONTHS *later*

Elena

I'd officially moved into Orion's new home just outside of Providence, where there was a huge backyard with a stargazing center for us to explore the sky. I still kept my farmhouse and used it to harvest my dandelions and other herbs for tea.

"What do you think?" I stepped back, admiring the lotus painting I'd purchased from the art show at the Mount Centauri Museum. "Nessa's art is truly unique. She invited me to her gallery to promote her next collection."

Orion came up behind me, slipping his arms around my waist. "You should have bought more of her work."

I turned around and looked at my love. "You bought the painting for me, remember?"

"How could I not buy it? You kept staring at it."

"Yeah, there was something about it. The flower and color scheme just resonated with me."

All my friends got a painting from their significant other as well.

"Nessa had twelve paintings on display. Our group bought six of them. She said an anonymous art collector bought the rest. That's not you, right?"

"No, Sunshine, it's not me. As you know, I collect other things. Why?"

I shrugged. "Maybe I want another painting for the house or the office."

"Why don't you commission her? Don't worry about the price."

"I'll ask her when I cover her event." I looked up at him. There was something in his eyes that spelled trouble. "What did you do?"

"Nothing." He laughed. "Can't a man love and admire his woman?"

"You can. But I see trouble sparking in your eyes."

"You know me too well. I made something for you, but it didn't turn out the way I wanted." He looked disappointed.

"Let me see." I was curious about what he'd made for me.

Orion had hired another team to assist him with his empire so he could spend more time with me. Not only that, he had started MuseWorks, a media company that owned Musepaper. He loved me and wanted me to be happy. I'd have my own TV show where I could report inspiring news. We would deliver the news with integrity and honesty and include more world news.

We walked out to the yard with some tulips and daffodils

already in bloom. I loved the atmosphere of spring, where new beginnings were everywhere.

Orion and I had survived a tumultuous storm. We were now enjoying the peaceful calm. All my dreams had come true because of him. He was my sun—warm, vital, and the center of my galaxy.

I yanked at his hand. "You seek me when you're cold and need me when you're lost. You measure my life in hours, and I will serve you until I perish. The wind is my enemy, and the shadow is my friend. Who am I?"

He answered without a blink, "I'm your candle, baby."

I smiled and whipped out another riddle. He replied without hesitation.

"Have you been studying my riddles or something?" I smiled, pride surging in me. This brilliant man was all mine.

"I studied Madame Sarcasm's old website."

Since he took care of all the tech stuff for my sites, he had access to all my information—all the old articles I'd ever written.

"That's a lot of studying."

"I can be an excellent student with the right teacher." He gave me a wicked grin that made me think about all the intimate things we'd done together since moving into this house.

An idea sparked in me, but then it vanished, replaced by a distressed bouquet of dandelions lying on the outdoor table.

Oh boy.

He definitely made the sad-looking bouquet.

I cupped his face. "It's adorable."

"Please help me make it better." He watched me as I unwrapped the paper and removed all the dandelions and accent plants.

A little box dropped out of the arrangement, and I looked at him, my heart racing.

His eyes gleamed with joy and mischief. "Open it."

I took off the lid and a lopsided paper star sat in the middle. It had my name written in small letters at the center. "It's adorable."

"Since you gave me hundreds of paper stars filled with lovely messages, I figured I'd make one for you. Mind you, it took me forever to make this star."

I could imagine him sitting at his desk, folding the thin strip of paper with his enormous hands.

"You did an amazing job. I'm not taking on new students, but I'll make an exception for you."

"Open it," he said, looking nervous.

I stared at the tiny star at the center of my palm. It pulsed with hope and love.

I unraveled the paper, arched an eyebrow, and read the question out loud. "I am the sun burning for you, the moon making sure you have a good night's sleep, and the stars making all your dreams come true. What am I?"

He stared at me, waiting for an answer.

I smiled at him. "I was going to say a dandelion, but you're asking for a deeper meaning." I placed the strip of paper on the table and placed two palms on his firm chest. "It's you, Orion. You're my sun, moon, and stars."

Then he pulled out a box from his pants pocket and dropped to one knee.

Orion

.   .   .

I'd never been so scared to see a reaction from anyone until now. What if she said no? What if she was happy living together without wanting to be my wife?

I opened the silver and gold box and pulled out a ring with the rare taaffeite gemstone. "I didn't know I was capable of this deep love until I met you. When you came into my life, I felt renewed. I love you with everything I am and everything I'll ever be. I'd love for you to join me on this journey. Will you marry me?"

"Yes! I love you so much!" Tears streamed down her face as I slid the ring onto her finger.

I rose to my feet as she placed her hand against the sunlight. "It's perfect. Isn't this the gemstone from your secret room?" The glow on her face proved she loved it.

"It is," I said, remembering how she kept staring at the gemstone.

She was the nebula that added color to my dark soul.

Elena embraced me. "I can't wait to be your wife."

I kissed her forehead. "You're the supernova that illuminates what I couldn't see within or around me. Thank you for loving me."

"Thank *you* for loving me. I'm so happy I don't have the words to express it." She smirked. "Why don't I show you?" She dragged my hand, leading me into the bedroom.

I paused and threw out one more riddle for today. "What kind of thief steals a glance at you?"

She angled her head and smiled. "A dead man—a dead thief."

I grinned at our unique way of communication. I could speak in riddles and my love would always understand me.

"I'm going to steal your sanity right now, thief."

She shrugged off my T-shirt with love and mischief gleaming in her eyes.

"Take whatever you want, Sunshine."

I couldn't wait to spend the rest of my life giving her whatever she wanted.

THANK YOU so much for reading Elena and Orion's story! If you enjoyed their romance, I'd really appreciate a review on your chosen platform.

Read about Elena and Orion's wedding **here**!

Order the final book, **The Maverick,** now!
https://nadiahan.com/books/

KEEP IN TOUCH

For exclusive content, new releases, and giveaways, sign up
to my newsletter.

https://nadiahan.com/newsletter/

Join my **Facebook reader group** for bonus features and exclusive giveaways!

https://www.facebook.com/groups/nadiahanselitebookworms/

ALSO BY NADIA HAN

WaterFyre Rising Series

The Mastermind (Book 1)

The Daredevil (Book 2)

The Innovator (Book 3)

The Inquisitor (Book 4)

The Strategist (Book 5)

Journals

Finding Your HeART

ACKNOWLEDGMENTS

As I finish the sixth book in this series, I reflect on my journey. There are so many wonderful people who have helped me publicly and privately. I'm so grateful for each and every one of you.

Anna, thank you for all of your spectacular suggestions and for being on this journey with me from book one.

Lindsay, I'm so grateful for your thorough copy edits and insightful feedback. I always look forward to your perspective.

Mindy and Dianne, thank you so much for your proofreads.

Jennesse, thank you for making sure my Spanish is correct.

Sharon, what would I do without you? Your friendship and support all these years mean the world to me.

To my wonderful PA, Mindy. Thank you for helping me manage all the crazy things behind the scenes. You're a true gem!

To my VIPP, Street, and ARC teams—you're all AMAZING! You have a special place in my heart. Your support and enthusiasm for my books motivate me daily.

To my readers, THANK YOU from the deepest part of my heart. Thank you for reading and sharing my books. I'm so thankful for your continued support! You've made my dreams come true, and I can't wait to share more stories with you.

Like always, I'm saving the best for last. THANK YOU to my remarkable husband, my best friend, my number one support system. When things go crazy, you always show up to make magic happen for me. Thank you for EVERY-THING. Love you! To my incredible children, thank you for all your love, understanding, and feedback on everything I do. I try my best to make you proud of me just as I am proud of you. Hugs and kisses!

Nadia Han is a contemporary romance author. She's a dreamer, a visionary, and a believer in karma and kindness. She lives in Massachusetts with her husband, two children, and a cat, and enjoys the unpredictable New England weather.

Nadia started out writing and illustrating children's books when her kids were small. But she decided to write romantic suspense stories featuring diverse characters for herself. She loves escaping into different worlds and for that reason, she also writes otherworldly romance under a different pen name.

When she's not writing, she practices yoga, reads, explores nature, watches K-dramas, and eats all kinds of foods. Nadia is also an artist. She loves spending time playing with paint and other artistic mediums. She believes creativity is important for the mind and the soul. It helps her become a better writer because she can guide the reader to see things from a different perspective.

facebook.com/authornadiahan

instagram.com/authornadiahan

bookbub.com/authors/nadia-han

amazon.com/author/nadiahan

www.ingramcontent.com/pod-product-compliance
Lightning Source LLC
Chambersburg PA
CBHW070230200726

48293CB00005B/1561